Never
Tear Us
Apart

Rowan Coleman is the *Sunday Times* and *New York Times* bestselling and award-winning author of fifteen novels, including the Richard & Judy Book Club choice, *The Memory Book*, the Zoe Ball ITV Book Club pick, *The Summer of Impossible Things*, and *The Girl at the Window*. Rowan also writes the Brontë Mysteries under the Brontë inspired pen name, Bella Ellis.

Also by Rowan Coleman

Growing Up Twice
After Ever After
River Deep
The Accidental Mother
The Baby Group
The Accidental Wife
The Accidental Family
The Home for Broken Hearts
The Other Sister
Runaway Wife
The Memory Book
We Are All Made of Stars
The Summer of Impossible Things
The Girl at the Window
From Now Until Forever

ROWAN COLEMAN

Never Tear Us Apart

HODDER &
STOUGHTON

First published in Great Britain in 2025 by Hodder & Stoughton Limited
An Hachette UK company

The authorised representative in the EEA is Hachette Ireland, 8 Castlecourt Centre, Dublin 15, D15 XTP3, Ireland (email: info@hbgi.ie)

1

Copyright © Rowan Coleman 2025

The right of Rowan Coleman to be identified as the Author of the Work has been asserted by her in accordance with the Copyright, Designs and Patents Act 1988.

All rights reserved. No part of this publication may be reproduced, stored in a retrieval system, or transmitted, in any form or by any means without the prior written permission of the publisher, nor be otherwise circulated in any form of binding or cover other than that in which it is published and without a similar condition being imposed on the subsequent purchaser.

All characters in this publication are fictitious and any resemblance to real persons, living or dead, is purely coincidental.

A CIP catalogue record for this title is available from the British Library

Paperback ISBN 978 1 529 37663 0
ebook ISBN 978 1 529 37661 6

Typeset in Plantin Light by Manipal Technologies Limited

Printed and bound in Great Britain by Clays Ltd, Elcograf S.p.A.

Hodder & Stoughton policy is to use papers that are natural, renewable and recyclable products and made from wood grown in sustainable forests. The logging and manufacturing processes are expected to conform to the environmental regulations of the country of origin.

Hodder & Stoughton Limited
Carmelite House
50 Victoria Embankment
London EC4Y 0DZ

www.hodder.co.uk

*For Maria Stella Borg Coleman,
the grandmother I never knew but think about often.*

PART ONE

'We are such stuff as dreams are made on, and our little life is rounded with a sleep.'

The Tempest, William Shakespeare

Chapter One

Wednesday 18th June 2025, 2.45 p.m.

'Slow down, Maia,' Dad says.

I speed up a little. We are arguing. Of course we are arguing – we are together: a rare occurrence that never ends well. The hire car has air conditioning, but my father insists on having the windows down, allowing the afternoon heat to swell into every crevice. Sweat trickles down my back from the nape of my neck. My thighs stick to the faux-leather trim. I should have coughed up for a better car.

'Dad, I'm not even over the speed limit,' I tell him, nodding at the dash, as I expertly take a hairpin bend of the road from Sliema to Mdina. The roads are lined with prickly pear trees. Wildflowers burst into random riots of fleeting colour, lighting up the dry and dusty landscape. 'I've driven in the Alps, in Ukraine, in Iraq, Afghanistan and the Gobi Desert. I've driven in *Paris*. I know how to drive.'

'You don't know to drive *here*,' he insists.

'Here? You haven't been to Malta for . . . what, thirty years? Everything has changed while you weren't looking, Dad. Amazingly, the world keeps going even when you aren't around.'

'Again, with the complaints.' He sighs. 'I don't know why I thought this would work.'

The *this* he is referring to is *us*: father and daughter together on a tour of the place where my dad, the great artist himself, David Borg, was born: the island of Malta. *This* was supposed to be our last great hope of having some kind of functioning relationship. No, scratch that – some kind, *any* kind of love.

'No matter how you feel about me and my numerous failings, you are still driving too fast for this road. You will kill us both.' He gestures, one arm extending out of the open window, rolling his head back against the headrest. 'I suppose then at least this torture will be over.'

At this, I pull over into a narrow lay-by. The red Prius that was behind us shoots past. I grip the steering wheel hard with both hands, taking a deep, steadying breath. I swore on my twenty-first birthday that I would not let him make me cry again. More than a decade on, I mean to keep that promise.

I turn to him when I'm sure I have my feelings under control once again. 'Why did you even suggest this trip?'

He crosses his arms and looks out of the window.

'Dad, if this is torture for you, then I'll take you back to the hotel and get a flight back to my life. Because I promise you, visiting Malta for the first time with the father I haven't spoken to for six years was not on my to-do list. So why put both of us through it?'

'You know why,' he says bitterly.

'I thought I knew why,' I tell him. 'I thought you had finally realised that life is short, that yours is almost over, and that now would be a good time to try to build a relationship with the daughter you abandoned, before it's really too late. That's what I thought when you called me out of the blue. You told me you wanted to take me to the island where you were born, to show me the places you knew and to introduce me to the relatives I've never met. I thought maybe you wanted to explain why you insisted Mum call me Maia, even though that's the only direct bit of parenting you have ever done.'

Three more cars whip by, and I wish I was in any one of them, speeding away from this moment. A lorry rattles past so fast and loud it makes me start.

'This is not a good place to stop,' Dad mutters.

'You called, and I came running, like I always do when you dangle me any sort of promise, even though I *know* you will break it. Because, despite it all, despite everything you have done or not done, I always hope we might . . .'

I can't finish the sentence, because I don't know what I hope, only that I do.

'You are your mother's daughter,' he says. 'You want to talk, to go over and over the past. You want reasons; you want apologies. You can't let it rest and move on.'

'I want to try to *understand*,' I cry, hearing the break in my voice and reining it in. 'I want to know you, before it's too late.'

'I'm eighty-eight,' Dad tells me. 'And in excellent health. I'm not dead yet.'

'Exactly,' I say. 'There's still time to make amends.'

'For what?' he demands.

'Oh, I don't know. How about leaving me to fend for myself for starters . . . ?'

'I never wanted children,' Dad says, his tone heating up now. 'I told your mother that when we married. She was thirty or so; I was in my fifties. I said, I do not want children. I told her that my first two wives left me because I didn't want children, even though I had made it clear right at the start. Women always think they can change you. She promises me it doesn't matter to her, and then she is pregnant despite my wishes. She leaves me for *you*.'

Every time I resolve not to give my father another chance to reject me, I fail. All I can do now is damage limitation.

'Right.' I check my wing mirror for traffic and indicate to pull out. 'Look, I know this trip was Vanessa's idea. I know she's always wanted you to try to build some kind of relationship with me. Vanessa is a nice woman. It consistently amazes me how you get nice women to marry you so frequently, but anyway . . . It's not going to work. You tried your best. You can go back to Vanessa and tell her you tried. You can live out the rest of your days with your fourth wife and a clear conscience. I'm taking you back to the hotel and I'm going back to London.'

'It's for the best,' he says with a shrug.

This is where I should check my mirror again, but I don't remember that until I see the speeding truck closing in on us – and by then it's too late.

Chapter Two

One Week Earlier

Wednesday 11ᵗʰ June 2025, 11 a.m.

Kathryn Borg and my father haven't seen each other for more than thirty years, and I've never met her before. Nonetheless, I spot her easily as she walks purposefully towards us through the crowd waiting to catch the ferry to Gozo: a neat, petite woman with an air of authority. She's a professor of archaeology and an expert in Malta's ancient temples and artefacts, and she has promised us a guided tour of all the ancient sites.

My first reaction is a rush of shyness, followed by relief. At least there will be someone else to break up the awful, stilted conversation between me and Dad, in which we circle around the black hole of our relationship, desperate not pass the event horizon and find ourselves with no way back.

My father seems untroubled by the decades of silence that have passed since he last saw Kathryn. He has never been concerned by the constant round of niceties many families consider essential: Christmas and birthday cards, round robins and postcards saying *wish you were here*. He told me once that he finds the very idea of such things a terrible burden, and for once, I have to agree with him.

But it seems like Kathryn is not the sort of woman to hold a grudge.

'You've got so old,' Kathryn greets him warmly, her eyes merry, as she takes his hand in both of hers. 'I'm surprised you're not dead!'

Dad laughs. 'Well, you look exactly the same. Do you have a secret way of cheating time?'

'Ah, you'd be surprised at the mysterious powers of the temples.' Kathryn looks at me then, hanging back, and swoops me into a tight hug. Returning her hug feels surprisingly natural, like I've somehow always known her.

'Maia.' Once she releases me, she steps back to scan my face, giving me further opportunity to study hers. Though we are first cousins, Kathryn is almost twice my age. Bright brown eyes, full of life. A heart-shaped face and soft lines that show a woman who knows how to laugh and how to hold her ground.

'You look like your mother,' she tells me, touching her palm to my cheek. 'I was so sorry to hear of her passing. It was so fast. And you were barely an adult, nineteen? It must have been hard for you.'

'It was.' I nod. 'The tumour hid itself very well in her brain for a long time. By the time they found it, it was too late.'

'My dear girl.' Kathryn squeezes my hand. 'You have her fair skin and smile. And you look a good deal like my mother, too, and our grandmother. Yes, there is a lot of the island in you, which is good. Malta will love you like one of her own.'

'That's nice,' I say. 'I've always wanted to be adopted.'

Kathryn smiles as she leads me onto the top deck of the ferry, where the cold, stiff breeze fights the strong, warm sunshine and wins. Dad pauses for a second before following.

And that's why we will never come to a place of peace in our lives: we just can't resist the urge to hurt each other.

* * *

The walk from the museum to the ruins of Ġgantija is garlanded with grassy meadows full of wildflowers that seem to thrive even under the intense heat. My father and Kathryn walk ahead. I hang back a little, taking everything in. I've never really cared for history, always preferring to find meaning in the present, but this time, it's different. This time, I am learning the history of me – or of half of me, at least. The half I have never known.

'Ġgantija comprises our oldest temples,' Kathryn explains when we stop to take in the huge structure. It stands proud against the golden plains that stretch far beyond, punctuated by domed hilltop churches dominating worshipful towns. 'They were made in the Neolithic period, so around five and a half thousand years ago. Older than the pyramids in Egypt and the second oldest man-made temples in the world, after Göbekli Tepe in Turkey.' She surveys the structure with pride, as if she built it herself.

'It's remarkable,' I say, taking in the enormous curving wall that bends gently away from us. Massive stones of all shapes and sizes are slotted together in perfect unity. 'It seems like it should have been impossible to build this back then!'

'Ah, well, legend has it that it was built by giants.' Kathryn grins. 'A Giantess, to be precise. A woman of enormous strength and height who could pick the stones up in one hand, while carrying their babies in the other, all while chewing on some broad beans.'

'Perhaps we are descended from a superwomen,' I say, smiling at Kathryn.

'We may no longer be giants in stature,' she replies, 'but we Maltese women are mighty still – in our hearts and minds. And, giantesses or no, you certainly are descended from impressive women,' she adds. 'Our grandmother is still a local legend to this day.'

'Really?' I glance back at my father, who has folded his clip-on sunglasses down over his specs. He has always behaved as if he came into the world fully formed, untethered by family or ancestry. We haven't spent a lot of time together, but when we have, he has never talked about his family or the country of his birth.

'Naturally,' Kathryn says, glancing at Dad. 'Don't you know anything about her?'

'Only that she died young,' I say. 'Mum told me that.'

Kathryn shakes her head, bemused. 'How can one know who one is without knowing where one came from?' She gives my father a pointed look. He ignores her. 'I'll tell you all about her before you go home, I promise. Giantesses don't seem so implausible when you consider that the wheel had yet to be invented when this was built. But we have found a number of large, perfectly spherical stones that we think might have been used like ball bearings, to help moves the stones.'

'And all for God or goddesses or whatever,' I say. 'It always amazes me, the stories that people are willing to live and die for.'

'Foolish and naive,' Dad says. 'Unable to face reality. We live; we suffer; we die. Most can't cope with it – they have to invent heaven.'

'Still a laugh a minute, I see.' Kathryn winks at me. 'So, the temple is built in the classic clover-leaf design, with a series of five apses or leaf-shaped chambers that were likely used for worship, perhaps burial. This temple, like the one in Mnajdra, is aligned with the equinox sunrise. They saw the heavens as their ruler, and they weren't far wrong. A drought, a blight, a cold summer would be enough to decimate a community. This huge undertaking was designed to placate and appease the sun and the stars, but it also had a practical purpose: when to sow seeds, when to bring in the harvest, when to fish . . . The sky and the temples together made up their calendar, too.'

Kathryn leads us across the wooden walkway that takes us into the centre of the temple. 'See, there – you can still see traces of the plaster and paint that decorated the chambers.'

'It's like they're still here,' I say. 'Just out of focus, billions of particles floating in the air.'

Kathryn tilts her head. 'You are poetic. Do you paint like David?'

'God, no.' I shake my head. 'No, I'm all hard-headed facts and economic prose.'

'Yes! I want to hear all about your career as intrepid war correspondent.' Kathryn loops her arm through mine. 'I've followed your work, of course, but now I get to hear about it from the horse's mouth.'

'Really?' I'm flattered. 'You've read my work?'

'Of course!' She smiles. 'Another brilliant Borg woman? I'm so proud of you – I boast about you all the time.'

Tears spring into my eyes. It has been such a long time since anyone has told me that; it makes me think of Mum, and coming from someone who was a stranger until today makes it all the more powerful. Turning away, I focus on a pattern of grooves etched into a huge block of stone.

Kathryn squeezes my hand briefly before turning to my father. 'You've never been inspired to create any art based on the temples, David?'

'Not my thing,' Dad says. 'Magnificent, nevertheless.'

'Well,' Kathryn says. 'Let me take you to see the "fat ladies" and then to a lovely place I know for lunch in Victoria. Then we can explore the citadel before we take the ferry back to the main island.'

'Thank you,' I hear Dad say as they walk away, 'for dropping everything to be our tour guide, especially when we haven't been . . . in touch all that much.'

'Family is family,' Kathryn tells him. 'Besides, I'm thrilled to spend some time with Maia. I only wish it hadn't taken this long.'

'Sometimes,' Dad says before they walk out of earshot, 'there never is a right time.'

Chapter Three

Three Days After the Crash

Saturday 21st June 2025, 5.30 a.m.

'You mustn't keep blaming yourself,' Kathryn tells me. Her voice is soft in the quiet of the early morning.

When I was discharged from hospital after a serious concussion but somehow with no other injuries, she was adamant that I would stay with her. She whisked me off to her harbourside apartment in Birgu, just across the blue water from Valletta, and embedded me in her guest room as if I were an infant niece and not a fully grown cousin.

Kathryn has surrounded me with every comfort she can think of, and I love her for it. It has been a long time since anyone mothered me. I hardly even remember what being truly cared for felt like. It has been a long time since I have rested feeling completely safe. Kathryn has given me that gift, and it feels like respite, even from myself.

Dad is still in hospital – his tibia is broken, but a clean break, thank God, but they're worried about his heart. A high-impact crash isn't good for an elderly man, even one who seems determined to live forever.

'It's hard not to feel guilty,' I say, rueful. 'The accident *was* my fault. Only I could go on a trip with my estranged father and end up almost killing him.'

'Nobody's perfect,' Kathryn says with a wink, and I find myself laughing as she flashes me a mischievous smile. 'Anyway, let's just focus on the fact that it wasn't worse,' she continues. 'You are up and about after a few days; your father is as strong as an ox. All of you, including the other driver, will live to see another day.'

'I don't know,' I say. 'Dad is eighty-eight. A head-on collision can't be good at that age.'

'Meh – my mum says that if living in New York in the 1960s didn't kill your father, then likely nothing can. She insists he will outlive us all, simply to spite her.'

'Were they ever close?' I ask. I know my father cut off what was left of his Maltese family a long time ago. Nevertheless, his little sister, Kathryn's mother, came to see him at the hospital the day after the accident, even if she did leave within twenty minutes.

'There's a photo,' Kathryn says. 'Mum keeps it tucked in the back of a photo frame – her as a baby sitting in this huge pram, and David holding the handle, smiling at her. He looked after her a lot when they were children during the war, though he was very young himself, only five. Perhaps they were close once, but they were separated young. After the war, David was sent to be educated in England, he was the son, so it was up to him to gain an education. My mum stayed in Malta, raised by neighbours. David rarely came home and when he did, it was clear he didn't want to be there. Mum says it was as if he'd decided never to look back. Perhaps it's understandable. The war was a terrible time for the people of Malta. For our parents particularly, they lost everything. David even lost his home.'

I know very little about what the Siege of Malta in the Second World War was like, but it wasn't so long ago that

I myself was hiding in a hospital basement in Mariupol as the ground was pounded with heavy artillery. There was fear and exhaustion in the darkened room, desperation and anger – but so much love between fathers and daughters, brothers, sisters, cousins and neighbours, too. It was palpable.

It was love that held together a universe on fire, fuelling courage and determination – love that would never surrender and love that would rage in bottomless grief when all was lost, because not even love can protect the weak and abandoned in the end.

To walk away from family. To walk away from love, and all the pain that comes with it. That's hard for me to understand. Then again, I suppose I am one of the people he walked away from.

'Look, you will go to visit him later. He will make you mad. I will take you for dinner and feed you wine. Until then, just be here, on this day, in this hour. Just be now. It's a magical experience, I promise you.'

It's almost dawn, and we are standing outside the ancient temple of Ħaġar Qim, perched on a hilltop almost above the edge of a cliff on the southern coast of the island. This is one of the ancient island temple sites that my cousin focuses her research on. She told me last night she had a gift for me: the gift of travelling back in time to when Malta was a temple culture that knew the sun and stars as gods. I'm about to find out what she meant by that.

The morning is perfectly still. Even the constant Maltese breeze has paused, as if holding its breath. The restless sea marks time like a clock that has yet to wind down, a constant distant movement. The sky bleeds from violet to a pale lilac. The promise of the sun is inked in coppery pinks on the far horizon.

I take in the remains of the temple, trying to imagine it as it would have been five thousand years ago, standing silent and stoic at the heart of change.

'It pleases me to think that our ancestors may have been led by women,' Kathryn tells me. 'These temples were filled with statues and sculptures of "fat ladies": beautifully corpulent women who held the power of creation in their big bellies and breasts.'

'Wow, these really are my people,' I say with a small smile.

Kathryn grins and leads me on.

A modern, open-sided canopy has been erected over the whole of the temple to try to shield it from the worst of the wind and sea spray, but I still get a sense of how impressive it must have looked, standing on the edge of the world.

'We should go in – sunrise is only a few minutes away,' Kathryn says.

I follow her into the heart of the temple.

'The people who built this temple were some of the first farmers, adapting from a life of hunter-gatherers to live off the land,' Kathryn tells me. 'And no land was harder to cultivate than this rocky island. The sun, the moon and the stars were their constant guides and must have been a huge comfort to them. Come what may, the North Star will always appear, the moon will always return to full bloom, and the sun will herald the beginning of summer by dawning on the longest day of the year. It's been that way for as long has human memories can reach.'

There is a small group of other people already waiting in the temple room, who greet Kathryn with smiles and warm hugs. Kathryn directs me to stand against one side of the chamber, and we fall into silence, waiting.

'Watch,' Kathryn murmurs, directing me with a gesture to the near-perfect circular hole in the south side of the main temple.

Around us, the sky lightens almost imperceptibly, and within a few seconds, the bright beams of the dawning sun are focused through the aperture so that they flow through the temple to the leaf-shaped room where we are waiting. A carefully placed standing stone means that when the light hits the back of the temple wall, it shows us the glowing image of a crescent moon. And as it rises through the sky, its beams travelling down the wall, it will move through the phases of the moon until the display is complete with a bright golden disc of light on the temple floor. One of the two most important celestial bodies in the universe is honoured and twinned with the moon in a ritual of singular simplicity and meaning.

As it is now, so it was then.

So it will always be.

'Magical.' I breathe the word on a long sigh as the sun begins her hours-long journey. 'It's almost as if you can feel the temple women here with us.'

'Oh, I'm sure they are here.' Kathryn puts her arms around me in a little hug, her dark eyes twinkling with pleasure at sharing her joy. 'When a ritual has been honoured for so many millennia, it connects us straight to the heart of our ancestors, don't you think? We are each only one link in the chain, after all. I work in many of these sites, sometimes quite alone. And there have been more times than I can count when I have felt . . . *something* is with me.'

'All these years, and I had no idea about the temples,' I say, pausing to stand still and looking around at the perfect morning. 'No idea about anything to do with Malta at all, and now I'm here, it . . .'

'Feels like home,' Kathryn finishes.

'How did you know I was going to say that?' I ask.

'I recognise that expression, and besides, home is a two-way street. You may love a place, but it can never be home unless the place loves you back. And you are born of this earth. Even before she met you, Malta has always loved you like a mother, waiting for you to remember her. Just as all of your Maltese family have been waiting to meet you.'

'Dad never talked about Malta or even being Maltese. It always felt as if it had nothing to do with me.'

'Ah, but it always has. No matter where you have been in the world, what you have done, Malta has always been with you; she has always had you in her heart.'

It's a romantic notion, but I like it. Not like me at all.

'Now, let me take you to my favourite of all Malta's temples: Mnajdra. It's smaller but somehow still so alive with ancient voices.'

'I'm sorry it's taken me all my life to get here,' I say as she leads me down the hillside towards the glittering sea. 'I'm sorry I've missed years and years of knowing you.'

'You don't need to apologise, Maia Borg,' she tells me, pronouncing it with a soft 'g'. 'Did you know that Borg is the most common surname on the island? There are dozens and dozens of us, and we will all claim to be your relative, you know. Our cousin Maia, the famous journalist from the BBC news.'

'Hardly famous,' I say, smiling anyway. 'I was on the BBC once, and that was just because I was in the right place at the right time. Anyway, thank you so much for bringing me here today to see the sunrise. I feel so lucky.'

'Not at all. Now, I must leave you to the ancestors for a while. I have a meeting at the visitor centre with the curator, it's the one time of year when we are both on site so early we can get all the week's work done before breakfast! Enjoy the peace of the temple in the early morning. Come and find me when you are ready.'

I thank her, smiling to myself as I begin the short descent down a white stone path towards the second, smaller temple that sits right on the cliff edge. Made of honey-coloured stone, it follows the same clover-leaf construction of Ħaġar Qim: five leafed chambers that come off a central stem.

Here, Kathryn has told me, it isn't the summer solstice that the positioning of the temple seems to echo but the spring equinox and the winter solstice, and, crucially for me, the constellation of the Pleiades or the Seven Sisters – one of which was named Maia.

Maybe here, in the dust and destiny of this almost forgotten place, is where my name was born – where, for perhaps even just a few minutes, my father imagined me as his daughter, a beloved child.

Chapter Four

The heat is already building as I wander into the temple. Birdsong fills the air under the canopy, the constant chatter of sparrows and finches accompanied by the constant rush and recede of the sea meeting the rocky shore. Harmonising with it all is the single constant singing note that has rung in my ears since the accident. The doctors tell me that it may eventually fade – or that at least I will stop noticing it's there, even if it remains: the ghost of a very bad day.

It's a privilege to have this ancient site entirely to myself. Even the security guard who usually watches over the temple hasn't arrived at his kiosk yet. For this short time, all that is left of it belongs to me. Its welcoming curves and secrets draw me into the heart of the temple, until I find myself at its centre. Somewhere above, a stray cloud covers the sun, the sky darkens, and I feel the keen chill of the breeze.

The fierce bright day dims and falls silent, as if something has scared all the little birds away. When I look up, I see a faultless clear sky, a dazzling sun that offers no light or warmth. Unease settles around my shoulders, like static building before a storm. A thought catches at the edge of my mind for an instant before flying out to sea: something isn't right here.

Once, one fiery evening years ago, I stood at the mouth of a cave in Northern Iraq, a place where the remains of Neanderthals had been found and excavated. This feels a little like that: like the shadows of the past are gathering near to remind me they once were, too, just as I am now. Lightness flows through the soles of my feet to the top of my head and I get the sensation that if I'm not very careful, I might float away somewhere into the sky where all the other ghosts are waiting.

Whispered voices echo off the golden stone, and I head towards them, desperate for the company of reality.

'Hello?' I call. 'Kathryn?'

When I enter the petal-shaped chamber where the voices came from, it is empty. The hair prickles on the back of my neck. I can't hear the crashing waves anymore. Even the ringing in my ears has abruptly shut off.

Something very bad is going to happen. I can feel it deep inside me.

Then I see it and recognise it, as if it has always been there – except I know for certain that it hasn't. A blank, black square, an entrance, has appeared in the opposite wall. It seems to look back at me.

This is the moment when anyone else would run towards safety.

But I have always sought out terror. There are stories somewhere in there, in the dark, and I want to find them.

The closer I get to the void, the quieter the air becomes as it thickens around me.

I let one last chance to turn back pass me by. Crouching low, I crawl into the dark.

The void widens, and I can stand up straight; a stone ceiling grazes the top of my head. The air smells of stone dust and heat, and singing that I cannot hear but can somehow feel vibrates against my skin.

This feels like unconsciousness. As I wade deeper and deeper into the dark, I see myself, growing smaller and smaller, until I vanish in a pinprick. This isn't reality anymore. It is something like death that leads me on.

Astonishingly, a clay oil lamp burns mutely in a small alcove carved into the wall, revealing a flight of steps tumbling down. The bottom is out of view.

If there was ever a world where the sun shone and the birds sang, it has vanished now. The one way forwards is descent.

It's only when I am already out of reach of the lantern's light that I can pinpoint the exact moment I left my body crumpled in the dust to be engulfed in this other world: it was when the canopy that covered Mnajdra vanished into thin air.

Whatever I am now is burning, aflame with pain and terror. I'm unravelling, being undone out of existence until all that remains is this thought:

I'm falling. Perhaps I will never land.

Chapter Five

The world solidifies around me, and I find myself braced with my hands against a rough stone wall in the perfect dark. Feeling my way forwards with a few faltering steps, I realise I'm in a low, narrow tunnel. The nothing behind me nudges me on.

There's something else: I am not alone down here.

My hearing seems to come back to me in increments: first the sound of my hands grazing the stone, then my soft, tentative footsteps.

Quiet murmurs emerge in the dark, woven with soft sobs. A piercing infant's cry cuts sharply through the dark and is swiftly stifled. Feet shuffle; bodies shift and sigh. Somewhere ahead, there are people crammed together. Even after a few minutes, my eyes can't make out any shapes in the gloom. Still, I know one thing for sure. I've been in perhaps a dozen places that sound and feel exactly like this: it's a place for the terrified and weak to take shelter.

The air fills with a roar of crashing, erupting noise. A direct hit. The world trembles and lurches. Screams crescendo as I'm flung hard against a wall, banging the back of my head. I crumple downwards, lost in fear. Rafts of dust rain down; I taste grit and blood.

Memory pulls me back through time, and I'm in Syria: Ma'arat al-Nu'man. A building collapses; we are entombed. Is this real? Am I there again? In that underground parking garage with a whole building concertinaed overhead. Stuck in those last few seconds before I realise the horror of what is buried beneath me in the rubble.

A wail rises in my throat. I clamp my hands over my mouth, battling it back with determined silence. This isn't then. This is a flashback of that day, not the first I've had.

This is different; this is now.

Understanding that brings little comfort, though. Taking a deep breath of pulverised stone, I listen. The pounding of bombs has receded a fraction, moved on a little. The tunnel shudders and buckles but holds. My trembling legs refuse to let me stand again for several long seconds until I find a gap carved into the wall, a handhold I can use to drag myself up. I must find a way out.

Logic dictates that I should be able to go back the way I came, up those stairs towards the burning oil lamp, out into a morning filled with warmth and song – but nothing is logical here.

Another ear-shattering noise rushes through me with a physical shove. Stumbling along the wall, I find another handhold and then another, guides in the dark to lead me on, though I don't know where I'm going. There's a sensation of small spaces crammed with people, shoulder to shoulder. I see the dim glimmer of wide eyes, smell the scent of sweat and urine. Pushing myself off one wall, I grope towards the room opposite and am met by shoulders and backs.

'*L-ebda spazju hawn.*'

I don't need to understand the language to know I'm being told to get out.

Then something low tumbles into me at speed, making me stagger backwards. I brace myself and feel small, narrow shoulders under my hands.

'Hey,' I whisper, trying to calm the frantic, small body that is desperate to crawl around me. 'Hey, it's OK. You're OK.'

'Mama!' a thin, light voice cries out as the child tries blindly to tear away from me.

'Are you lost?' I make myself sound calm. 'I'm lost, too. How about we stick together until we find out where we are supposed to be? Does that sound good?'

'English?' the young voice asks.

I pat the top of a small head, hair cut short. A little boy, I think. 'Yes,' I say. 'I'm scared, too. So will you stay with me, kid?'

His slim frame twists under my hands and then stills. 'I will stay.'

A bony hand wends its way into mine, dry and hot. I hold it tight as much for my sake as for his. At least the worst of the pounding has receded now. The sound of explosions rolls continuously, like thunder growing distant.

There's footfall in the direction the child came from. I place myself between him and the sound. Then I see the flare of a match, and a moment later, a small lamp is lit. Its light is feeble, but it's enough to reveal the rough niche it's placed in and the tall figure that lit it.

'Out?' I ask incoherently, pretence of any calm snapped like a taut thread, as I take two steps towards the stranger. 'How do I get out?'

'You don't want to go out there yet, ma'am,' says a male voice – American. He moves into the glow of the lamp. His shadowy figure is bent almost in half in the tight space. 'From your accent, I guess you were trying to reach one of the military shelters? Me too – but seems like our friends up there don't much care where we are when they try to kill us.'

'This kid is lost; we need to find his mum. Can't you tell me which way is out?' I ask again. I can just about tell he's wearing some kind of uniform, and a cap with a bent peak sits on the back of his head. 'Point me in the right direction?'

'Ma'am, please stay calm. The raid will be over soon. We've just got to wait it out. You don't want to alarm the good folks down here, do you?'

Somehow, his good-natured calm only serves to peak my anxiety. The last thing I need is some stranger mansplaining trauma to me. I *know* trauma.

'This isn't right. I need to get out, and you can't stop me. This boy needs his family. What happened? When did this start?'

I can't see his expression in the dark, but I see him shake his head and sense his bewilderment. His shoulders square.

'Look, lady, you've got to keep it together.' He moves a little closer. I get the impression of light eyes and a long, roman nose. 'You Brits like to lead by example, right? These people are scared. The last thing they need is some delicate English lady losing her you-know-what when they can barely keep it together themselves.'

'What the—?'

Another rumble, another tremor, and I stumble towards him. His hands catch my elbows, and he tilts me back onto my feet. The boy clasps my arm in a bear hug, and I see the child's face clearly for the first time in the orange light. Two huge, dark eyes stare up at me, full of fear and sorrow. I know that look, I've seen in the eyes of so many children trapped in wars they don't understand.

'Get me out of here,' I tell the American.

'Fine,' he says, short. 'If it means you will relax a little, I'll take you close to the entrance. Maybe we'll pick up the kid's mom on the way. But the warden's not going to let you out, not even if you turn out to be Princess Elizabeth, which you sound like you might be.'

'Thank you,' I say. 'Wait—'

He blows out the lamp, and we're blind once again.

'It's dark as hell, and there are tunnels upon tunnels down here,' he says, his voice soft, 'so you keep hold of my jacket hem, OK? You hold on to me, and make sure the kid's got a hold of you, and we might just avoid breaking anything.'

'Fine.' I take a couple of inches of the rough cloth between my thumb and forefinger, and he starts to shuffle forwards, with me in tow. The boy holds on to my wrist with both hands. There is nothing to do but follow; all I can think about is being close to the exit, close to escape.

To consider how this happened only tilts me even further out of my mind. Not that long ago, I was standing in the ruins of a temple in a peaceful, sunlit morning. Wherever I am now is far from there. Could this be another ghost of PTSD? They said psychosis was rare but possible. But what does a psychotic person consider reality?

'Which . . . which war is this?' I ask.

He stops abruptly, and I walk into the back of him.

'Do you mean which front?' he asks.

'Er . . . yes.'

'Well, we're trying to keep Malta from the Axis powers. If they get hold of this rock, that's the end of North Africa. Don't you know where you are?'

'I hit my head in the first impact,' I tell him. 'Things aren't clear.'

'Hell, hold on.' He stops, turns and strikes a light. His face, younger than I imagined – he's maybe in his twenties – appears in the glow of the flame. Worried eyes scan my face. When he takes my chin with his thumb and forefinger, I don't flinch. He turns my head from side to side, winces when he spots something and fumbles in his pocket with a handkerchief. When he presses it to the side of my head, pain burns down my neck.

'That was a hell of a bump,' he says. 'Can you keep it compressed and keep a hold of the kid?'

'I can,' I say.

'Good, stay close to me, OK? We'll find a doc to look you over.'

'Doctor!' The little boy leaps at the word. 'Doctor! Mama!'

'Your mom hurt, too, son?' the American says as we resume our slow journey. 'Don't you worry. We'll get help to her – we'll get you both help. Almost there.'

I keep my eyes fixed on the shape of his back. Strong but supple, it fills out the rough material of his uniform. I follow him for what seems like an age, my arms grazing against the stone walls again and again. We pass signs in English and Maltese: *no smoking, no swearing, no spitting*. Gradually, the air gets a little fresher and the light stronger.

Eventually, we reach a sort of cubby office, lit by a lamp, with a wooden desk and a rickety-looking chair. There's a chart on the wall and an ancient-looking radio system, as well as one of those old-fashioned telephones.

'What you doing 'ere?' An older Maltese man with a bald head and grey moustache looks my guide up and down. 'You should be up there giving Jerry hell!'

'I'm supposed to be on rest leave, for all the good it does me,' the American explains. 'Got caught out, I guess. Ducked into the first port of call, sir.'

'You'd think you lot would know better,' the man huffs. 'Anyway, go back to your cell – can't have people running around willy-nilly. Is hazard.'

'Sir, this little boy is lost – he is asking for a doctor for his mom. And this lady has a nasty cut and may have some concussion or something. Is there a doctor here?'

'Is that . . . ?' The older gentleman peers at the boy concealed behind me, smiling broadly as he talks in Maltese. They know one another.

Slowly, the boy emerges and nods in understanding, his expression still very serious.

'He's not asking for a doctor for his mother,' the gentleman tells us, with a chuckle. 'His mother *is* a doctor. He must have got bored and gone exploring and lost his way, yes? Very bad.'

The boy nods, bowing his head.

'No harm done,' the gentleman tells him kindly.

'I give you light. You follow the boy. He takes you to the doctor for the young lady.'

'No!' I say a little too abruptly. 'I want to stay here, please. By the exit. I will be fine if I can stay here. And as for the child – he's already got lost once. It doesn't seem like a great idea to let him get lost again.'

'That's more like it – sounds like your brain cells are waking up.' The American grins at me; I see dark hair curling beneath his cap and a crooked smile. 'Let them stay here a while, huh? I'll take responsibility for them. Maybe you've got some water they can have?'

The warden – I think that's what he is – sighs.

'I only do this for you,' he tells the American. 'Because you are hero. You come while I fetch; you tell me about last dogfight.'

'You got a deal.' The American shakes the warden's hand, and the warden beams.

'Stay right there on that chair.' The American points at me and the boy in turn.

Gratefully, I take his seat. Unbidden, the boy climbs onto my lap and rests his head against my shoulder. All sounds of attack seem to have receded. The adrenalin that has kept me on my feet and unaware of my injury starts to drain away, leaving a deep exhaustion in its wake. Mustn't sleep. Not when I have the care of a child. Mustn't relax – that's a mistake I can never make again. Must get out before all of this falls down on top of us. But what about the boy?

The American said I could leave when it was all quiet – that's what he said. And now, it *is* quiet. Just beyond them, I see a staircase leading upwards – the same milky stone of the tunnels but edged with bright daylight behind a metal door. What I want more than anything is to be out there in the world, where I can tell up from down and make sense of this insanity.

'Hey.' I lift the slight child off my lap. He rubs at his eyes as he frowns at me.

'You sit there and wait here for your mum, OK? Do not move.'

'You are going outside?' he asks, grabbing at my hand. 'It's very dangerous!'

'I'm just going to look,' I tell him softly, as the American regales the warden with an animated tale of some description. 'You stay here, though. Promise? You need to wait.'

The boy sits on the chair and watches me. 'It's very dangerous,' he repeats in a whisper.

'Your mum will come and get you,' I assure him. 'You're going to be fine.'

Then I dart for the exit. The door is harder to open than I expected. Bolts need dragging back, and a wheel lock needs turning. But then it moves, and I'm out.

Reflexively, I gasp in lungfuls of air, and it's a mistake. I breathe in burning oil, noxious smoke and clouds of stone dust. There's another smell, one I can taste, sweet and metallic. I don't want to think about what that is.

Piles of rubble are haloed with dust that glares in the sun. Where am I?

Somewhere far away, a high-pitched wail rises. There's the noise of a distant engine. Looking up, I spot a small plane in the sky, growing larger and louder by the second. Where am I? What is that plane doing?

'I come with you,' the boy – this very little boy of maybe five – appears at my side, tugging me back towards the shelter. 'I make you safe.'

Then he catches sight of the aircraft. His eyes widen.

'Messerschmitt,' he gasps.

My gaze turns back to the plane screaming right towards us.

It's mesmerising. I want to run and hide, but I seem to be fixed to this spot, my eyes glued to the oncoming winged demon that rips down towards me. Its shape fills up the sky, now so low I can see the two black crosses painted on the underside of its wing. It swoops right down the centre of the ruined road towards me, the ground ahead of it pitted with tiny, rapid-fire explosions. Too late, I understand that in the next three seconds, the plane's machine-gun bullets will reach us. It's happening again. And all I can do is stand here and wait.

'Jesus H. Christ!' I hear the American growl as he charges at us, knocking me out of the path of fire, scooping the kid up under his arm and throwing us all as far as he can into the unforgiving rubble of a broken house. Our attacker screams into a sharp turn as the American drags us further in under a cave formed out of a collapsed ceiling.

'So, you wanna die?' he asks me angrily. 'You want to kill the kid, too, while you're at it? What the hell is wrong with you?'

'He . . .' The world swims and dissolves in front of my eyes, and, touching my hand to my head, I am intrigued to see blood glazing my fingertips.

'Oh,' I say. 'That's not good.'

I look at the American. The world melts all around him.

'There's something really wrong,' I tell him.

Then there's nothing.

Chapter Six

Saturday 21st June 2025, 10 a.m.

'Maia? Maia? Can you hear me?'

The voice just reaches me from very far away. I don't recognise who it belongs to, so I ignore it. Is this sleep or death? The distinction seems very hard to make. Pain throbs throughout my body in sharp pulses. Not death, then. At least, I hope death isn't like this. Is it birth or rebirth? I feel as if I'm encompassed in a thick, viscous fluid that wants to rock me back to sleep.

'Maia, Maia, open your eyes please.' A woman's voice, a stranger.

'Maia, wake up at once please. You are scaring me.' Kathryn's voice sounds urgent and demanding.

I remember her kindness. For her, I start to slowly fight my way back from the dark. It hurts.

'What's happening?' I squint against the bright light. A woman is bending over me, shining a torch in my eyes – I think it's the same doctor who saw me after the crash. I bat my hands at her. 'What the hell . . . ? Go away!'

'Oh, my dear.' I feel Kathryn stilling my flailing hand, holding it to her lips. 'Hush now, hush. Dr Gresch is just trying to help you.'

I work hard to bring her face into focus.

'Is this . . . ? Was it . . . the crash?' I ask, my voice dry as dust.

'No, dear, no. You were with me at Mnajdra, remember? I left you for a little while, but I got worried when you didn't come to find me. Then soon after the temple opened to the public, a visitor found you unconscious, bruised, and with these deep cuts on your head. We brought you right back to the hospital. We're not sure how long you were out for.'

'I don't know.' I shake my head and pay the price as pain burns down my nerve endings. 'I was down there for at least an hour, maybe more.'

'Down where?' Kathryn asks.

'In a shelter, in the middle of a war.' Then I realise: it was all a dream. I am in that most hated of clichés. Still, the sense of relief is a blessing. Just a dream – just my damaged brain conjuring images to haunt me with.

'Our best guess is that you fainted and knocked your head on a rock or perhaps fell onto stones and cut it that way,' Dr Gresch tells me. 'Though it's odd you have cuts on the back and front of your head. Maia, considering your family history and your mother's illness, I'm concerned that I missed something after the accident. I want to do some more tests.'

'But you said my scans were all clear?' I ask, raising a tentative hand to my forehead. 'I've been diagnosed with PTSD previously, Doctor. Do you think that's relevant? I'm a war correspondent. But that doesn't usually show up on scans.'

'Well, actually, it depends on the scans, but I have ordered more to be safe,' she says. 'According to your records, from your insurers, your anxiety, the flashbacks and insomnia have been well controlled with therapy. Are you coping well?'

'I am,' I say.

'Still, I will keep you overnight, I think.'

'I don't want to be kept in overnight,' I protest, looking at Kathryn. 'I'm fine, really. Well, I will be. The dream I had – it was so vivid . . . I saw a door, Kathryn, at the temple. And the stairs leading down, and then, somehow, I found my way into the Second World War, I think? There was this American and a child . . . I could hear the bombs falling – I could *feel* them. It was so real . . .'

'The Second World War, really?' Kathryn asks gently, quickly adding, 'Not surprising, I suppose, given your experience in war zones. I should have taken better care of you. I shouldn't have left you. Your father told me you can be a little delicate.'

'He did?' I ask, baffled. 'I'm a lot of things, but delicate is not one of them.'

Then I realise he must have been talking about my mental health, how my mind has constantly teetered on a knife-edge ever since Syria. Is Dad ashamed of my 'issues'? Delicate? Fuck that.

'Perhaps you didn't have enough water, or you're not used to the heat,' Kathryn goes on. 'I should have stayed with you. This is all my fault, Doctor.'

'No, I'm fine,' I insist, trying to prise a clear thought out of my head. It feels like time is stuck in a short-running loop.

'I will be the judge of that.' Dr Gresch sits on the edge of the bed, frowning. 'You need stitches. I'll arrange it. It could be delayed shock, your body reacting to a drop in adrenalin. Or perhaps I missed something, so I need to keep you tonight. We will have more tests – agreed?'

'I don't like hospitals,' I say.

Kathryn hands me a glass of orange juice.

'Neither do I,' Dr Gresch admits. 'But you are injured, and I'm a doctor. What are you going to do?'

She smiles; I smile. It hurts.

'What about Dad?' I remember a little too late to ask after him. 'How is he doing?'

'Your father is doing exceptionally well for a man of his age who has devoted so much of his life to smoking and drinking and other pursuits,' Dr Gresch tells me. 'He is frustrated and bored, but I take that to be a good sign. Would you like to see him? I can arrange for a porter to take you in a chair once we've got you properly cleaned up?'

'Oh no,' I say at once.

'Not today,' Kathryn says, tilting her head to look at me. 'You don't need any more agitation.'

'I'm an adult woman in a perfectly safe place,' I reassure her. 'I'll be OK. The doctor here is probably right – it's a delayed reaction or something. I'm fine, honestly – a bit groggy but fine. I could probably come back to yours tonight, Kathryn, and come in for another scan tomorrow . . .'

'No,' Dr Gresch and Kathryn say in unison.

'You *are* like your father in some ways,' Kathryn chides me. 'You think the laws of physics don't apply to you, that you are invincible.' She reaches for her bag and brings out a large, glossy paperback, which she lays on the bed. *Malta: The George Cross Island at War.* 'No reading today, but I bought this for you at the museum earlier. I have my own copy at home. There's quite a bit about our grandmother in it. But no reading today – promise?'

'Promise.' I nod, picking up the book to look at the cover image of Spitfires flying over the harbour. They blur, double and refocus. No reading today.

'I'll come again tomorrow, in the morning. Do as you are told.' Kathryn kisses me briefly on the back of my hand as she leaves.

'Ugh, I hate doing as I'm told,' I grumble under my breath.

Dr Gresch remains after Kathryn has gone, reading something on the iPad that's attached to the bottom of my bed. She's in her forties, I think, tall and attractive, with the kind of glossy, neat hair that I have never managed to achieve. She gives off an air of calm confidence that is reassuring.

'So, Doc?'

She looks up from the iPad.

'Give it to me straight. Did you miss something bad? Am I going to die?'

Dr Gresch smiles. 'I don't *think* so.'

'Not quite as much reassurance as I'd hoped for.' I laugh.

'The brain is an enigmatic organ,' she says. 'Any serious injury should have shown up on the scans, but sometimes the effects of an accident can be invisible. It's possible, though unlikely, that slight bruising or some swelling has developed since the scans. Or the incident could have triggered the PTSD, reactivating some of the more distressing symptoms.'

'Oh good,' I say.

'Count yourself lucky – sometimes after an accident like yours, people start speaking a new language perfectly or their personality changes completely. I once authored a paper about a woman who lived the rest of her life with a constant sense of déjà vu.' She shudders at the thought and gives me a slight smile. 'It's more likely to be like the ringing you mentioned you are experiencing in your ears – an after-effect of having your body thrown around. You might experience a little dizziness and some fainting, and you will perhaps need to take extra care for a while. Try not to be worried, and if you start to speak fluent Maltese, let me know. I'll take you to meet my mother.'

'What, not even dinner first?' I quip weakly.

'You should sleep,' she says, smiling generously at me. 'The nurse will bring you some meds for the pain in a little while. There is nothing to do but rest.'

'I've never been very good at resting,' I explain. 'I'm not keen on having time to think.'

Dr Gresch pauses for a moment, as if choosing her words carefully. 'Your doctors in the UK sent me your records. I see you were injured in Syria.'

'It's not as if I'm a veteran – just a reporter who was in the wrong place at the wrong time. Anyway, I've done the therapy; I'm fine now. Basically.'

'As I mentioned, the shock of the crash may well cause a resurgence in symptoms: flashbacks, anxiety, perhaps even hallucinations. Please, tell me if that happens. Don't try to brush it off. Listen to your body and ask for help. I am a world-leading neurologist and psychiatrist, I'll have you know, and I'm at your disposal. Make use of me.' She raises a commanding finger at me just as she leaves the room.

Of course I will do no such thing, but even so, I like Dr Gresch. If I were ever to truly confide in a medic, it would be her. But experience has taught me never to tell them everything – especially not how I can never forgive myself for being alive when so many innocent lives have been lost around me. One because of me.

For a moment, I feel a pang of guilt about not being able to see Dad today, but he'd probably prefer me not to. I imagine his irritation at being confined to bed will only be compounded by seeing me, the architect of his downfall.

There's a little part of me that worries, though. A nagging thought that it wasn't *just* that I forgot to check my mirrors when I pulled out of that lay-by. An idea that it was more that I simply didn't care what happened next.

After all, it wouldn't be the first time I'd played roulette with my life in the years since Syria.

Chapter Seven

Insistent pain wakes me once more, slicing down through my temple in a throbbing, repetitive slash, prodding its way into my fractured dreams. A white room filled with bright light. A sensation of floating and comfort.

Touching my hand to my forehead, I feel thick cotton bandages tightly wrapped. A safety pin holds the dressing in place. Did the cut get worse in the night?

'Bet you feel pretty terrible.' A cut-glass English female voice.

It takes me a few attempts at blinking to unpeel my lashes, then another moment or two more for my sore and swollen eyes to focus. A slender, light-haired young woman is standing over me, her head tilted slightly to one side. I have a blurred impression of a curious songbird.

'Why the bandage?' I ask. My mouth is dry.

She pours me a glass of water from a tin jug and helps me sit up, supporting the small of my back as she lifts the glass to my lips. The water tastes metallic, but it refreshes my bone-dry mouth and throat. This nurse – if that's what she is – smells of old-fashioned soap, lavender, and lily of the valley, just like my nan used to.

'You were knocked out by a bit of flying rubble,' the woman tells me matter-of-factly, peering at my bandage. 'At least, that's my best guess. Not shrapnel, thank God. That likely would have seen you off. You'll have concussion, but you'll live – though you will have a scar,

I'm afraid. Shouldn't think it will scare off prospective husbands – not if you style your hair over it.'

'What are you talking about?' I ask, noticing the raw scrapes on my arms. 'Flying rubble? Shrapnel? I fainted and hit my head.'

'I think you are in rather a muddle, dear,' she says kindly. 'You were in the Vittoriosa public shelter when you had something of a moment and decided to run outside before the all-clear, the boss's son in tow. Good job nothing happened to him. If it had, I'm not sure you would have made it through the night.'

Is this a dream, or something else? The room flexes and morphs into another place, a place made of glass and white tiles, where a vase of cut flowers sits in the window. Each flowering of reality blooms and dissipates into another until finally the walls settle, the floor rises to meet the feet of the bed and this shabby, hot room solidifies around me, bringing every scent and sound with it.

My nurse sits on the edge of the bed and takes my hands. Hers are cool and smooth. 'Look, we have all had to develop nerves of steel here. But really, putting others at risk with your own silliness is not the done thing – not the done thing at all. You need to screw your courage to the sticking place, as Lady M would say. Can you do that?'

'It's normally my thing,' I tell her. 'Don't know what happened.'

'Well, never mind. All's well that ends well. I say, I am being Shakespearean today! Now, who do you belong to?'

'I don't have a husband,' I say, trying to make sense of who I am in this world my brain has created. 'I have a cousin. I'm staying with my cousin.'

'And who is your cousin? You didn't have any papers on you. Nothing at all. And some people might find that rather troubling. After all, it's not long ago that we had all that bother with the spy.'

'The spy?' I frown. Frowning hurts. 'What about my cousin? She knows me.'

'There's no cousin come to check on you.' Her face softens. 'You seem to be quite alone. Don't worry – we'll get to the bottom of all this. In the meantime, I expect you have rather a terrible headache. We are short of supplies, but take some aspirin, and I'll see if I can find you some penicillin. Wouldn't do to have you die of an infection after Danny did such a sterling job of saving your life.'

'Danny?' I ask, taking another sip of water.

'Danny Beauchamp, the pilot who saved your life? It was him who knocked you clear out of the path of that aeroplane. Quite a few of the young ladies on the island would have been pleased to be in your position, I can tell you, even accounting for the brush with death.' She chuckles. 'If I wasn't already spoken for . . .'

A vague impression returns of a tall man in unform with an American accent. Why him? I can make sense of where much of this wartime narrative comes from, but there has never been a handsome rescuer of any description in my life. I've always had to rescue myself, even when I've thought of just letting go and losing myself to oblivion. In those moments, I think of Mum and how she would never forgive me.

I catch the woman studying me closely, trying to interpret my thoughts.

'Anyway, where are my manners?' She offers a bright smile. 'I'm Christina Ratcliffe. You may call me Christina. I am volunteering here at the Floriana medical inspection room today. It's Vittoria, the usual helper's, day off. I used to be a dancer, and now I'm a plotter. But when my Warby's away – he's a pilot, too – I like to keep busy, so I help here, too. Better than dwelling on things, don't you think? Anyway, that's where you are: Floriana. The doctor doesn't usually keep patients overnight here, but we thought we'd better hang onto you as you refused to wake up and no one came to claim you.'

'I'm in wartime Malta,' I reflect.

'Yes,' Christina says, rather perplexed. 'Of course you are.'

'What's . . . the date?' I make myself ask.

'August 1942, of course – I forget the day. They all rather run into one another these days, don't they? Dear me, how hard did you hit your head? In any event, the Germans and Italians are trying very hard to kill us, and we are trying very hard to kill them. One wonders what the point of it all is. I just hope someone knows.'

'August?' I latch onto the single word, unable to process the '1942' she said after it. 'That's interesting.'

She doesn't appear to hear me. 'It's hellishly hot, desperately dangerous, and we are all starving to death. Certainly never a dull moment!'

I study her face, blinking in the bright light. Christina is young, perhaps in her late twenties, and very pretty, even though she looks like she hasn't slept properly in an age. Her face is thin and gaunt, her wrists frail and bony. Even so, she's smartly dressed in a skirt and blouse, though both are showing signs of wear and seem to have once belonged to someone who carried quite a few more pounds than Christina. Her skirt is secured at the waist with a safety pin just like the one holding my bandage in place, and there are empty pockets of air in the tailored shirt that was made to fit neatly over a fuller bust. She wasn't exaggerating when she said she's starving.

'Do you know your name?' she prompts me.

'Maia,' I say. 'Maia Borg.'

'A Maltese name and an English accent,' she says thoughtfully. 'As you must be aware, security is something of an issue at the moment, after we hanged that traitor in March. The head honchos are in a terrible fret about espionage.'

Christina pauses, offering up an apologetic smile. 'Perhaps I'm already saying too much if you *are* a spy . . . But I'm rather afraid that either way, you are an unfamiliar face in these parts, without any identification or anyone to claim you, so as soon as you are fit, you're to be taken to HQ just to tidy up the loose ends. Nothing to worry about – just a formality. Unless, of course, you *are* a spy? But honestly, what kind of spy would run around in the middle of a raid? Not a very good one, that's for sure. Mind you, the other chap *was* a terrible spy. Landed at midnight in a boat by the cliffs, then realised he couldn't climb them and nearly starved to death. Poor, silly boy.' Christina goes on, as if she is talking to herself, more than me. 'His name was Borg, too. The island is full of Borgs – it's a terribly common name. Like Smith is back in England. Are you a terrible spy, Maia Borg?'

'I'm not a spy. I'm not even here!' I sit up, ignoring the pain that shoots down into my neck. Maybe my brain is swelling again, and somewhere in the real world, the good Dr Gresch is checking me over right now. The one constant that connects every reality is the ringing in my ears, low and steady – it follows me everywhere.

'Steady on, old girl,' Christina says. 'You'll do yourself a mischief. Did you say you had a cousin? Let's start there.'

'Yes, Professor Kathryn Borg at the university,' I reply. 'But she's almost a century away.'

'I say, you are a funny duck.' Christina shrugs. 'Well, there's a telephone at Lascaris. We'll have this all cleared up in a jiffy and find a safe place to put you. Now, I'll make you a nice cup of tea, and you see if you can get dressed. How does that sound?'

'Fine,' I say. 'Thank you.'

'You know you made half the women on Malta sick as dogs when Danny brought you in yesterday, carrying you like he'd just swept you off your feet. He's regarded by many a poor girl as the most eligible bachelor on the island, but he's a heartbreaker is Danny. Not a cad, you understand? Quite the opposite. Won't have anything to do with a girl. I did wonder, but he's not *that way* inclined either, if you know what I mean? Too focused on the job, he says. Oh, the girls that have cried themselves to sleep over Danny Beauchamp . . .'

She chuckles to herself once more as she walks away.

When I'm alone, I take a good look around the small room. This metal-framed bed is rickety and old, the sheets rough and coarse. The room is barely furnished. There is a sink, a lantern, a small cupboard – and no electricity at all. It is a little odd to be so immersed in whatever this is and yet kind of detached from it. Nothing exactly like this happened after Syria, but I've experienced enough for me to know that something is misfiring somewhere to create this illusion. I'll take this over the terrifyingly real and sickening flashback that would floor me in an instant, leaving me a sobbing wreck. Instead, *this* delusion feels somehow *healing*.

Perhaps it's because it's years and years before I made that terrible mistake. Perhaps in this world, I am a clean slate with no penance to pay.

Chapter Eight

Tentatively, I swing my legs out of bed and put my feet on the cool tiles. They are firm beneath my feet. A stiff breeze wanders through the broken window shutters, which fight against their rusting latch with every gust of wind. Over the sink, there's part of a mirror attached to the wall by a twist of wire and a nail.

Bracing myself, I peer into it to see my forehead wrapped in white bandages like a headband, with a small dark flower of blood at the centre where I was wounded.

What came before feels vividly real: I was standing there, staring at this plane flying so low it felt like it was coming straight down the street. There was gunfire churning up the ground beneath me. And then the American – Danny, she said his name was – he came out of nowhere and knocked me out of the way. He saved my life, she said. My life before life, I suppose.

Hastily, I pull on my jeans and T-shirt, looking around to find my shoes placed neatly under the bed. Interesting that I'm wearing my usual twenty-first century clothes when I am in a bedgown in a hospital bed somewhere in 2025 and apparently in 1942 in this moment.

Slipping my feet into my sandals, I open the door an inch and peer into what must be a waiting room. The windows are cracked and filmed with dirt. Sunflower-yellow paint peels off the plastered walls; the hot, still air is thick with debris. An older woman, all in black, sits on one of several rickety-looking wooden chairs that line the walls of the room. She rubs at her knees, muttering fretfully under her breath. A young mother cradles a fitful baby against her shoulder, murmuring low, soothing words. Silent tears roll down her cheeks. Two seats away from her, a small boy of about five sits alone. His dark head is bowed over the scraps of paper he has rested on a book. He draws intently with the stub of a short pencil. I recognise the tilt of his head: it's the kid from the shelter, the one who followed me into the path of a murderous plane.

'Hello, kid,' I say.

The boy looks up and smiles. 'You are alive!' he says. Scrambling up, he trots over to me, wrapping his arms around my hips with a tight squeeze. 'I am glad you are not dead.'

'I'm glad *you* are not dead,' I say, disarmed by his easy affection. I must be careful; this is dangerous ground to tread. 'I did tell you to stay put.'

'Yes, but I had to save your life,' the little boy says. 'Be a hero, like Papa.'

By all accounts, it was the pilot who saved both of us, but I don't bring that up. In the full light of day, the boy is a thin but healthy-looking child. His clothes are a little big but clean, his shoes almost worn through.

This is a world of deprivation, where even everyday things are hard to come by. I understand the resourcefulness and determination it takes to live in these worlds. I've travelled through so many versions of the same place: ordinary people brought low by power grabs and political egos out of their control, while I report their hardships to the world.

I am, as ever, acutely aware that I have always been fortunate enough to be able to fly away back home to a world of new shoes and running water. I don't know much about the history of wartime Malta, but just from looking at the kid's shoes, I know there is no flying away from here, not for him.

There's no sign of Christina, and I think about trying to leave, except I'm not at all sure the kid won't follow me. Still, I start strolling towards the exit. Sure enough, the kid is on my tail, a sweet, fond smile on his face. This is stupid, but I can't run out on him again.

'Where do you think you are going?'

I turn around slowly to find a new woman questioning me: in her early thirties, about my age – dark hair, tall, with midnight eyes. Everything about her tells me at once that this is a woman you mess with at your peril.

'She leaved again, Mama,' the boy says. 'I will stop her again! Just like Papa.'

'Was leaving,' the woman corrects him, without dropping her gaze from me.

Christina suddenly appears, standing a few paces behind, holding a cup and saucer. Her eyes are wide, signalling that now I'm for it. The kid's doctor mother, of course.

'Thank you so much for taking care of me, Doctor,' I say.

'The least I can do,' she says, without a hint of a smile. 'After all, you took care of my boy after he disobeyed my specific instructions and ran off in the shelter.'

The boy's shoulders droop; his chin folds onto his chest. 'I'm sorry, Mama,' he says.

'He's a good kid,' I say. 'If anything, I was the careless one.'

'You were.' There is the briefest nod of affirmation. 'Nevertheless, you will not go anywhere *now* until you are seen and cleared by the authorities. You have been entrusted to our custody and will remain here until you are collected.' She points at a seat next to where the kid was drawing. 'You will sit there and wait.'

'This is insane,' I say, frustration bubbling up. 'I'm not sitting anywhere. Thank you so much, but . . .'

'You have no papers; you are dressed like a sailor.' The doctor gestures at me, her expression somewhere between cross and bemused. 'No one knows you or has ever heard of you. We have every right to detain you. It's a matter of national security, especially after the last incident, the spy. The shame of it.'

I have always found it very hard to follow an order. The urge to bolt grows.

'Doctor, if I may?' Christina steps lightly in front her now, as if reading my thoughts. 'Let me sit with Miss Borg while she drinks her tea. I'll keep an eye on her. And there's a very nice sergeant outside waiting to take her off your hands once she has had some refreshment.' Christina directs me to the chair.

The boy eagerly retakes his seat. 'I will show you my drawings,' he says happily.

The tea Christina gives me is lukewarm but dark brown, strong and sweetened with sugar. I finish it in two gulps.

The doctor looks like she has something else to say, but suddenly the cry of a baby starts from within her consulting room.

'Qalbi, your sister,' she tells the little boy.

He puts down his drawing and hurries into the room. A moment later, he reappears, carrying a screaming child of about one in his arms. His sister is almost as big as him.

'Shh, Eugenie,' he whispers over and over again, rocking the child back and forth.

The doctor returns to her office and shuts the door.

'You really are such a helpful little boy, aren't you?' Christina says to the boy. 'Would you like me to rock her for a while?'

The boy shakes his head. 'My . . . responsibility.'

'And your English is coming on in leaps and bounds,' Christina praises him, then turns to me. 'The doctor is a marvel, really – widowed while expecting her daughter, two children to care for all alone, and still working every day. Remarkable. Whenever I feel like complaining, I think of her.'

For a moment, I stare from the closed consulting-room door back to where the little boy struggles with the enormous whimpering baby.

'I'm a bit freaked out, to be honest,' I tell her.

'Freaked out?' Christina repeats, chuckling softly, her grey eyes searching mine. 'That's a new one on me. Look, I'm sure you are who you say you are. I'm a good judge of people, and I can tell you are not the traitor type. But just be careful what you say. No one just arrives on the island any more without everyone knowing about it, especially not a pretty young woman.'

'It's just that . . . I don't think this is real,' I find myself muttering aloud.

'Nonsense. Does the pain in your head feel real?' Christina asks me.

I nod reluctantly.

'And the taste of the tea? The heat of the day?'

I nod again.

'Then pull yourself together. Look, war does strange things to people. It drives us all a little mad. But I can promise you it will be better for you to cope with what is real rather than be labelled a lunatic and locked up somewhere – do you understand?'

'Don't let anyone see you're having a breakdown. Got it,' I say. 'I've heard that one before.'

The door swings open, and a gruff British soldier in khaki shorts peers in. 'Right then – this her?' He gives me an appraising look and clearly finds me wanting. 'I was hoping for more of a Mata Hari.'

I notice he is wearing a black armband reading *MP*. He's military police. Something about those stark white letters sends a shiver down my spine.

'With your permission, may I accompany our patient?' Christina asks the sergeant. 'She is rather fragile, and I should like to make sure she is looked after.'

'Certainly, Miss Ratcliffe,' he replies with a bashful smile. 'Anything for you.'

Christina smiles at him, then turns to the little boy. 'Darling.' She bends down until her face is level with his. 'Tell your mother I'll come back again if I can when she needs me – she can send for me anytime.'

He nods as his baby sister sucks unhappily on her fingers.

I find that I don't want to leave him, sitting there alone grappling with things he's too young to understand. He has that particular sadness of a small, ignored child: dutiful and good, but so very sad, with a sea of anger just beneath the surface, waiting to boil into adulthood.

I look at him and see myself.

'Hey, kid, you are a cool dude,' I tell him, with a thumbs up.

He blinks at me but smiles, too.

'Come along, Maia,' Christina says, giving me a look. 'We haven't got all day.'

She guides me outside into the searing heat, where a battered jeep idles on the road. A line of what look like bullet-holes punctuate its flank. Reluctantly I get in.

'Chauffeur-driven.' Christina smiles as she climbs in next to me. 'We *are* living in the lap of luxury, are we not?'

The jeep shrieks into gear and judders away.

Chapter Nine

Our supremely uncomfortable journey comes to an end in what I learn is the heart of Valletta, or at least what's left of it.

It's almost impossible to understand what I'm looking at. The last thing I remember in the waking world is looking at the black-and-white photos in the book Kathryn gave me. But those grainy, distant images have nothing to do with this shattered landscape. This is no repurposed memory.

This *is* Valletta. And it is on fire.

The sun is covered by clouds of smoke and dust; the air is so thick with oil that I can taste it. Grief surges upwards from my gut into my mouth – that, and the horror of total devastation. For me, this loss is happening *now*. This whole place ravaged in an instant. I want to cry for a city I have only recently learnt to love as it will be, rebuilt, decades from now. But that has been swept away by rewinding time, and in this hour, we can't know if Malta will survive. Memories of reality are no protection against the fear and tragedy of now.

As soon as I step out of the jeep, I start racing towards the Upper Barrakka Gardens, running from Christina and the sergeant, just needing to see. The elegant arches that once framed the perfect blue of the harbour are broken and shattered. The lush planting and colourful flower-beds are gone, replaced by rubble and heavy artillery. The military policeman shouts at me to stop, but I run on through the drifting clouds of debris. I need to see the harbour and the sea beyond. I need to know that *that*, at least, is still there.

Christina hurries behind me, calling for me to come back. I'm not doing very well at convincing her that I'm not a spy.

We stop dead against what's left of the wall looking out over the harbour. The pale rock is scorched by fire.

Dust rises in clouds. Smoke permeates all. Ships burn, giving off noxious black fumes. The three cities across the harbour, Vittoriosa, Senglea and Cospicua, are smouldering craters, torn open for the world to gape at. Ruin is everywhere I look. I can taste the dust on my tongue, smell the fumes of a thousand fires. I can see and touch the devastation.

'How did this happen?' I find myself asking no one in particular, because here in this moment, it is all too real.

'I ask myself that again and again,' Christina says; she's caught up with me and is leaning over the balcony to survey the scene. This isn't new to her. She has that world-weary look of a person who is exhausted by survival. 'You know, I arrived here by ship in '37. I had never seen anything as beautiful as this harbour at night. I felt like Titania being sailed into fairyland. The moon was full, and its light turned each of the towers and bastions silver. And the sky was full of twinkling, golden lights, from the stars in the sky to the thousands of lanterns on the anchored ships. I felt that Malta was a timeless, magical place where knights still fought for the hand of fair ladies and where history had stopped. I never would have dreamt then that I would still be here now and that all that splendour would have been smashed to smithereens. It seems that history never stops for anyone, doesn't it?' Then Christina thinks for a moment. 'But you *must* have seen this before?'

'I only just arrived in Valletta,' I tell her, which is true in a way.

The sight of this devastation has fired something in my racing heart: a furious, passionate anger. This is my land, whether I have known it or not. And I can't stand to see her bleed when the future is so very far away.

'I heard of the destruction, but this is . . .' I expand my hand across the panorama in a hopeless gesture. Looking over my shoulder I see the MP waiting for me, arms crossed.

'I know,' she says. 'I have never loved a place or a people as fiercely – its borders are etched on my heart. The Maltese have shown me how to fight a battle against the odds; it's for them that we battle on together. What else can we do? Come on – I'd better take you back, or the sergeant will have us both shot for insurrection.' She purposefully takes my arm and nudges me to follow her back towards the jeep. 'Sergeant,' Christina says when we reach it, addressing the flustered soldier. 'No need to trouble yourself any further here. I'll escort Maia for her interview. Now, Maia, you said you are staying with a cousin?'

'Yes,' I say slowly. 'Professor Kathryn Borg.'

'Oh, I know a Professor Borg – a delightful gentleman,' Christina says. 'I wonder if it's the same one. Oh no, how silly. A lady professor? That is marvellous.'

'A woman professor – don't sound likely,' the sergeant says.

'More likely than you knowing the sum of two plus two,' Christina tells him sweetly. 'Run along now – there's a good fellow.'

The sergeant harrumphs, mutters 'four' under his breath, but nevertheless turns on his heel and goes off to do her bidding.

'This way.' Christina leads me up the steps of a grand-looking building. 'Ordinarily, you'd be taken off to the prison to be interrogated, but as you are a woman, we have brought you here to see General Gort himself . . .' Christina has taken a few steps when she realises that I'm not following her.

'Come along, now,' she says, beckoning me. 'What are you doing?'

'Considering the nature of what constitutes reality,' I tell her honestly.

'Come on, you silly goose.' She beckons me impatiently. 'The general is a busy man, and I expect he has hardly the time or the ammo to muster a firing squad for you, even if you *are* a spy. Besides, I'll look after you. Promise.'

A promise from Christina seems like a solid thing, so reluctantly, I walk to her side.

'All you need to do is tell the general that you are here staying with your cousin the professor, and when your cousin arrives, all this will be cleared up.'

'Right,' I say.

Except, of course, there is no cousin to vouch for me here.

Chapter Ten

'So, you see the problem we have, Miss Borg?' General Gort tells me as he leans back in his chair, stroking his impressive moustaches, a pipe smouldering in one hand. 'Can't possibly afford to let any intel get back to Axis HQ in Sicily, so we must take every possible threat seriously, no matter how . . .' He gives me a lingering look. '. . . unlikely.'

Before reaching the general's smoke-filled office, Christina led me through a series of elegant and regal rooms bustling with activity. Quiet and intense men and women were labouring over matters of life and death with all the laser-focused concentration those kinds of stakes demand.

Now, as the general waits for my defence, I catch Christina's eye and read the note of caution. Christina seems to be the expert on navigating this world; I'd be a fool not to heed her.

'I'm not a spy,' I say. 'I got lost and, as you can see, suffered a head injury, and now everything is a little fuzzy. I'm not sure what happened to my papers . . .'

'*Well, that's not good enough, is it?*' The general slaps his hand on the desk. 'I've got a lot more important things to deal with now than a little lost English girl who can't keep hold of the most basic items. I should probably just send you off to the prison and have done with it.'

Perhaps he wants me to cry. I'm not going to cry; I've dealt with so much worse.

'What I did at the shelter was foolish; I could have got two other people killed . . .'

'Not just any person,' the general tells me. 'Flight Lieutenant Daniel Beauchamp is our best pilot. He's taken down nigh on twenty enemy aircraft here and saved dozens of lives by doing so. Damn fine man, for a Canadian.'

'Oh, *Canadian* – I see,' I say.

The general scowls at me.

'It's just that I thought he was American.'

'Men from all over the world have come to Malta to fight, madam,' he tells me. 'Americans, Canadians, Free French, South Africans, Polish, and of course our own chaps are the best of the lot. There's nowhere in the world where pilots risk their lives hourly like they do on Malta, and . . .' He checks himself.

'I realise that, and I just want to say that I really am truly sorry. I lost my mind for a moment, but I'm better now, thanks to Miss Ratcliffe and the doctor. I swear to you that I am not a spy.'

'And is there any reason why you appear to be dressed like a navvy?'

This man really is quite something.

'Clothes shortage, I expect,' Christina jumps in helpfully, looking up and down at my cut-off jeans and T-shirt. 'Some days, I wonder if I shan't have to start wearing brown paper bags – my frocks are all but worn to threads as it is. I admire Miss Borg, not bowing to the impulse to keep up appearances during wartime. Good for her, I say.'

I feel a rush of warmth for her.

'There's the other thing,' Gort mutters.

'The other thing, General?' Christina asks him.

He gestures at me.

'Ah, I see.' Christina gives me an apologetic look. 'You do look very well,' she says. 'Very well indeed, considering that food is so scarce.'

It's just sinking in that by 'well' she means 'fat', when someone new arrives.

'It runs in the family, you see.'

I turn around to see an older, rather short gentleman in a threadbare three-piece suit and round, wire-rimmed glasses. He is almost entirely bald except for a ring of neatly trimmed silver hair.

'Hello, my dear.' He addresses me directly. 'I've been worried sick about you.'

Sensing I should not allow my shock to show on my face, I smile weakly.

'Oh, my Professor Borg *is* your Professor Borg. Well, how lovely.' Then Christina catches herself as she remembers that my Professor Borg was a woman. But instead of mentioning that, she simply smiles, repeating, 'Lovely.'

'Of course – I am her cousin. You sent for me yourself, Miss Christina. Professor Borg at the university was summoned. Here I am.'

'I didn't put two and two together – silly me.' Christina looks from me to the gentleman, clearly wondering what is going on. She's not the only one.

'Well, there are many Borgs on Malta, my dear. And, General, if I may,' this other Professor Borg goes on, 'you will see that I am still rather rotund, despite not having seen pasta in months. My mama always used to say to me, "Salvatore, you are as wide as you are tall." A family trait, I suppose.' He chuckles, patting his belly.

'Well, there we are, then,' Gort says, standing up abruptly. 'Miss Ratcliffe, this woman is clearly this man's cousin.

We will need to see her papers, of course, Professor Borg, at the earliest convenience. Where do you live, sir?'

'I used to live in Senglea, but now . . .'

'Yes, now?' Gort barks impatiently.

'Well, I have a makeshift place in Valletta, General. The young lady is my responsibility. If her father were still alive, he would be cursing me for failing his daughter, and let me promise you, you never wanted to be on the wrong side of that formidable relation of mine.' He shudders theatrically. 'Why, I remember one occasion when . . .'

'Right, well, that's that matter closed,' the general says, already halfway out of the office. 'Take better care of the girl, Professor. She is clearly rather delicate of mind. Don't let her wander off and get hysterical again.'

'You have my word.' Professor Borg bows slightly at the waist.

Christina ushers us out of the office, and we follow her in an awkward silence outside.

'So, you are Cousin Kathryn, Sal?' she asks the old gentleman, crossing her arms as she frowns at him.

'Ah yes, Cathrinus, my formal name,' he says without missing a beat. 'Though I go by Salvatore. Sal more often, as you know, my dear.'

'And what do you call her?' Christina asks.

My eyes widen. There's no way he can know my name.

'Maia,' he replies at once. 'She was named for one of the stars in the Seven Sisters, you know.'

How did he know that?

'I see . . .' Christina seems unconvinced as she turns to me. 'I like you, Maia, and I don't think for one moment you are a spy. But I also know something fishy when I smell it. It would be better for you both to come clean so that I can stop worrying about you. But in the meantime, I'll be keeping an eye on you and your charming *Cousin Kathryn.*' She says the last two words in a mocking tone, making it clear she doesn't believe us, but also isn't going to argue. She pauses before adding, 'Count on it, won't you?'

'Miss Christina,' the professor implores her, 'I swear to you that I am here to take care of Maia, and you have my word of honour that we pose no threat to Malta.'

'I choose to give you the benefit of the doubt,' she says. 'For now.'

'Christina.' I take her hand impulsively. 'Thank you. For everything.'

'Don't make me regret it,' Christina says. 'For some reason, I feel like you and I have already met, even though I know we haven't! And while you're thanking people, you should probably find Danny Beauchamp and thank him for saving your life. Don't leave it too long. Danny's an ace, all right, but we lose so many of our boys fast round here. You never know when it might be too late.' She says this matter-of-factly, as though it is a completely normal thing to say, then looks down at an elegant gold wrist-watch. 'It will soon be time for the one o'clock raid, and I'm due at work. Make sure you stay in the shelter this time, Maia.'

'I will,' I say, desperately trying to get my head around what is going on. I look up at the sky, so serene and clear. It seems impossible that so much violence and death can be concealed in the blue.

Professor Borg nods and bows, and then he turns to me. 'Shall we?' He gestures for me to follow him.

I fall into step beside him. After all, I have no idea what else to do.

Chapter Eleven

For ten silent minutes, I try to work out what to do now as I follow the surprisingly fast-paced professor through the rubble-strewn streets of Valletta, taking turn after turn after turn.

Every sense I have tells me that I am actually *here*, on this street, in this place, in 1942. And my gut says I should believe it. But then again, maybe I'm crazy – maybe this is what psychosis is like. Either way, I know already that to try to game this, or act like it is a place where no action has any consequence, would be a rookie error.

Somehow, my head has put me *here*, in this time and place, and I need to try to understand *why*.

Especially why I am following a strange man ever deeper into the less salubrious narrow streets and alleyways of wartorn Valletta, like a lamb to the slaughter – a man who somehow knew my name. If my head made him up, that would make sense.

But what if it didn't?

I've followed more overtly threatening men in the past: men with covered faces, carrying weapons and issuing threats. I've followed them for a story, content to risk my life to get it. This is different, though. There is no truth here – it's all a mirage. Sal doesn't glance back at me as we walk. He is certain I'm following behind, and I don't like that kind of certainty. It implies that he knows I have no choice.

Eventually, we turn onto a long, narrow, straight street that runs first downhill then inclines upwards again. It's lined on each side by shuttered buildings, apartments, nightclubs and bars. It has an air about it – the sort of atmosphere that even in the strangest of circumstances might make a woman wonder where she's being taken and why. Wary, I stop.

I know this place. I had an Aperol Spritz here on my second night in Malta, about a hundred years from now.

'Is this the Gut?' I ask.

Professor Borg falters to a stop and looks at me as if he's half-forgotten I'm here. I read about this place before my trip. Once, it was Valletta's most infamous street, home to cabaret bars and ladies of the night.

'Er, yes – but you have no need to worry for your reputation, Miss Borg. It is just a short-cut. Besides, during the day it is perfectly safe for respectable young ladies such as yourself.'

'Hey, it's you! The woman who almost did what the Nazis haven't yet and got me killed.'

Coming out of one of the narrow houses in front of us is the man I now know to be the Canadian local hero and Spitfire ace who saved my life: Danny Beauchamp. He looks like he hasn't slept a wink. His hair is a mass of tangled brown curls beneath his battered peaked cap. His frayed shirt has more buttons undone than I would imagine is regulation, revealing a tanned, toned chest. The bottoms of his shorts are rolled up, revealing muscular thighs. And seeing him here gives me a chance to tell someone where I am going and who with – just in case.

'So, you're not dead, huh?' He grins at me, before nodding at my bandage. 'Though you took quite a hit. Where you going now?'

'I'm going with Professor Borg here – I'm not sure exactly where,' I tell him pointedly.

'Oh, hi, Prof!' Danny tips his cap at the man. 'I didn't see you there, sir. Wait a second – you know this gal?'

'Ah yes, Flight Lieutenant. She is my cousin. I didn't take proper care of her, and I can only apologise that she caused you such inconvenience.'

'Excuse me....' I begin, put out by being spoken about like I'm a naughty child.

'Don't worry about it,' Danny says, glancing at me with a lopsided twist of a teasing smile. 'Ladies are delicate creatures, after all. Especially English ones.'

'Look, I'm quite capable of looking after myself and apologising when I have to,' I say firmly. 'And I am sorry. Truly. Thank you for – I don't know, saving my life I suppose.'

Danny shrugs. 'I'd have done it for anyone.' He pushes his cap to the back of his head and squints at me in the midday sun. 'Christina wouldn't let me see you yesterday, and then I heard they'd carted you off to General Gort, under suspicion of being a spy. I told Christina it'd be an awful shame to shoot you after I nearly died to save your life.'

'I strongly agree,' I say, 'but it's all been cleared up now. A misunderstanding. You know. . . my cousin, well?'

'Sure, the prof is a stand-up guy. Comes and reads with our injured men and helps them write letters and such. Teaches the local kids who don't have schools to go to anymore. A genuine local legend.'

'You go too far, Flight Lieutenant.' The professor bows his head, blushing with pride. 'You are the real hero.'

'We're just doing our jobs.' Danny removes his cap and runs his fingers through his curls, before replacing the cap. 'Each one of us is proud to do our duty, sir. Especially for the people of Malta. There ain't none braver that I've ever met.' Danny flashes another smile at me. The ice-cold blue of his eyes reflects the sky he spends so much time in, as if he has brought a little bit of the heavens back with him.

'Well, I shall wait a little way down the street for you, Maia,' the professor tells me. 'I know you would like a chance to speak with Flight Lieutenant Beauchamp in private. We are going to the half-house first on the right-hand street at the end of the Gut, Flight Lieutenant. That is where Maia will stay while she is in my care. Once again, my deepest thanks for your service.'

'Champ,' Danny calls after the professor as he heads into the shade. 'My friends call me Champ.' He turns to me. 'So, you OK, Stitches?' he asks. 'OK with the prof?'

'Do you really know him?' I ask.

Danny raises an eyebrow. 'He's *your* cousin, ain't he?'

'Yes, but I only met him . . . recently. And I don't have anyone else here. I suppose I only just met you, too, but you did stop me from dying, so . . .'

'I'm pretty sure you're in safe hands with the prof,' Danny assures me. 'As safe as you can be anywhere in this war. But I feel kind of responsible for you now, so I'll keep an eye on you, if that's OK with you?'

I nod. It irks me ever to need help from anyone, but it seems sensible to make allies until I understand what's happening.

The professor has walked a few steps down the street to shelter from the sun in a doorway. The moment he stops, he fishes what looks like a notebook out of his pocket, and the stump of a pencil. He licks the end of it, then begins to take notes.

The sun is fierce. I can feel the skin on the back of my arms stinging with sunburn. The smell and taste of dust in every breath is chalk and oil. The way Danny Beauchamp stands, head cocked to one side as he waits for me to talk, is both assured and boyish. The scent of his sweat, his height, his golden skin, a graze of stubble and a crooked smile. He's both so young – mid-twenties, at a glance – and so world-weary all at once. Life flows out of him with a barely repressed energy.

'Oh, it's Maia, by the way. My name, that is. Maia Borg.' I offer him my hand.

'Named after a star,' he says.

I nod. 'Good guess.'

The professor coughs from his doorway, and when I glance at him, he shows me his pocket-watch.

'Oh, I know stars,' Danny tells me. 'They are my compass and companions. You have a pretty name. I might still call you Stitches, though. It suits you.'

'Ahem.' The professor is rather more insistent this time.

'I'd better go.' I hesitate. I have no idea what's coming or even when.

'You better had.' Danny nods. 'Next raid due any minute. Try not to die before we next meet, OK?'

'Same goes double for you,' I tell him.

'I'll do my best, Stitches.' Danny tips his hat and strides away.

'Not much time now.' Professor Borg taps his watch-less wrist as I walk towards him. 'Hell by clockwork. It's how the Nazis want to wear us down. Get us softened up nicely for invasion.'

'I need to ask you something before we go any further.' I stand assertively, refusing to follow him for now.

He looks anxiously towards wherever we are going, but I stand my ground.

'Very well,' he says.

'Am I safe with you?' It may seem like an odd question, but I've discovered that people don't often lie when you are direct.

'Yes, you are safe with me, Maia.' He nods, and I think I believe him. 'I am the only person on this island who can help you.'

What does he mean by that?

'But we must go,' he says.

'One more thing: how did you know my name?'

'That much is easy,' Professor Borg tells me. 'I know your name because I read all about you. And I've been waiting for you for a very long time.'

Chapter Twelve

'What do you mean by that?' I ask after a pause, taken aback.

'Not here – we must get to safety,' he insists, sharper now, with increased urgency. 'Then I will tell you everything I can.'

We stop outside what was once a four-storey house in an elegant street that wouldn't look out of place in Paris or Prague. The top storey has gone completely, and the first and second floors are exposed to the air like a kind of obscene doll's house. Someone's once-beautiful home and precious belongings are on display for every passer-by to pore over. A pink kimono hangs from a splintered floorboard that juts into mid-air, fluttering in the breeze like a flag.

'Through here,' the professor tells me. He opens the solid-looking front door onto a hallway that leads through to a surreal landscape of rubble bathed in bright midday sun. I look up again at the ruin balanced over our heads. As I look, an air-raid siren wails outside, and already I can hear the droning hum of planes. I can see waves of aircraft, steadily making their way closer, so many that they seem to fill the sky.

'Hurry,' he urges. 'There's a private shelter off the courtyard through here. Follow me.'

I step into the torn-open hallway, where the stairs ascend to daylight. A clock stands against the wall, still ticking. I wonder vaguely who continues to wind it.

He leads me past a room that once would have been a comfortably appointed parlour. I glimpse shelves lined with books, a family photograph in a heavy mahogany frame over a mantelpiece. The professor isn't in it.

'Here.' He opens a gate, revealing a set of steps leading down. Biting my lip, I peer into the close darkness.

'I told you I won't hurt you, Maia,' he tells me, as the drone of the planes grows louder. 'You need not be afraid of me. I'm trying to keep you safe.'

Still, I hesitate.

'I know there is more you need to know. Why I came to help you when you and I have never met and do not know one another,' he tells me. 'Whether any of this is even real.'

'Is it?'

The thunder of falling bombs sounds very close, and finally, I run down the steps and into the dark, the professor just behind me.

He lights a candle, revealing a sparsely furnished room.

'You are not dreaming, Maia,' he tells me. 'You exist in this time, just as you exist in the time you have come from. Here you will grow old, as I have grown old. Here you burn under the hot sun, as your skin has burnt today. Here you live as best you can; here you may very well die at any hour or on any day. I do not know if death in one reality means death in all. I do not have that answer.'

'What are you talking about?' I ask. 'How do you know my name?'

'I read about you – in a time that is very far into the future for both of us.'

'What do you mean?' I ask as the explosions grow louder and the walls shake.

'It's hard to explain,' he says. 'I've found myself in so many times or realities. I'm not sure if they are within this universe or linked to others but . . . for now I should start at the beginning – my beginning, anyway.

'You see, I woke up in 1909, thirty-three years ago,' he says. 'Which was surprising because I fell asleep in 1992.'

The world trembles in fear.

Chapter Thirteen

Sunday 22nd June 2025, 12.30 p.m.

I'm in a coffin. There's no air. I can't see anything. All I can hear is this loud, booming clanking. Its volume is so great that it fills the air, suffocating me. The building must have collapsed on me. I am buried alive.

The din is so all-consuming that when I scream, I can't hear my own voice. I can only feel the words vibrate and grate in my bone-dry throat: 'Get me out, get me out, get me out!'

'Maia.' Dr Gresch's voice crackles in my ears, shocking my eyes open in the dark. There's light somewhere out of reach.

'Can you get me out?' I plead. 'Can you dig me out? Am I dead?'

'Don't worry – we are bringing you out now. Take a deep breath. It will just be a moment or two. You are safe. You are in an MRI scanner at the hospital. You are safe and well.'

I can't move my arms to touch my face, but I realise I have an eye mask on and, if this is the same as my last scan, a sort of cage over my face. Tears roll down my cheeks, falling onto my earlobes and neck: I am back.

Dr Gresch takes my hand as soon as I am out of the machine.

'I'm so sorry, Maia. It must have been a shock, coming back to consciousness like that, but you are OK. You are safe.'

A nurse removes the cage thing from my head, and then my eye mask. Bright light makes me screw my eyes shut for a moment, cover them with the palms of my hands. They smell of something unfamiliar: smoky and sharp.

When the nurse removes the ear plugs from my ears, the ringing fades a little into the background.

'What the hell?' I say, sitting up too fast; the room tilts and spins a little before settling back on its axis. 'Couldn't you have woken me up first?'

'Paula, would you fetch . . .' Dr Gresch nods discreetly at the door. 'That was the problem,' she continues, turning to me. 'We couldn't wake you up. The nurse came to take your vitals this morning, and you slept through them, slept through breakfast, and when your cousin came, she couldn't rouse you. All your vitals seemed fine, but you would not be woken. We were very worried. I'm sorry you came round in the machine – it must have been very frightening.'

'What do you mean you couldn't wake me up?' I ask her. 'Why not?'

'We don't know,' she admits. 'And I'm afraid that I need to ask you to go back into the MRI machine so that we can complete the scan and try to find out.'

'No.' I shake my head. I'm still wrapped in the horror of those last few minutes between waking and sleeping, when dreams and reality became one.

'Maia, please—' she begins.

'I'm awake now, right? So, problem solved.'

'Maia, something is going on that we don't understand. Please. I beg you. We need to be certain that nothing has been missed.'

'She's begging you, and I'm telling you.' Kathryn appears at the door with the nurse who fetched her. She hurries over to my side, hugging me to her bosom.

After a moment, I put my arm around her waist. My arms are stiff and sore. When she lets me go, I notice they are bright red.

'You scared me to death, Maia. Now, let them finish the scan. I'll stay in here with you, OK? I'll talk to you through the thing, but you *are* going back in for that scan. End of.'

When I run my fingers through my hair, little bits of grit and dust film my hand. I stare at my palms for a long, confused moment. It's not normal to bring a little of your dream back with you, is it?

'OK,' I say. 'I'll go back in.'

***

'It was so real,' I tell Dr Gresch, back in my sun-drenched hospital room. 'I felt like I was there, in real time. The heat, the smells. And then I wake up smelling of smoke, with dust in my hair? And with sunburnt arms. People don't get sunburn in their sleep.'

'No.' Dr Gresch is thoughtful, her dark brows knitted together in a frown. She taps a silver pen against her bottom lip. 'Yet your scan is clear for physical anomalies or concerns.'

'What does that mean?' I ask. 'Does that mean I'm going mad?'

'No.' She studies the results of my scan again for a long moment, while Kathryn sits down next to me.

Getting up suddenly, Dr Gresch calls to a nurse in the hallway. A slight young man in scrubs steps in.

'Gi, who did Maia's stitches?' the doctor asks.

'I am not sure,' Gi replies. 'They were done when I came on shift. I did notice . . . but I thought perhaps an older member of staff or . . . ?' He shrugs.

'What's wrong with my stitches?' I ask, touching my fingers to where a sterile pad is fixed to my forehead. It stings.

'Nothing.' Dr Gresch comes round and, bending down carefully, removes the pad. 'Fetch me another, please, Gi.'

The nurse departs.

'Your stitches are very neatly and expertly done,' Dr Gresch tells me, 'but in a way I haven't seen practised for . . . well, ever! Very old-fashioned, using silk. We haven't used silk to stitch wounds in *decades*. I'm not sure how this happened. We sometimes have older agency nurses, but where would they find silk stitches?'

'What does this mean?' I ask.

'Nothing, really – just another little anomaly to add to the mystery of Maia.' She smiles at me. 'I'll take them out for you in a few days. You'll hardly notice the scar.'

Kathryn is looking at me thoughtfully. 'You were in Malta during the war?' she asks me. 'In your dream?'

'Yes, and it was so real . . . I can hardly believe that my brain could come up with the details. I woke up in this place in Floriana, and there was this woman there. Her name was Christina Ratcliffe. And she told me my life had been saved by this flying ace called Danny—'

'Beauchamp,' Kathryn finishes.

My mouth falls open. 'How do you know?' I ask.

'Because they are real people,' Kathryn tells me. 'Famous on the island. You must have read about them or heard about them somehow.'

'I didn't read that book, though,' I protest. 'So how could I have dreamt about real people I knew nothing about?'

'It's very possible that you know about them without knowing about them,' Dr Gresch tells me. 'You must have absorbed this information in the time you've been on the island, and while you slept, your subconscious brought them to life for you.'

'And the dust in my hair?' I ask, running my fingers through it again.

'You have an abundance of beautiful, long dark hair,' Dr Gresch says. 'It was probably already there from when you fainted at the temple.'

'But the sunburn?' I ask.

'Sometimes your body can manifest the physical attributes of a mental . . . event,' Dr Gresch suggests, somewhat half-heartedly.

'Well . . . why?'

'I don't know,' she says. 'And I also don't know that the redness on your arms and face *is* sunburn. I will need to consult a dermatologist and also, perhaps . . . a psychiatrist.'

'No, thank you,' I say firmly. 'I've seen enough of those to last me a lifetime. If I'd been wandering around imagining this world was real, maybe – but it was a *dream*. So I'm fine. Look, my head looks OK to you, right?'

'Yes,' she says, 'but considering your history, we should exercise caution . . .'

'Yes, I agree, but I've been under a lot of stress: coming to this island in the first place; seeing my father, with whom I have had a very difficult, practically non-existent relationship; then the crash; then I looked at the photos in the book Kathryn gave me and my brain went to town on me, right?' I look at Kathryn. 'I've always had really vivid dreams, and now . . . well, now it's like all the things added up and created the perfect storm inside my head. It's hit me hard – delayed, but hard.

'I needed to sleep, so I slept deeply. But it's like the physical trauma has sent my immune system into overdrive, which, instead of giving me psoriasis, which is what it usually does, it's given me this hot, stinging rash. And my past experiences of reporting from war zones all added up to a really, really vivid dream, and now it's done. And I could stay here and have a load of tests and talk to your psychiatrist, but I am pretty sure they would come up with the same conclusion after a few days and a lot of euros. Aren't you?'

Dr Gresch sits back in her chair and thinks for a moment. 'Without you undergoing the appropriate diagnostic tests, I can't say conclusively that that is the case,' she says. 'But I am conducting a sort of sleep study at present. It's to explore the link between consciousness and . . .'

'No, thanks.'

'I understand your reservations, but if you would consider letting me enrol you . . . ?'

'No. Thank you, but no. Discharge me, please,' I ask. 'I'll stay in Malta until Dad is OK to fly home, but I think all I need is rest and time and space from all this past – his past, my past. I've never been very good at thinking about all of that – I'm very much more of a now person.'

'I see that.' Dr Gresch smiles softly. 'Very well – I will get your discharge papers ready. But if, in the next few days, you get any new symptoms, you will come back – agreed?'

'She will, Doctor,' Kathryn assures her. 'I'll keep an eye on her.'

'Great,' I say. 'I guess I'd better go and see my dad while I'm waiting. I think it will help ground me. He has a way of bringing me down to earth with a bump.'

'Want me to come?' Kathryn asks.

'No,' I say. 'Dad telling me what he thinks of me is something I'd prefer not to have an audience for.'

Chapter Fourteen

'I'm fine – don't come here,' my dad is saying to his iPad as I enter the room. 'You don't need to come here. I don't want you here. I will be home soon. Oh.' He looks up across the top of the screen at me.

'Oh, what?' I hear Vanessa's voice from the other side.

'Maia.' He says my name as a single, self-explanatory word.

'Oh, that's good! You talk to your daughter then. I'll FaceTime you later,' Vanessa says, hanging up before my father can protest or get out of talking to me by making me small talk with his fourth wife instead. In all honesty, I feel as aggrieved by her evasive tactics as he does.

We observe each other for a moment with apprehension.

'How are you feeling, Dad?' I ask from the doorway. It's the best I can come up with. I look at him, and I want to feel love. The best I can manage is a sort of vested interest. He is half of me, after all.

'Like I've been in a car crash,' he says dryly.

Over his bed, there is a whiteboard with his full name written on it in capital letters: DAVID SIMON SAVIOUR MICHAEL JEREMY BORG. Jeremy? I'm pretty sure that's not on his Wikipedia page.

'I'm sorry.' I don't want to apologise. I hate apologising, especially to him. But it *was* my fault. And I never back away from things I'm responsible for, even when there is no way to repair them. He taught me that by doing the opposite.

'You should have looked,' he agrees, but his tone isn't combative. He looks weary, almost defeated. 'But it wasn't just your fault. I brought you here. And I . . . failed at making it what you wanted it to be, which in turn made you feel angry and hurt, which meant you didn't look.'

The insight and generosity of this comment can only have come from Vanessa. Even so, that he listened, retained and spoke it aloud to me is something unexpected.

'Thank you,' I say, taking a few hesitant steps into the room. 'I expected you to be angry. I deserve it.'

'I'm not a monster, Maia. I'm . . .' He lets out a long, wistful sigh. 'I don't know what I am – only that what other people find easy, I find hard. I know you wanted a reunion, a moment where I apologise to you for not being the father you deserved, where you forgave me, and we healed the past. I wish I was that man, but I suspect, if I were, then we would not be here in the first place.'

'That's not quite right,' I say, choosing my words carefully. 'In an ideal world, yes, I'd love that scenario. But the world is not ideal. It's broken and painful. *We* are broken and painful. All I wanted was to try to understand you.'

'Hm.' He shrugs, leaning back into the pillow. In the afternoon light, he looks so old: small and frail and impossibly mortal. But my dad can't be mortal, can he? Not this man who has strode across decades, a thousand feet tall. 'I'm not that interesting.'

'Well, for someone who's not that interesting, you've had three books written and one documentary made about you,' I say, tentatively taking a seat at the side of his bed. Any conversation with my father involves an invisible hair-trigger, and you are never sure when or how you might trip it.

'They are all about my paintings,' he says, with a wave of his hand. 'Not me. I'm not important. I'm nothing.'

That isn't true, and he knows it isn't. My father has been a celebrity since he hung out with Andy Warhol. His various addictions, affairs and marriages have been as enduringly fascinating to the world at large as his art. Even I, the child he never wanted, have been a hot topic for debate on Radio Four art shows. It's strange, to say the least, when the world wants to know all about the absence of someone in your life. I have never commented, despite dozens of requests – not out of respect for my father, but just because I don't know how to explain what I don't understand. And because I wanted to be someone apart from him. Look at how I've succeeded, despite you, I wanted to say.

Then something terrible happened, and instead of building a life of my own, I imploded on myself.

'Dad, can I ask you one question?' I phrase it as if I expect never to speak to him again.

'You can ask,' he says, with a shrug. His eyes are closed, a frown stitched between his brows.

'Did you call me Maia after the star? The Pleiades?'

'Good Lord, no,' he says. 'Only a mawkish idiot would do such a thing.'

'Then why did you?' I ask him. 'Mum said it was the only thing you fought for when it came to me. You fought for my name. And I just want to know why.'

'Honestly?' When he looks at me, I see genuine sorrow in his face. His hand, frail and spotted with age, touches the back of mine, just for a second. 'I'm afraid I don't remember.'

Chapter Fifteen

The heat of the day has subsided into a gentle warmth. Somewhere, fireworks are lighting up the sky with crackles of glitter. Boats bob in the harbour, illuminated by fairy lights and lanterns. It makes me think of what Christina told me about the first night she entered the grand harbour. Perhaps that came from looking at this view – it would make sense.

Kathryn pours me a glass of ginger ale over ice. We have decided against wine, at least until I can be really sure that I am as fine as I told the good doctor I was. It seems prudent to be cautious, which does not come naturally to me. I have always been inclined to risk. The more I've seen, the more I've risked, as if I might be able to barter myself in exchange for a better world.

'Is that a wedding?' I ask Kathryn as we watch red and silver lights blossom in the lavender sky. Each display is followed by a deafening boom, and I have to hold myself very firmly not to flinch.

'A *festa*, for a saint,' Kathryn tells me. 'We have a *festa* every month here, sometimes twice,' she says. 'A parade, flags, food, fireworks. Our cities and towns are always dressed to celebrate. We take our dedication to the saints seriously.'

'Are you a very devout Catholic?' I ask, tilting my head in query.

'Not really.' Kathryn scans the gold horizon. 'I don't suppose I am, by traditional standards. But then the women in our family have never really been traditional.'

'You mean our grandmother?' I ask, intrigued.

'I mean you and me,' Kathryn says. 'But yes, our grandmother, too. I'm amazed you don't know about her – you are so like her, both of you with a thousand times more courage than most.'

'Dad didn't like to talk about her,' I say. 'And also, he didn't like to talk to me, so, you know . . . I have quite a few gaps. I know only that she died young.'

'So tragic, poor Grandmama. Such a tragic loss. I think it broke your father's heart for good.' Kathryn presses her lips together in disapproval. 'Even so, it's important to know where you come from.'

'Tell me about Gran, then?' I prompt.

Kathryn thinks for a moment. 'Read the book I gave you first,' she says. 'I never knew her, of course. And Mum was just a baby when Gran was killed. All I know about her comes from family lore and stories handed down. They provide wonderful colour. But the book is impartial, and I think you will be impressed and amazed, if not a little sad.'

'Only you would refuse to spoiler the story of my own grandmother.' I laugh. 'At least tell me why she died so young.'

'Oh, she was killed by enemy gunfire,' Kathryn says. 'The day before the siege was broken. The tide turned, the next day. She might have been safe. It breaks your heart.'

'This is why I don't have any faith,' I tell her. 'If there is a God, he is cruel.'

'You don't need to adhere to a religion to find something to have faith in,' Kathryn says, dropping more ice into my drink. 'I do have faith in something greater than us, but maybe it doesn't have to be more than that we exist. I'd rather pay homage to those ancient women, who knew nothing of Christ but understood the skies and seasons well enough to guide the people who depended on such things through when to plant a crop, when to take in a harvest.' She shrugs. 'But that's just me.'

'I like your version of faith,' I say. 'I was raised a heathen. My mum believed in . . . well, in fairies, mostly, though sometimes I wonder if that side of her – the mystical and slightly mad side – was really her or the tumour all along.'

'Your mother was just who she was,' Kathryn says. 'I remember her at your parents' wedding – well, handfasting ceremony, she called it. They got married in a clearing in a forest, and she had bare feet and daisies in her hair. That was your mum through and through. A lump of gristle in her head couldn't change that.'

Kathryn's words are full of warmth and comfort, but I'm not sure I can completely believe them, even if I wanted to.

'And my dad believes in nothing at all.'

'I like the sound of your mother.' Kathryn smiles. 'You must miss her.'

'I do, I do, I do.' There is nothing to add to that constant acknowledgement that is never far out of reach.

I take a sip of the ginger ale and wish it had whisky in it. It's hard to imagine the faces of people I never knew or feel the pang of their absence. But my dad must have felt that loss keenly. I have never thought to put him in context before, and it shifts something in my heart. Perhaps there is a reason he is as he is, after all.

There's something else weaving a subtle chill into the evening – something about Malta that scares me. It's a kind of pull, an almost physical tug that started the moment I got off the plane: a longing I have never known before but for something I can't identify.

It's almost like I'm pining for something or someone. But I don't know what or who. Like I'm missing a lover I have never known. I can't explain it exactly. I only know that it makes me feel vulnerable, somehow – open to loss, when I've been so very careful to make sure that I have nothing to lose.

'Well, it's late, and I have two lectures to give tomorrow,' she says. 'So, I'm off to bed. Will you be OK?'

'I am a bit nervous about the whole sleeping thing,' I confess. 'It suddenly feels like an unknown state.'

'Well, it is, I suppose.' Kathryn thinks for a moment. 'We can never know for sure what was truly on the minds of ancient peoples, but there is a strong case for the theory that they saw dreams as portals – ways to travel to the stars, to visit their ancestors and to communicate with the universe in the form of their gods. Perhaps they felt dreams were like horses, riding through the sky. Try to think of it that way. Like an adventure.'

'I won't, if you don't mind. I prefer to choose my own adventures. I'm just going to hope for my usual dream of not having done enough work to pass my exams – or a classic zombie apocalypse.'

'Well.' Kathryn gives my shoulders a brief hug. 'Come to meet me, for lunch tomorrow? I have the afternoon off. I can take you to the knights' city of Mdina – the Silent City, it's often called. You'll love it.'

'Yes, please.' I smile enthusiastically, but in my gut, I have a premonition. Something's coming.

* * *

Once Kathryn is in bed, I dawdle on the balcony for as long as I can, until the air carries a hint of cool and my eyes are tired and long to close. I procrastinate over going to bed, cleaning my teeth for a little too long, deciding to brush every tangle out of my freshly washed hair, and then take a second shower before starting the process all over again. I have a sense that I want to feel completely clean, to have washed away every last trace of my unnerving wartime dream.

Finally, I am sitting up in the guest bed, leaning back against the pillows.

Malta: The George Cross Island at War lies innocuously on my lap.

Honestly, what kind of a woman am I, to fear a book – a history book, too? Picking it up, I flick through to the central section of photographs again. There is Christina, just as I dreamt her, beautiful and bold, even after years of war and starvation. This image must have taken root in my mind. That makes perfect sense. I turn the pages, looking at images of the harbour on fire, the opera house destroyed.

My eyes catch on a group photo, not posed but candid. A crashed aircraft smokes in the background; there's a bus and a large group of passengers have climbed off to see the destruction. In the foreground, a very grimy pilot stands with his hands on his hips, looking down at something, maybe a map, that someone is showing him. Around him, there's a straggled group of bystanders, all smiling. There's a lot of text under the photo printed very small, but the name *Danny 'Champ' Beauchamp* is in bold. I peer at him, trying to get a sense of the man I met in my dreams, but the image feels exactly like what it is: a document from long ago that has all but lost its meaning.

My head is heavy; exhaustion drags my body down into the comfort of cushion and pillow.

Sleep is a constant traveller; there are no borders in dreams.

Chapter Sixteen

Thursday 6ᵗʰ August 1942, 2 p.m.

'Are you quite all right, my dear?'

Professor Salvatore Borg lights an oil lantern, which illuminates the small, vaulted shelter. It must have been used as cold storage once. Chisel marks can still be seen in the stonework. Now, there is a rickety-looking bookshelf in one corner, a chair and a small school desk with papers and notebooks balanced precariously across its surface. Some of them are open and scrawled with notes. In one corner, there is a metal-framed bed with a slim mattress and a battered-looking pillow. In another is a bucket. I don't want to think about what that's for. There's also a small table with a covered jug and a bread tin on it.

'I'm not sure,' I say. I'm lying on the cool stone floor. There's a battered-looking brown velvet cushion under my head. I can see by the creases in the material that it was once ruby-red and trimmed with gold.

'You fainted,' the professor tells me, peering at me. 'Did you return? To where you came from? Or another place?'

'Another place? How long was I out for?' I ask.

I struggle to sit up, and he helps me with a gentle hand under my elbow. My instinct is to shuffle away from his touch, leaning against a wall for support.

He seems to understand and backs away a step. 'A few minutes, perhaps five. Maybe one or two more.'

'That proves it – you're just in my mind. I was awake for more than twelve hours back in my real life, and then I went to bed. I was back for a whole day. That's why this must be a hallucination or a delusion – a dream. It's my fucked-up brain making everything too real again.'

The professor frowns fleetingly at the swear word but says nothing. 'Yes, I recall thinking much the same thing when it first started happening to me,' he tells me. 'At first, it only occurred when I was asleep – easy to dismiss. Vivid dreams, I told myself. And then later, time started to come for me at any moment.'

Wincing a little, he crouches and then sits on the floor against the wall opposite me. He produces a handkerchief from his pocket and mops his brow. I hardly know him, but I know enough to know that the initials sewn into its corner are not his.

If this was real, everything about him would be waving red flags at me. But this is not real.

'What do you mean: "Time comes for you"?'

Part of my therapy was to keep a dream diary. My therapist told me it might help me make sense of the secrets my brain was keeping from me. So it makes sense to try to understand why here, why him, why this.

'It's hard to explain, but you will understand soon enough. At its peak, it happened often, and it was always shocking. You should prepare yourself for that. It felt like constant vertigo: the ground would not remain beneath my feet and the world would disintegrate and reform itself around me, and I would be in another time. Still in Malta, but always in another time. Once, all I saw was the dark sky and a billion stars. I heard the roar of something in the night. I don't know for certain, but I think that is the earliest time I was ever taken to.' He pauses. 'Like you, I tried to explain it all away. I told myself that I was simply dreaming, that any moment I would wake up at home beside my wife.'

'You're married?' I ask.

'I am,' he says. 'Or at least, I was. Or I will be. The only thing I know is that I miss her. Anyway, I didn't die. Instead, the fluctuations, as I call them, started to slow down. But it wasn't my own time that I seemed anchored to. I've lived almost permanently here now for thirty years – long enough to become part of the community, to almost forget that war was inevitable and that one day the siege of the island will end – which it will, though of course I can't be certain it will end the way it has before.'

'What do you mean?' I ask.

'I mean that whenever you are, there is only now. And in the now, nothing is predetermined. I mean that anything you do here might change everything. You might even erase your own existence, which would mean you had never travelled in time at all, which would make your present self something of an anomaly and present us with the kind of paradox that makes Einstein very unhappy.'

Noise crashes through the earth, filling the tiny room for several long seconds with a sound so powerful I feel it in every cell of my body. Fear flushes through me. Everything feels as if it is twisting and tearing apart. I long for one second of quiet, just enough to take an inward breath. I want to go back to a world where this horror belongs to other people.

'You are quite safe,' the professor assures me as the roar gradually dies away, leaving the air quivering in its wake. 'That was close, perhaps the closest for now. Yes, I think the worst has passed.'

Sinking to the floor, I fold in on myself, tucking my head between my knees, searching for the courage I used to know.

When I made that terrible mistake in Syria, I had been there a month. From the roof of my hotel, I could hear the sounds of warfare like the boom of distant thunder. Not that one powerful aggressor bombing his own people to oblivion can really be called a war. I bore witness to plumes of smoke that curled into the sky, knowing only in abstract that each one grew from a place of devastation. I reported on children sheltering in bunkers, wrote stories about how they would sing to pass the time. I experienced the rolling blackouts across the country, the acute medical and food shortages. I sent news home, hoping my articles might help raise awareness, influence politicians.

I'm not sure that anything I've ever done has really helped anyone. The only solid evidence I have is of the harm I've done. So, the war my mind has dropped me into is hardly a subtle metaphor. My brain bombards me with guilt formed by experience. It was my fault. I put her in harm's way.

There is no recovering from a mistake that cost a child her life.

Chapter Seventeen

'Here.' The professor passes me a tin mug of water. He listens for the next explosion. It's a little fainter. 'See, it will be done soon enough, and you are not dead. Some have died; some will die. But here on the island, the houses are made of stone, so fires, like you have had in England – they are rare. The shelters hold firm. Many live. Take comfort in that.'

'Professor, I need to get out of here . . .' I feel my throat tightening, refusing to let more air into my lungs.

'I understand, and you will. But please, call me Sal,' he says. His tone is calm, lilting. 'Sal to my friends. For we will be friends, in time – when you have come to realise the truth and that you can trust me. So, call me Sal in anticipation of that moment, please? Let me explain a little. If you listen and think about what I say, your anxieties will calm, and begin to recede. Do you agree?'

'OK.' I nod. He's right; I need distraction to get through the next ten minutes without screaming.

'As far as I know, we are the only two people in the universe who have happened upon this phenomenon, and through my research, I have come to believe that what is happening to us is somehow connected to the islands. But with only myself to study, I have very little evidence to help me understand *why us*? So, I would like to know everything that happened to you before you first found yourself here, if you please?'

Taking a deep breath, I focus on the question. 'It wasn't like you described it, like being pulled out of reality,' I begin. 'It was like falling into a deep sleep, which is what makes the most sense. I was in the hot sun; I had recently had a head injury. I saw a doorway, and I walked through it. At least in my mind. In the real world. I fainted. That's what happened to me.'

'A head injury. Interesting,' Sal says. 'I also suffered a blow to the head before I first fell. I don't imagine that a bump to the cranium unlocks time travel by itself. But perhaps it is a catalyst, shaking loose some unknown realm of the mind, which in certain people, perhaps people with a particularly coded DNA, thins what we understand of reality.'

'Or I fainted,' I say, trying not to notice that he is successfully distracting me from my own fear. 'And this is my brain making me process trauma all over again. It likes doing that. The crash triggered it.'

'Ah, you were in a crash. What sort of crash?'

'Car accident.'

'I was knocked off my bike,' Sal tells me, as if he's just discovered we are secretly related. 'I do believe there is something unique about the island, its topography and geology that may create this gateway – I have studied as best as I am able, and I have theories . . .' He catches the expression on my face, which I imagine is bewildered and uncomfortable. 'But that is enough for now. You need to understand, and the best way to understand is to see.'

He gets up with the same stoic grimace he sat down with, returning to his table to write something down with the stub of his pencil. His concentration is intense as he goes through piles of papers and notes, until he finds what he's looking for. Then he takes the chair and pulls it to be opposite where I am huddled.

'When I'm . . . *relocated*, I never know how long I am going to be there. So, I have two policies, and I suggest you adopt them also. If I find myself in what I recognise as the further past, I leave a mark, something where it will still be found in centuries to come. I have written my name in medieval illuminations. I drew my initials on the very edge of a painting. Something that will last and can be verified. If I go into what I perceive as the future, I read. Sometimes, this means going to a library and reading everything I can about history and committing it to memory. In another future time, I have found all I need on a small device. And once, I was able to place a small disc on my temple and learn French in under a minute.' He smiles. 'It was quite marvellous.'

'Like Keanu Reeves in *The Matrix*,' I say. 'So you're saying you can go into the future too?'

'I'm unfamiliar with that title,' he frowns. 'Clothes travel with me, but only once have I succeeded in holding on to an artefact. I have yet to determine why this item, on this occasion. Multiple experiments have not yielded any concrete evidence.'

Fear is encroaching on me again. I feel the crushing weight of the stone above my head, breathe in the thick, acrid air that's billowing outside. It feels, smells and tastes so real.

'Prof— Sal, I really need to get out of here.'

'I am going too fast.' He smiles gently. 'I must remember that you know nothing yet. So, from the beginning . . . I am a professor of physics. I was born in Malta in 1962, but in my first life, I moved to Milan to study and ended up staying. In the summer of 1992, I came back to Malta to visit my mama, and for the celebrations – fifty years since the end of the Siege of Malta. I hired a bicycle while my wife rested – Elena was pregnant with our first child at the time, you see – and I was caught by a truck on a sharp bend. All was well; I was thrown and hurt but not too badly. I didn't want to scare Elena or cause a fuss, so I dusted myself off and pushed the bike back to town. A few days later, as we were preparing to go out, something happened – I don't know what. All I know is that when I came round, I was in the same place but another time – this time, but more than thirty years ago – 1909, to be precise. And then I was thrown about across space-time with no rational explanation, as I have outlined. Yet this timeline is the one the island wants for me the most. This is where it returns me to most often, where it keeps me – where I hope I am meant to be for some greater reason that I do not understand. That is all I can do to ease the pain of missing my Elena and never knowing what the face of my child would look like. To hope I have a purpose here.'

A thin siren sounds somewhere close by, signalling the end of the raid. Scrambling to my feet, I stumble up the steps and into the bright daylight, not waiting to see if Sal is following. The sun shines fiercely, even if the sky is hazed with pulverised debris. Desperate to get away from this mutilated house, I plunge into the cool dark of the hallway and fall out of the front door onto the street.

People emerge from somewhere, tentative and careful, squinting at the sky. There's a terrible familiarity to it: ordinary people trying to live ordinary lives when the world refuses to let them.

'Here.' Sal arrives behind me, clutching something. 'This is what I wanted to show you. My evidence.'

Sal hands me a battered leaflet with the dates *1942–1992* printed on it. *FIFTY YEARS SINCE THE END OF THE SIEGE OF MALTA.*

'I got back to my own time only once.' His voice is low. His body shields the paper from passers-by. 'I was metres, minutes, from finding Elena. But the island took me again. It let me bring this with me.'

Then, in the corner of my eye, I notice something spinning, spiralling, growing larger and more intense. Everything around me disintegrates into atoms, and all that is left is an idea of me lost in the darkness.

Chapter Eighteen

Cold tiles rest under my palms. After a moment, my eyes adjust to the dark, and I see that I am no longer in the bright daylight outside the half-house that Sal lives in. I'm inside; somewhere above me, jazz music plays on scratchy vinyl. Low lanterns light a stairway. The air smells of perfume and beer. Outside the door, I can hear male voices shouting and singing in languages I don't understand.

As I start to straighten up, the world collapses again, and I am plummeting down, accelerating into nothing until I am delivered into a field of barley.

Soft, long stems of green flow like tides under the wind, back and forth, side to side. The sun is bright, and in the distance, I see figures working in the field.

Then I am jerked out of that moment, upwards, so fast I swear I see the curvature of the earth. My stomach churns; my head spins; my heart races. I breathe in, and there is nothing to inhale.

Music vibrates the freezing thin air: male voices singing in Latin. Calm, cool marble rises to meet the soles of my bare feet. I have lost my shoes somewhere in the tumult. The scent of incense fills the air, and somewhere far off, I can hear shouting. Slowly, I realise I am in a church or a cathedral. Cautiously, I turn towards the sound of the commotion and see a small, dark-bearded man bearing down on me, a sword raised above his head. A short cape flares behind him as he swings the blade. His eyes are filled with fury.

Instinctively I cower, but just before the blow comes down, I am disintegrated and strung out like pearls across the cosmos. The only thing that follows me is the singing, though I hear female voices now and not Latin: it's some other language, distant and strange, a powerful chorus drawing me into its harmony. My single discordant note becomes part of a beautiful whole. For a moment, there is perfect peace.

Then bright light glares, fires burn, voices cry in torment. I collapse, and when I do, it's Sal who catches me, staggering a little as I fall into his arms.

'I think I'm dying,' I tell him, tears streaming down my cheeks.

'Not quite,' he says. 'Not quite death, not yet.'

Chapter Nineteen

Sal leads me back through the still-trembling half-house. I follow him into the cool of the tiled hallway, where he pauses in front of the longcase clock, looking up at its face as if in apology. Opening the body of the clock, he begins to wind it with some kind of chain mechanism. I watch as he sets the pendulum in motion, restarting time.

'This isn't your house, is it?' I ask as he carefully closes the case, dusting off the latest shower of debris with his handkerchief. It's a pretty clock with a painted face – once someone's pride and joy.

'It isn't anyone's house anymore,' he says very solemnly as he leads me into a simple kitchen. 'The family who lived here . . . they were on the bus when it was targeted by a Messerschmitt Bf 109.' He sighs deeply, bowing his head. 'I often think about the young man who attacked them – what must have been in his mind when he turned around and bore down on that bus. They can't all be monsters, those boys up there in the sky. And yet there is such cruelty. This war has numbed so many to their own humanity. They have become so lost that even after a bombing raid is complete, some of the pilots still search out victims to plough down in the street. Well, you have experience of that tactic yourself.'

'I have a lot of experience of the cruelty of war,' I say, looking up at the sky. 'It frightens me how very little it takes to make men into monsters.'

'You are a . . . soldier in your own time?'

'I'm a journalist, and I work in war zones. I try to find individual stories amidst the conflicts, to show other people these awful things in a way that's relatable. Or I did. I lost nerve after . . . well, I lost my nerve after . . .'

I won't share her; she is my burden to carry.

Sal looks at me with a profoundly sorrowful expression.

'And here you are, in one of the most sustained and heavy bombing campaigns of the Second World War. Our creator is mysterious indeed.'

'I read once that a dying brain can create a lifetime's worth of dreams and images in its last few seconds,' I tell him. 'That's what I think this is. Somewhere, outside of my head, something catastrophic has happened to my body, and this is the film my mind is showing me.'

'Perhaps it is,' Sal says gently. 'I wouldn't be surprised to discover I am a figment of someone's imagination.' He glances around. 'In any case, you are quite right: this is not my house. I had an apartment in Senglea. It wasn't much, but it was all I needed. Unfortunately, it was turned to dust some months ago. We moved what we could of our studies and archives underground. It was my colleague's brother's family who lived here. He asked me to move in, take care of it for as long as it's safe to do so. He can't bear to come and see it himself. So, I live on the ground floor and in the shelter to protect it for him. One day, my friend will want to come and retrieve the belongings of the people he lost. I am no looter or thief, Maia. Do you believe me?'

'I do,' I say, feeling quite suddenly profoundly at ease. I have given up fighting whatever this is, deciding to let the current take me where it will. It's not as if I have anywhere to be or anyone left to miss me. Dad would rather be rid of me, and I've only known Kathryn a short time.

'I live as quietly as I can,' he continues. 'No wife, no family – not here. Not when I still love the woman I lost, or who lost me.'

'It sounds like a sad existence,' I say.

'I am sad, yes, but not for myself,' Sal tells me. 'Sad for my people. Sad for my island that must endure so much. Sad for that future young man who will leave behind the woman he loves – a woman who is carrying their child – without even realising he will never see her again. As for myself, I take pleasure where I can in books and my work and the camaraderie of people I never thought would become my dear friends. People like Christina. And you' – he snaps out of his more wistful state and instead into one of productivity – 'well, you will need the right clothes and papers while you are here. We must take you to Christina. We will see what the dear girl can do with . . .' He gestures at my entirety. 'If anyone can work a miracle, she can.'

'She is onto us, you know,' I tell Sal. 'Christina knows that you are not a Kathryn. She half-thinks I'm a spy already. She just likes me for some reason. Taking me to her for a makeover might not help.'

'Perhaps,' Sal says. 'But Christina always looks so lovely, even when there is nothing on the island. I don't know anyone else who might be able to pull it off.'

Chapter Twenty

'Christina only lives a few streets away,' Sal explains as we bisect the Gut again and turn onto a wide, elegant street – or *triq* in Maltese, 'in an apartment on the edge of Floriana. The grand buildings that line the street look as if they have escaped any severe damage from the air raids. The lines of palazzos and palaces hide courtyard gardens and cool vaulted rooms.

I follow Sal, grateful with every step that my feet meet solid ground. People who just minutes ago were crammed into shelters emerge blinking into the sunlight. Store owners open their shops. Children gather in a loosely organised group on the street in front of a rickety blackboard, where a woman begins to teach them their times tables. Older ladies, all dressed in black, sweep the grime off their front steps or sit on chairs, talking and making complicated-looking lace in their laps.

This is the other side of war. For every violent fury spent, there are just people, picking up the shards of their lives two or three times a day, every hour a little more diminished. Perhaps it's just surviving, as we are all programmed to do, even in the midst of horror. But I like to think it's more than that: it's ordinary people refusing to let go of the ordinary freedoms some stranger is bent on depriving them of.

'Professor!' A young girl looking hardly more than seventeen skips up to Sal. She's wearing a slash of red lipstick that looks as if it's been stolen from her mother. 'I finished the book you gave me – may I read another?'

'Of course.' Sal smiles benignly at her as he gestures at me. 'This is my cousin, Maia. Maia, this is Vittoria. I taught her at school until . . . well quite recently. Vittoria often assists the good doctor and wishes to be a nurse after the war. You still do, yes, Vittoria?'

'I do.' Vittoria nods. 'When the war is over.'

'Did you enjoy *Tess of the d'Urbervilles*?'

'So much,' Vittoria tells him. 'Though the end made me cry. The world is very cruel to young women, Professor.'

'Thomas Hardy, rarely cheerful,' Sal says fondly. 'But, Vittoria, you were always such an enthusiastic pupil.'

'I had to leave school,' Vittoria explains, turning to me, unalarmed by the fact that we've only just met. Perhaps when so many people are taken from the city on such a regular basis, sharing with anyone you can find becomes commonplace. 'My father dies, the war comes. I am alone. I help the doctor when I can, and in the evenings, I . . . work in the bars, you know?'

I do know. I have known many young women like her, out of options and forced to trade the one thing she has left.

'After the war, I am going to leave Malta and go to England to train as a nurse, and I will wear a bright white starched cap and marry Lawrence Olivier.'

'Sounds like a plan,' I say.

'I will bring another book to you tomorrow,' Sal tells her. 'Are you well, Vittoria?'

'I am well.' Vittoria nods. 'I have a special friend now. He is kind and says he will take me to England after the war. I wonder if he might even fall in love with me? Well, I'd better go. I have a date with him tonight! Thank you, Professor. Goodbye!'

She races off to her date as though it is with a boy who has courted her with sweet nothings and not with a stranger paying for her survival.

'She's very young to be making those kinds of hard choices,' I say. 'Couldn't people have helped her?'

'We all help her as we can. The doctor cannot pay her, but she can teach her and keep her hope of nursing alive. And I'm afraid some of our good people turned their backs on her when they realised how she had been earning her keep. Not all are as modern as we are, Maia. Or indeed as Miss Christina and her friends.'

We stop in front of a door that has been recently painted green, but its weathered surface reveals layers of colour peering through. Straightening his tie, Sal raps the mottled-brass dolphin knocker smartly, and we wait. And wait.

'Perhaps she's out,' I suggest. 'At the place where she took me to get interrogated.'

'There is always someone in – we must wait.' Sal knocks again.

After another minute a tall fair-haired young man in a crumpled RAF uniform opens it, leaning on the doorframe like it's the only thing that might keep him upright. He is clearly rather the worse for wear.

'Prof, old chap!' He swings out and claps Sal on the shoulder. 'Nice to see you!'

'Flight Lieutenant Warburton,' Sal replies formally. 'I have brought my cousin, Miss Maia Borg, to call on Miss Christina. Is she home? They've met before.'

'Well, hello to you, too,' Flight Lieutenant Warburton says to me cheerfully. 'Chris! You have a gentleman caller requesting an audience with you. Oh, and his "cousin"!' He grins blearily at us both in turn. 'She'll be down in a minute when she's dressed, old chap. That damn raid quite ruined our rest. Now, if you please, I'm about to lose a year's wages to a bloody Canadian and his northern sidekick.'

'Of course.' Sal steps inside at Adrian's gesture, and I see Danny at a table in a small sitting room, alongside another young man, one who looks to me like he should hardly be out of school. He has the smooth complexion and ruddy cheeks of a very young man and a swathe of blond hair so fine you can see the sunburnt pink of his scalp through its strands.

'Stitches!' Danny says, getting up. 'Hey, are you following me?'

His companion blushes a deeper shade of plum.

'I thought you were up there?' I say, pointing at the ceiling.

'I was meant to be, but the erks couldn't figure out a way to get my engine to stay *inside* the Spit. Mac here's out for the same reason. That's the problem when you have a finite number of Spitfires in an air war and no spare parts. Every day, we have to find new ways to stick 'em back together. Considering how dangerous it is up there, Command sure are fussy about letting a feller fly a plane with a loose engine. Damn frustrating if you ask me. Anyway, we're grounded until tomorrow. Good to see ya, again, ma'am.' He tips his hat and winks at me.

'Don't mind Champ,' Warby says, pouring himself a large neat whisky. 'He's as sober as a vicar, just plays along with me so that I'll let my guard down. Works every bloody time. Mac, on the other hand, is sozzled after half a mild stout.'

'Hey, that's not true.' Mac laughs, his eyes glittering in a way that suggests Warby might be right in his assessment.

'Please to meet you, miss.' He straightens his shoulders. 'I'm Flight Officer James Mackay.' He offers me a smooth young hand, and the blood in his face reaches his temples.

'Hello, Mac,' I reply. 'Yorkshire accent?'

'That's right, miss.' He nods. 'Scarborough.'

I nod. 'Lovely spot.'

'Taking a bit of a beating from that lot at the moment,' he says. 'Still, every plane we take down here is one less to bother them there, right, Champ?'

'Right, son.' Danny pats Mac on the back in a firm and fatherly way that makes Mac beam. There's maybe four or five years between them, but it's clear that Danny is the elder statesman in this friendship and that Mac is his loyal, adoring squire.

'Christina, are you coming?' Warby shouts upstairs once again.

Danny smiles at me over Warby's shoulder as he settles back into the game. It's a nice smile, more confident and relaxed than it has any business being in the middle of a war, and I get the sense he wears it like a shield.

'Warby, the hero,' Sal mutters as we leave them to their game and return to the foot of the stairs. 'And yet so . . . undisciplined. I'm not familiar with the younger gentleman. I'm afraid they are often not around long enough for one to get to know them.'

'The hero?' I repeat. I have a feeling I've heard about Warby in my real life.

'He's a quite brilliant reconnaissance pilot,' Sal tells me. 'And a singular young man – a rebel and often insubordinate but so good at his job that Command takes a lenient view. And he seems to make Christina very happy, though I do believe he has a wife somewhere in England.'

'Honestly, who hasn't got a spouse they've forgotten about these days?' Christina appears at the top of the stairs wrapped in a silk robe printed all over with pink roses. She looks like a movie star, frail but luminous.

'Miss Christina.' Sal breaks into a wide smile. 'You said you wanted to keep a close eye on Maia, and I thought perhaps you might start with some sartorial advice. She worked on a farm, you see, until very recently. It was an isolated life, and she has very little notion of feminine style – unlike you.'

'Oh, Professor, you old charmer.' Christina giggles, smiling broadly at me. 'I think Maia here is perfectly stylish in her own way. But yes, I'd be happy to help. Could do with a bit of light relief. We are at sixes and sevens here, as always. But that's what you get with former theatricals, I should say. Actually, as one of my housemates is our chief costumier, he might be just the ticket.'

'Christina and her friends once entertained at the cabaret,' Sal tells me as we follow her upstairs. 'After war broke out, they formed a concert party, the Whizz Bangs, to entertain the troops.'

'We still perform when we can,' Christina tells me. 'But now we all have other more important jobs, doing our best for the island that has been so kind to us. What are you doing for the war effort, Maia?'

'She has been helping on her aunt's farm on the other side of the island, but she's come to stay with me now,' Sal says. 'We must find her a role here. She has experience in reporting, so I will take her to meet Miss Strickland when she looks appropriate.'

'Oh, gosh, she needs a suit of armour to meet dear Mabel,' Christina says. 'Amazing woman. Terrifying.

She's kept the *Times of Malta* in print every single day during the war. I don't know how she's done it, but I am in awe of her. And a tiny bit terrified.'

I remain mute as Sal and I follow in Christina's wake. Her dancer's grace hides her acute thinness with fluid movements, but it's easy to see that she is near starving. Her high cheek bones are razor sharp, and her grey eyes look huge in her heart-shaped face. Still, her elegant eyebrows have been perfectly drawn on under her bleached-blonde curls, and there is not even a hint of roots showing. Her lips are painted a resolute red.

She graces me with another smile as we reach the second floor and a square of open doors to rooms that lead off the central hallway. The definition of putting a brave face on it, I think.

'This is my place, but my Warby stays with me whenever he can, and I have a lot of friends . . . We do have a rather anything-goes attitude here, Maia. I hope you are not too easily scandalised.'

'Hardly ever,' I say as I go into a small but serviceable kitchen.

'She does rather look as if she has been living on a farm,' Christina says, without any cruelty, as she looks me up and down. 'And that will never do, not for such a pretty girl. And certainly not for Mabel Strickland! You remind me of someone, Maia – I can't place who. But perhaps it's just the Maltese women – they are so very lovely.'

'Thank you?' I say, uncertain. 'I'm only half Maltese. My—'

'Her father was Maltese,' Sal puts in, as though afraid I may get our cover story wrong. 'I thought perhaps you might help Maia make herself a little more . . .' He gestures vaguely at me once again.

'Naturally, I don't have any clothes that will fit her. I have hardly any that aren't threadbare and worn through.'

Sal nods sombrely. 'Of course.'

'But I do know a haberdasher in St Paul's Bay who still has a good stock of material, and in the meantime, of course our Alex is a dab hand with a needle, you know. Let's go and see Alex now and see what he says. Coming, Professor?'

'I cannot stay.' Sal bows. 'I am teaching the older children this afternoon at St Peter's. Of course, they would prefer I didn't, but mathematics is still important even in a war. You understand.'

'I do, Sal,' Christina says. 'You leave her with me – I'll get her sorted.'

'It's good of him to teach the children,' I say, once the professor has departed.

'He's a good man,' Christina observes as we head to find this Alex. 'As well as teaching, he takes the bus and visits the chaps at the hospital in Mtarfa. Reads to them, plays cards with them, that sort of thing. Gives them a bit of a pick-me-up. Of course most of them would prefer to be visited by Rita Hayworth, but what can one do?' She turns to me, eyes twinkling. 'But perhaps you already know that – after all, he is your "cousin". Anyway, my friends and I do our best to keep up morale – or at least we did when the troupe was touring. Now I am a plotter, and it's serious work. Especially when my dear Warby is in the air.' She hesitates for a moment, a brief expression of pain passing over her delicate features. 'Well, all the boys, really. There are so few of them, and so few of them last very long. One does what one can.'

I want to ask her what a plotter is, but I decide that I should probably know, so I just nod sagely.

'Here's Alex!' Christina claps her hands with delight as if she has never seen anyone as remarkable as Alex, and I think she might be right.

Alex is a strikingly beautiful young man sitting in a string vest that shows off his toned torso to a tee. He is bent over a sewing machine, which dominates a small bedroom strewn with colourful scraps of material. At first glance, he seems to be hemming some sort of garment with it.

'Alex, this is Maia. We are tasked with making her presentable.'

'Marvellous,' Alex says. 'Pleased to meet you. My, you are a solid girl, aren't you? Look at those breasts, Christina! More than a couple of saucepan lids' worth there.'

'I know, darling – infuriating,' Christina says. 'And here we are, flat as pancakes!'

They both laugh uproariously, and I smile, very much like the awkward kid hanging out with the cool crowd at school.

'I thought you might measure her up and work your magic with a needle on her clothes while I set her hair and sort out her eyebrows. What do you think?'

'I do love a challenge,' Alex says. 'As long as the usual rules apply.'

'The usual rules?' I ask.

'In here, I'm just me – take me as you find me. Out there, I'm Alex, army driver and drag-comedy turn in the concert party. Also, I have a fiancée at home called Dorothy. My life does rather depend on it, darling, if you don't mind.'

'I understand,' I say. 'I can't imagine there is much diversity around here.'

'You what, love?' Alex asks.

'Never mind,' I say.

'Well, come on then, Tessie – come over here and let me measure you.'

'Tessie?' I look at Christina, who double-snips a pair of scissors at me.

'Two Ton Tessie, darling. Now, come here and let me have a go at turning a sow's ear into a silk purse.'

I don't take offence at their jokes. Like everyone who has ever known Christina Ratcliffe, I am instantly in her thrall.

Chapter Twenty-One

'Not my best work,' Alex says, looking me up and down. 'But not my worst, either.'

'You really must stop flattering me,' I tell him wryly.

Smoothing down the rough material of my custom-made skirt, I vaguely wonder what time it is in my own world. I set my alarm for nine o'clock, and though more hours have passed here than they would have done in the night, I try to picture that quiet, air-conditioned room, full of blue shadows. If I could manage to wake myself now, would Alex and Christina be blinking at the thin air where I had stood moments before? I know they are not real – they can't be real – but they *feel* it.

Christina has cut my hair quite short. She was delighted when it sprang into its natural curls. She then tamed it into something she considered far more fashionable. I watched, fascinated, as she created great solid curls that she stuffed with something she called 'rats'. I felt considerable relief when she told me they were stuffed stockings tied off to keep the curls in place.

She has pinned the roll with as many bobby pins as she's willing to spare and doused me with a liberal spray of something that smells a lot like beer.

'Because it *is* beer, darling,' she tells me now. 'A girl has to improvise. And with the shortage of hops, we'll be looking for something else to set our hair with soon, won't we, Alex?'

''Fraid so,' Alex says. 'One dreads the day.'

'And I think we'd better take off this ugly old bandage,' Christina says, snipping it off with her scissors. 'There, that's healing nicely. Lovely, neat work from the doc.'

'Like the bride of Frankenstein,' Alex adds approvingly.

Christina and Alex made a great and, honestly, hysterical show of not finding any clothes between them, not even costumes, that would fit my hips and bosom, making me laugh so much that tears rolled down my face. Christina has promised that the next time she's at St Paul's with her Warby, she'll obtain some fabric for Alex to make me some frocks.

In the meantime, Alex has remade my T-shirt into more of a blouse by resetting the sleeves, adding buttons and putting in some darts under the bust. Then he ran up the skirt out of an old, thin red blanket that was burnt down one side so no longer fit for purpose.

The effect is surprisingly convincing, but I'm not at all sure it's better. A least now I look like I fit in – frumpy as hell, and looking ten years older, but you can't have everything. I suppose that feeling lumpy and itchy and trapped by my clothes with newly short hair is temporary, but I have to keep reminding myself of that.

'Let's give the boys a show!' Christina says, leading me by the hand. 'Get the RAF seal of approval.'

'Oh, no thank you,' I say, dragged along behind her. 'They don't want to look at me.'

'Perhaps not,' Alex says, 'but I want an eyeful of Danny Beauchamp. He's good for the soul, so he is.'

'Ta-dah!' Christina yanks me out from behind the door and into the parlour. The card game is over, and the men are sitting back in their chairs. Warby is smoking, and Danny seems to be writing or drawing in a notebook.

Mac has flopped back in his chair, arms hanging loosely at his sides, head tipped back as he gently snores.

Alex stands just outside the room, his arms crossed.

'I say!' Warby gets up as we enter the room, as does Danny. 'Yes, scrubs up all right, doesn't she?'

I don't know where to look as Christina insists on twirling me.

'Well, Champ, what do you think?' Christina demands his opinion.

'I think Stiches here is just about as pretty as a girl can be,' Danny says, with a polite bow. 'But I thought that before all the gussying up.'

A flush of heat rushes up my neck and into my cheeks.

'Well, sit down, won't you?' Christina directs me. 'I don't have much to offer you, but I have some iced water you can partake of while we wait for the prof. Alex, will you join?'

'None for me, love. I've had about as much excitement as I can stand for one day,' Alex says. 'Besides, I'm on night watch. Goodbye, dears!'

Danny and Warby bid him a cheerful goodbye as he takes the stairs two at a time.

'Warby, help me with carrying the tray, will you?' Christina beckons her boyfriend rather pointedly. Is she deliberately trying to leave me more or less alone with Danny and the sleeping Mac?

'I'm not sure I'm fit for carrying anything,' Warby says, but nevertheless, he gets up to follow Christina.

'You OK, Stitches?' Danny asks once they have departed. 'It can be quite the whirlwind round here.'

'I'm good,' I say. 'Everyone's very kind. This whole thing is very strange, but at the same time, it is starting to feel sort of normal.'

'Normal, huh?' Danny smiles slightly. 'I am pretty sure I have forgotten what normal feels like.'

There's a sadness to him, so gossamer-fine that it's nearly impossible to see. It's there, though, adding a faint sheen to every smile and confident, sardonic remark.

'Are Warby and Mac your best friends?' I ask.

'Warby's a legend round these parts. Flies over territory that others don't dare to cross. Couldn't do what we do without him, that's for certain – but I'm not sure he's anyone's friend. Not even his own. And Mac.' He glances at the boy. 'Malta is a hell of a place to end up after twelve weeks of training. I'm trying to keep him alive as long as I can. That's about all I can do.'

Somewhere, a clock ticks, and I can hear the muted sounds of a radio.

'Were you glad?' I ask him on impulse. 'To be grounded?'

Danny frowns deeply, and I think for a moment that I've offended him.

'Not glad.' He shakes his head. 'A man doesn't want to think that he's not there to back up his buddies. But truth is: I'm no use to them dead either. Got to at least start a flight with a chance of making it back, right? And I'm kinda glad Mac isn't up there. Some of those young kids aren't going to make it back today, and that might have been different if I'd been up there with them; at least he's safe for now. But it's a relief to know you're more than likely still going to be alive in the morning, if you know what I mean?'

'I think I do,' I say.

'Well, time for me to get the kid on his feet and get him back to our digs.' Danny stands up just as there's a knock at the door. 'And that sounds like the prof has come to pick you up. Nice to see you again, Stitches.'

'Nice to see you, too,' I say.

We hesitate, as if not sure how to end this encounter.

Christina ends it for us, flinging open the door. 'Prof, wait until you see what we've done!' she calls. 'It's a miracle!'

Warby drops a tray of glasses, sending them clattering down the stairs. 'Bugger!'

Chapter Twenty-Two

'Better,' Sal tells me once we have said goodbye to Christina. 'You look presentable.'

'Presentable for what?' I ask.

'For Miss Strickland. It's too late this evening, but we'll go first thing in the morning. Mabel Strickland is the editor-in-chief of the *Times of Malta*, and *Il-Berqa*, two very important publications for the island. You will offer her your services as a reporter.'

'Sal . . .' I catch hold of his wrist. It feels so real. The frayed hems of his suit jacket, the small dark hairs on his wrist, are rendered in such detail, as is the heat on the back of my neck, the feeling of this shirt rubbing on my upper arms. It's all so real that I almost forgot for a moment that it can't be.

'You wonder why I take you to get a job when you are still sure this is a dream or a hallucination?' Sal asks. 'Even after everything you have seen and experienced yourself?'

'It still makes more sense than suddenly being at the whim of some mysterious force of the universe,' I tell him.

He thinks for a moment, rubbing his hand over the top of his head.

'Like I told you, I've had problems with my mental health before. Depression and quite severe anxiety, flashbacks – did they use the term PTSD in the nineties?'

'I've heard of it.' Sal smiles, possibly because even as I insist this is a delusion, I am talking to him as if it's all real.

'Well, that can make you think you see and feel things, though I've never had anything like this before. But it makes sense for this to be connected to that or the crash. And I need things to make sense, Sal.'

'Very well. If you prefer to believe this is a fantasy created by your dying brain, Maia, or a dream after eating too much cheese, or some side effects of medication, then I understand. But even so, your mind did not choose a resort or castle for you to exist in, but a war. And in this war, everyone must do their part. Perhaps you won't be here for very long before you fall through time again or wake up in your own time – or die, though I sincerely hope you do not. Either way, it hardly matters. What else are you going to do while everything around you is like this?'

He raises his eyebrows and hands in question. I have no reply.

'Fine,' I say. 'If I'm still here in the morning, let's go and see Mabel Strickland.'

* * *

The next morning, after a dreamless sleep, I wake in the little bed Sal made up for me in the half-house. I almost expected to find myself in 2025 when I opened my eyes, but I'm still here . . .

We find Miss Strickland sitting behind a desk that is positioned literally in the street, bashing away at a typewriter with a fearsome focus. Dark-haired, with thick brows and a fierce expression, Mabel Strickland is perhaps a decade older than me. She is smartly dressed and sitting at her desk as if it's perfectly natural to be working in what is more or less the middle of a ruin. Beyond her is an office – or the remains of one, anyway – where two young women are working, in some kind of meeting with an older gentleman, perhaps piecing together the layout of the paper.

'Miss Strickland?' Sal approaches her almost sideways, as if he is caught between wanting her attention and rather hoping she doesn't notice him. 'If I may have a moment of your time?'

'There are no spare moments of my time, Professor,' she says, without looking up from her typewriter. 'We are updating the casualty lists, and as you can imagine, it is essential that we do not make any mistakes.'

'Ah yes – I have brought you a young lady who has experience in journalism, and I thought perhaps she could offer you and your staff some assistance with the paper.'

'What?' Mabel stops typing and squints at Sal in the bright afternoon sun. 'What someone?'

'Hello.' I step forwards. 'My name is Maia Borg. I've previously worked as a reporter in the UK. The professor, my cousin, thought that as I'm here, I could be of service.'

'Why have you not come to me before?' she asks, affronted, sitting back in her chair, just as at ease in the rubble and mayhem of the street as she would have been in a well appointed office.

'I was helping at my aunt's farm on the other side of the island until recently,' I explain, hoping I've got the story right. I see Sal give a faint nod and let out a sigh of relief.

'I see. How many words per minute?' Mabel asks. Clearly, she has little time for sentiment either.

'Ninety,' I say off the top of my head, although I have never typed on a typewriter before.

'Shorthand?'

'Naturally,' I reply, although honestly, I only learnt it for a qualification for one of my first jobs, and can't remember anything.

'It is our duty to bring the truth to our readers,' she tells me, gesturing at the ruined building behind her. 'Even when our office took a direct hit this April, we still went to print that day. We have never missed an issue, not ever. Paper is finite, ink is scarce, so we publish only what is essential to our readers on one sheet of newspaper. You will be information-gathering and fact-checking across the island. It will be boring and hard and very badly paid. Are you still interested?'

'Yes,' I say, glancing at Sal.

Mabel gets up and comes round her desk to look me up and down.

'Are you the girl they thought could be a spy?' she asks, incredulous.

'I'm not a spy,' I tell her.

'Of course you're not,' she says. 'Look at you – the very idea! Well, I'm far too busy to talk to you anymore, so come back here first thing tomorrow morning, and I will assign you duties. Agreed?'

I nod. 'Agreed.'

Sal links his arm through mine and hurries us away.

'I'm not at all sure I know what I've just agreed to,' I tell him once we are out of earshot.

'Whatever Miss Strickland tells you to do,' Sal replies.

Chapter Twenty-Three

'Where are we going now?' I ask Sal.

'Rabat,' he tells me, 'in the centre of the island, next to the ancient city of Mdina. I have a friend there who will help us with your papers. But it is dangerous, Maia. You must stay close and don't speak if you can help it. I use the term "friend" very loosely.'

'Right,' I say. 'I'm not traditionally good at not speaking, but I'll try. Why is it so dangerous?'

Sal glances around, simply shaking his head, from which I gather that he doesn't want to talk about it when anyone might overhear us.

'How will we get there?' I ask, looking up at the burning sky. Sweat is already tracking its way down my back and beading around my hairline. 'Are we walking?'

'It would be a very long walk, even if it weren't so hot,' Sal says to my relief as we stop at the edge of a dusty trail on what seems to be the outskirts of Valletta. 'There is a bus.'

'The same bus that your friends were shot and killed on?' I ask.

'Yes.' He nods. 'But we have some time until the next raid, so no need to be afraid yet.'

It is the word 'yet' that lodges in the middle of my chest.

When the bus – a small, squat, rickety vehicle – all but staggers into view, I see that any remaining glass has been removed from the windows and that it is pocked along its visible side with bullet-holes. I'm certain the far side looks the same, and it seems more than likely to be exactly the same bus the family was travelling on when they were attacked.

I think about them: a small, close family, getting on with things; the threat of death from above must have seemed like an abstract thing – real enough, but not meant for them. Not until it was. It's hard not to think of their last moments, of desperate confusion and fear.

And yet the weary people still take the bus, because they must. Trusting that this time, they will reach their destination. Hoping that when death comes, it will not be for them.

The other passengers sit in silent exhaustion.

Sal nods to a few people as we edge our way down the aisle. He signals for me to sit in a vacant seat while he stands at my shoulder, holding on to the back of the seat. Doing as I'm told, I slide into the stiff, wooden bench-like seat, next to a very young, slender woman, who is holding a sleeping baby cradled against her chest. Her lovely face set in a frown of concern and deep worry, she rocks and murmurs to her infant. I get the sense she is comforting herself. The weight of the world rests on her narrow shoulders.

'What a beautiful little one,' I tell her, with a gentle smile. For a moment, her features lighten. Her arms tighten around her precious bundle. Tears shine in her eyes.

The bus squeaks and rattles onwards. Outside, a parched landscape rolls by, an ombre of creamy yellows descending to deep, dark red, punctuated here and there by dark-green trees and row upon row of prickly pears. Bright wildflowers dazzle in the muted landscape with starbursts of colour: remarkably similar to the Malta I saw with my waking eyes. Not surprising, I suppose.

Long, narrow fields are marked by drystone walls, running in terraces that echo the contours of the land, each containing the hard-fought-for crops of cabbages and potatoes, presenting their own personal battle for life over death in the endless heat and violence.

Despite this – perhaps even because of it – the landscape is beautiful.

Truly, I didn't expect to feel anything when I set foot on this island. But now, as I sit here with these people in my own personal film, produced and directed by my tender brain, I do feel . . . *something*. Not that the battered, bomb-blasted land I'm watching unfurl around me belongs to me. More that part of me belongs to it and always has. And I don't mean just to the island, but to this precise moment in time and each of the seconds that follows after. Somehow, I feel these coming minutes, hours and days from the past have been waiting just for me.

So, despite the heat, the jolts of the transport, the surreal uncertainty of everything, I feel something I have hardly ever felt before: I feel as if I belong.

* * *

From quite a way out, I see the medieval citadel of Mdina perched on the highest point in the centre of the island. Until now, I've only read about it in guidebooks, though I saw it presiding over the island from a distance as we drove past.

Sal taps me on the shoulder, and I follow him off the bus outside the grand gates of the citadel. As we leave, the baby begins to cry.

'Wow, this is so beautiful,' I say, stopping in front of the stone bridge. It crosses a now empty and overgrown moat, leading to the grand entrance to the city, which is flanked on either side by a great lion holding the livery of the Knights of St John.

'Mostly, the airmen are billeted here now,' Sal tells me. 'Flight Lieutenant Beauchamp, for one – I believe he is here. But there are still a few old families, some clergy and an order of nuns who will not be moved from the city, not for anyone.' Sal chuckles. 'One wonders how the airmen and the nuns get along as neighbours.' His demeanour changes in an instant, and he lowers his voice. 'Now, follow me closely – we are going into Rabat. You are not to talk. These people cannot be trusted, and they are dangerous, understood?'

'Understood.' I nod. I can feel something building, something beyond the heat of the afternoon or the collective grief and resilience of the people around us. There is something else. It's coming for me.

* * *

Rabat seems like it is – or would have been before the war – a charming little town of picturesque squares and café life. There is a church on almost every corner, and as with Valletta, the buildings are elegant and beautiful, concealing the promise of shady courtyards and cool, vaulted rooms beyond.

Sal seems to know where he is going, and soon leads me into a cemetery crowded with tombs, and then to a mausoleum that seems to be the entrance to the underworld. A rusty, barred gate stands open, and when I take a tentative step forwards, I see a flight of steps leading down into the dark. The last time I'd ventured into a cellar staircase on the island, it didn't go so well.

'Where are we going?' I ask. 'Because I am not keen.'

'We are at the St Paul's Catacombs,' Sal tells me, glancing around to check we are not being overheard. 'The people who have inhabited this island have been burying their dead underground here for many thousands of years. There are pagan, Christian and Jewish burials here. At the beginning, local people would use them as a shelter, but we do not like to disturb the dead.'

'There are still remains down there?' I ask.

'Naturally – where else would they be?' He shrugs, as if I've asked a foolish question. 'There are tunnels and rooms in there that have yet to be explored and many corners that most people would not concern themselves with. That is where we are heading. Stay close – don't lose sight of me. It is possible to become lost down here and not be found again until it is too late.'

It's not the prospect of mortal remains or a labyrinth of tunnels that gives me pause, though. I look at that entrance, the steps leading down, and it is not Rabat I see, or even the shelters I've taken refuge in over the strange two days I've spent in this fever dream. I see a fateful decision, a moment where my choice would end a life. I took a little girl's hand and led her down a flight of stairs just like this to get her out of harm's way. At least, that's what I thought I was doing.

Now, these stairs remind me how one wrong turn can change everything.

'Come, Maia,' Sal says, reading my expression. 'You are the intrepid journalist. You are not scared of the dark or a skeleton or two, are you? Not when very real evil rains down from the heavens?'

'I feel like something very bad is coming,' I tell him, too tired and afraid to pretend to be brave.

'Something bad is always coming, Maia,' Sal says, taking my hand. 'The trick is to be ready to meet it.'

Chapter Twenty-Four

At the foot of the steps, Sal produces the stub of a candle from his pocket and lights it. The glow thrown by the flame is not huge, but it doesn't need to be. I can sense the vast spaces that echo with shadows around us. The air smells of earth and dust and something ancient.

'There have been burials here since before the Roman times,' Sal tells me in a low voice. He holds the candle up and circles slowly to show me a series of open-sided, arched chambers, each with one or two plinths. 'Maybe even before. Centuries of grave-robbing mean there are fewer remains here now than there once were, and even so, there is nothing to fear. Just our ancestors – that's all. Proof, if you like, that we have come from somewhere other than a dream.'

He keeps the candle high as he makes his way between the tombs, sending flickering shadows to dance along the hand-wrought stone, and every now and then, I find myself caught in the blank gaze of a skull or resting my hand close to a scattering of disarticulated bones.

'Watch your step,' Sal warns as we turn a corner. Every last trace of daylight vanishes. 'We descend.'

There is nothing to do but follow him, feeling the echo of a child not yet born following in my wake, the child whose life I will not save. The dark thickens; the air grows heavy and hard to breathe, and somehow, even Sal's candle seems to dim. As we pass an alcove, I glimpse the figure of a woman on her knees, shawl around her shoulders, her hair covered with a scarf. She weeps.

'Don't look,' Sal whispers. 'We must not disturb the ghosts.'

I steal another glance at where she was kneeling. There are only empty shadows now. Despite being below ground, the air feels thin, as though we are at altitude.

Following the curves of another set of tombs, we pause by a large, flat, circular surface carved into the floor.

'A kind of table. For the funeral feast,' Sal tells me. For a span of seconds, he is gone, and the circular table is surrounded by people, speaking softly as they eat, linen hoods drawn over their heads. In the low light of a simple oil lamp, I see a child at rest on the plinth, a little girl being guided to the afterlife by her family. I recognise her.

Then up ahead, I see a faint glow of light, and Sal reappears.

'I think I just . . .'

'Quiet now,' Sal warns. 'We have arrived. Elias! It's Sal Borg, your friend. I bring another with me. We need your assistance.'

There is silence, and then a figure comes out of the gloom, hardly more than a shadow. I get a glimpse of lantern-light reflecting their eyes, the collar of their jacket turned up to hide a portion of their face, out of shame or subterfuge – it's hard to know which. Whoever it is might not even be from this time. They may have come from a time long ago or a time yet to be – that is, if I let myself believe Sal's theories. But I refuse to let that happen. Following him down here isn't admitting this is real. Like he said before, what else am I going to do? Sooner or later, I will either wake up or pass into nothingness. I'm not sure which outcome I long for the most.

The figure slips away, receding into the darkness of the catacombs, and a deep voice booms from within the room they have just left. 'Come then, Salvatore.' The words reverberate jarringly through the chamber. 'Come into my office.'

Quite improbably, this Elias has occupied one of the chambers of the catacombs and filled it with every requirement for black-market administration. He is sitting behind a wooden desk, on which a number of ledgers make an unstable tower. He is working by the light of a lantern, and it throws large shadows on the wall behind him. Stacked all around his desk are piles and piles of what I imagine are black-market goods: tins of all kinds of food, bags of rice and pasta, and a variety of other items I can't make out in this light. Standing on a tripod in one corner is a very old-looking camera that long predates this war and possibly the last.

'Sal, my old friend.' Elias grins. 'I never expected to see you here. But then, even a man of principle like you may need the help of old Elias from time to time, no?'

Sal smiles, his discomfort plain. 'It is so.'

As little as I know Sal, it's obvious that Elias doesn't seem like the kind of man he'd be truly close to. Any man who would set up their racketeering operation in a grave must have quite the question mark over his character, and he is not the first of his type I have encountered. In every war, there is always someone turning a profit from suffering. I'm also sure that Sal wouldn't have brought me here if it wasn't absolutely necessary. Needs must – that's what Mum used to say.

'My cousin.' Sal gestures at me. 'We need papers. Everything. Hers are lost.'

'Cannot you then apply for replacements?' Elias asks, looking me up and down very slowly. I feel the creep of his gaze on my skin. 'Oh, is this the spy?'

'Maia is not a spy, but there are complications,' Sal says, with a wave of his hand. 'It must be resolved quickly. I know you have people who can provide good-quality documents.' He is trying to look and sound as if it is not a matter of life and death, knowing, I suspect, that Elias will put the price up as soon as he sniffs out a trace of desperation or fear.

'Have you brought money?' Elias asks.

Sal nods.

Elias turns one of the ledgers to face us and pushes it across the desk, holding out a pencil in his other hand. 'Write all her information here,' he tells Sal. 'You.' He points at me. 'Stand up against that wall.'

Turning, I see a square of rock that has been whitewashed. I stand in front of it.

'Don't smile,' he says. That's an easy command to follow.

A moment later, the glare of a flash fills the room, with a second of blinding light and the scent of smoke.

'Will you take another to be sure?' Sal asks.

'No,' Elias replies, without further explanation. 'Come back the day after tomorrow.'

'Very well.' Sal nods. 'How much?'

Elias gives him a figure, and Sal patiently counts out the fee, or at least half of it.

'The rest on delivery,' Sal tells him sternly over the top of his glasses.

Elias shrugs. 'And what else can I tempt you with?' He gestures at his treasure trove.

'Where did you get all this from?' Sal asks. He is doing his best to keep his anger hidden, but his tone is stiff and halting.

'Some I "find"; some is sold to me,' Elias says, unconcerned. 'You disapprove, my old friend, but in times of war, there is always a need for a man like me, as you yourself have demonstrated. Those who sell to me are desperate. Those who buy, the same.'

Sal nods curtly. 'Do you have another candle?' he asks.

'For you, on the house.' Elias takes a fresh candle out of his desk drawer and rolls it across to Sal. 'To remind you that I am not a monster, eh?'

'Not a monster.' Sal picks up the candle, lighting it from the lantern.

'Two days and all will be ready,' says Elias.

Sal sighs deeply as soon as we are out of earshot of Elias.

'I'm sorry,' I tell him. 'It's my fault you have to deal with him. That was a lot of money.'

'It's not the cost.' Sal waves that away with a gesture. 'To protect you is my honour, Maia. You are my compatriot in more ways than one. No, it's this war – any war. How can Elias be a monster when the world is populated by far worse? We are all monsters now.'

'Not you,' I say, 'or Christina or Warby. You've lived after the end of the war once already. You know how many heroes there always are.'

'Have I the courage to be a hero here and now?' Sal says sadly. 'When a choice must be made, who knows how we shall make it?'

Chapter Twenty-Five

As we emerge from the profound dark of the catacombs, the glare of the bright afternoon light makes my eyes sting. I raise my hand to shield my gaze as I squint at the spot where we exited. It's different to the place we went in. Long, brittle golden grass stands hard against the grey mausoleums like bright spectres. Somewhere hidden in the scant traces of shade, insects chirp and drone, oblivious to the havoc of men. For now, the sky is empty, peaceful and still.

I wonder about the sky in the time when I am supposed to be – where I *am*. Has the sun risen there? I wonder if Kathryn is worried, waiting for me to wake up. Or perhaps hours here are just a few seconds there. That sense of foreboding that has been following me since we arrived at the catacombs intensifies, vibrating like the beat of a drum. I'm overcome with the strongest sensation that I might never return to that world, as difficult and as painful as the thought is. Guilt and fear swarms over me.

'You tremble.' Sal frowns, putting a calming, paternal arm around me. Something about him is inherently trustworthy, and not just his stories of time travel or his kindness. There is something more, something obvious. My subconscious has created the Maltese father I always wanted, the one I so badly want right now. Turning into his arms, I rest my forehead on his shoulder and allow a few tears to fall, just between the span of one breath and the next.

'There, there, Maia,' Sal says gently. 'All is well. All will be well. We will find the solution to all our troubles.'

'I'm sorry.' I straighten up, wiping my eyes with the edge of my thumb. 'I'm not like this. I don't usually fall to pieces. Well, not recently, anyway. Thank you, Sal.'

'There is no need to thank me,' Sal says. 'As far as I'm concerned, you are the only other person in all the stars and galaxies who knows what I know. You are my proof of sanity.'

'Well, that's a first,' I say with a watery smile. 'Even so, you are kind.'

'What is kind, except deciding not to be cruel?' Sal says. 'Kindness is easy – it should be natural.'

'What now?' I ask as we walk out onto the dusty road.

'There will be a bus in an hour, perhaps two,' Sal says, checking his pocket-watch. 'We will be back in time for the evening raid.'

'Wouldn't want to miss it,' I say. 'An hour or two of waiting?'

'Yes, not long! I expect there is no waiting in your time,' Sal says. 'I expect all is perfectly on time, and you may travel anywhere and everywhere you want at the drop of a hat . . .'

'Not exactly . . .'

'But here, petrol is rationed, and buses are few and far between. We must make adjustments and accept our lot. And when I say we, I mean you.'

The Silent City of Mdina looms ahead, a citadel set within a deep, now empty moat. The grand gateway stands proud before us.

'It's so beautiful,' I say, looking up at the golden stonework. A lion bares his teeth at me. At the foot of the gate, two British soldiers stand guard. 'It feels like the knights might be just about to thunder over the bridge on their horses.'

'Perhaps they are,' Sal says. 'Time is a wide river, with all her currents flowing as one. I have been in the citadel in the time of the knights . . .' A thought occurs to him. 'I will show you the Silent City and, with it, more evidence – you will see I am telling you the truth.'

'I get the impression it's not open to the public,' I say, following Sal as he approaches the soldiers with an added spring to his step.

'Nonsense – a Tommy is always a friend to Salvatore Borg.' As we reach the soldiers he peers at the young men, his face lighting up. 'Ah, Private Wilson, we meet again!'

'Prof!' An achingly young man of about nineteen or so grins happily at Sal. 'We never got to finish our match! And I was winning.'

'Well, when the good doctor instructs a man to leave, he leaves, if he knows what's good for him.'

Sal and Private Wilson chuckle, and I wonder if they are talking about the terrifying doctor I met yesterday. Was it really only yesterday? I've lost all sense of what is up and what is down.

'It was good luck for me,' Sal tells him, warmly shaking his hand. 'You are a master of chess, Eddie.'

'The prof here came and visited me when I was all beat up after the harbour took a pounding,' Eddie tells his mate, who nods and grins.

'And the book I gave you? Have you finished it yet?' Sal asks.

'Nearly,' Eddie says proudly. 'Never thought I'd read a book, Prof, but it's proper good. Takes my mind off missing home and Ma.'

'A good book will do that,' Sal assures him. 'Eddie, it is very hot. May I take my cousin to sit in the cathedral a moment while we wait for the bus?' He indicates me, standing just behind him.

'Don't see why not,' Eddie says. 'Tell you what – I'll give you a shout when the bus comes, and my mate Bill here can keep it from leaving until you're on board – how does that sound?'

'It sounds marvellous.' Sal claps Eddie on the back, and the young man beams. Sal leads me under the grand stone archway and into the Silent City.

Silent it is not. Troops march double-quick to the shouted orders of their sergeant. Servicemen come and go, and some local people, too. Some look like support staff – cooks and cleaners – and a few seem like regular residents. One elegantly dressed woman, wearing an air of resignation with as much style as her deep, wine-red lipstick, looks as if she is living cheek by jowl with the army as best she can. Yet it's also somehow true that everything inside the walls of the citadel is a little more still, a little more serene – as if it has its own invisible defences against time.

'It's beautiful,' I say, looking around me at the honey-coloured buildings.

'Yes,' Sal says. 'Little ever changes in the Silent City, except the people who pass through here. No car or horses allowed you know, that's how it got its name.'

He leads the way across a small, square courtyard, enclosed on three sides by an external, ornate stone staircase, and through a low, arched entrance, closed off with a wrought-iron gate. On the other side, I find myself confronted with a beautiful domed church.

'Michelangelo designed the dome of St Peter's Basilica, you know,' Sal tells me as I gaze upwards. 'It made rather an impression on the Knights of St John. Our little island is graced with a good many such marvels. In the miracle church of Mosta, we have – *had* – the third largest unsupported dome in the world.'

'Had?' I ask.

'Back in April, the Nazi bombers had one left over, so they dropped it on their way home. I suppose the Mosta dome must have made a pretty target. And mass was in full swing.'

I gasp. 'Were many people killed?' I ask him as we walk up the church steps and into the blessed cool of the interior. At once, my eyes are drawn up to the ornate gilded mouldings and frescoes that line the magnificent dome.

'That's the miracle,' Sal tells me softly. 'The bomb fell through the dome and into the middle of the congregation – but did not detonate.'

'That's so lucky.' There's something about being in church that makes me whisper my reply.

'Or it was divine intervention.' He tilts his head as he crosses himself and bows to the altar. Not knowing exactly what to do, I nod my head at the statue of Jesus on the crucifix, like we are casual acquaintances – which I suppose we are.

Sal takes a seat on a pew at the back of the church, and I sit beside him.

'Should we pray?' I ask him.

'Always,' he says.

'I mean now?' I ask. 'Are there rules? Do we have to pray to be in here?'

He turns in his seat to look at me. 'You're not Catholic?' he asks.

'I'm not anything,' I tell him. 'I think my dad was raised Catholic, but he never went to church as far as I know. And my mum was very much more of a . . .' An image of my mum flashes: she has flowers in her hair, singing under the full moon to welcome in the solstice. 'A pagan, I guess.'

'Ah.' He nods. 'Well, I pray all the time. No need to be in a church to speak to God. Naturally, I have many questions for him.'

'And the cruelty of this war? The fact that in the future, there will be another war and then another and another? None of that shakes your faith at all?'

'Shakes it? No, why would it?' Sal frowns. 'I've spent my life trying to understand the fabric of the universe. Not to disprove God, but to be a little closer to him. What has happened to you and me – and maybe more, who knows? – it's all part of His great mystery.'

'I suppose I don't really get why any of it has to be mysterious,' I say. 'Why make life into a crossword puzzle?'

Sal looks as if he is about to answer me when we are interrupted by the sound of clicking, striding footsteps. At first, I think the dark-suited figure that is walking towards us is a priest; then I see a man of around forty in an exquisitely tailored suit. Somehow, this gentleman has escaped the ragged fate of the rest of the island, which must mean that he is important or rich – or both. There is something about him that is curiously familiar.

'Signor Conte.' Sal stands up and offers his hand with a slight bow of his head. 'A pleasant surprise.'

The nobleman – if that's what he really is – is just a shade taller than me, with a strong roman nose and a dimple in his chin.

'Not such a surprise, my friend. My palazzo is only across the square.' The count looks at me with polite enquiry, his dark eyes making a quick assessment.

'May I introduce my cousin, Maia Borg?' Sal says. 'She has recently come from the other side of the island to stay with me, though I have little to offer her in the way of home comforts. Maia, may I introduce you to Count Nicoletti Landolina. His family are Italian nobility, from an ancient lineage, but have lived here almost since Mdina was built.'

'Pleasure.' The count takes my hand and shakes it firmly with both of his. 'Please, call me Nicco. We do not stand on ceremony in Malta. The professor is quite right, I am an Italian at home in my beloved Malta. It hurts me to see our two nations so divided, when we ought to be as brothers. Delighted to meet you, Miss Borg. All this time, I was certain that the professor had no family, and yet here you are!'

'Then please call me Maia,' I ask him, hopefully deflecting his attention from Sal's new-found family.

'Maia – a beautiful name,' he says. 'But tell me, what brings you to the Silent City this afternoon?'

Sal and I look at one another. Neither of us has thought to prepare a reason.

'History,' I say. 'I love history. And there's something so magical about Mdina. It feels out of time, almost, as if you can step through the gates and the rest of the world, even the war, fades away. Sal thought a trip here would give me a little quiet, a chance to breathe.'

'Ah, yes.' Nicco nods, as if he has heard of my panic in the shelter. Perhaps he has. 'But now, the day grows late. Will you not join me for dinner? I'd be so delighted to have some civilised company. The rations are so strict, but my cook really can make miracles. I even have a few bottles of good wine left. Please, agree, and I will have my driver return you to Valletta when it is safe.'

'A most kind invitation, Count,' Sal says. I expect him to turn it down, but he surprises me. 'We would be delighted to accept your hospitality. And I wonder if I might ask a further favour?'

'Of course.' The count smiles. 'If it is within my power to gift.'

'The manuscripts, the illuminations made by the monks long ago, the ones you let me see before? Are they safe?'

'There is nowhere safer than here,' the count says. 'Hitler will not allow bombs to fall on Mdina. It's here that he envisages Nazi headquarters on the island will be, you see. He does so like his grand buildings.'

'I see.' Sal nods. 'May I show them to Maia? She is so interested in history, you see, and I remember that there were some lovely annotations and details. The cat's paw prints, for example.'

'Yes, so charming. Of course, let me find Father Patrice.'

At the mention of his name, a small, svelte gentleman with immaculately groomed silver hair appears as if from thin air.

'Ah, there he is. Father, will you take my guests to the crypt and let them peruse our manuscripts, then perhaps guide them to my home when they are finished?'

'It would be my honour, Count,' the priest murmurs, deferential, before turning to us. 'Please, follow me.'

Sal follows the priest as I glance over my shoulder at the retreating count. He opens one of the huge cathedral doors, letting a slash of bright afternoon light intrude into the interior. Our eyes meet, and that's when I recognise him.

The count was the secretive figure with their face hidden that we met outside Elias's den. I can see it in his bearing and the turn of his head. More than that, I know that he recognises me, too.

Chapter Twenty-Six

Father Patrice takes great pleasure in unlocking the ancient cabinets that hold the illuminated manuscripts, many of which date from the arrival of the Knights of St John on the island; few are from even earlier.

'There is a particular book of hours? A book of prayer?' Sal asks the priest. 'With the elephant?'

'Ah yes,' Father Patrice smiles. 'The elephant is always our visitors' favourite.'

'The elephant?' I ask Sal.

The priest brings out a large heavy book, one that I imagine would have been designed to rest on a ledger, a page turned every day to reveal a new prayer, meditation or catechism. Sal and I stand each side of Father Patrice as he turns the heavy pages, showing glimpses of exquisitely inked and gilded illumination until he finds the page with the strangest looking animal on it I have ever seen.

'That's an elephant?' I ask, looking at the grey lumpen creature that is sitting on its hind legs, like a begging dog. His very human face sports a wide grin that seems to understand he is somewhat ridiculous. What I can only guess is a trunk erupts from the top of his head and spouts a fountain of silver water.

'You see, the artist had heard elephants described but had never seen one for himself. Rather sweet, if you think about it,' Father Patrice says, smiling at us in turn.

'Or the stuff of nightmares,' I say, glancing at Sal.

'Oh, and might we see the New Testament, the one that belonged to Caravaggio?' Sal asks.

'Ah.' Father Patrice thinks for a moment. 'I will ask. It's annotated, you know, by the master's own hand, and so is kept in another location. One moment.'

As soon as he is gone, Sal flips through the book a few more pages.

'It was Brother Phillip who produced that elephant,' he tells me as he finds the page he is looking for. 'A most stubborn man. Certainly lacking in the humility that one would expect from a monk.'

'Are you saying that . . . ?'

'I was here when this book was being made,' Sal confirms. 'Not for long. Three days – enough to get to know Brother Phillip.' He finds the page he wants, pressing down firmly to reveal the tightly bound margins. 'And here is the evidence . . . Look, and tell me what you think.'

★ ★ ★

Nearly an hour later, I'm still thinking about what Sal showed me, as the count – or Nicco as I must learn to call him – gives us a tour around his beautiful palazzo. If Sal were to tell me we've stepped back in time now, I would believe him, for although the palazzo is rather frayed and dilapidated, it is dripping with old-world money and expensive taste.

'My drawing room,' Nicco says as he leads us through a high-ceilinged room lined with pink silk wallpaper. Peering up at the dark corners of the vaulted stone ceilings, I can see it peeling in some corners, and there are one or two large patches of damp and mould, but somehow, in the lamplight, it only adds to the glamour.

'My ancestors.' He gestures expansively at a long line of oil portraits that seem to cover two or three centuries, judging by their styles and number. They are linked only by a marked family resemblance to Nicco himself.

'And my library.'

We pass through a small but beautiful room filled floor to ceiling with blue-painted cabinets full of books, some of which look older than the manuscripts Father Patrice showed us in the crypt. I want to linger and run my fingers down the spines of the books, to pull one out at random and leaf through the pages. Nicco doesn't seem to be the lingering type, though.

'And finally, the dining room.' Nicco smiles as we enter a long room with vaulted stone ceilings. 'Please.' He gestures to the end of one long refectory table, where there are three place settings.

'You are too good,' Sal says as he takes a seat. 'To share food in this difficult time is a kindness indeed.'

'There are only me and Santa, my housekeeper,' Nicco says. 'And though I am of Italian blood, I am little concerned with food. It is but a necessary fuel.'

'I wish I felt the same,' Sal says a little mournfully, placing a hand on his belly. 'I am always hungry.'

I've barely thought about food all day, but when the scent of something rich and earthy reaches me, my empty stomach lurches with pangs of hunger. I'm ravenous.

'Rabbit stew and a little pasta,' Nicco tells us as his housekeeper, a rather beautiful woman, sets a large pot down on a skillet. She lifts the lid to allow the aroma to wend its way into the room and sinks a ladle into the stew.

'Please, help yourselves,' she says with a smile as she takes a step back.

There's a strong ladies-first sense, so I stand up to reach over the pot to serve myself some of the rich broth. A boiled-bare, blind-eyed rabbit's head floats upwards.

'Christ!' I say, dropping the spoon.

'Santa!' Nicco shoots the woman a look, and she shrugs and represses a smile.

'Ah,' Sal says, fishing the head out of the pot for me. 'Not a cruel trick, Maia, dear. The head is left in the stew so that guests can be certain they are not eating dog or rat. Even before the war and rations, this was tradition, you have been saved from such privations on the farm.'

'Oh, of course.' I sit down and let Sal serve me. 'Well, sorry. I just wasn't prepared.'

'Santa, bring your plate and sit with us,' Nicco tells her. 'We always eat together when we don't have guests, and besides, I think poor Maia needs a little female company now. And bring us another bottle of wine – whichever you prefer.'

When she returns a few minutes later, Santa smiles at me from across the table.

'I apologise,' she says sincerely. 'I didn't think.'

'Don't be, this is delicious,' I say. It's too salty, what little meat there is is chewy, and I have to keep picking bone fragments out of my teeth. Even so, my hunger is such it tastes like the most delicious meal I have ever eaten.

'I only wish we had more,' Santa tells me. She exchanges a look with the count, and I get the distinct sense she is a little more than a housekeeper to him.

Wine flows with abundance, and I feel its heady warmth running through my veins. My stomach is full, and suddenly everything around me comes into sharp focus.

This *is* real. Somehow, I *am* here – I'm here as much as I have ever been anywhere.

What Sal showed me in the margin of that book was something that should not, could not have been there. His name and date of birth were etched on the very edge of a piece of vellum, so close to it that when the sheet was bound with all the others into a book, several hundred years ago, it was hidden deep in the margin. It could only be seen by someone who knew it was there and could not have been added after the book was bound.

All the atoms of the universe have rearranged themselves to bring me here. I don't know why, how long for or when I might be torn out of this world and flung to some other corner of another time.

It's terrifying.

Chapter Twenty-Seven

When the wave of impossible fear hits me, I have a sudden pressing need for fresh air. Excusing myself, I get up from the table and head towards the staircase. Both men rise from their seats as I do, and Sal offers to follow me, but I wave him away. All I know is that I need to find a place where I can feel the weight of this reality and try to place myself within it.

A cool breeze beckons me to the central marble staircase, and I follow it up until I find myself on a verdant roof terrace, full of night-scented plants that must need a great deal of care to remain so green in this heat. From another building somewhere nearby, I hear young men singing a song I don't recognise. Walking over to the balustrade, I lean against the stone and tip my face up to the moon.

Is it the same moon I have seen all my life or some other satellite?

Perhaps, like Sal, I will always be eighty years late now. And what does that mean for the people I have left behind? Would Dad care or notice? What about Kathryn, who gave me so much care from the moment she met me? It hurts that I can't think of anyone else who would truly notice my absence. Is there a body – my body – prone and empty, waiting to be found? When they find it, will it show all my scars. Not only the physical ones, but the scars of the harm I did.

There is a burden of guilt that I carry.

The name of a seven-year-old girl that is etched on my ribs.

If I were delivered to that moment and given a chance to turn a different corner and make another choice, then this would make perfect sense.

But here? This time and place makes no sense – not for me or for Sal. And yet this is all the sense that I have.

'Hey there!' a familiar voice shouts up to me from below. 'Stitches? Still following me?'

'Danny?' I call out, leaning over the railing as far as I can. I see his face in late-evening purple, gazing up at me from a balcony below.

'Damn, there you are, just like Juliet,' he says. 'But soft! What light through yonder window breaks?'

'Bit old for Juliet,' I tell him, as surprised and pleased to see his face as he seems to be to see me. 'Sal and I are having dinner with a count.'

'Oh, *the* count,' Danny says. I sense a hint of dislike in his voice. 'He's a handsome fellow, I suppose.'

'Is he? I hadn't noticed.' In the dark, I can just make out the pale shape of his uniform, the glint of his eyes, reflecting the moon. 'You're billeted here?'

'Yeah.' Danny looks over his shoulder into an orange-lit room. I can just make out a group of young men standing shoulder to shoulder around a piano. 'We're raising a glass to the guys who didn't make it today. We lost four.'

'I'm so sorry.' Even as I say it, I know it sounds empty, meaningless.

Several still and silent seconds pass, and then I hear him say in a soft, low voice, 'Can't help but think if I'd been in the sky . . . then things might have gone different.' And then, 'Wait there. Don't move, OK?'

'Why? I should probably go back to . . . oh!'

Before I can finish my sentence, Danny has leapt up onto the low wall surrounding his balcony and climbed up on the flat rooftop of the building next door.

'*Boghod mieghek, xitan!*' A nun in full habit happens to appear from inside at that very moment and takes after him with a broom. Danny escapes her assault by bounding, climbing and swinging up onto the roof next door with terrifying fearlessness. She shakes her fist at him until she spots me, waiting for him either to arrive or die. Finally, after a suspense-filled second, in which he balances precariously on the low rooftop wall, he jumps down lightly to meet me, and she claps her hands in delight.

'That was very silly,' I tell him, smiling all the same. In all the madness and confusion, this man seems to bring a sense of calm and peace with him in every breath.

'Not dashing, exciting and impressive?' he asks, a little hurt.

'What if you'd broken your neck? Then what?'

'Oh, I wasn't going to break my neck,' he says. 'I know how I die, and it's not falling off a building while trying to impress a girl.'

'What do you mean?'

He's being glib, but there's a dark undertone to his words, one no doubt coloured by the death of his comrades.

'Oh, it's no big deal,' he says lightly, with a throwaway gesture. 'It's just that we pilots . . . we know that when our number's up, it's up. There's nothing you can do about it. It's a way of getting through it, I guess, accepting fate.'

'I'm having kind of a hard time accepting fate, right now,' I say.

'What – dinner with a handsome count not good enough for you?' he asks, taking a step closer to me. 'A man risking his neck to come and say hello not satisfactory?'

There's no way to explain to him that I am lost in time. My fear of fate is incredible; his is made of brutal reality.

'You must feel awful about your friends.' I turn away from him, looking towards the pale gold light of the moon.

'I do, and I don't.' I feel the brush of his arm against mine as he shrugs. 'They were hardly around long enough for me to get to know 'em. And if I'm honest . . .'

We turn our heads to face one another. One side of his face is cast in gold, glowing and full of deep sorrow.

'Can I be honest with you, Maia?'

'You can,' I tell him, somehow knowing it's true.

'I saw them on their first day, green and fresh out of training, and I didn't try to get to know them. There wasn't any point. Those kids weren't gonna last, and I knew it.'

Neither of us speaks. We hold each other's gaze for one long heartbeat before turning back to look at the island, her golden skirts spread out around us in all directions. Slowly, slowly, she is falling into darkness. There are no twinkling lights in the villages and towns that I know stretch below us. Instead, thousands of fragile lives go on behind tightly closed shutters. Families hold one another close and hope to see the dawn.

'You are doing your best to protect yourself,' I say into the soft night. 'Maybe it's the only way you really can.'

'And don't that make me the coward?' Danny's voice is laced with quiet anger. 'So damn keen on keeping my head on straight that I don't even take the trouble to ask a kid about his ma or if he has a sweetheart back home? Make him feel like he's not alone in this whole show?'

'Not a coward,' I say. 'Careful.'

'That's me, Stitches. Captain Careful.' He laughs, short and wry. 'Begging your pardon, I didn't risk my neck to come over just to make it all about me. I can't be all that careful. If I was, I would have stayed over there, safe and sound.'

I smile. 'I told you it was dangerous.'

'Oh, it's not the fall that's dangerous,' he says.

I feel his gaze on my cheek. I keep looking at the moon. 'Christina told me that you had sworn off women for the duration of the war,' I say, 'which is weird, because if I didn't know better, I would swear you were flirting with me.'

Danny laughs, perhaps taken aback by my boldness. 'Maybe I am,' he admits. 'Best to ignore me. You listen to this silver tongue of mine, and before you know it, you'll be all moon-eyed and in love with me, and I'll be forced to break your heart.'

'Oh, you are in no danger of me falling in love with you,' I tell him, allowing myself to look at him at last. It makes me smile to see his mouth fall open.

'Not even after I just Errol-Flynned it up here to impress you?'

'I think you did that to take your mind off the four colleagues you lost today,' I say softly. 'I think that you try hard not to care and that you think you don't. But a man who doesn't care doesn't beat himself up the way you have. And I think that taking a stupid risk to see a virtual stranger was a way of inviting fate to even the score.'

'I never met another woman like you, Stitches,' Danny tells the moon. 'I mean that – you are fresh out the box, one-of-a-kind – an original.'

'That's because I come from eighty years in the future,' I tell him. He's been so honest with me, I feel compelled to be the same, even though I know he will laugh it off. 'I'm not meant to be here. I just fell through time and landed right now.'

Danny thinks I'm joking. 'Funny,' he says, 'cos, I get the feeling you were never meant to be anywhere else but right here, right now.'

'Maia?'

I look around, and Nicco is standing at the stop of the staircase.

'Signor Conte,' I say, repeating what I heard Sal say earlier. 'I'm so sorry. I came up here to get some air and happened on an acquaintance. Do you know . . . ?'

'Flight Lieutenant Beauchamp? Of course,' Nicco says coolly. 'The whole island knows him. I do not know how he landed on my roof terrace, though.'

'Forgive me, sir.' Danny offers him a hand. 'Just letting off a little steam.'

'I see.' Nicco is smiling, his voice warm, but even so, his irritation is clear. He does not accept Danny's hand.

'Well, I guess I'll be going then.' Danny hops up onto the railing.

'I would prefer you go out the front door,' Nicco tells him. 'If you don't mind. One has certain standards.'

'Of course.' Danny comes off the wall. 'Goodnight, Stitches,' he says as he jogs down the staircase, calling as he goes, 'I'll see you around.'

For a moment, Nicco and I listen to the sound of Danny's steps receding. I expect to be admonished or asked to leave, but neither happens.

'You are close to the flight officer?' Nicco asks, with a kind of curiosity I can't exactly place.

'Not really,' I say.

'But you could be,' he observes.

'Unlikely.' I'm guarded.

He nods and changes the subject. 'Well, it seems like there will be no raid tonight,' Nicco says, reminding me for the first time that the raid Sal mentioned earlier never came. 'One can't help but wonder if it's not the calm before the storm. One hears rumours, doesn't one?'

'I don't,' I tell him. 'I'm so sorry – it was rude to leave the table early after you've been so kind. I think perhaps the wine went to my head. I had no idea that Danny would . . . well, do what he did.'

'Please.' Nicco offers me his arm to escort me back to Sal. 'No need to apologise for the Canadian. I find North Americans always think they own whatever part of the world they are in.'

'And yet here he is, risking his life for us,' I say.

'Of course,' he concedes.

When we reach the entrance courtyard, the door to the street stands open, and there is a sleek-looking black car outside.

Nicco inclines his head. 'The professor is waiting for you in the car.'

'Thank you again,' I say. 'I know petrol is short . . .'

'I have my ways,' Nicco replies. He takes my hand and kisses it. 'I think we all do, don't we, Maia?'

'I suppose we do,' I say, knowing that he is referring to seeing us in the catacombs.

'I hope you won't mind if I seek out your company again,' Nicco says finally. 'I feel that we have much to talk about.'

'Of course,' I say politely, intrigued but instinctively wary.

'I will see you again,' he says.

There's something about the way he says it that feels like a threat.

Chapter Twenty-Eight

Monday 23rd June 2025, 10 a.m.

Sitting up with a jolt, I gasp in air like it's my first breath.

'Maia.' Kathryn grabs hold of my wrist. 'Thank God, at last. I've been sitting by the bed for an hour waiting for you to wake up.'

The air vibrates around me. I see her face dissipate and reform, catching glimpses of lidless eyes and the bone in her jaw.

Nothing is real.

That's the single thought I have in my head: nothing is actually real.

'I don't think I'm staying long,' I say urgently, grabbing onto her hands in the hope they will anchor me. 'Kathryn, I need you to listen to me, please. This is really important. I need you to look for me.'

'What do you mean? You're right here,' Kathryn asks anxiously. Tears stand in her eyes. 'I'll take you to the hospital as soon as you feel able to travel.'

'No, no. This isn't real – nothing is real. Soon I'll be taken again. I can see it all dissolving. You're floating away.'

When Kathryn shakes her head in dismay, she leaves a trail of herself caught in gravity's web. My mind is a fragile thing, flowing in a liquid state. Thinking seems impossible.

Frantically, I scrabble for information. 'Have I been here? Has my body been here?'

'Of course – where else would you have been?' Her voice fragments, splintering into almost indecipherable shards. I don't have long now.

'Your hair.' Her frown is disjointed and broken. Her expression becomes incredulous. 'When on earth did you cut you hair?'

'It doesn't matter,' I say. 'I think you know what's happening, even if you don't believe it yet. I need you to look for me. Look for me in 1942.'

'Maia, I think you are very ill,' she says, each word echoing a thousand times.

'Maybe, but just look for me in 1942. If I see you again, I need to know if you find me. Promise me you will look.'

'If?'

Then she's gone, almost entirely – a vanishing point at the end of an expanse of dark – and I'm being dragged through the grit of starlight so fast I feel it graze the surfaces of whatever it is I am now, even though I know I am nothing.

★ ★ ★

I come to a stop with a lurch. My body coalesces around my mind. A kitchen, modern and bright white. A little girl of about three with light-brown curls and pale grey eyes frowns at me. Behind her, a woman stands with her back to the girl, chopping something. Long dark hair caught up in a hair clip.

'Who are you?' the little girl says, sounding not scared but intensely curious. She glances at the woman and then back at me. 'Where did you come from?'

'Where did who come from?' the woman asks her. The sound of her voice frightens me. 'Are you talking to Mimi again?'

'Who's the lady, Mummy?'

'What lady?' The woman turns around, and I glimpse her expression of horror and shock before I am unravelling again.

Her face looks just like mine.

* * *

There's no air in my lungs, and I can't breathe. Sal slaps my face. It seems to reanimate my body. Pain arrives on delay as I suck in a deep breath of oxygen. Clutching the edge of the table, I cling to its solidity. All I want is for the universe to stay still for more than a moment.

'Where did you go?' Sal asks me urgently, as I stare at my surroundings. 'When?'

I'm in the sitting room of the half-house. It's night outside; I'm not sure if it is the same night as when I left. Unable to form words, I ask the question I need an answer to with my eyes.

'In the back of Nicco's car,' Sal tells me. 'You collapsed, as if your soul had been ripped from you. The driver carried you in. I told him you'd had a little too much wine and not enough food. We laid you on the couch. You were not here, Maia – not for the last four hours or more. It was as if your body was a shell, emptied of all meaningful life.'

'Hours?' The first word comes at the cost of a sore, parched throat. 'It felt like I was gone for only a few minutes.'

'Where this time?' Sal asks, intense.

'Forwards, to Kathryn. For a little while. I was able to ask her to look for me here.'

'Yes, good – good idea.' Sal nods. 'Anywhere else?'

'Yes, but . . .' I think of that child's face and the face of her mother. My face. 'It doesn't make any sense. It was somewhere in the future. A future, I think. But I couldn't go to my own future, could I? Especially not one that I have ever dreamt of for myself.'

'I never have,' Sal says. 'But I haven't travelled for decades. You are still settling. Perhaps here isn't where you will land?'

'Nothing is real,' I say, frantic. 'Nothing. Not you or me, and perhaps all of this is just insanity. In a way, I wish it was, because at least then I could stop feeling the spin of the earth under my feet. Except . . . except that nothing is real, and there is no meaning. Not to anything!'

Tears come then, all at once and in force. Dropping my forehead onto the table, I sob into my folded arms.

Sal pats my shoulder. 'There, there.' He pours me a glass of water and presses a clean handkerchief into my balled fist. He waits.

Before long, exhaustion and dehydration empty me utterly. I take a few deep shuddering breaths and take comfort in the calm made by the remnants of me.

'I haven't felt comfortable in my own skin . . . ever,' I confess to him. 'But I really want to go home right now, back to the world I understood and the me who didn't care anymore. I don't want to know the secrets of the universe. I just want to be still and ordinary again.'

'I know, Maia, I know.' He sighs deeply, and in that sigh, I hear all the years of his loss.

'Together, we will try to find the answer,' he says.

'And in the meantime . . . I need Kathryn to be able to find me. If she can find a record of me here, at least then she will be able to see what's happening – which means I need to get noticed by history.' I sit up straight and wipe my face dry. 'I think I might have a story for Miss Strickland.'

Everything I do here is waiting to be written in the future. So, it's time to make some waves.

Chapter Twenty-Nine

Saturday 8th August 1942, 9 a.m.

'Are you certain?' Mabel sits back in her chair. Operations have been moved inside the paper's ruined office once more. The windows are shattered, with shards of glass still protruding from the wooden frames and plaster that was once on the ceiling now scattered across the floor, but I don't get the impression the building is about to fall down. I'm not sure that Mabel would leave her beloved paper, even if it was.

She watches me as I go to every window and doorway to check once again that we can't be overheard.

'No, not at all,' I tell her. 'It's just an . . . instinct. One I'd like to explore.'

'Your gut?' She smirks. 'Do you like to pretend you are a hard-boiled PI?'

'No.' I take a deep breath and hold her gaze. 'I like to think that after years in the job, I can tell where there might be a story. Since I arrived in . . . Valletta . . . the fear of espionage has been constantly present. The island's on its knees. There are probably plans being put in place by both the Allies and Axis forces that you and I know nothing about – maybe aid coming from the UK or America. And if those plans were discovered somehow and intercepted, then the fight for Malta would be over.

So, if there is even a slight chance that an influential and trusted figure on the island could be in a position to pass information and secrets to the enemy, then wouldn't that be worth knowing?'

'My dear.' Mabel uses the term like an insult. 'I think you misconstrue the purpose of our work here. The army takes care of intelligence. The *Times of Malta* is a tool to inform the people and to lift them up, to fortify their spirits by connecting them to the outside world and telling them that victory is certain. We report the news; we don't make it. If you have any evidence that the count is collaborating with the enemy, then you should take it to HQ – though I am certain they will laugh in your face and arrest you for good measure. The count's family has lived on this island for centuries!'

'And yet he still calls himself an Italian,' I remind her. 'And anyway, victory isn't assured, is it? We both know that. The island is on her knees. The people are tired, heartsick and hungry. It's not the people's stoicism that is going to save Malta: all it does is prolong the agony. Malta has no control over her fate, but if there is a traitor living in plain sight, then let me at least look for evidence. If I find any, I will give it to General Gort, and you can break the story. All I want is a by-line.'

'I have never even heard your name before,' Mabel says.

'Is it because it's a Maltese name?' I ask her archly.

'How dare you!' She stands up, and suddenly I really understand where she gets her fearsome reputation from. 'This island runs through my blood, and when I tell you that I would die for Malta, I am not exaggerating.'

'I'm sorry,' I say.

Her eyes blaze for a moment longer; then her fury recedes as quickly as it rose. 'Apology accepted,' she says, taking her seat again. 'I'm not blind, Miss Borg. I see how some of the English treat the Maltese – like they are naive peasants. But you must remember that I *am* Maltese.' She presses her hand to her heart. 'In here. I am a woman who has carved a path for myself from the rocks beneath my feet. It is my sincere hope one day to be prime minister of an independent Malta in a world free from the terror of fascism.'

'You would be a great prime minister,' I tell her.

'I would.' She accepts the comment as a statement of fact, and I decide I like her very much. 'The truth is that every attempt to break the siege by sending supplies from Gibraltar has failed. Our only chance is a heavily armoured convoy with the aid of the Americans, and it's already underway. What everyone wants and needs to know is what route it will take and when it will arrive. What mustn't happen is that they find out too soon. Every hour counts in this war. Every mile a convoy can travel unnoticed improves its chances of making it to Valletta. Therefore, if you believe that you can gather evidence on a potential spy in our midst, you must do it. However, I insist that you talk to HQ first, or you could find yourself with a noose around your neck.'

'I can't.' I shake my head. 'You do things your way, Miss Strickland, and I have to do things mine. If anyone other than you and I know what I'm up to, there's a chance my cover will be blown. No one else can know, not even Sal.'

'And if *you* are a spy, as a good many in Valletta already think?' Mabel asks.

'Time will tell.' I shrug. 'But you don't think I'm a spy, do you? And I think you don't make mistakes when it comes to trusting your gut.'

Mabel smiles. 'Touché. Very well, Maia Borg. But take care, please.'

When I leave her office, stepping over the rubble on the staircase that takes me out into the bright sun, I have a sense of purpose, a sense of being alive, that I haven't felt since Syria. It's not the moral cause or an urge to do the right thing; it's the risk I am attracted to. It's playing roulette with my life and knowing that I might lose.

Chapter Thirty

As I'm leaving, I hear the sirens mount their call and the radios playing through open windows, announcing that a fleet of bombers is incoming. I can already hear the distant thrum of the approaching aircraft. The sound vibrates in my bones. It's deeper and more sonorous than the fighter jets I heard over the skies of Ukraine or Syria, but it brings the same message, one of mindless death and destruction.

For a few seconds, I freeze. I am back in the collapsed building, trapped under rubble with a small girl's hand in mine. It's growing cold to the touch.

The Maltese hurry towards the shelters, parting around me as though I'm a rock in a stream. This is not a moment to lose my grip, I remind myself. If anything, here in this time, I am absolved. That terrible day is decades in the future.

I haven't killed her yet.

That thought gives me strength enough to move my feet. Moving against the flow of the crowd, I head towards the half-house, where I think Sal will still be. There's a familiar comfort now in the deep, dark shelter, but more than that, there is an unfamiliar comfort in knowing him. He is like my one fixed point in time, somewhere I can return to and know he will welcome me.

Just as I get to the door, the first of the bombs drop on the harbour. Turning towards the sight, I see that the sky is black with heavy bombers slouching towards us. Just above their massing swarm, I can make out the trails of distant dogfights cutting swathes in the clear blue sky. Up there are men like Danny – and Danny himself – fighting for us and their lives far above the earth. Bombs fall from the bellies of the aircraft, gliding softly down beyond the horizon. The ground shakes under my feet as snakes of smoke and rubble unfurl a few streets away. When I look up, the planes are right overhead.

It hasn't happened yet. I don't deserve to die. Not yet. The girl I will one day kill isn't born and won't be for decades. It hasn't happened yet. Maybe it never will – maybe the future can change.

Throwing myself through the unlocked door, I race through the hallway as the cloud of planes blots out the sunlight streaming through the broken building. The gate to the shelter is propped open, waiting for me.

'Maia?' Sal shouts above the din as I clang the gate shut behind me.

'I'm here,' I say, almost falling down the steps into the small shelter. 'I'm safe.'

Sal nods. 'Your meeting with Miss Strickland?'

'Yes, she will give me a by-line if I uncover the right story. Now I just have to find one.'

'Excellent.'

It's remarkable how my body has already learnt to tolerate the noise of the raid, recalibrating and reassessing the new normal. Taking a second chair that Sal must have brought down here, I join him in the near-dark, and we listen, our gazes directed upwards as each pounding explosion releases another wave of fine dust to rain down on us. We brace our bodies against the noise and fear, and we wait for the raid to pass.

The noise recedes in slight increments until we can tell the worst is over. I wonder about the bright blue sky above, now filmed with the grit of battle. I wonder if Danny has made it back in one piece.

And finally, right here in the shelter, on my fourth day as an accidental time traveller, I accept it all. The relief of not fighting to make sense of it is profound. It just is this: this life and the other one. If you think about it, I'm lucky. How many people get to experience two lives? Perhaps I am meant to be here, perhaps there is a hidden purpose to all of this, or maybe the ancient universe got her wires crossed. It doesn't matter, not in this now. This is the only now I have.

The all-clear sounds, breaking me from my thoughts, and Sal gets up at once, dusting himself down. 'I must go to the church – the children will soon be waiting for me to teach them mathematics.'

'You really have made a life here,' I say with admiration. 'After you were ripped away from everything, you started again and made it work; people love you.'

'Eventually, there was no other choice.' Sal shrugs, a brief shadow of sadness passing over his face. 'Oh, I had word that your papers are ready earlier than expected. We will fetch them tonight.'

'No need to come with me,' I say, seeing an opportunity. 'I know where to go now. I'll get the bus this afternoon and pick them up.'

Sal frowns. 'I'm not sure. Elias is not a good man . . .'

'Exactly,' I say. 'I'm looking for stories, remember? He is a good story.'

Sal's frown deepens. 'The Mafia are here on the island, Maia. Perhaps for now, the war has stopped some of their business. But Elias . . . he is dangerous.'

'And I am used to danger,' I tell him. 'I can take care of myself.'

'Can you?' He twists his hands with worry. 'You are coping with a lot. And . . . forgive me – I know little of your life before – but you said you had some problems with your . . . mental well-being.'

'Well, yes,' I reply, not wanting to discuss how broken I was before I ever arrived on this island. 'But it was my job to work in war zones and seek out stories, even when I was in danger. Don't worry – I'm tough enough.'

'And if you fall out of this time, while you are on the bus or in the catacombs? You will be undefended and vulnerable.'

'You're right.' I nod. 'But I can't sit still. You've had more than thirty years to try to find out what has happened to us, and now it's my turn to take up the mantle. I'm not embedded in this time yet, so we need to be ready for if – or when – I go back to my time, so that I can show someone what's happening and get some answers. You want that, too, don't you?'

'I do,' he concedes. 'Though it's too late for me, I'd rather not die without knowing.'

'Then trust me.' I offer him a smile that's braver than I feel. 'Now, go and make your poor kids learn maths in the middle of a war.'

* * *

You'd think I'd rush out into the sunlight. Instead, I sit in the dark for a while, letting the minutes wash over me. Am I a different version of me, or the same me in a different universe? Or the same me in the same universe? I don't see how it can be the last, because I have a body here and a body there – and perhaps in a thousand other times. And yet I don't think it can be a parallel universe either: everything that happens here seems to have an impact there. Either way, perhaps there are millions, maybe billions more of me reprinted throughout the universe. And perhaps, out of all those versions, one is living in perfect happiness. I smile for her, whoever she is and whatever she's doing. Suddenly, I have infinite sisters.

When I get upstairs and into the house, I find a covered pitcher of fresh goat's milk on the table and a small loaf of bread.

Drink milk quickly, a pencil-scrawled note on a page torn from Sal's notebook tells me, *before it turns.*

Hungry, I do as I'm told.

'Hello? Anyone home?' I hear Christina's voice calling in the hallway.

I hurry to greet her. 'Hello!'

'Oh, *there* you are.' Christina greets me. She looks beautiful in a light cotton blouse and long, wide-legged trousers that gape at the waist. 'I'm on my way to work, but I just had to drop by. Last night, Alex had a perfect brainstorm! He remembered our old landlady's cotton sheets down in the basement – bright yellow, don't you know? We'd thought about running something up with them before, only yellow makes me sallow and Alex says he'd rather die than be compared to custard. But then we thought of you, with your complexion – when it's not red – and your dark hair. You can carry it off very well. So, he stitched you a frock in double time, and I'm delivering. I had him put pockets in it. A woman needs pockets in time of war, darling.' She thrusts her hands into her own, as if to make a point. 'And so much better in this heat than what you've got on.' She notices that I'm still in the same altered outfit

I left her house in the day before yesterday. 'And now you have a change of clothes, though I'm not sure what we are going to do with your hair. None of my setting lasted on that mop.'

'I quite like it as it is,' I tell her, touching my hand to where my hair has sprung back into its natural curls, sitting lightly on the nape of my neck. 'Easy to care for.'

'It does rather suit you, I suppose, in a sort of rural way,' Christina says. 'Well, come on then. I want to see how it looks.'

She presents a neatly folded garment to me, which I take with delight, shaking it out so that I can hold it up against me. A simple cotton shirt-dress, darted at the bust and gathered at the waist – and after being stuck in this uncomfortable skirt and blouse, it's the most beautiful thing I have ever seen.

'Well, go on!' Christina urges me. 'Put it on. No need for modesty – it's only you and me. It's stitched in blue thread, because that's the only colour we had to hand, but I think it's rather nice. See how Alex made a feature of it on the collar and buttonholes?'

'It must have taken him hours,' I exclaim as I strip off. 'How will I repay him?'

'Not hours – he's a whizz. Wants to go to Paris after the war. If there still *is* a Paris, that is. And you know, it takes his mind off things. It's not easy for Alex, being two people at once. What a stupid world we live in, when a man isn't supposed to love another man, but war and power and violence is something to be proud of.'

'I hear you,' I say.

Christina cocks her head. 'Well, of course you do, darling, I'm standing right next to you. I say, your brassiere is marvellous.' She leans in to peer at my M&S plunge underwire. 'All that cleavage with no corset. I used to have breasts once, you know? Nothing like your ample bosom, but perfectly respectable. Of course, since rations, they've gone the way of my shapely behind.'

'They'll come back one day,' I tell her.

'Perhaps, darling, but being dreadfully thin never goes out of fashion.'

Hastily, I button up the dress. There are ten white buttons – no two are matching, but they are all of almost equal size. And it fits perfectly.

Christina holds a fragment of broken mirror for me to look at myself in, moving it up and down so I can get the full effect.

'This is so kind,' I tell her. 'I must do something to return the favour.'

'I am sure we will think of something,' Christina tells me with a laugh. 'Actually, you know, we need another plotter at Lascaris. One of the local girls has gone down with "Malta dog" dysentery, darling, and we have no backup at all. And as you are at a bit of a loose end, perhaps you could apply?'

'Oh, I've just started working for Miss Strickland,' I tell her. 'Words are my thing. I have all the hand-eye coordination of a rock.'

'Well! That is a good way of supporting the war effort, I suppose. We all need the morale boost of the *Times* every day.' Christina observes me with her grey eyes. There are a dozen questions there that she wants to ask me, and yet for some reason, she refrains.

'Christina . . .' I begin.

'No.' She shakes her head. 'I know there's something mysterious about you, Maia Borg, but I also know that whatever it is, you aren't here to spy on us. If you are, then everything I thought I'd learnt from a lifetime in music halls is wrong. I trust you. I don't know why. I can't explain it, and it makes no sense, but from the first moment I set eyes on you, I felt as if we had always known each other and that you were my friend.'

'I feel that, too,' I say.

'So, don't tell me anything. But if it turns out that I'm a deluded fool and I'm wrong about you, then it won't be the military police you have to fear. I'll put you up against a wall and shoot you myself.'

'It won't come to that,' I tell her.

'It had bloody well better not. Well, I'm late, so I'd better run.' She kisses me lightly on each cheek. '*Ciao!*'

It seems to me that, if nothing is real, then nothing is a lie and nothing is true either. And yet I have met very few people as palpably alive as Christina Ratcliffe, and not to tell her everything feels like a betrayal. So, I promise myself – and her – that one day I will try to explain this impossible thing. When the time is right. One day, I'll tell the truth to everyone who matters. It won't matter if they believe me, just as long as I have stayed true.

Chapter Thirty-One

The gate of the catacombs is locked with a thick chain and heavy padlock. I stand for a moment in the long, dry grass and hot afternoon sun, staring at it, trying to work out what to do next. I didn't account for this.

Then I hear a short, sharp hiss.

Looking towards the sound, I see a small boy wearing a cap several sizes too big for his head, peering through the railings. Glancing around, he beckons furtively.

'Hello?'

He frowns at me from below the peak of his cap. 'You want Elias?' he asks.

'Yes.' I nod. 'Do you know when he will be back?'

'I know. I know everything,' he tells me. 'You follow.'

There's something about him, the way he's deadly serious about living this adventure, that reminds me of *her* – a child flirting with danger and the dangerous, because no harm can possibly ever come to them. Confident and frightened in one breath, living in make-believe to get through another day. My instinct is to scoop him into a hug and take him home to his family. And yet the last time I followed that instinct, it caused all the harm.

So, I don't try to save this little boy. I follow him instead.

He leads me through dusty, empty streets, the residents of Rabat having taken shelter inside out of the worst heat of the afternoon. The boy marches on, setting quite the pace, occasionally lifting his cap to wipe his brow on the sleeve of his shirt, revealing the prominent bones in his neck and shoulders. By the time he leads me into a quiet shaded courtyard, I am desperate for water, my hair is clinging to my head in damp curls and my yellow dress sticks to my back and breasts.

In one corner of the courtyard, sitting at a table under the shade of an old grape vine, is Elias with two male acquaintances. They are eating from a plate of *pastizzi*, little pastries filled with ricotta or mince and peas, and drinking bottles of beer. The bottles glisten with perspiration, like they have been chilled. How much does Elias charge for a cold beer, I wonder.

But when I start towards the table, the boy bars my way with his skinny arm.

'Name?' he asks.

'Maia Borg.'

He removes his hat as he approaches the table, then whispers in Elias's ear. His eyes go wide and round with awe as Elias makes a gesture to an unseen waitress, who brings over a small packet wrapped in newspaper. Meat, probably. I've seen more than a dozen children just like this boy, looking for a hero amidst terrible hardship. He is in awe of these men drinking cold beers at a shaded table who can give him food as if they are gods dealing in manna. I fear for him.

I wait as he trots back towards me, holding his prize close against his chest. The two men that were at the table melt away into the shadows. It seems Elias wants to be alone with me.

'You may go,' he says, and the boy leaves, presumably to go back to his station at the catacombs.

'Miss Borg!' Elias greets me with an expansive gesture. 'Take a seat. I see you are not used to the heat of the afternoon. Here, let me send for another beer.'

He gestures at a slender girl standing in the doorway, who turns on her heel at once to do his bidding.

'You have my items?' I ask him, glancing at his two companions lurking under the arches, each openly leering at where my dress sticks to my damp skin. I take the balance of payment that Sal gave me out of my pocket and place it on the table.

'Ah yes, they are here.' Elias picks up the folded notes, takes a small packet from his shirt pocket and lays it on the table.

But as I reach for it, he closes his hand over my wrist.

'There is an extra charge,' he tells me with a smile, his gaze travelling to my breasts.

'We have paid what was agreed,' I remind him. I try to pull my wrist away, but he holds it firm. Any fear I might have felt is washed away by fury.

'Yes, but you see, you need these papers. And I suspect the reason you need them isn't one that you would be happy for the authorities to know. So, I'm *renegotiating*.'

'I don't have any more money,' I tell him. I learnt a long time ago never to let men like this see any fear or weakness in you. The moment you show vulnerability, they will treat you like prey for the taking.

'I will accept payment in kind.' His wet lips curl into a smile, revealing yellow teeth with flecks of peas caught between them.

'I suggest you let me go at once,' I say evenly. 'If you don't, you will regret it.'

I have no idea what my next move is, but I know enough to push my luck until it has run out. This time, it hasn't.

'Unhand that young lady!' The count appears at the entrance of the courtyard, striding towards us.

Elias drops my hand and stands to greet the nobleman. I find my legs don't quite have the strength to do the same.

'You will give my friend her items immediately, Elias.' Nicco looks cool and elegant in white slacks and a shirt open at the neck. His black hair is concealed under a Panama hat.

'Signor Conte,' Elias bows, grovelling. It's pleasing. 'Of course. I didn't realise that she . . .'

'You embarrass me,' Nicco tells him. 'Your role is to provide a service for those already in hardship. Once a bargain is struck, the deal is done. Don't let me catch you trying such tactics again – on friends of mine or on anyone on this island, do you hear me? We want the goodwill of the people, not their hate. Now, get out of my sight.'

Beckoning to his associates, Elias half-stumbles, half-runs away, no doubt back to the underground tombs where he is a king of sorts.

Taking a breath, I compose myself as Nicco takes a seat at the table.

'Please accept my sincere apologies,' he says, picking up the envelope which he opens.

Waiting, I watch him take out the documents and examine them closely.

'These are good,' he says. 'You will pass muster.'

He refolds them and hands me the envelope. Cautiously, I take it.

'You need not be afraid of me, Maia,' Nicco assures me. 'I will not betray you for being on the island without the proper papers. Were you not provided with any before you arrived?'

It seems that Nicco might suspect I am a spy after all – an agent who has landed on one of the island's remote rocky shores in the dead of night, come to spread disinformation and propaganda just like the foolish young man they hanged. And if he believes that and hasn't turned me in, then he must think of me as an ally.

The count isn't working for the good of the people of Malta. He's working for the triumph of Italy.

'Thank you.' I lower my eyes, saying nothing. If I am still and quiet, it's more likely he will talk. 'I lost my papers at sea. A difficult crossing.'

'I'm sure,' he says, 'though I'm surprised that the professor has taken you in.'

'We are cousins,' I say as if that is a sufficient explanation alone. 'Sal wants to protect me.'

The more I can re-enforce the assumptions he has made about me without telling him anything, the better. Let him do the talking.

'You wonder why a man of means such as I is running a black-market operation, profiteering from others' misfortune? It's a fair question.'

Silently, I raise my eyes to meet his; they are as dark as a moonless night and as impenetrable.

'I am a man of layers, Maia,' he begins to explain. 'A count from an old family, but really, what does aristocracy matter in this modern world? It's a relic of another age, and I am a man who believes in radical progress. Freedom and opportunity for all kind.'

It's clear that this is a speech he has made a few times before. It's well-rehearsed and polished. I'm sure the people he usually performs for are in awe of him. He *is* impressive.

'In addition, I am a grocer of sorts. Finding ways to obtain what is very scarce for those who can afford it leaves more for those who cannot, does it not?'

An argument I've heard a thousand times before.

'But the man I really am, at the heart of everything, is a patriot determined to help my country win the war.'

The question is: which country?

'You had no papers – no need to tell me why. No need to explain why you didn't seek replacements through the more formal channels,' he says. 'We all have secrets that we would like to keep, do we not? I will keep yours, and you will keep mine – agreed?'

I nod. 'Yes.'

'Then we are friends who understand one another, Maia,' Nicco says. He signals the waitress. 'And perhaps we will find a way to help one another when the time is right. Now, we will enjoy a nice cold beer on such a glorious day.'

'Nicco.' I pause, uncertain if what I am about to say is the right thing. I need something to tempt him with, something harmless but risky that means he will trust me with all of his secrets – some information that will show him I am who he wants me to be. I remember what Mabel said. 'A huge convoy, protected by the US Navy, is already on its way,' I say. 'It won't be long now.'

'Do you know when it will reach the harbour?'

I shake my head.

'Well, I wish them godspeed – they will need it.'

That Nicco is at the top of the profiteering and black-market operations run by Elias is not in doubt, but that doesn't necessarily make him a spy or a traitor. If anything, it's quite possible that the senior members of the British army know what he's up to and even discreetly avail themselves of his services. The count is cautious and careful. He sees me in exactly the same way I see him, as an asset ripe to be exploited at the optimum moment.

And so we play on, sipping cold beer in the late-afternoon sun, each of us biding our time.

Chapter Thirty-Two

There's a small group I recognise waiting for the bus: the doctor who stitched up my head, her little boy, her baby fussing in the pram, and Vittoria, sheltering under the branches of a meagre-looking tree a little way apart from the other travellers, who are pressed into the embrace of a large, dense yew.

Vittoria is holding a large, battered doctor's bag that looks like it might weigh at least as much as she does, if not more.

'Maia!' Vittoria sees me and waves me over, shuffling up to make space for me in their patch of shade.

'Maia!' The little boy beams when he sees me. Racing to my side, he takes my hand. 'I saved you.'

'You did, kid.' I smile at him, then remember the name his mother called him. 'How's it going, Qalbi?'

He beams at me, delighted. 'You are funny,' he says. That's good enough for me.

'Ah, it's you. Let me see.' The doctor takes my face firmly in her large hand, turns it this way and that as she scrutinises my cut. She seems pleased.

'A few more days and the stitches can come out,' she says, admiring her handiwork. 'Healing nicely, no infection. The scar will be quite discreet. You will come to Floriana in three days, and I will remove the stitches.' She releases my jaw and goes back to waiting.

The kid swings my arm back and forth. The baby starts to whimper and fuss in the deep pram and Vittoria sings to her, leaning over the hood. Her voice is high and thin, as sweet as a child's. She is hardly more than one herself, after all.

'Doctor?' A young woman nervously approaches. 'Will you take a look at my boy? He eats all we have but still grows thin.'

The doctor barely glances at the child. 'Does he complain of an itching anus at night?' she asks bluntly.

The young woman lowers her eyes and nods.

'Threadworms – there are many cases in the children at present, especially the boys. They do not wash their hands. Castor oil – you have some?'

The young woman nods. 'Yes, Doctor.'

'Good. It is scarce. Castor oil, twice daily, and plenty of fluid to keep him hydrated. Repeat each day for a week at least, even if you stop seeing worms in his faeces. But you must give him water and milk and keep feeding him. Don't allow him to dehydrate.'

'Thank you, Doctor.' The young woman looks at her oblivious son as she takes his hand perhaps a little more gingerly than usual.

'And you, boy.' The doctor points at the child. 'Wash your hands every time you defecate.'

His mother pulls him to the back of the crowd.

'Not so hot on the bedside manner, is she?' I murmur to Vittoria, who jiggles the pram with the heavy bag slung over one bent arm. We walk a little way from the doctor. 'Here, let me take that bag for a while.'

'Oh no, Maia – the bag is my responsibility. You could rock baby Eugenie, though. See how she is red like a tomato with a face like Churchill? I know this face. Soon she will be screaming, and no ear will be safe.'

Eugenie's name suits her, for though she is little, she is mighty. Somewhat reluctantly, I take the pram and try to wheel it back and forth. It's heavy and stiff.

'You must be much stronger than you look, Vittoria,' I tell her.

'I work all day and all night,' she tells me. 'But the doctor teaches me, and so, when the war is over, I will be a nurse somehow.'

'And are things going well with your friend?'

Vittoria's face falls, and I realise at once my mistake. No one at the bus stop has greeted, smiled or even glanced at her. Clearly, when she took up with lonely young servicemen with money in their pockets and a will to live all the life they had, she let go of the only thing she had left: her reputation.

'Sorry.' I bend closer to her. 'I didn't think.'

'I am nothing to them.' She lowers her eyes. 'An outcast. And as for him, he . . .' She turns her face away from me. 'His plane went down yesterday. He is dead. No matter. My friends in the Gut have taken me in. I can work there a while, and I will be a nurse after the war. Life is not easy, but my friends . . . they know how to help me.'

She means her friends in the brothels of the Gut, I presume. They probably do know how to navigate life's difficulties better than most.

I look down the road in the hope of seeing the dust cloud of the bus lumbering towards us, but the road is empty except for a heat haze that twists and distorts the landscape like a dream.

Eugenie is not keen on the way I rock her. She is gulping air in preparation to caterwaul, so I scoop her out of the pram and pull a face at her, a trick I learnt from my mum, who never met a baby she couldn't charm. The baby's plump mouth falls open, and she stares at me as if I am crazy, but at least the great lump forgets to cry. When I blow a raspberry, she even smiles.

'She likes you, see?' the boy says. 'We are all friends.'

'We are, Qalbi.'

He hoots with delighted laughter.

The doctor glances at her watch and sighs. Gesturing to me with one hand to pass her the baby, she unbuttons the front of her dress with the other. With one swift movement, she latches Eugenie onto her breast, and the baby begins to feed as her mother stands in the heat. Vittoria produces a shawl from the bag and drapes it over the baby's head, covering any vestige of bare bosom.

The baby is heavy, the air is scalding, and yet the doctor stands unflinching, feeding her child. Perhaps people skills aren't top of her list, but she is an impressive woman.

'The bus.' Vittoria points to the battered vehicle as it rattles and shakes to a juddering stop.

'Vittoria, the pram please.' The doctor gets on the bus, her baby at her breast. The little boy tugs at my arm to follow him.

'You get on with your mummy,' I tell him. 'I'll help Vittoria.'

Everyone streams past us to get onto the bus. Vittoria and I are last, but we're just about able to jam the pram beside the driver and find space to stand between the seats.

'You can always come to me,' I tell the girl suddenly. 'If you need someone to talk to, a friend or help, come to me.'

The smile that she gives me in return is so radiant, it breaks my heart. 'You are a friend,' she says happily. 'A good friend. I am lucky.'

Her definition of luck and mine are completely different.

Chapter Thirty-Three

No one even tries talking over the rattle of the bus's engine or the clatter of its suspension against the potholed road. Then someone by the window gasps, and suddenly four or five people are leaning forwards, craning to try to see something. When the other half of the bus shift towards whatever they are looking at, the bus lurches, tips and crunches to a halt. Vittoria and I force the pram back out onto the road so that everyone can get off. Standing side by side, we shade our eyes and squint into the sun.

Then I see it: a small plane is half-flying, half-falling downwards, smoke trailing from its engine, and it seems to stop and start in mid-air.

'British!' someone cries as the aircraft rises and falls as if buffeted by invisible forces. 'Spitfire! Must be on patrol. Something's gone wrong.'

The aircraft descends further, gathering pace as it hurtles towards us.

'He has not ejected – he will die,' another cries.

'Why doesn't he eject?'

'Must be trapped . . . a malfunction.'

'No hope of landing safely,' says another. 'It will crash. He will die.'

Scanning the surroundings, I realise they are right. The terraced fields around us are long but narrow and edged with low stone walls. The chances of putting anything down safely on the uneven terrain at that speed must be negligible.

'Oh, God,' I whisper.

I want to look away, but as with everyone else in the road, my eyes are glued to the Spitfire as it looms ever bigger in the sky. In a few heartbeats, I can see the markings on the underside of its wings and the outline of the pilot. Perhaps he is already unconscious. I hope he's already unconscious.

Then it lurches down into the field next to the road. One wing dips so low it ploughs a furrow in the dry soil, sending rocks and earth exploding into the air. Somehow, the impact seems to right the dangerously listing aircraft just as it contacts the ground. There's a sickening crunch as metal folds and falls apart.

Smoke billows out of its engines as it skids the length of the field on its belly. Any second now, the nose of the plane will smash into the stone wall.

As one, we all clamber over into the field, racing towards where the impact will be Only Vittoria stays behind with the children.

Then, at the very last second, the Spitfire's tail slides to the left, slowing its speed and bringing it horizontal to the wall. It slams against the stone, finally breaking its speed and comes to a juddering stop.

For a moment, everything is still and silent. Then a fire blossoms into life in the aircraft's nose.

'Water – fetch buckets of water,' someone calls, and a group of men run off towards a simple low structure, where I hope there's a well or a pump.

'He can't get out,' a woman next to me gasps as small bright flames leap into view in the engines. 'He will burn to death!'

Stella, me and a couple of the men run forwards. A man nearly as old as Sal leaps onto the wreckage of the wing, dragging and smashing at the cockpit as flames nip at his ankles. Then I see the doctor wrench a loose piece of wood from a decaying gate. Climbing onto the remains of the wall, she bashes it against the glass.

From the other side of the field, the water-bearers are running, caught between urgency and keeping their buckets full. The fire suddenly roars its intent, and the bus driver grapples the doctor from the wall, dragging her to a safe distance. At the same moment, the other would-be rescuer dives off the wing, rolling in the dirt to put out the flames on his clothes.

The pilot is going to die, I realise. He made it all the way here, and now he's going to die in front of my eyes. Before I know it, I'm running towards the flames, just as the men with buckets throw their precious load. But the water does nothing, and the ferocious heat stops me dead; I can smell my hair singeing.

Then two boots appear, kicking violently at the windshield. I can't tear my eyes away from that last desperate bid for life. When the hood finally comes free, the second run of water is thrown at the wings, just as the pilot scrambles out of the cockpit and half-falls half-jumps into the field. At once, we all grab hold of a corner of him, because he belongs to us now. As one, we lift him and carry him far away from the burning wreckage.

A boom sounds just behind us as the fuel catches and a blast of hot air races over and through me, its fingers reaching to the far corner of the field.

The doctor is at the fore, helping him sit, pulling at his jacket, loosening it around the neck as he coughs and splutters and gasps in air. She tugs off the pilot's goggles and flight mask.

Bright blue eyes stare at us from his smoke- and oil-grimed face. My hands cover my mouth in shock.

'What luck,' Danny Beauchamp splutters as he takes in his surroundings. 'A bus! It looks like I'm gonna need a ride back to base.'

In amongst the throng of people, he sees me and smiles. 'Stitches, we meet again,' he says. Then he collapses in the doctor's arms.

Chapter Thirty-Four

'Stand back,' the doctor tells them, beckoning to Vittoria who hands the baby to an older lady, racing towards us with the bag. 'Bring water. Vittoria, my bag.'

'What can I do?' I ask, refusing to move back with everyone else.

'Be near – he knows you,' she says. 'He will be in shock. Take his hand. We need to check for injuries.'

I pick up Danny's hand, pulling off his charred gloves.

Quickly and efficiently, the doctor opens his jacket and the shirt underneath. His torso is lean and tanned, no blood that I can see. Vittoria hands her a stethoscope, and she listens to his heart.

Then the two of them roll him onto one side, Vittoria keeping him in place as the doctor checks his back and legs for wounds, pulling off his scorched boot. They repeat the process on the other side. It takes some effort but I keep his limp hand in mine throughout this, unable to pinpoint the exact meaning of the swell of emotion tightening my chest. His fingers are bruised; one nail hangs loose.

'Remarkable,' the doctor mutters. 'Hardly a scratch. Bring me water.'

Someone hands her a flask, and she promptly tips half of it over his face.

'What the fu—?' Danny splutters awake, sitting up abruptly. 'Am I dead?'

'Somehow, you are alive, and apart from smoke inhalation and the odd scratch, completely uninjured,' the doctor tells him.

The passengers erupt into spontaneous applause as Danny looks at us with an expression of mild bemusement.

'Stitches,' he says, breaking into a lopsided grin as he realises that I'm holding his hand. 'You sure I ain't dead?'

'You're not dead.' I squeeze his fingers a little too tightly, and he winces. 'You made it out of there.'

'The flying ace Danny Beauchamp!' someone shouts.

'The hero!' another.

The small crowd of passengers hug one another, shaking hands and clasping arms. Somehow, from somewhere, someone produces a camera and tripod and sets it up to take a photo.

'Whoa there.' Danny holds up a hand when the would-be photographer approaches. 'Let a man button his shirt and get his boots back on before you snap him for posterity.'

'Get back!' The doctor stands up, shooing the crowd away. 'Give the man a moment.' No one dares defy her.

I watch for a few painstaking seconds as Danny's trembling hands attempt to button his shirt.

'Let me,' I say, gently pushing his hands out of the way.

He watches me as I do barely a better job than him, my own fingers clumsy and foolish. Between us, we dress him again. I put the heavy flying jacket back onto his shoulders and return the boots to his bare feet, pulling them on with some effort.

'Awful embarrassing to admit I don't got no socks,' Danny says, a little sheepish.

'Can you stand?' I ask him, glancing at the milling crowd, in which a sort of festive air has broken out.

'My legs ain't broke,' he says. 'But I got a feeling they might be made of water.'

'Then lean on me,' I say. He hooks his arm through mine as he makes it slowly to his feet, tests first one and then the other.

'I should be dead,' he mutters. 'Why the hell ain't I dead?'

'I'm glad you're not,' I whisper, turning to look at him. 'Really glad.'

'Maybe you are my lucky charm, Stitches.'

'No such thing as luck,' I say. 'Your expertise got you out of that.'

Once we've managed to get to the line of passengers, all waiting to be photographed with the miracle pilot, Danny is walking unaided. I watch as he shakes hands and thanks everyone there, before standing in the middle of the passengers to have his picture taken. I tag on at the end, feeling like I don't belong here but wanting to be part of the celebration. Just as the photographer snaps, the kid hands Danny a battered old comic to look at. It's *Biggles*.

Laughter and relief spread through each of us as we make our way back to the bus, Danny leading the way, holding forth on every exciting and dangerous detail of his crash landing.

It's more than just his escape that has thrilled them, I realise. He has survived – he has cheated death. And if he can, then so can anyone. We all need to believe that.

Chapter Thirty-Five

By the time Vittoria and I get the pram back onto the bus, Danny is already sitting in the back seat, his arms outstretched either side of him, as if he's on a pleasant Sunday-afternoon trip, like he hasn't a care in the world.

The other passengers have crammed into every other part of the vehicle, letting him have the whole back row to himself. The doctor's little boy stares at him over the back of the seat in front. His mother puts her hand on top of her son's head and turns it away.

Danny gives me a bone-weary smile and pats the seat next to him. I gesture down at the pram that is blocking my way.

'You must go,' Vittoria tells me, lifting the pram out of the way just enough so that I can squeeze past. Everyone on the bus is looking at me. 'It's so romantic! Go,' she urges, her eyes full of stars, as I roll my own.

I make my way up to Danny, doing my best not to look anyone in the face, especially him.

'How are you coping?' I ask as I sit down next to him. At once, his weight leans into mine.

'I'm in shock, I guess,' he replies, keeping his voice low so that only I can hear. 'Like nothing seems real, and maybe all this – you, even – is a trick. Sometime later tonight, I'm gonna cry for my ma and tremble and shake, and even take a goddamn drink. But I ain't gonna let these good folk see that. They don't want no shaking wreck patrolling their skies. They need to believe I'm Errol goddamn Flynn, a bona fide hero, and not just some no-good fool trying to stay alive.'

His honesty shocks me, and moves me too.

'You *are* a hero.' I turn to look at his profile. His skin is still streaked with smoke, his eyes red-rimmed and bloodshot. His sweaty hair falls matted over the bridge of his nose. 'How the hell did you get that plane down? It looked hopeless.'

'Well, you got to know your Spit like she's the love of your life, see?' Danny says, with the ghost of a smile that shows genuine affection. 'So, you know what's gonna make her smile and what's gonna make her purr. That's what it's like when it's you and your gal in the sky – it's like a marriage: one part intuition, one part heart, and then the rest is hard study. When you know her, when you *really* know her, then when the time comes, you don't have to think about what to do. Your body already knows. You put her in a sweet spot, and even if she's on fire, she'll still give you anything you ask of her. If you know how to ask her right, that is.'

'Do they teach you flirting at pilot school, or are you just a natural?' I ask, wanting to give him some distraction.

But when his eyes meet mine, they are intense and full of fear.

'That goddamn plane wasn't shot at – just something loose in the engine. That's no way to go in a war.' Barely repressed anger threads through every hushed word. 'There's no honour in death by rivet. I fought that goddamn rivet harder than I've fought any Nazi. I guess I could have just sat back and let it happen, but that ain't me, Stitches. I was gonna wrestle that bitch into the damn ground and make sure that when it's my turn, it's for a good reason.'

'You did it. You are an incredible pilot.'

'I am.' He nods, swallows hard; tears threaten. 'But no matter what you say, it takes a damn good slug of luck to walk away from something like that.'

On the last word, his voice catches, and on instinct, I take his hand. This time, it's him squeezing my fingers hard.

'You fly better than anyone else on this island. You just proved that.'

'Not that hard,' Danny says. 'I ain't like a lot of those other boys that only learnt to fly a month or two ago. I've been flying since I turned eleven and got a job dusting crops out at the local aerodrome. It's as natural for me to be up there as it is for fish to swim in the sea. I know that's where I'll meet my maker someday. But I'll be damned if it's over a goddamn rivet.' He shakes his head. 'My ma would scold me over all that cussing.'

'I've heard worse,' I tell him.

'Can I tell you something?' he asks.

'Go ahead.'

'When I saw your face today, right there when I opened my eyes, I thought I was dead. I thought it *would* be you I'd see in the second I died – the girl I can't stop thinking about.'

The bus jolts to a sudden stop. Two army jeeps block the road. A handful of men in flight dress scramble out.

'Shucks, the fellers must have seen me falling out the sky and come to see if I'm toast,' Danny says, clambering up, swaying his way down the aisle of the bus and out onto the road to another round of spontaneous applause.

For a minute, I stay in my seat, stunned by what he just said. Then I follow him.

'Hey, fellers, sorry to disappoint you, but Danny Beauchamp is still the ace round these parts. You all are just gonna have to play second fiddle to me some more.'

'Good God, man.' A Brit claps him on the back. 'Felt sure you'd bought it when I saw your tail go up.'

'Damn near did. Where's the CO?' Danny asks.

'On the blower to the general, trying to scare up more Spits,' another tells him. 'Trouble is: we keep crashing them faster than the erks can repair them. Come on, we've come to take you back to base for a debrief.'

He's being cajoled back into the jeeps when he stops suddenly, as if he's forgotten something. He turns around and walks back to where I'm watching from the doorway of the bus.

'I ain't gonna dress it up,' he says. 'Truth is, I like you, Stitches.'

'I like you, Flight Lieutenant,' I tell him.

'Maybe we could take a walk, you and I, sometime, if we're both still alive on my next rest day. See if we might like each other some more?'

'I think that would be nice, if I'm here.'

Danny considers this for a moment. 'Hard to know if any of us will be here tomorrow.'

Taking my hand, he makes a deep bow and kisses it. His friends cheer as he jogs back to the jeep, and in a couple of minutes, they are leaving at speed, a cloud of dust following on behind.

'Flight Lieutenant Danny Beauchamp likes you,' Vittoria says, clasping her hands to her chest as I step back into the bus. 'You will marry a hero!'

Suddenly, her wide eyes seem to float away from her face, and I feel something stronger than gravity grabbing onto my ankles and pulling me down and down. The sky rolls back to reveal stars burning fiercely in the void. I see an infinite number of moments raining all around me, a version of me in every one of them.

'Vitt . . .' The words come thick and half-formed. 'I'm . . . fainting. Get me to Sal. To Sal. Just Sal . . . No doctor.'

There's no chance to see if she understands before I'm raked out of this body, feeling the tear and wrench of every severed nerve ending burn through whatever it is I am and cast into who knows where.

Chapter Thirty-Six

Monday 23rd June 2025, 11 a.m.

'You're back!' Kathryn grabs hold of me as I sit up, gasping in air.

My heart is pounding against my ribcage. I cling to her as pain throbs through me in waves. It feels as if I am reinhabiting this body atom by atom.

I fall back against the pillows.

'How long since last time?' I ask.

'An hour? I couldn't leave. I just stayed here with you. We need to get you to the doctor.'

'An hour.' Hot tears start to flow down my face, and it feels as if they belong to someone else. All I can think about is the place I just left, the people I left behind, in a version of my life that feels a thousand times more vital and real than this one.

'Do you feel strong enough to get dressed?' Kathryn asks. 'I'm taking you to the hospital right away.'

'I don't think they can help with this, Kathryn.'

'What do you mean?' She grasps my hands, her face full of concern. 'What on earth do you mean?'

'You could have called an ambulance to take me to the hospital while I was out, but you didn't. Why?'

'I was going to,' she says, lowering her eyes briefly. 'Another thirty minutes and I would have.'

'You know something,' I insist. 'Something you're not telling me.'

'No.' She shakes her head. 'Not really. Nothing based on fact. Just stories – old and forgotten stories, nothing but whispers now.'

'I'm not so sure about that,' I tell her.

Looking around the room, I see the book she gave me. Snatching it up, I open it to the photograph I looked at before.

It's a row of smiling people standing in front of the smoking wreck of a crumpled plane.

It's not a great reproduction – the image is a little grained and blurred – but it's good enough. Turning the book to face Kathryn, I point at the young man in the centre of the group of people.

'That's Danny Beauchamp,' I say.

Kathryn looks perplexed. 'Yes, it says so in the caption.'

I run my finger across the people. There, in front of Danny, is a little boy, holding out what I now know is a copy of *Biggles*. And there, on the left of the frame, I can see a woman watching the photographer from amidst the crowd. I didn't even notice her last time I looked at this picture, but now I see the way she is standing on her left leg, right hip jutting. I feel the ache in her feet in her flat and worn tennis shoes. In the photograph, her dress looks white, but I know it's bright yellow.

I point at a photograph of myself, taken more than eighty years ago.

'That's what I mean,' I tell her.

Kathryn's eyes widen. The book falls from her hands.

'It's real,' she whispers. 'All the stories are true.'

PART TWO

'Was it a vision, or a waking dream? Fled is that music: – Do I wake or sleep?'

'Ode to a Nightingale', John Keats

PART TWO

Chapter Thirty-Seven

Monday 23rd June 2025, 5.45 p.m.

'Tell me again.' I turn to Kathryn. We're sitting in the courtyard of a little café, waiting for it to be time to visit Dr Gresch's office. I didn't want to go, but Kathryn has insisted on it.

'If you want me to meet you halfway with the things you are experiencing, then you have to do the same for me,' she told me sternly. 'I'm not saying I don't believe you. I might be the only person who has reason to. Even so, we need to make sure there is nothing else happening.'

Reluctantly, I agreed. She told me about 'the stories' once already, back at her flat, in a halting and disjointed way, as if she were really trying to convince herself of something. Whether it was to decide to believe in me or the opposite, I'm not sure yet.

'Everything begins and ends with the Ħal Saflieni Hypogeum,' Kathryn begins again. This time, her tone is even and collected, working through everything I've told her and everything she knows step by step. 'It's the oldest Neolithic site on the island, perhaps as much as eight thousand years old – we can't really be certain. We do know that for thousands of years, it was forgotten, lying silent underground while life went on above it. And then in the early 1900s, a builder broke the roof of the site, and the complex was uncovered – a truly remarkable discovery that tells us so much about the ancient peoples of the island and just how much we still don't know about who they were or how they lived.'

'Is it a temple? Like the others you've shown me?'

'A temple, yes, a place of burial, and perhaps people lived there alongside the dead, as if they were never really gone. There are three layers, the earliest at the top of the complex, then later chambers were dug deeper into the rock. It's the only site on Malta where the ochre decorations are still preserved, red spirals painted onto the walls. And then there is the oracle room, a feat of engineering that seems all but impossible considering the tools and knowledge they had.'

'Why?' I ask, leaning forwards, intent on finding some answers, any answers.

'If you sing into an opening in the chamber at exactly the right pitch, your voice can be heard amplified throughout the complex,' Kathryn explains, 'perhaps so worship could take place wherever you were. It resonates at one hundred and eleven hertz exactly. They say it's the frequency of the universe.'

'Huh.' I take a long draught of cold Coke and press the glass bottle to the back of my neck. 'That's amazing, but I don't see how it's connected to what's happening to me.'

'I'm still trying to get my head round your haircut,' Kathryn says, shaking her head. 'It happened to you in 1942 and to you here, too? It makes no sense.'

'Don't think about that,' I tell her. 'Just explain what you do know.'

'The best documented case of vanishing happened in the 1930s.' Reaching into her bag, she brings out an old copy of *National Geographic* magazine, its distinctive yellow cover dog-eared and faded. Taking care of the loose pages, she opens to an article and hands it to me.

'What happened?' I ask, skimming the article, which seems to be about two young American men on a cycling holiday round Europe.

'Here.' She points to the bottom of the article. 'It reports that at some time in the late 1930s, thirty schoolchildren and their teacher were taken into the hypogeum by a guide and never returned. Then, some months later, they were discovered sleeping in a cave on the other side of the island. They were hospitalised and cared for over years but never regained consciousness. The doctors at the time were baffled. They thought it had to be a kind of sleeping sickness, perhaps from insect bites. When they died, they all died on the same day, within an hour of each other.'

'So, do you think that this whole group of children – their "souls" maybe – fell into another time, leaving their bodies behind?'

'I don't know what I think,' Kathryn says. 'I've investigated it, searching for more evidence that it happened at all. The article goes on to claim that the cries of the children could be heard from within the caves and tunnels of the island for weeks afterwards, until they just died away . . .'

'Jesus,' I say. 'If what happened to me happened to them, they'd be flung backwards and forwards with no idea what was happening . . .'

'But there is no other evidence, beyond this article. *If* it happened – and that is a big if – then it's as if the whole island decided collectively to forget it.'

'Why would they do that?' I ask.

'That's the question,' Kathryn says. 'There are other cases, hardly documented at all. A doctor who appeared on the island during the Napoleonic wars, who knew more about advanced medicine than he had any right to. He saved hundreds of lives. When he died, it was discovered that he'd had surgery – top surgery, we call it nowadays – to remove breasts, but his genitalia were still female. That much is documented on his death certificate.'

'A trans man in the 1800s? There is nothing new under the sun,' I say.

'Except that the surgery wasn't developed until the twentieth century,' Kathryn says.

'Oh . . .'

'And then there is the strange woman of Attard.'

'Who was she?'

'She appeared in Attard in the 1980s, wearing a dress that seemed to come from medieval times. She spoke only archaic French and Latin. She was terribly distressed, so she was taken to hospital, but she died on the way there – a heart attack, even though she was probably only in her twenties. No one ever discovered who she was.'

'Someone with mental health issues?' I ask tentatively.

'More than likely. Her clothes were thought to be authentic to the period and got boxed away in the archives of the museum. I tested them a couple of years ago. The threads were at least five hundred years old.'

'Maybe she found them hanging about in an attic of a palazzo . . .'

'Yes, that's probably it.' Kathryn nods. 'Except there's a story of a young woman in the 1500s who was being forced into marriage with the man who raped her. Rather than marry him, she leapt off the top of a tower to her death.'

'Oh, God! Poor woman!'

'Yes, poor woman,' Kathryn says. 'Except the story goes that she never landed, that she vanished mid-leap. Even though there were dozens of witnesses to her jump, she was found in a deep sleep in her bed – a sleep she never awoke from.'

I can't say I understand, but a slow blurry possibility is starting to form in my mind.

'So, you were right,' I say slowly. 'The stories are true, and it's something about Malta itself: the people who used to live here, the temples, the hypogeum. The island is a portal. Not always, and not for everyone, but sometimes, some of us find our way through.'

I think of Sal and Christina and the look in Danny's eyes the last time I saw him, and I feel an unfamiliar ache, a longing. I so desperately want to go home to wherever, whenever it is. Whoever it is.

Chapter Thirty-Eight

'I don't feel like I've really got time for this,' I tell Dr Gresch, already on my feet with my hand on the door-knob. The thought of staying overnight as part of her sleep study makes me feel trapped and anxious. How can I explain to her that I have no idea where my mind might travel next, or when?

'I think you might change your mind if you just sit down and listen to what I'm saying,' she says, gesturing at the chair next to where Kathryn is sitting.

'Why?' I ask.

'Because I've listened to everything you and Kathryn have told me, and I'm not paging the psych ward. Because there is a theory, one grounded in real science, that might – just might – prove that everything you are saying is true.'

Staring at her, I sit down. '*How?*' I ask. I try to stay focused and present in her neat, bright office, but at my back, I can always hear the stars burning and the planets turning and feel the ever-present grasp of time pulling at the hems and seams of me.

'For decades now, the scientific community has been trying to understand what consciousness is and how it works, both in the structures of our brains and bodies, but also beyond. It's a field of science that, even though it's been around since the 1990s, when the theory was first proposed by Nobel prize-winner Roger Penrose, is felt to be somewhat . . . speculative. Neuroscience has traditionally rejected it, as has physics, until recently. Now, something we have always thought of as science fiction might actually be true.' Dr Gresch gets up, walking around her desk. 'And I think that perhaps you and I could be the first people to practically test that theory, together.'

'Explain,' I say.

'Of course.' Dr Gresch nods, taking a moment, clearly deciding where to begin explaining something very complex to two laypeople. 'So, what we would be doing is conducting an experiment that attempts to understand the mechanics of consciousness, to identify what it is and what it's capable of on a universal scale.'

'What *is* it capable of?' I ask. 'Because I have to warn you, I failed GCSE physics.'

'Well, it's a bit more than that.' She smiles briefly. 'We are testing the theory that consciousness is a quantum process that passes through these tiny structures in every neuron in the brain called microtubules. If we can prove that theory, then we may be able to show that consciousness has other quantum properties. Such as superposition.'

'What's superposition?' Kathryn asks.

'Put very simply, it is being in two or more states at exactly the same time. In a nutshell, we might be able to prove the theory that human consciousness can connect with anywhere or any*when* in the universe at the same time as being here – or in other words, what we generally understand as the present.'

'What?' I ask her, reaching for Kathryn's hand.

'And,' she goes on, clearly warming to her subject, 'that our universe is not the only one. That our daily experiences, our perception of time as linear and fixed in one dimension, is just an illusion. That what we understand as dreams – might conceivably be our consciousness receiving information from other versions of us, in other parallel worlds, and all other consciousness across time and space.'

'Maybe I'm still asleep,' I mutter, 'because it seems like an impossible coincidence that you are an expert in the very weird thing that is happening to me.'

'Oh, I agree,' Dr Gresch says. 'It would be a coincidence, if I wasn't a neuroscientist and we weren't all in Malta, where, as Kathryn knows, there have been legends and rumours of a thinning of realities for centuries. It's not a coincidence, Maia. It's a confluence of events that presents an opportunity – for all of us. You see, we are beginning to think that consciousness is like gravitational waves: they should go on across the universe forever, but they *decohere*, or collapse. The wave pattern that keeps our version of reality separate from others' ideas of their own reality might also decohere, revealing that we all share some kind of communal consciousness. So, if we are basing your experience on that very new and largely untested premise, then maybe your consciousness *can* travel through time and space and somehow the physical variations of you all align to meet your mind when it arrives.'

Kathryn and I look at each other.

'So,' Dr Gresch says. 'Want to find out?'

'Hell, yes,' I tell her.

Chapter Thirty-Nine

The room Dr Gresch shows me into is modest but comfortable. There's a sofa and a TV and a large window in the wall that looks out onto a corridor. Kathryn is standing there, watching.

'We will start with observing you for a few waking hours and then overnight,' she says. 'I'm sorry it's not the most exciting way to spend your vacation.'

'I'm excited,' I tell her.

'Excellent.' Dr Gresch nods, her expression neutral. 'The thing to remember is that previously these observations have only ever been made in a lab with simulations, and what we are doing here isn't as accurate, but we are trying to replicate those studies in a "real world" setting.' She encapsulates the two words in air quotes.

'Why do you say "real world" like that?' I ask, imitating her.

'Well, what is reality?' she says as her assistant brings in a trolley laden with equipment that is about to be fitted to me. 'All we really know is that this incredibly complex lump of hot wet mush in our heads takes what clues it can from our five senses to construct a reality that we are able to live with. We don't know – we can never know – that it is actually real.' She gestures at a chair. 'Now, if you could take a seat here for me?'

'Am I dead?' I ask her as she begins to pull a sort of hairnet over my head.

'Why do you ask?' she says.

'Because I have this constant ringing in my ears. It sounds a bit like when a heart monitor flatlines – and because everything that has happened to me in the last few days would tie in with your brain flooding you with hallucinogenic chemicals when you are on your way out the door and making your last seconds of life seem to last a lifetime.'

'Did you see that in a movie?' she asks. Now she's attaching sticky pads to my chest and back.

'Probably,' I say.

'Well,' she says cheerfully, 'I feel like I am alive and real; therefore, you are alive and real, too. Mind you, I would say that.'

'Comforting,' I reply.

'It's meant to be.' Dr Gresch laughs. 'If it seems real, if it *feels* real, then what does it matter either way? Human experience is mostly emotion. It is real to you. That's really all "reality" is.' Those air quotes again. 'Now, you're all hooked up. So, take advantage of the free streaming services – and there's a load of books. Just relax. I'll see you in the morning.'

Turning to the window, I wave at Kathryn, who blows me a kiss goodnight.

'If I'm in another reality when I dream, and I get stuck there, say, what would happen to my body?'

'I don't know,' Dr Gresch says. 'I guess we'd find out.'

'Will you do something for me?' I ask.

'Yes,' she says.

'Will you look up a Professor Salvatore Borg for me? He was a physicist in Milan in the nineties. And maybe also in Malta in the early twentieth century.'

Dr Gresch raises her eyebrows but says nothing.

'Of course.' She smiles. 'See you on the other side.'

'But the other side of what?'

Chapter Forty

Sunday 9th August 1942, 9 a.m.

'Maia? Maia?' I hear Sal's voice through the emptiness, a nothing that seems to go on forever in all directions, even inwards. It's not dark exactly, just a sense of being nowhere and not existing, of nothing being present but his voice crackling in the distance like a faint star. His voice speaking my name becomes a fixed point, a spark to focus on, and I direct all that is left of me towards it, concentrating hard.

As the light of that single word grows, others come into being, competing for my attention. My mum shouts out my name, the way she used to when I was little and had been playing for too long in the woods at the bottom of the garden. I hear the whimpers of a little girl crying for her mother. Voices and words I don't know call to me, too, but I fix on that one coppery spark, turning the whole of my being towards it the only way I can: with intention.

'Sal?' Opening my eyes is difficult, almost like I am a newborn.

'You are here.' Sal's blurred face looms before me. 'You are back.'

'I'm back. I've got so much to tell you,' I say, coming to life almost immediately. Reaching for the water jug on the table, I pour a little into my palm and pat it over my face, blinking. I feel myself arriving at the very tips of my fingers.

'There are these things called microtubules . . .'

'Wait.' Sal stops me with a calming motion. 'Tell me on the way. If you are able. We are already late.'

'I'm fine,' I say, standing up, looking down at my body. I'm wearing the same yellow sundress, but stuck just below the neckline is one of the plastic disc things that the doctor used to attach me to the machines. How on earth could that happen? Just when I think I am making sense of any of this, there's another curveball or direction change that makes it all the more mysterious.

'What are we late for?' I ask.

'You are to present your papers at HQ,' Sal tells her. 'Rumours are rife on the island, and you are at the centre of a few of them, I'm afraid. People simply don't know you, and that is a little strange.'

'Oh, I see,' I say, patting myself down. I wonder what happened to the envelope I got from Nicco. 'Oh, no. I think I . . .'

'Here.' Sal hands me my ID card without the envelope. He's folded and creased it a little, and stained it, perhaps with some coffee, to make it look as if it's been in a purse or a pocket. 'Vittoria got a group of army men to carry you to me when you fainted on the bus yesterday afternoon. The doctor wanted you to be taken to the medical room, but Vittoria was adamant you came here. The doctor was astounded that Vittoria wouldn't obey her orders! The poor girl was quite worried she wouldn't have a job the next day when she left here. I hope it'll be all right – I believe the hope of going into nursing is the one thing she has left.'

'I'll go and talk to the doctor,' I resolve. 'It was me who insisted. I knew I'd be safe here.'

'I'm glad you did,' Sal said. 'Vittøria gave me your papers, too. If she looked inside the envelope, she didn't say anything to me. But we must be careful, Maia. Word is going round that there might be a British and American convoy on the way to break the siege. Of course, you and I know exactly when that will be, but if we say the wrong thing to the wrong person, there is a chance we could alter history and give the island to the Axis.'

'I actually don't know the dates,' I tell him, a little shamefaced. 'History wasn't ever really my thing. I sort of regret it now.'

'I see.' Sal smiles. 'Well, that at least narrows the risk. I will keep what I know to myself. Come along then. We must hurry.'

Just as we leave the house, we see Christina walking towards us along the street.

'Prof!' she calls. 'I was just on my way to call in and see how Maia was after the crash and fainting on the bus.'

Cheerfully, she hooks one arm through mine and another through a delighted Sal's, so that we are walking three abreast.

Looking around, I see shopkeepers opening up their bare-shelved shops and little children heading somewhere to learn something. I seem to be in the morning, the day after I saw Danny nearly die. It is already incredibly warm. The sun beats down on the top of my head, seeking me out through the narrow alleyways and tall buildings. *What is reality?* Dr Gresch mused. *If it seems real, if it feels real, then what does it matter either way?* I feel the hot road underfoot, the touch of my hair on my neck, the thinness of Christina's arm in mine, and in my heart, there's a quiet desperation to know how Danny is today. I can't remember the last time when I felt anything so keenly as everything I am feeling here and now.

'Is Danny OK?' I ask Christina, trying to sound casual. 'Have you heard anything?'

'Oh, yes, he was back in the sky last night,' Christina says, shaking her head. 'Those boys – they are so exhausted, but they refuse to stop, even for a second. He'll be up there again today before long, I don't doubt.' Christina pauses. 'My Warby's off somewhere today, too. Can't say where, but I know I'll be holding my breath until he lands again.' She looks at me briefly, her smile growing wan. 'Don't fall in love with a pilot, Maia. It's a fool's game and one that can only end in heartbreak. One way or another, I will lose him. All that remains to be seen is how.'

'Come, now,' Sal intervenes. 'There are some young men who are like gods in the sky, and Adrian Warburton is one of them, as is Danny Beauchamp. These young men are like Icarus: they have the sun in their thrall.'

'I don't think you've heard quite the same version of that story as me,' I say.

'I have, but you see these men are pilots. They don't fly into the sun; they fly out of it.'

This thought enormously cheers Christina, whose smile is restored as she listens to Sal reinvent Greek mythology just for her. As they talk, she treats him to a succession of dazzling smiles. Every now and then, she hugs his arm a little closer to her body. It's clear that Christina has real affection for Sal, just as it's clear Sal is very fond of Christina – and so am I. Now I can fully believe that there are a million of me spread out across a multitude of realities. What I find harder to fathom is that there could possibly be more than one version of someone as spectacular as Christina Ratcliffe.

I've almost wilted completely away by the time we reach the administration building, where Christina drops us off before heading down into the tunnels and the war rooms.

'Now, don't let me down in there,' Christina tells me, brushing me off and hastily applying a dab of a blunt lipstick to my mouth and cheeks, before rubbing it in. 'Remember I've vouched for you.'

'I promise I won't,' I tell her.

'That's the spirit!' She claps me on the shoulder before walking off to work, whistling a show tune. The sunlight follows in her wake.

Chapter Forty-One

The administration building is grand and ornate, presiding over the surrounding destruction with a kind of detached aloofness. Sal seems confident in my papers, but still, my stomach knots in anxiety as we make our way up the steps to the entrance and inside. To calm myself, I think of that other me, sleeping in Dr Gresch's sleep lab. Is she an empty vessel, or is she dreaming me? Perhaps I am just a series of dreams, echoing across the universe. Perhaps we all are.

In the first room we are shown into, there are several women sitting at typewriters. The mechanical noise of fingers hitting keys fills the room with an industrial symphony. One noticeable exception is a young, fair-haired woman, who seems to have managed to keep up a certain level of glamour, despite shortages. She sits with her fingers poised to type, but her blue eyes that gaze towards the window are somewhere else entirely. I suppose you don't always need to fall through a portal in reality to time-travel – her way is much better.

An older Englishwoman, probably an officer's wife, notices me and Sal right away and clicks over to us with the air of someone used to giving orders.

It's the British who seem to hold most of the positions of authority here. The Maltese fight side by side with their allies, but I still get a sense they are very much considered lesser in the partnership. It makes me bristle with injustice.

If Sal feels it, though, he keeps it well hidden behind his gentle smile and perfect manners. He is a natural diplomat – he's had to learn to live incognito, not something that is easily done if you are prone to drawing attention to yourself, especially not in a country about the same size as the Isle of Wight.

'Miss Maia Borg,' Sal tells her, gesturing to me. 'Come to me just recently – before that, she was staying with an aunt on the other side of the island. We have brought her papers and are presenting them as required.'

'Thank you, Professor Borg.' The woman glances up at him over the top of her wire-rimmed glasses as she examines the papers. 'These seem to be in order. Please give me a moment to have them verified further. Take a seat.'

She glances at me, giving me a quick once-over before disappearing into an internal office.

'What does that mean?' I whisper to Sal, as I take a seat next to him. He looks down at my once-white tennis shoes with dismay. 'Next, we must ask Miss Ratcliffe to find you presentable shoes,' he says. 'Perhaps I might yet find some in the house.'

'I don't want to wear a dead person's shoes,' I say.

'No time for a sensitive disposition now, my dear,' Sal says. 'There is nothing on this island except for what we already had when the raids began. We must make do and mend.'

A door opens at the other end of the long room, and a tall woman enters. I recognise her at once by her stride: the doctor, and she seems to be alone. I'm not sure now is the perfect time to talk to her about Vittoria, but if there's one thing I've learnt, it's that sometimes second chances never come.

I step into her path. 'Doctor.'

'Maia. Awake – good. I was worried. You were in a dead faint and not coming round, not even with smelling salts. It is concerning.'

'It's fine,' I tell her. 'Normal for me. I didn't want to waste your time, so I made Vittoria promise to get me back to Sal.'

'Yes.' Her expression is tight. 'She was insistent, despite my direct orders to the contrary.' A hint of a smile twitches her mouth. 'I'll be honest – I didn't think she had it in her. Perhaps she will be a nurse one day after all.'

'You'll still train her?'

'Of course.' Now she seems rather offended. 'But these dead faints – they are not normal, not for you or anyone. Come to the medical room. Let me check your blood pressure at least.'

'I will,' I agree readily, hoping to see another hint of her elusive smile before she goes, but it doesn't return.

'Good.' She nods at Sal, walking into the room where I imagine my counterfeit papers are being examined under a spotlight. She doesn't even knock.

A moment later, the superior woman re-emerges.

'Thank you, Maia. Your papers are in order.'

'Thank you,' I say, taking them and getting ready to go.

'You are also English?'

'Yes,' I say, glancing at Sal.

'Your papers say you were born in Malta, but your accent . . . ?'

'Oh, my father was Maltese,' I say, 'and I was born here, but after he died, my mother moved back to England. I grew up there, living with Mother until just before the war, when I came to stay with my aunt.'

I hope I've got that right. I don't dare look at Sal in case I've missed anything.

The woman holds my gaze for a long second. 'I see . . .'

'You people!' The doctor opens the door, her attention still turned into the room. 'You think I can magic medicines and supplies from thin air? That I can make what little we have go any further? General, we treat your pilots with the greatest care and respect, and in return, you let our people suffer and die. *You* should be ashamed.'

She walks out, her eyes flashing. 'You, why are you standing over my patient?' she asks the superior woman. 'Is she not sick enough for you? Would you like to injure her more with your haughty stare? Or perhaps you can find something that is of actual use to do?'

'I beg your pardon?' the woman asks, wonderfully affronted.

'Come,' the doctor tells me. 'We are leaving.'

Without another word, Sal and I follow in her wake, as she mutters furiously under her breath.

'Thank you, Doctor . . .' I offer as I follow her.

'I swear,' she says as we come out of the building into the full force of the August heat. 'The English – if they could, they would have let this island burn. Do they defend us because it is the right thing to do? No, but because they need to win something, somewhere, *anywhere*. And here we are, dying from dysentery, disease and starvation, while bombs fall all around us. Every single islander here is disposable to them. There must come a time when this island stands for its own self, for its own people, under its own sovereignty. And that time must be soon.'

'Careful,' Sal says, lowering his voice. 'You don't want to sound anti-British.'

'I am anti-everyone who is not pro-Maltese!' the doctor says at the top of her voice. 'I love my home and my people, and it is for them I fight, and no one else.' She paces back and forth, her hands on her hips, elbows bent back, her head bowed as she does her best to contain her feelings.

It's then that I see her children waiting alone in a scant patch of shade, no sign of Vittoria. The boy, Qalbi, wrestles Eugenie in his arms, the big old-fashioned pram standing in the sun.

'Wait there,' she tells her son. 'I have one more person to see.'

'I'm thirsty, Mama,' he calls.

'I'll be one minute.' She waves him away.

The baby begins to kick and cry.

'Hey there, kid,' I say, glancing back at Sal, who follows me over. 'Would you like me to hold the baby for a moment?'

'She is my sister – my responsibility,' the little boy tells me with huge solemn eyes. I get the feeling that he is repeating something he has heard a hundred times.

'Where is Vittoria today?'

'Sick.' The kid struggles with the restless baby. 'Mama sent her home.'

'Here, let me hold Eugenie for a minute. You can keep an eye on me.'

He lets me take her with a look of relief.

'Such a pretty girl,' I say, hefting her onto my hip. She sticks a plump fist in my hair.

The kid looks at me like I'm crazy. 'She looks like a great big potato,' he exclaims. 'I get thinner every day, but the baby gets fatter. Sometimes I think she eats me while I'm sleeping.'

'More likely it's your mum feeding her,' I say, wondering how the doctor stays on her feet while trying to care for the island and nurse a baby. 'Don't think you need to worry about your sis eating you, Qalbi.'

'Why do you call me that?' The boy giggles. 'Only Mama calls me that.'

'Isn't it your name?' I ask.

'No – it's a thing that mamas say. It means "my heart". You keep calling me *your heart!*'

The kid and Sal break into delighted laughter.

'Oh!' I laugh, too. 'Well, I am quite fond of you. That will teach me to think I'm clever. So, what *is* your name then, kid?'

'David Simon Saviour Michael Jeremy Borg,' he tells me proudly, finishing with a flourish.

My blood stops dead in my veins. That overlong, grandiose name that I have been familiar with all my life. All I can think to say is: 'Jeremy?'

'My father liked the name Jeremy – it was his best friend's name. He's dead now. And so is Papa. My mama is called Stella, like a star. What's your name?'

My mouth opens, but no words sound.

The proud, impressively terrifying doctor is Stella Borg. She is my grandmother – the woman who, Kathryn told me, will die the evening before the siege is broken.

And this sweet, funny little boy will grow up without her and go on to become my father.

Chapter Forty-Two

'This changes everything,' I say the moment Sal and I are alone. 'I was starting to believe this, when Kathryn told me her stories, and there was Dr Gresch and her microtubules.'

'What stories, what microtubules?' Sal asks me. 'You haven't had a chance to tell me what you've found out, Maia. And what difference does a little boy's name make?'

'That little boy is my *father*,' I tell him. 'And now it all makes sense. You, the island at war, Danny, Stella, all of it – it's just my poor broken brain trying to find a way to fix all the shattered pieces of my life. It's all an illusion, one made for me *by* me.'

'That's not what's happening here,' Sal tells me urgently. 'I have lived thirty hard years in a time that doesn't belong to me, Maia. I know what is real. I know that I am flesh and blood.'

His words swirl around me, but none of them strike home. All I can think of is how I am lost in a delusion of my own making, and I can't find a way out.

'My father has always rejected me. Something is so broken in him that he can't find it in himself to truly love anyone: not my mum, not even his current wife, but especially not me, the kid he never wanted.' Even though I have known this to be true my whole life, saying it still slices like a knife through my tender heart. 'So I dreamt up you, Sal – a man who is the epitome of what I think of as an ideal father.'

'Really?' Sal's face softens as he smiles, but I'm too wrapped up in what I'm saying to acknowledge it further.

'All of my relationships – if you can call them that – have been brief and detached. I've never fallen in love. I've never known how to until . . . I meet a perfect hero pilot with the sweetest smile and hope in his eyes. And then I start to think maybe . . . maybe I do have a heart after all.'

'It's not a good idea to fall in love with a pilot, as Christina said . . .'

'Even Christina,' I interrupt him as I pace up and down, tugging on my thread of logic and unravelling it at pace. 'Even she is like the ideal best friend that I never really had. I was always a bit too weird, a bit too different and shy to have one of those. The way Christina accepted me and took me in – that's just what I've always secretly wanted. And *then* my dad as a kid, my dad who, according to this fantasy, started out as this sweet, funny, brave little boy and grew up to be this cold remote man who doesn't even take an interest in his own daughter. He's here, because in my fantasy world, I can save him, *change* him, help him grow up to be the kind of dad I've always wanted. Don't you see, Sal? This is all just my stupid, pathetically needy subconscious. I can't have a life in the real world, so I made one up in my head.'

Sal guides me out of the heat of the day, under one of the great stone archways built into the fortified city walls, left over from the rule of the Knights of St John. Seeing the tears that track down my face, he reaches into his jacket and produces a handkerchief, which he gently dabs at my cheeks.

'Come now,' he says, gently catching my hands. 'Breathe. In and out. Deep and slow. You are having a panic attack, I think.'

'But if this isn't . . .'

'Whatever this is, you are feeling overwhelmed. So: breathe. With me. In, one, two, three, four, five, six, seven. Hold it. And out – this time count to eleven. Really empty your lungs.'

I keep my gaze fixed on him as I follow his instructions.

'Good, and again.'

Slowly but surely, I feel the muscles that have contracted around my ribcage release. I see the blue sky, cut into a wedge by the arch we are under, feel the pebbles jutting through the thin rubber on the soles of my feet, and Sal's hands holding mine. My shoulders fall in increments until I can think again.

'To meet your father here as a little boy, knowing what he has endured and has yet to face – that has frightened you, Maia. It frightens me, too, if I'm honest. And perhaps it does make sense, especially to a modern mind that has grown up in a world where the unexplained is so often sidelined as nothing more than smoke and mirrors. Believe me, I went there myself. But I know something you don't yet, Maia.'

'What?' I ask. 'What do you know that I don't.'

'That I *was* sent here for a purpose. I was sent here to atone.'

In the shade, his glasses reflect the blue of the sky so I can't see his eyes.

'What do you mean, atone?' I ask.

'I didn't come back to Malta to see my family,' Sal says. 'I came back to escape a terrible thing I did – something I tried to run away from.'

'What terrible thing?' I ask, anxious.

'Before I came here, I drank. A lot. And when I found out that my dear Elena was pregnant, I got very drunk. I was so happy, you see, and that's what I did when I was happy – I drank. I never thought myself an alcoholic. I was never angry or cruel. I never drank at work, or during the day, only when I had a reason to. And I always had a reason to. Elena was quite rightly angry with me. On this most important day of our lives, I went out to get wine, met a friend at a bar on the way and didn't come home until the early hours. I told her I was wetting our child's head. She said it had to be born first. We fought – I left the house and got in my car and . . . I woke up with my head on the steering wheel, the horn blaring into the night. When I got out, there was another car, run into a ditch. The driver wasn't moving. There were children crying in the back, shouting for help. I reassured them, walked until I found a payphone and called for help. And then I thought of my job, my baby, my Elena, and I hung up when they asked for my name. I went back to my car, and I left those children crying behind. I ran away. I left those crying children there all alone.'

My mouth falls open. 'Sal!' I gasp. I can barely believe that this sweet man would do such a thing. But panic in the worst of situations does that to people, I would know.

'The shame has followed me all my life,' Sal tells me, tears in his eyes. 'That doesn't fit in with your perfect vision, does it?'

'So, you think this is some kind of . . . cosmic punishment?' I ask him, turning away from him.

'No, I think it's a chance to atone,' Sal says. 'To make amends and restore balance, to all that is, and to my soul.'

'But you've been here for thirty years, and you haven't atoned yet?'

'Because the time has not yet come,' Sal says. 'But I believe it will. And when it does, I will be ready to pay the price for what I did. Whatever it is.'

Sal takes a step towards me. 'I was a different man then, selfish and scared. I've had more than thirty years to learn how to be the kind of man who deserved all the things I lost and will never regain.' He bows his head. 'It was nice to be seen the way you saw me, if only for a little while. The man you saw – that is who I have tried to be. For my sake, for my wife's, for my child who I will never know.'

This is impossible. I want something to believe in. I *need* something that I can know is absolutely true, and there is *nothing* – nothing but the beat of my heart in my chest, hard and fast. Wherever I really am, that at least proves I'm alive.

'But why here? Why, in this one corner of the world, would there be this unique system of punishment? Or chance for redemption? Why only on the few square miles that are this island?'

'The ancients lived another life, by another set of rules,' Sal says. 'They understood a reality that we can't even imagine. And they ingrained their interpretation of the universe so deeply into the rock that it became part of it. They carved and painted it into the fabric of the island with such conviction that it lives on still. Even after everything that has come since, it lives on underneath it all, waiting. And sometimes, somehow, people fall through the gaps that remain – for a purpose.'

'Not those thirty children,' I mutter. 'You can't tell me thirty eleven-year-olds all had something to atone for.'

'What children?' Sal asks.

'Have you never heard of the children who were lost in the hypogeum? My cousin told me about them when I was last back in the present. *My* present, I mean.'

'Whispers and rumours, I suppose,' Sal says. 'A ghost story, of sorts. You think it really happened, and that it's connected to this?'

'Don't you?' I ask, incredulous. 'You think you are here to atone, Sal, but perhaps you are just *here*. And perhaps you are a figment of my imagination.'

'Or . . .' Sal thinks for a long moment. 'Perhaps we are both wrong. The modern mind assumes it knows more than all those that came before, but perhaps it doesn't. I thought of the island as a sentient thing, but perhaps it's just an anomaly; a passing-place in time that the ancients learnt to live with, but which we don't even recognise; a mouth that knows exactly who it can feed on and takes what it wants.'

'If that's true, then you will never atone.' I find I can't look at him, this frail man who ran away, even though he and I are so much the same.

'Is there nothing in your life that you regret with every breath?' Sal asks me.

For a second, I can feel a small hand growing cold in mine. But I can't speak of her aloud. Not yet. Maybe not ever.

'I don't know,' I say. 'I only know that you are my friend. You made an awful mistake – I've made them, too. When I was, back there, in my own time, I was out of place and lost. I missed you. I missed all of this.'

'I'm still the same man, Maia,' Sal says sadly. 'A man who has done wrong, once. In the past, in the future – I'm not sure. But I am the man you think I am now. That's all I can tell you.'

'You're right,' I say, remembering a thought I had, the one that gave me the courage to keep going. 'Sal, you're right. What you did, what I did. It hasn't happened yet. And if you and I are here, then . . .'

'We have decades to make sure it never happens.' Sal's eyes light up. 'Do you really think that can be true, Maia?'

'I know that we have time. Maybe enough time to change what will happen somehow.'

'But don't we risk changing everything? Tearing up the world for our own benefit?'

'No,' I say, 'because there is no future to alter yet. There is only now.'

'Maybe . . .' Sal thinks, a glimmer of new hope on his face. 'Perhaps you could be right.'

'All I know is that I just met my father. I know the little boy who becomes my father – or a version of him at least. Whatever kind of real this is, it doesn't matter. I have a chance to save a child – two children if you count the fatherless little girl I was. Maybe it's ancient wisdom or cosmic fate or just that my neural pathways have brought me here, but I am here. In every way that counts. I'm going to save my father from all the loss and pain that changed him. And that starts with making sure that Stella doesn't die on the day she's supposed to.'

Chapter Forty-Three

'Kathryn said that Stella was killed the evening before the siege was broken,' I tell Sal once we are again in the cool and relative comfort of the half-house.

Our walk back from the truths we told one another under that arch was silent and somehow distanced.

We both know things have shifted between us, that we see each other in a different light now – one that casts us as we truly are, instead of in the images we want to be true.

That I have grown to care about Sal in the days I've known him hasn't changed, but now I see him for what he is: not a perfect paragon but a man as fallible as any one of us, as capable of doing great good and of making mistakes. In his two lifetimes, Sal has done both. Somehow, that makes me love not only him but my own father even more. It makes me want to redeem them both – and myself – even more.

As for what he thinks of me now . . . Sal seemed a little wary and preoccupied on the way back, mulling over thoughts that perhaps he hadn't dared to allow before.

In realising that David will grow up to become my father, we have both found a reason for hope. Because it is surely possible to undo any harm if it has not yet been done.

'The evening before the siege was broken,' Sal says thoughtfully, mopping his furrowed brow. His frown is deep and etched with sadness.

'Do you know what date that is?' I ask.

Sal doesn't answer at once, which makes me wonder. He stands up, then seems rooted to the spot for a moment before making a decision about something only he knows.

'I do.' He nods, then goes to a bookshelf and retrieves a small brown notebook from between two large hardbacks where I never would have noticed it. 'I don't suppose I need this to remember that particular date, but when I first arrived, I wrote down everything I could remember in this book, and I've added to it. When I was still taken to other times, I would write down everything I could learn then. Some things that I read about the siege, well . . . I do my best to forget what I know. If you ever need answers, Maia, and I can't help you, look here.'

'Can I look now?' I say.

Sal holds the book to his chest. 'I'm not sure.'

Frowning, I look at the notebook, and one of the first things he said to me – something that was quickly lost in the confusion and chaos – comes back to me.

'On the day we first met, you said that you had been waiting for me – that you knew I was coming because you'd read about me.'

Sal nods. 'Yes.'

'Well, what did you read?' I ask him. '*When* did you read?'

'I wish I had never mentioned it,' Sal says. 'It was foolish of me, but in the light of what we think is possible, I think you have to see it.'

'If it's about me, I want to know!' I say, laughing. 'I hope Mabel gave me a by-line, and I delivered a huge scoop and got a medal, or something. There is only now, remember? Whatever is in the book, it's fine.'

Sal looks at the book for a moment longer.

'It was not very much,' he says. 'A line on a website, in . . . 2040, I think it was. I was there briefly, many years ago now. The site was on historic women of Malta.'

'Really?' I say, impressed with myself. 'I'm a historic woman?'

'Not exactly. You were in a footnote on the page about Mabel Strickland,' Sal says.

I shrug. 'Oh, oh well.'

'When I read your name, it seemed to shout out at me from the screen. Borg, of course, I am familiar with. But Maia – I have never met a Maia, not in any of my lifetimes. It felt too modern for the 1940s, so I searched for it, and I found your articles. They were very good, Maia. I knew you were no ordinary woman even before I met you.'

I smile and shrug.

'But there was no photo of the 1940s Maia Borg that I could find, just the twenty-first century one. I thought that maybe, if someone with such a particular name *was* in two timelines, then perhaps this Maia Borg might be like me. So, all I had to do, once I was back in 1942, was to write down the information I'd read about you and wait. I never thought . . . it didn't occur to me . . .'

'What?' I press him. 'What did it say, the line about Maia Borg? You have to tell me. To leave me wondering would be too unkind, and you are not an unkind man, Sal.'

Sal sighs, turning his face away as he opens the book on a marked page and hands it to me. Taking a deep breath, I brace myself and read.

Maia Borg, who had been living on the island since before the war, was commended for her acts of bravery and life-saving heroism in August 1942

DOB unknown
DOD 14th August 1942

I read the words again and again. They feel like they are about someone else, but at the same time, I know they aren't.

'When was the siege broken? When is Stella meant to die?' I ask Sal, stopping him before he can answer. 'No, don't tell me – it's 14th August, right?'

Sal nods. 'Yes. The convoy arrives on 14th August and the ships finally make it through to the harbour on the 15th.'

I stare at the words again. 'So I die on the same day as Stella.'

'The future isn't written,' Sal repeats. 'It can change.'

'I die, and Stella dies,' I say. 'Everything that has happened points towards exactly that. I come here, decide I must save Stella to save my dad – and I fail. Badly.'

'Impossible to know what will happen,' Sal tries again, but without much conviction.

There should be fear or tears or anger, but none of that happens.

'I don't want to die,' I say slowly, the realisation coming to me like a slow dawn creeping over the hills of my childhood home. 'I don't want to die.'

'Maia, I know.' Sal reaches for me. 'You must remember that it's not—'

'No, you don't understand. Until just now, I was really certain that I didn't mind either way.'

'Maia . . .'

Incredibly, I hear my own laughter bubbling out.

'But now I know! I know I *don't* want to die, Sal,' I tell him happily. 'I *want* to live. For the first time in . . . well, somehow time seems irrelevant now. All I know is that

I *want* to live life, that I *love* life. And it's taken this' – I wave at the book – 'to show me that.'

'I'm not sure I understand,' Sal says. 'Are we happy or sad?'

'The book says that I die that day,' I tell him. 'But *I* say I don't. *I* say that this Maia Borg, the one who is here to save her grandmother's life, is not going to fail. I *will* succeed. That is the new plan. The 14th of August 1942 is not going to be the day I die. It's going to be the day I live.'

Chapter Forty-Four

Monday 10th August 1942, 9 a.m.

The next morning, Danny turns up on the doorstep.

'How are you feeling?' I say, coming to meet him.

'Me?' Danny shrugs. 'I'm peachy keen. I've got a few hours off today, so, I thought I'd come and see if you're free for that date we talked about the other day.'

He nods behind him, where sitting outside on the street is a clapped-out old motorbike that seems to be held together with wire and rust.

'You suggested we go for a *walk*,' I say, eyeing the machine.

'We will when we get there,' Danny says. 'And good!'

'Good what?' I ask.

'You didn't say it's not a date!' He smiles, pushing his cap back on his head. 'Look, I traded in all my chocolate and cigarette rations for a quarter tank of gas and this bike for a day. I know we're on this tiny dot in the middle of the sea, but I really want to get as far away from the war as I can, at least for a couple of hours. Don't you?'

Shielding my eyes from the sun, I can see the traces of the worn and worried expression on his face, camouflaged by his tan and wide smile. His body language is open and confident, but there's something else in his voice: a need. I find myself longing to answer it.

'I do,' I tell him. 'I want to come with you.'

The expression in his sky-blue eyes is unreadable as he climbs onto the bike, the sleeves of his khaki shirt rolled up to reveal his strong brown forearms. 'Get on the back and hold on tight.'

To say that swinging one leg over the bike in my yellow dress feels awkward is something of an understatement — to call the rear part of the bike a seat, even more so. I have no choice but to move in closer to Danny. My thighs press along the back of his. My breasts cinch into his back. As my arms wrap around his ribcage, I feel his stomach muscles flex against my wrists, the warmth of his skin under the worn cotton of his shirt. The urge to run my hands under his tattered shirt and over his skin is almost irresistible. But I do resist, leaning my chin on his shoulder instead, so that his curls brush and tickle against my cheek.

Danny kicks the bike into action. There's a roar of the engine; wheels spin, kicking up dust and gravel, and then we are in motion. It takes a concerted effort for me not to scream.

It's too noisy to talk. For the first minute or so, I don't even want to open my eyes. The moment the bike accelerates, my arms tighten hard around Danny, and I press my cheek between his shoulder blades. As we whip through the hot air, I am acutely aware of his body, how the muscles in his thighs and buttocks are tensed and taut, fitting tightly between my legs.

I prise one eye open and take a moment to get used to the wind full in my face, then open the other. Danny leans into the twisting roads, and I lean with him. The landscape streams past in rapidly unfurling ribbons of gold and turquoise. I catch glimpses of people at the side of the road, some waving, children shouting, their cries carried away before the sound can reach us.

Is this a little like flying? Everything is warm: the breeze, the heat of his body, the sun on the back of my head, the rush of speed taking my breath away. Closing my eyes again for a moment, I feel like I am flying, free of everything, even my flesh, soaring and speeding away from every bad thing – and I realise this moment is something perfect.

Finally, the bike slows and comes to a stop. Danny tilts it slightly, steadies us with his booted foot as he kicks down the prop.

I climb off first, a little unsteadily. My legs and arms are silted with dust, my hair tangled and thick with it. Danny turns off the engine and climbs off after me.

'That was actually really . . . not as bad as I thought it would be,' I say, batting dust off my dress as an excuse not to look him in the eye. I'm not sure it's the heat that's making my cheeks flush.

He nods, taking off his cap for a moment, running his fingers through his dark curls and repositioning it in exactly the same place.

'Blows the cobwebs away, as my old ma would say,' he says. 'Well, welcome to Mellieħa.'

When finally I take a proper look around where we've arrived, I see we're in a beautiful village made up of traditional Maltese houses that line a series of gently scalloped bays. The dwellings climb leisurely up a steep hill, crowned at the top with a domed and towered church.

The colourful fishing boats, *luzzus*, are pulled up onto long, golden beaches or moored in the shallows. The sea is crystal clear and the brightest cyan blue, lapping gently against the boats, which rock and sway together on the tide with a comforting clank.

'It's so beautiful.' I sigh. For a thousand reasons, none of which I can name, I feel calm. Tears roll down my cheeks. Embarrassed, I turn from Danny, wiping them away with the heels of my hands.

'Sometimes it's not until you take a breath,' Danny says gently, 'that you realise you've been up against it. It's OK to cry – there's a lot to cry about.'

'Christina would say my stiff upper lip needs some reinforcing and blame my Maltese half for being overemotional. But that's not right – my mum was English, and she'd cry at the drop of a hat. I once found her sobbing over a daisy she'd picked in a field, the mad old hippy.'

'Hippy?' Danny smiles. 'That's a new one on me.'

'Oh, just a family joke,' I say, brushing it away.

We begin to stroll slowly along the shoreline. The beach and front are busy: fishermen hauling in their catch, women gutting and salting the fish. Everything carries on as normal, at least in the snatches of time where there is space enough to pretend for a while.

'Well, my ma is just the same as yours,' Danny says. 'When I told her I was running away to join the RAF, she cried for a week.'

'It's not exactly running away if you tell people in advance,' I point out, with a small smile.

He laughs. 'Well, you'd think, but the truth is: it was my second attempt, and I needed my birth certificate, so I had no choice but to tell her.'

'What *do* you mean?' I ask, glancing sideways at him.

He's walking with his hands behind his back, holding his cap. His head is tipped forwards so that his curls fall over his eyes.

'Well, I'd been trying be a fighter pilot since long before the war.' He chuckles. 'I don't know – I was sixteen, and I just figured that was my calling in life, you know? I tried to join up with the Chinese and the French, but I was too young, so it was back home for this kid and another few years spraying crops and hauling cargo. Then this shebang kicks off and I'm more than old enough to play a part. No way I was going to wait for the Canadian Air Force to get its act together. I wanted in with the RAF. I couldn't figure how I'd get to England, though. The passage cost more than I earnt in a year. And then a pal of mine, he tells me that if I work on one of the merchant navy ships, I'll get free passage and some wages. Course, I'm supposed to work the voyage out and back, but I don't concern myself with that detail. My plan is, once we dock in Liverpool, to jump ship and make my way to the local airbase to sign up and save the world.'

'Wouldn't you be in trouble for running out on the ship?'

'Only if they caught me.' He grins and looks about a decade younger.

As I watch, he relaxes. His shoulders settle, and that now familiar smile creeps back into his expression. He's himself again, or at least the young man he was before this war got hold of him, full of energy and certainty.

'So, I get my logbook, right, showing all my hours of flying – more than enough to join the RAF – and I work my guts out on that goddamn ship, and in three months, I'm in Liverpool. Jump ship, easy as can be. Find a place to join up. Danny Beauchamp is finally on his way! The CO looks at my logbooks and all my hundreds of hours, and he's pleased as punch. And he says, "Now all I need is your birth certificate."'

'You'd forgotten your birth certificate?' I ask him, unable to stifle a laugh.

'Sure had,' he says. 'I begged, I pleaded, but he was insistent we did things by the book. So, I turn on my tail and I run back to the ship, hoping like hell no one had noticed I'd gone, and luck was on my side for once. Worked my way all the way back to Canada. And that's how I had to tell my ma that I was running away to join the RAF.'

I'm wide-eyed. 'You made the whole trip again?'

'You bet I did, except this time when I jumped ship, the captain saw me and a policeman got hold of me. The crew's coming after me, and this fat old bobby had me by the arm, and I say to him, "Please, sir, let me go – I've come all this way to fight for England." And you know what?'

'You got coshed on the head and made the whole trip again?' I laugh.

'He let me go, that bobby. I'm running off as fast as these skinny legs will carry me, and he shouts after me, "Good on yer, son!"'

It's impossible not to laugh at his attempt at a Liverpudlian accent. Lost for a moment in our mirth, our eyes meet, and the laughter falters to a stop. It's like when we see one another, we remember.

'You really, really wanted to be a fighter pilot,' I say after a beat of silence.

'Sure did, still do. Up there, it's the only time I feel like I'm really being me, if you know what I mean. All the noise falls away and it's just me, the Spit and the angles.'

'Do you mean angels?' I ask, confused.

'No, ma'am, I mean angles,' he says. 'That's what this whole business is about: figuring out the angles. I taught myself watching the birds floating on the updraught, watching them dive for fish and prey. I knew all about the angles even before I set foot in a plane.'

'I don't think I've ever really felt that way about anything,' I say. 'It must be nice to know you are born for something.'

Danny draws to a stop on an empty stretch of beach and kicks off his boots. He is still barefoot underneath.

'If I could, I would knit you some socks,' I tell him.

'Knitting socks don't seem so very like you, Maia Borg,' he says. 'Besides, I kinda got used to it now. Want to sit on the beach for a while?'

'Yes.' I nod, slipping off my battered shoes, and dance for a moment on the hot sand as my soles make the adjustment.

Danny pulls his tattered shirt over his head, revealing toned biceps and the ripple of dozens of small muscles in his back. It must take a lot of physical strength to fly a Spitfire. He flops back onto the sand, flinging his arms about his head. His brown torso must have been burnt and tanned a hundred times by now, and I notice the white tide-mark that peeps just above the waistline of his shorts and stop myself from wondering how far that untanned stretch goes.

Not nearly as comfortable in my own skin, I opt for a spot in the shade of the boat, hugging my knees to my chest as I look out at the quiet bay. Digging my toes into the sand, I lean my chin on my arms. Here is exactly where I want to be, and yet at the same time I would like to make myself invisible – to be with Danny, but not to be seen by him. He is like some kind of god, a man at the peak of his beauty. Next to him, I feel fat and ungainly, entirely unworthy to be in his company.

'Everyone's born to do something,' Danny says, rolling onto his side to look at me. His roving gaze coaxes me to uncurl a little, still uncertain that he can really want to look at me, when every bit of me is soft and pink, sunburnt and glistening with perspiration. Leaning back on my hands, I twist towards him. His eyes travel over my torso to the tips of my fingers. With every millimetre of my body that his slow and lingering gaze takes in, I reveal a little more of myself to him in a deliciously long unspoken conversation.

'You chose to be a journalist, right? Pretty bold move for a dame, if you don't mind me saying so. Didn't you choose it because you knew that was what you were born to do?'

'No, not really,' I admit. 'It's funny. Dad always knew what he was meant to be, and as for Mum, well – I've never met anyone as comfortable in her own skin as she was. But me – I've always felt kind of aimless. Kind of an outsider. Always like I'm drifting along like that tiny cloud up there. And then one day, I found myself accidentally in the middle of a war, and I had the turn of phrase to make it into a report and that was that. I'm good at it, but it never felt like a calling. Not like you and flying.'

'I'm sure glad the wind blew you here, Stitches,' Danny says, rolling onto his back. His hand drifts through the sand until his fingertips almost touch mine. 'And I'm a little annoyed, too.'

'Annoyed?' I ask with a laugh.

'I told you I wasn't fixing to fall in love until this whole thing was done and dusted. Well, you upset that apple cart all right.'

Chapter Forty-Five

'God, it's hot as all hell,' Danny says, suddenly leaping to his feet before I can even really process what he just said. 'Come swim with me.'

Climbing to my feet, I watch as he gallops into the sea, splashing spray in all directions. As soon as he's waist deep, he dives headlong into the water, emerging a few seconds later, shimmering and wet.

'It's all right for you,' I call to him. 'I don't have a swim-suit.'

'Come as you are.' He laughs. 'You'll dry off in a couple of minutes in this heat. You're safe with me – promise, Stitches.'

I believe him.

Glancing around the beach, I see it's almost deserted, save for a couple of fishermen mending their nets. I have no sense of what time it is, but the sun isn't high in the sky yet. There must be at least an hour until the expected lunchtime raids. An hour without noise, fear and confusion seems like something truly miraculous.

'I'll paddle,' I say as if I'm making a concession, when I really want to be in that water.

Danny leans back into clear, blue water until his feet bob up and the back of his head is submerged. The water is warm but cool enough to soothe my hot and dusty feet. Gathering my skirt up in my hands, I walk in a little further and then a little more, until the sea circles my thighs.

I hear myself sigh long and low for a moment of simple pleasure.

Closing my eyes, I hear the water lap and the boats gently clanking. There's a gentle breeze and constant birdsong on the shore. From somewhere further away, I can hear a woman calling to her child, loving and cross all at once.

If I could isolate these few minutes from all the madness that has defined my life in the last few days, they would be the definition of serene. I think of all the bored and empty minutes I have spent in my other life, without realising what a luxury they were.

There's a *swoosh* in the water; Danny grabs my hand and pulls me hard towards him. Losing my footing in the sand, I'm dunked into the water and swimming.

'Bloody cheek!' I tell him, laughing.

'You looked like you were thinking too hard,' he tells me. 'Today is not a day for thinking hard. How well do you swim?'

'Not bad, I guess?' He points to a little cove, hardly more than a spoonful of sand and rocks across the bay. 'Can you get there?'

'I think so. Race you!'

Before he can move, I plunge back into the water, diving under the glassy surface and into the blue.

Silvery bubbles escape my clothes and hair, cascading into the aquamarine. Tiny iridescent fish shoal around my outstretched fingers, darting away. My one yellow dress flattens and billows with each stroke I take, making me feel like a golden jellyfish.

It doesn't take long for Danny to beat me into second place with just a few strokes of his long, strong arms. His tanned, bare skin has turned pale as moonlight under the water. With his dark curls becoming gravity-defying tendrils, he looks like the kind of creature that might sing a siren song.

When he reaches the tiny beach a minute before me, I slow down, lingering with the sea at my shoulders as he climbs out onto the sand. Two things are true: I am shy of him seeing me wet through in a clinging dress; and I want an excuse to look at him. I am only human, after all.

'This is my perfect spot,' he tells me. 'See? There's a little bit of shade here to lie in, nice soft sand, big flat rocks if you want to sunbathe. And it's just a short climb to the top of that cliff, and there's a farmhouse where they will sell you a quart of milk and a little bread for only two or three times the market value.'

'How many poor unsuspecting girls have you brought here?' I ask him, still wrapped from his view by the sea. His body shimmers in the sun, a glorious thing as beautiful as a Michelangelo

'Precisely none,' Danny tells me. 'I haven't brought anyone here before – it's my place.' He crosses over to the rocks, rummaging around, and brings out an old leather knapsack. 'I come here to just be plain old Danny Beauchamp. It's where I like to draw or read.' He takes out a stack of what look like sketchbooks and a collection of pencils.

'An artist, too,' I say.

'Not really – more of a doodler. An artistic temperament doesn't do well in war – not when we are required to be cold-blooded killers six days a week.' He pauses for a moment, staring at his feet. 'Anyhow, I stashed my stuff out here when I first found this spot, and I keep it to myself. Got a couple of books out here, too, if you want to read?'

'It's lovely,' I tell him.

'So, are you going to come out of the sea, or will you just stay there until you dissolve?' Danny asks.

'Will you turn around then?' I ask. 'This dress will not leave much to the imagination.'

'No,' Danny says. 'I don't think I will. I want to see you, Maia. I want to look at you, if you'll let me.'

Even in the cold water, I feel the heat of desire kindle in the pit of my belly. Slowly, half afraid and half impatient, I peel myself out of the shelter of the sea. It takes effort not to cover my body with my arms, but I don't. Instead, I watch Danny as I wade onto the shore, aware of how the fabric of the yellow dress clings to every curve and dimple of my body.

He lets out a long yearning sigh as I walk across the sand to stand just before him.

'May I?' he asks.

I nod.

With infinite care, Danny unbuttons the mismatched buttons, his hands trembling just as they did after the crash. This time, I don't try to help. I stand perfectly still until he has opened my dress to my navel, letting him peel it off my shoulders and lower it until I am able to step out of it. With great care, he spreads the dress out on a rock in the full glare of the sun, before turning back to me.

'Can I hold you, Maia?' he asks, his voice hoarse.

'Yes, please,' I say.

First, he puts his hands on my waist; his eyes meet mine. I expect him to kiss me, but instead he just draws my cold and shivering body close to his. His arms tighten around my waist, and mine curve up to encircle his back. The top of my head fits neatly under his chin, my lips rest against the salty skin of his neck, and I feel the pound of his heart against my breasts, crushed against his chest.

Our bodies dry and warm in unison as we hold one another close and still, each aware we have something very precious and fragile in our tender grasp, something we both want to protect.

'I would like to kiss you very much,' Danny says. 'Would that be all right?'

Pulling away a little, I look up at him, and wrapping my arms around his neck, I kiss him. When our lips meet, they seem to know exactly how to fit together. I feel a moan vibrate in his throat as my mouth opens for him, and we press our bodies even closer together, lost in the most delicious connection I have ever known. It feels like we could stay here in this embrace for the rest of time, whatever order it might come in, but Danny steps away.

'This is not what I intended, I promise,' he tells me, running his hands through his hair. 'I had a plan to woo you – nice and gentle and slow. I wanted to share this place with you and talk about art and books. I thought maybe, later today, I might try to hold your hand. But there you are looking like you do, and I can't think straight.'

'It's OK,' I tell him. 'I feel the same way about you, Danny. I want you, too.'

Danny takes a step back. 'Maia, I need you to know, I'm not the kind of guy who takes advantage of a girl. That's not how I want it to be between us. I want it to be right, proper and good. For us to get to know each other, like folk should, with walks and picnics and holding hands, before we ever get to . . .' He looks at me standing there in my underwear. 'It's just that you are so goddamn beautiful, and I can't take my eyes off of you.'

All I want is to lay him down on this beach right now and let my tongue explore every inch of his body. But Danny wants to do it 'right' the way that is right in his mind, in his world, in his time, and to him, we mean more than desire and longing and lust, all of which are pulsing in the air around us like little sparks of lightning.

For Danny, we mean love. We are in love. And for Danny, love is an endless thing that has a lifetime to discover the hows and whys of its existence between the two people that created it. He wants to wait to show me how much I mean to him. I can only adore him all the more for that.

I reach for my dress and find that it is almost dry already, so I slip it on over my head, buttoning it up as fast as I can.

'I'll wait for you, Danny,' I tell him simply. 'We don't have to hurry as much as we might like to.'

'Here.' He scrambles up to a small, high cave in the cliff wall to retrieve some books and sketchbooks, along with a battered, sandy and motheaten old rug, which he lays out on the sand. 'This will stop you getting sandy some. And here's a cushion for your head.'

Longing still hums in every fibre of my body as I lie down on the rug, and Danny takes his place next to me. He stretches out his arm and I move into the crook of his shoulder, my head resting on his chest. His hand rests on my hip.

'How long till the tide comes in?' I ask, trailing my fingertips down his chest.

'This is as far in as it gets,' he says. 'When the tide goes out, we'll be able to walk back to the bike and our shoes. I kind of hope the tide never goes out, though, and that time will stand still forever. But I guess that's not how it works.' He sighs. 'It oughta be.'

'Can I look at your sketchbooks?' I ask, seeing the pile on the other side of him.

'You can, but remember, I'm just an amateur.'

I reach over him for one of the books, kissing him as I take one. He catches me to him and kisses me back, his body rising to meet mine.

'Now, now,' I tease, breaking the kiss. 'We're getting to know one another, so let me look at your books.'

He smiles at me ruefully as he lets me go, looking away as I open the book.

Each page is covered in drawings. Some pages are devoted to a landscape, some of them the view from this cove, others of Valletta and Mdina, as well as places I don't recognise. What amazes me is that even though the drawings are all black and white, I can feel the colour and heat in each, see the movement of breeze. He weaves the same kind of mercurial magic in the many swiftly drawn portraits that fill the books, too: pilots, local people of all ages, from the most elderly gentleman to the youngest baby. When I see a sketch of Christina, her arm swung around Warby's neck, her head thrown back in laughter, I can hear her giggles. Then there's a drawing of an older woman who I guess is Danny's mother – she has the same-shaped eyes and serious set of the mouth. There's a snow-bound farmhouse with mountains behind. And dozens and dozens of tiny drawings of Spitfires, on the ground, in the air, crashed into fields or sand – page after page filled with little visions of curiosity.

'They are really good,' I tell Danny after a while. 'My dad is a painter. He's good, too, but these have a life to them. His art is all about death.'

'He makes you mad and hurt,' Danny says tenderly, reading me at once.

'Yes,' I admit. 'We were never close. I loved my mum, but I lost her a few years back.'

'I'm sorry,' Danny says. 'My folks are as good as they get. I'm lucky.'

'Dad is Dad. Mum was at peace in the end. They both lived the lives they wanted to. So many don't get that chance.'

'I've come to realise that chances to be happy don't come in one big go,' Danny says. 'They are small and fleeting, and you've got to recognise them when they are here. Like now, with you. This is just about the happiest I've ever been. And that I might die tomorrow or even later today can't take that away from me.'

All my resolve to be patient slips away in an instant.

'Then why don't we do everything right now that we should wait to do until we're better acquainted?' I ask him. 'We can hold hands and go for walks and to the cinema after all this is over. If we both make it out, we can do that until we are old and grey. Why don't we live forever right now?'

Danny doesn't even reply. Instead, he drops his sketchbook and pulls me into his arms, his kisses urgent and hungry, his fingers fumbling at my buttons again, while his other hand slides up my thigh and under my skirt. Hungrily, my hand travels under the loose waistband of his shorts, grabbing buttocks and pulling him closer to me.

Then the sirens start to wail. We freeze, our eyes closed, paused as if we are hoping it might be a mistake. Eventually, Danny rolls over beside me, his face turned to mine.

'I guess we're just going to have to stay alive until the next time we can be alone,' he says, breathing heavily. 'I promise you I ain't gonna die, and you promise me you will stay alive, Maia. Don't you let me down. Swear it.'

'I swear I will stay alive for you,' I tell him, hoping and praying to everything and anything that I am not telling a lie.

Chapter Forty-Six

'It's not usually too bad out here,' Danny tells me as we reach the bike, 'but you never know where they're going to plant their stray bombs. There's a public shelter under the church. Come on – this way . . .'

We are walking, part of a steady stream of people all heading for the shelter, when I stop. I can hear something. I feel Danny's hand slip from mine as he's pushed on by the steady movement of the crowd, but I tilt my head, listening for the noise. Then I hear it again: the sound of a child whimpering. Somehow, the quiet cries cut through the wail of the siren and the noise of people hurriedly making their way to the shelter.

It's David, sitting alone on the step of a closed-up shop, his arms wrapped around his knees, his head in his lap. His shoulders are shaking. Weaving my way against the flow of people, I finally get to him.

'David?' Crouching down, I lightly touch his shoulder. 'What are doing here?'

He jumps, looks up at me, startled.

'Hey, Qalbi, it's me!'

Not even that makes him smile; his dark eyes are wide with fear.

'Where's your mummy and your sister?' I ask. 'Or Vittoria?'

He starts to cry again, shaking his head. He's talking in fast, sobbing Maltese, but I know that he's lost. Desperately,

I look around for Stella, as Danny continues on, lost in the crowd. There's no sign of her anywhere, and the crowd is dwindling as the locals gradually disappear into the shelter. I can already hear the distant hum of plane engines.

'Come with me,' I tell David, offering him my hand and a smile. 'I'll take you into the shelter, and afterwards we'll find your mummy together. Is that OK?'

He curls up on himself, as if he's trying to armour himself against the world.

'It's all right.' I offer him my hand again. 'As soon as it's over, I'll help you find your mummy, OK? You know me, right? It me, Maia Borg, right, kid?'

David nods and fits his narrow hand into mine. It's hot and wet with tears. I can feel the bones of his slight fingers and feel the pulse in his wrist under my thumb.

We follow the shouts of the warden to make it into the shelter just as they are closing the doors. I know what to expect now: the long, low tunnels, carved out of rock; an alcove every few feet holding a flickering oil lamp; and the scent and press of humanity all around. Almost identical to every other public shelter.

'Move in, move in,' the warden tells us. 'There are spaces further in.'

Leading David, whose lips are pressed together in terrified silence, I take us deeper into the shelter. There's no thought of searching for Danny, though I'm sure he's in here somewhere. I just feel certain that he will find me and I will find him, over and over again.

After a few minutes, we reach a narrow room with one space on a bench. The occupants call us in, telling me to take the seat, so I do, pulling David onto my lap. The woman next to me speaks in Maltese. I don't understand, but somehow I do.

'We lost his mother, Dr Borg? Do you know her? Did you see her before the raid?'

'Oh yes, everyone on the island knows Dr Borg. But I haven't seen her today,' the woman tells me in English. 'You must be related. You look alike – same chins, no?' She places her forefinger on her chin just below her lip.

It's true – David and I both share the same shallow cleft there.

The shape of his hands echoes mine, too. Or rather, mine echoes his.

The ground doesn't tremble – the sound of the bombs falling is still loud, but distant enough for us to know it isn't on top of us. Quiet chatter fills the room. A father sings his baby to sleep on his shoulder; his wife leans silently into his chest. Packed into this narrow room are at least a dozen life stories, each one balanced between tragedy-in-waiting or a fragile happy ending, depending on the whims of war.

At length, David leans back against me, and my arms encircle his slender waist. He tips his head back on my shoulder. The bombs fall; the pilots fight for their lives above us; families cry and cling to one another. And here in the deepest dark, I hold in my arms the little boy who will grow up to be my father and give him the shelter that he never afforded me. Here, I love him in a way I never have before. Seeing him as small and unprotected makes that possible, and more. I forgive him, too.

'Here you are!' Danny appears in the doorway, breaking me from my thoughts. 'I missed you.'

That he wasn't cross or worried, that he trusted me to be safe, makes me want to kiss him, and if I could, I would.

At once, a man gets up to offer Danny his seat, but Danny shakes it away, kneeling on the floor in front of David. 'Hey, you're the doctor's boy, right?'

'They must have got separated somehow,' I explain, kissing the top of David's head.

'Hey there, champ,' Danny says. 'You got to help me out, because I am the greatest rock paper scissors champ this side of the world, and I can see that you might be the only serious challenger I got.'

Uncertainly, David shakes his head.

'Are you telling me that a kid with your natural talent does not know how to play rock paper scissors?' Danny gasps. 'Well, I guess I'll have to teach you.'

The next few minutes pass with Danny showing David the rules of the game and then artfully losing every single time they play, pretending each time to be more upset, until David laughs and cheers. Then he slips off my lap and sits on the floor between Danny's crossed legs, leaning his back against Danny's chest.

'You're a pilot,' he says. 'You fly like this?' David twists his hand into the air, making it bank and turn.

'Sure, sometimes like that. Let me show you a neat trick for the next time you're flying your plane.' Danny shows David how to take off, to turn and loop the loop, their hands following one another in the dim light. David's eyes track each movement of Danny's hand, a smile playing on his lips.

Somehow, in this place I was never meant to be, I have found my heart.

Chapter Forty-Seven

When we come out of the shelter under the church on the hilltop, we can see columns of smoke rising in the sky from the direction of Valletta. Danny stares at them as if he can somehow discern their cause. Perhaps he can.

'I got to get back to base,' he says, looking at me. 'I'm due on duty.'

'Can we fit David on?' I ask. 'There's no sign of his mother here, so I'll take him to Sal. He'll know what to do.'

'You gonna come and fly with me on my motorbike?' Danny asks the boy, who nods, hopping from one foot to another. 'Come on then, kiddo. We got places to be.'

'Miss Borg!' At first, I don't pay attention to the male voice calling out the name. 'Maia, Maia Borg.'

It's Nicco who approaches me, in a pristine white suit. I don't suppose he took shelter with everyone else and still stayed so clean. He must have a private shelter somewhere.

'Nicco.' I smile, uneasy, confused as to where he's sprung from. I wonder what he's doing here in Mellieħa, but I suppose his black-market exploits must take him all over the island.

My association with Nicco feels dirty and secret, and it is. Danny doesn't know what I am trying to find out, and that feels wrong. I want him to know everything about me, even the things that he won't be able to believe. So even being in the proximity of this duplicity makes me feel sordid and unworthy.

'How fortuitous to see you.' Nicco takes my hand and kisses it. 'What brings you to Mellieħa?'

I might ask him the same thing. I don't reply. I look towards Danny and David, leaning on the bike, waiting, but Nicco completely ignores them.

'As it happens, I wanted to ask you to come and see me at the palazzo in the morning, if you will. I have a favour to ask of you.'

'Of course, if I can,' I say.

'I will send my car,' Nicco tells me. His gaze passes over David to Danny.

'I hear you caused quite a spectacle the other day, Flight Lieutenant,' he says coolly.

'Active duty will do that,' Danny replies.

'We all have our ways to serve.' Nicco gives me a little bow. 'Tomorrow, my dear,' he says, vanishing into the crowd as quickly as he appeared.

'I do not like him,' Danny says. 'Something is off about him. Look, I'm not going to tell you what to do, but I'd be real careful about doing favours for a guy like that.'

'Don't worry,' I tell Danny. 'I have the measure of him. I've met a hundred like him. He's the kind of man who thinks he is the main character.'

Danny laughs, kisses me lightly on the cheek, the warmth in his eyes telling me he wishes we could be alone.

'We need to go,' he says. 'I hate to say it, but we do.'

As I lift David onto the bike, Danny grabs my hand, pulling me close. His blue eyes search mine for a second. I feel the thrill of possibility bubble up from my stomach.

'I'm in love with you, Maia,' he says. 'I know it's fast and stupid, but I'm not gonna pretend it's not true – not gonna not say it every chance I get. You came out of the blue and knocked me flying. And that's just the way it is.'

'Same,' I say.

'Same?' He laughs in delight. 'That's all you're going to say: *same?*'

'I'm in love with you, too,' I relent. 'No one is more surprised than me.'

'You are a real piece of work, Stitches,' Danny tells me.

He releases my hand and gets on the bike, David sits between us, both of us winding our arms around Danny's waist. My heart is racing, my skin is singing.

The drive back seems shorter, perhaps because all three of us are heading towards uncertainty. Danny doesn't turn off the engine when we stop outside Sal's half-house; he steadies the bike with his boot. I lift David off and hold his hand.

'Stay alive,' Danny says as he drops us off.

'You too,' I tell him. 'I mean it.'

He's turned the corner at the end of the street in a matter of seconds, clouds of dust flying up behind the bike's wheels. I would like to stand here waiting until he comes back again, but David needs help.

'Well.' I look down at David, who looks up at me. 'Let's get you something to drink and see if we can find your mum, shall we?'

Sal is in the kitchen of the half-house, sitting at the table, his hair and jacket covered in a film of dust. There is a selection of open books spread out before him, and he is scribbling furiously in his notebook. The stump of his pencil is now barely more than the width of his fingernail.

'There you are,' he says without looking up. 'I'm glad you weren't in Valletta today – two British pilots lost. Our boys shot down three Italian fighters – the airmen went into the sea. The army has gone to pick them up. There's more bad news, too . . .' Sal stops when he sees David peering out from behind my skirt.

'You remember David?' I say brightly. 'I found him all alone and lost on the other side of the island. We're not sure where his mummy is, so I brought him back with me until I find her.'

'Do not worry, little one,' Sal says kindly to David. 'I know where your mother is.' He turns back to me. 'Christina came in today to ask me to help find her. Christina has the baby at her lodgings. Stella is at a house in the Gut. My former pupil, Vittoria — she is in terrible trouble.'

'Vittoria?' My heart drops as I remember her sweet smile the last time I saw her. 'What happened?'

'Christina will tell you.' Sal waves his hand, turning his face away as his voice breaks.

Whatever has happened, it's serious.

* * *

Christina opens the door with the baby in her arms and bends down to kiss David on top of his head.

'Oh, I *am* glad you are here,' Christina tells him. 'We are putting on a play and we need a leading man. Run upstairs, will you, and get fitted for your costume? You can take this great lump with you.'

Christina sets Eugenie down, and David lifts her as best he can as they make their way slowly up the stairs together, Eugenie tottering with her brother's arms around her waist.

'Dr Borg said someone would bring him,' Christina says, watching the children.

'That's all she said?' I ask, incredulous. 'Like he's a bag she's left behind somewhere? He was crying his eyes out, poor little mite.'

'You're right, of course,' Christina says regretfully, watching the children meet Alex at the top of the stairs, where he immediately wraps them both in something satin. 'But I am rather afraid we get hardened to all the tears. Perhaps the children's tears especially. As if all this terror and death have become just another part of life. But he's safe now, thanks to you. He can stay with me until the doctor collects him.'

'Where is she?' I ask. 'What was so important she didn't go back for her son?'

'It's my fault,' Christina says. 'Vittoria is in a bad way. She wouldn't let the women she lives with call for help, so things got worse and worse. Then one came to me and told me the trouble. I knew Stella was in Mellieħa today, so I telephoned a friend there and asked her to fetch her. I begged the doctor to see Vittoria. There was nothing I could do to persuade her to go to the hospital – she was too ashamed. The poor thing.' Christina lowers her voice. 'Seems she's pregnant. Her friends tried to help her get rid of it yesterday. With a bottle of gin, a coat hanger and a hot bath. But the bleeding wouldn't stop, and infection's set in so quickly.'

'David said she wasn't feeling well yesterday, but I had no idea . . . Why didn't she ask Stella to help?'

'Shame, fear,' Christina says, with a sad shrug. She points down the street. 'Right at the top, on the left – the house with the red door. It will be open. Stella is with her now.'

'Right,' I say. 'I'll see if I can help.'

'Maia, darling.' Christina pulls me back. 'The boy is safe. No harm done – he'll forget all about it by teatime. But what you'll find in there . . . It will be harder to forget.'

'I know, but I'm not afraid,' I tell her. For the first time in my life, I think that might be true.

Chapter Forty-Eight

The red door is standing slightly ajar, just as Christina told me it would be.

It leads into a narrow hallway, and beyond, a splintered door stands open, leading onto a small, square, open courtyard. Here are the steps that lead to the first floor. Washing, covered in dust from the earlier raid, hangs on a line stretched between two balconies. The whole courtyard is in shadow except for one corner, which is lit by a slice of late-afternoon sun.

A young woman sits in that light, her blue dress made more vivid by it. Her head has fallen to her lap, and she is weeping. A cigarette held in a limp hand burns down.

'Hello?' I enquire softly from the foot of the steps. 'I'm Maia, looking for Dr Borg and Vittoria.'

The girl looks up at me, her face gaunt, and gestures to the hallway behind her. I take the steps quickly, but as I move around her, she catches my wrist. I look into a haggard face stained with exhaustion and tears.

'Are you a nurse?' she asks. Her accent isn't Maltese, though I can't quite place it. 'Are you here to help Vittoria?'

'I'm not a nurse,' I say.

'We moved her to the big room – better light, you see, and the air from the sea? We left her during the raid – we had to, didn't we? Do you think she knows we left her?'

Things seem very bad. I can hardly believe it. I only saw her the day before yesterday.

'I don't know.' I wish I had something to tell this frightened woman, something to comfort her with, so instead I've chosen honesty. It dawns on me that I have walked into this situation as a twenty-first-century woman with no idea that death can be so near or so certain.

The hallway is lit at either end by a long, shuttered window. Another two women wait outside the room I was directed to. One leans her forehead against the door, her palm flattened against it. The other sits on the tiled floor, her chin resting on her chest.

I'm about to turn away when the door opens, and Stella looks at me.

'Oh, good,' she says calmly, handing me a bowl of bloody water. 'I need fresh, boiled water and more towels, linen. Anything will do as long as it's absorbent, and I need it fast. Can you do that? These young ladies will help you.'

'Of course,' I say.

The door is closed.

'This way.' The girl who was sitting on the floor leaps to her feet, desperate to do something, anything. 'I'm Daphne. This is Gloria.'

'Hello, I'm Maia,' I tell them.

'Thank you, thank you for coming,' Gloria says. 'We were afraid no one would come to help Vittoria. When Dr Borg came, we were so grateful. And now you. There are good people, truly.'

She crosses herself, glancing briefly at the heavens.

In a basic kitchen, they show me a pot of water simmering over a fire. Gloria's face pales as she looks at the blood in the water, and she throws it out into the yard. She begins to tear down the washing.

'It's no good,' she cries. 'It's covered in dust. Nothing stays clean!'

Daphne washes and refills the bowl with hot water. 'Our sheets – they were fresh yesterday, and we have not slept in them. Strip the beds!'

Gloria runs upstairs, and Daphne and I carefully carry the water. Gloria opens the doors for me into the bedroom. Daphne thrusts a bundle of sheets into Stella's arms. I notice she is careful not to let the girls see into the room. She steps aside slightly to let me pass.

'Set it there,' she tells me, pointing to a small chest of drawers.

It's the smell that hits me first, the sharp scent, followed quickly by the sweet sickly smell of infection and sour sweat. The windows are open, the curtains billowing in the breeze, but somehow it seems as if the fetid air will not be moved, as if it has its own mass. A pile of bloody towels slumps at the foot of the bed. Stella sits down on the edge of the bed, holding the girl's hand.

'What should I do?' I ask her.

'Very gently, take the towels between her legs and replace them with what you have brought. Gently. She is in pain.'

As I move around the bed, I see Vittoria properly for the first time. Her dark hair clings to her face, which is sheened in waxy sweat. It's hard to match this near-dead girl with the young woman whose eyes shone the last time I saw her, just two days ago. Vittoria's complexion is a very pale grey, her parted lips dry and bloodless. When I lift the sheet that covers her lower half, I see the wad of linen already in place is saturated with red. She groans quietly as I remove the towel and gently press the fresh sheets into place.

'Thank you,' Stella says. 'I don't want to let go of her hand again – she thinks I am her mother.'

'Will she recover?' I ask, already knowing the answer.

'She will die,' Stella says. 'The water, the sheets, are for her friends' benefit rather than hers, so they will be able to comfort themselves after she has gone.'

'Jesus.' I cover my mouth, my throat suddenly full of grief. 'I said I'd help her. She promised she'd come to me if she ever needed help.'

Stella's expression is implacable, detached somehow. She watches Vittoria struggle for another breath like an angel in a stained-glass window, sad and remote.

'Her pain is eased now, at least,' she says eventually. 'I had a little morphine left. Now I have none. She has lost a lot of blood, and sepsis has set in. Her organs are failing. But she is young and was healthy, so her body clutches at life. We must pray that her death is swift.'

'No penicillin?' I ask.

Stella shakes her head.

'I could find some – I can search the island.' I think of Nicco. 'I think I know someone who might help.'

'There is none,' Stella tells me. 'I have already sold everything I had of value to buy what stocks Elias had.' She says this matter-of-factly, as though she already knows I know of Elias and his ways, and is unshocked by it. 'There is none, and even if there was, it's too late now, Maia.'

Of all the incredible things I have been through, this is the hardest to believe.

'Listen, will you go and find Father Vincent at St Paul's? Many would not come, but he is a good man. He will give her the last rites.'

'Where will he be?' I ask, focused by Stella's commanding tone. 'I don't know the area that well.'

'Of course.' Stella thinks for a moment. 'You stay with her. I will fetch him. Hold her hand. Talk to her as her mother would. Do not let her feel alone.'

She stands up, and I take her place, picking up the girl's hand. It's freezing cold, even though her body radiates heat.

'I will return presently,' Stella says as she closes the door, and I'm alone with Vittoria. She is not the first dying person I have sat with.

Mum was the first, and then . . . then Saria. The little girl I met that day far away from now. The little girl I took with me into the underground garage to escape the missiles. When the building collapsed, she was fatally crushed, but she didn't die immediately. For a little while she cried asking for her mother. So even though I could not see her, I knew she was alive – and dying – her tiny body trapped somewhere beneath mine. I had sat with Saria, holding her hand until it went cold, pinned in the dark until aid workers came. Knowing for each long second that I had led her to her death.

With Mum, I talked her through her last morphine-fed fantasies. We marvelled together at the opening of the starry firmament of heaven she told me she could see right above her head.

With Saria, I sang nursery rhymes, long after she could hear them.

For Vittoria, I am lost. What have I to give this girl, who should have had so much more? In the end, all I have is the kindness of lies.

'Mama?' Vittoria whispers, breaking my train of thought. 'Mama?'

'I'm here,' I say softly, wishing I could speak Maltese. 'I'm with you.'

A wail sounds from outside the open window, soon joined by more sobs outside the door. A few seconds later, Stella ushers in a young priest, who crosses to the bed, his solemn gaze settling on Vittoria's face. I start to get up, but Stella shakes her head.

'Keep talking,' she says. 'Let her hear her mother's love.'

In the minutes that follow, I hold her hand, murmuring gently under my breath, repeating all the words of comfort my own mother used to whisper to me when I lay awake, afraid of the dark. I listened to the prayers spoken over her, watching the priest anoint her forehead with oil. Finally, Stella lets the others in, and they take turns to kiss her goodbye.

We wait together until the air-raid sirens wail again, and we hear the sound of aircraft in the sky. No one leaves.

Outside in the open, the world explodes in a roar. The building vibrates; plaster showers down from the ceiling. Fires from the harbour cast their dancing shadows across the wall. As the hours pass, Stella comes to stand with me, her hand on my shoulder. The priest continues to pray, and her friends, the last family she will ever have, kneel at her bedside, keeping vigil. We all understand the danger of remaining here, and yet we stay. Perhaps the others feel as I do: that this room, in these hours, exists outside time and space, as if the universe has bowed its head just for Vittoria.

And then finally, just as the evening falls silent once again, Vittoria lets out a long rattling breath and the room becomes profoundly quiet.

Vittoria Palermo, seventeen years of age, has gone from this world, and perhaps from all the others, too.

Chapter Forty-Nine

'Thank you for your help,' Stella says sometime later. We are sitting on the steps of Christina's house, waiting for her to come back from the shelter. The street is twilight-purple, still quiet after the raid. Stella is smoking. 'You were steady and strong. Why did you come?'

'Christina told me where you were,' I say.

Stella doesn't respond; she simply shrugs, as though accepting this as enough of an answer. And I know it's because, for her, it is: she would have done exactly the same. When I look at her profile, I see my father, a little of Kathryn and quite a lot of myself: the long, narrow roman nose and dimpled chin; the strong jaw-line and thick dark hair. I inherited my mother's pale complexion, but that's all. The rest of me is my father, from the shape and colour of my eyes to my enduring ability to hold a grudge.

I never knew Stella. I barely even know *about* her. She died when my father was a child – that much I always understood, and it never mattered really, until now. I've never known her, not even through his memories, and she never seemed real. But now, I know that this brilliant, determined, compassionate woman will be killed just a few days from now, and behind her, she will leave a devastation that spans generations. There is no one else in the whole of existence who can change that but me. Fear and fury pulse in my veins.

'It's hard to say this after what we have both just been through, but it's important, Stella. I need you to listen.'

Stella takes a deep drag on her cigarette, shoots me a querying look.

'I'm angry with you,' I tell her.

'Everyone always is,' she says, with a shrug. 'They want me in a hundred places with all the medicine in the world. But I can only ever be in one, and whatever I bring, it is never enough.'

'No, that's not why.' I drop my head. I know this isn't the right time. After all, I just watched her do all she could for a young woman we both liked and cared for. That was the best of Stella. Who am I to find fault with her now? But there will never be a right time, and soon there will be no time at all, not for Stella.

'I found David, alone and crying, at the other end of the island.' I gesture in the vague direction of Mellieħa. 'You just left him. He's five years old, and you left him all alone.'

Stella turns to look at me, her expression one of deep weariness. 'Ah, I thought perhaps you were different,' she says, dropping her cigarette stub and grinding it under her toe.

'What do you mean?' I ask.

'I thought you British women were progressive. You do your bit, yes? Christina at the war room, you a journalist. I thought you understood my work is vital. Especially now.'

'I do understand that,' I say. 'Not only do I understand it, but I admire you, more than you know. But . . . just to forget him, like a piece of unwanted baggage?'

'I did not abandon him,' Stella says, stamping out the stub of the cigarette. 'We were in Mellieħa to see a patient, the mother of a friend of David's, when we had to leave quickly. I got word Vittoria was very sick. We had to get back to Valletta. So, we all get on the bus, all three of us. But David – so like his father – he didn't want to leave his friend there. So we all get on the bus – he gets off again. It was crowded. No one saw. I didn't see him get off. But he did, because he wanted to. And then he regretted it. Perhaps next time he will think twice.'

My mouth falls open in disbelief. 'There was a raid – your five-year-old son was alone in the middle of a raid!'

'And so was Vittoria,' Stella says. 'And a hundred other children. Young men burnt half to death or with their limbs torn off. Old women trapped under rubble. Which of these souls should I save first? You tell me. Where do I go first? Who do I let die? Or should I let all of them die because my son got off the bus?'

'Vittoria died anyway,' I say, and regret it at once.

'She did.' Stella lowers her eyes. 'But at least I was there to ease her pain, as were you. I knew that David would be safe.'

'How? He's hardly more than a baby himself, and yet you drag him around the island with you, leaving him to take care of his sister, as if . . .'

'As if I am a mother, doing her best for both her children in the middle of a war,' Stella finishes for me. 'Do you think I don't know how this war harms him and my daughter? Two years ago, he was a happy little toddler with a father and a mother and a sister on the way. Now, his father is gone; his home is gone. His mother must travel the island day and night to help the injured and the sick, when there is no one else. I tried to leave him with a neighbour at first, but David will not be left, because he knows that one day his father left and never came home.

So, I take him with me. I take them both, wherever I go, so that we are always together – at least until my stubborn little boy forgets he is afraid and decides to get off a bus.'

Stella's shoulders drop. 'At the end of each day, I believe that tomorrow will be the day I break, the day I cannot fight any longer. But at the beginning of each day, I make a promise to start again, to fight for my country and my people and for my children. To keep us together. As we are meant to be. You can think what you want of me, but I knew that David would be safe, because he is my son. And the people of Malta know me, and they know my son. I knew someone would take him to a shelter and bring him to me, and I was right, wasn't I?'

I nod.

People are starting to walk down the street, weary and sad in the aftermath of the raid.

'I also knew that Vittoria would die alone and in pain if I got off the bus to go and fetch him. I made a decision – it's one I can live with. If you can't, then that is your problem.'

Christina comes around the corner with the children. As soon as David sees his mother, he tugs free of her hand, racing into Stella's arms. She scoops him up as he flings his arms around her neck, talking excitedly in Maltese. Any trace that he was alone or abandoned seems forgotten as Stella hitches him onto her hip and Christina brings the little girl to her.

'Here she is,' Christina says, bouncing the baby as she walks. 'Here's Eugenie.'

The little girl's eyes light up, and David scrambles down as Eugenie is passed into Stella's arms. The love between them is almost palpable. Stella isn't a cold, neglectful mother – she's a woman stretched almost to breaking point, who still manages to find love and compassion every day in the middle of relentless violence.

Then the words Kathryn said come back to me, suddenly perfectly clear: *So tragic, poor Grandmama. Such a tragic loss so young. I think it broke your father's heart for good.*

'Stella.' She looks at me, defiant. 'You are the most remarkable woman, but you need to know how important you are. Yes, to everyone you treat – but to your children, too, and to me. You can't save the world.'

Stella lifts her chin and gives me a scathing look. 'What kind of a mother would I be if I didn't try to do just that?'

Chapter Fifty

When I return to the half-house, Sal is sitting at the kitchen table, picking at a single fillet of fish. Another is sitting in a pan. Going to the stove, I collect the fish, slide it onto a plate and sit down opposite him.

'You did not come when the raid began,' he says almost accusingly. There is a sheen of sweat on his tanned forehead. His eyes are lowered.

'Vittoria.' I make myself say her name. 'She was . . . dying. None of us could bear to leave her in her last minutes.'

Now, he looks up at me, and I am startled to see tears in his eyes.

'She's gone?'

I nod. I'd almost forgotten how much the professor liked his young student. I should have been more careful with my words.

'I watched her grow up, so full of hope and promise, and how quickly the world brought her to this.' He shakes his head. 'Sometimes, I just feel the weight of it all. Of being where I am not meant to be. Of having lost my future, my love, my child. And the war, and the violence that falls from the sky, and in the middle of it all, a young woman driven to an act that has killed her. Much of the time, I am able to shoulder it, but not today. When you did not come back when the sirens sounded, I was afraid I'd lost you, too.'

'Sal, I'm so sorry,' I tell him, reaching a hand across the table to cover his. 'We're trying to make sense of something that has no rhyme or reason.'

We sit in silence for a long moment.

'If you could, would you want to go back? To find your wife, your child, to try to begin again?'

Sal shrugs. 'I am sure she has moved on. What could I do but hurt and shock her?'

'I want to be *here*, Sal,' I tell him. 'Here right now and for the rest of my life.'

Sal looks up at me.

'My very long life,' I tell him with a bravado that I don't feel just in this moment.

'Maia, are you sure? You would be safer if you . . .'

'I wasn't safe, Sal,' I tell him. 'Back there, I put myself in harm's way all the time, not because I was brave, but because I was *afraid* – afraid to be alive in a world that didn't feel like mine. I don't feel like that here.'

'This could simply be love talking,' Sal says. 'I see the look in your eyes after a day with Flight Lieutenant Beauchamp. It's easy for the young to get swept away. But for you, it's a matter of life and death.'

'I won't pretend that doesn't come into it,' I say. 'But so what if it does? Isn't love the best – no, the *only* reason to cross universes? Love and one incredible chance to save someone who truly deserves to be saved?'

'Stella,' Sal says.

'My grandmother,' I agree. 'But before that, before I build a life here, I need to find a way to go back to 2025 on my terms,' I tell Sal, and the room, the sky at large, as if I might have the ear of the universe. 'I want to explain, to say goodbye to the people I'm leaving behind, but I also need more information. I won't be able to save Stella without it.'

'If wishing was enough to ride time as if it were a bus, I would have been gone a long time ago.'

'I know,' I say. 'But I was thinking about one of the stories that Kathryn told me. And I have an idea. Will you take me to the Ħal Saflieni Hypogeum?'

Chapter Fifty-One

Sal and I leave the half-house in silence, each of us feeling the weight of a possible goodbye and all the uncertainty that comes with it. Of course, it might not work; it probably won't. All I have to go on are Kathryn's stories and not one shred of evidence. But this is the only way I can think of to try to take some control over what is happening to me, because I have found a home here. I have found a family. I have found something I never really believed was true: I have found love. And I will be damned if some mindless cosmic force gets to show me all of that and then rip me away from it any time it wants.

At the 10 p.m. curfew, the streets are quiet and completely dark, save for when a door cracks open on the Gut to reveal a brief slash of light accompanied by the sound of raucous laughter and the scent of perfume and sweat. A warm night air, hoping we can tame the impossible, that we can bring the universe to heel.

'There,' Sal whispers as we stop across the street from a place cloaked in slanted shadows. We are in the heart of the small town, Paola. Light from inside the buildings is blotted out, but somewhere nearby, I hear a radio playing and a family talking. There are no soldiers posted outside the entrance gate to the site as I had expected. Sal and I look at each other.

'It can't be this easy,' I say.

'I hear the local people use the lower levels as a shelter,' Sal says. 'The army has nothing to fear from islanders, remember. Wait here.'

Very slowly, with his hands clasped behind his back, Sal saunters over to the gate. I watch as he looks up and down the street and then tries it. The creak it makes sounds deafening in the still night, but the gate opens. Sal looks towards me and beckons.

The night seems to lean in, and I hesitate for a moment, afraid that this time the universe will not let me go, that I'll never see Danny again.

Chapter Fifty-Two

Sal leads me down through a circular entrance to where a ladder descends into the gloom below. It's impossible to make out any detail of what might be down there – just the tips of the ladder reaching upwards. This raw and somehow still wild temple feels dangerously alive, and alert to our intrusion. It seems to prowl, searching for something or someone to sate its hunger.

As we feel our way carefully down each rung of the ladder, absolute dark waits for us below. I hear Sal's feet on stone, and a moment later, I realise I am also at the bottom, my feet meeting the ground. All traces of light are lost, and there is no way to tell what lies in any direction. There is something very old and primal that is not quite in this world or outside it but somewhere in between. There's a sensation that I am in the mouth of a living creature who is just about to swallow me whole.

'I'm afraid,' I confess, whispering out loud, desperate to prove to myself that I am still here and attached to a body. My light voice falls dead into the air, a separate, alien thing.

'Don't worry,' Sal's voice comes back, comfortingly normal. 'I feel it, too, but people have been using this part of the temple recently. There will be lanterns. Stay where you are while I find one. It will just be a moment.'

His cautious movements sound around me in the dark: a footstep here and there, the sound of a pebble falling. Then

I hear the worldly clank of metal and glass, followed by the drag of a match across stone. There's a brief flare of light.

At once, I focus on the steady flame of the match illuminating Sal's hands, which are working to light the wick of the lantern. Finally, an orb of amber reveals his face, serious and full of intent. The globe radiates outwards, revealing a series of handcarved passages and chambers. Slowly, I look around, gradually getting my bearings.

'And here's another.' Sal locates and lights a second lantern, holding it out towards me.

There is a pile of neatly folded blankets on one vacant shelf that must once have been occupied by the dead; some chairs stand around, as if they've just been caught doing something they shouldn't. There are buckets and candle stumps: nothing you wouldn't expect to see in any other shelter, but they feel intrusive here, almost obscene.

'This layer is the oldest part of the temple,' I tell Sal. 'Kathryn told me it's perhaps even eight thousand years old. But I think the part we need to visit is at the lower level . . .'

I take a moment to superimpose this room on the descriptions of the temple that Kathryn gave me.

'This way.' Taking the lantern from Sal, I lead the way. The tunnels were made for smaller people and we bow our heads as we make our way deeper into the temple.

The path tilts downwards at a shallow angle, but it's still steep enough for me to be acutely aware that we are descending deeper into the earth. Everything that seems so unlikely and unreal on the surface feels entirely possible down here.

At last, we walk out into a slightly larger space, where the ceilings are just high enough for me to be able to stand up straight. Looking around and holding my lantern up high, so that it casts a light around as much of the room as possible, I gasp, awestruck by the red-painted spirals turning and twisting into infinity, the bowed pillars carved to make the room appear much larger and grander than it is.

'Astounding,' Sal says, pausing for a moment to gaze at the decoration. 'To think that thousands of years ago, our ancestors stood here and made these marks with intention and purpose. It feels as if they are standing very near, doesn't it?'

'I think they are,' I whisper. 'I think they're just a hair's breadth away. One glimpse out of sight.'

We go on, the lanterns casting a tight circle of light around us. Perfect dark precedes and follows us at close quarters. There's no fear here, though, just the sense of profound peace left in a place that was created for perpetual dreamers.

When I enter the oracle chamber, I'm sure I feel a slight sense of resistance in the air, as if it has coagulated. My soft footsteps disturb the intense quiet as I find my way to the echoing niche. I recognise it from Kathryn's description, a miracle of ancient engineering.

'If you speak into this niche,' I tell Sal, 'at exactly the right pitch, then it can be heard throughout the complex and beyond. Even in 2025, archaeologists aren't sure how they created this effect. It resonates at one hundred and eleven hertz exactly.' I turn to look at him. 'The frequency of the universe.'

'So you will speak into the niche?' he asks.

I shrug and turn to it. 'I am Maia Borg,' I say. 'You know who I am – you brought me here. You know why I am here and where I need to go. Take me there.'

Sure enough, my voice flows through the stone structures of the temple, amplified into every crevice and corner.

Gasping, I turn around and listen to my own voice echo and repeat until, at last, the words fade into silence.

I'm not sure what I expected to happen, but nothing does. Sal and I stand in the dim glow of the lanterns, waiting, and the temple turns her back on us.

'There should be something more,' Sal says. 'An offering.'

'I am the offering,' I say, 'and nobody asked me first.'

'That's it,' Sal says. 'You are angry; you are making a demand. But instead, you must harmonise with the temple itself. Sing at the same frequency as the temple, as the whole of space and time.'

'I have no idea how to do that,' I tell him. 'I have no idea what one hundred and eleven hertz even sounds like.'

'But the temple does. The temple knows exactly. Sing – sing to her until you discover her song.'

'Blow the lanterns out,' I say.

'But . . .' Sal looks perplexed.

'I'm not going to sing if you can see me!'

Sal blows out the lights, and darkness envelops us, soft and quiet. To break the velvet dark with my voice feels like sacrilege, but I can't think of any better ideas, so I close my eyes and sing, tentatively at first, and then I let it build.

As I sing, I picture everything I love, everything I need to do, projecting my heart and mind onto the fabric of the underworld. The way Sal takes his battered glasses off his nose and cleans them with a hanky. The way Christina's smile and energy radiate around her like a beacon. Stella's laser-focus frown, her stride that breaks for no one and nothing. David, holding his sister in his arms with the kind of small strength that can shoulder the world. And Danny: the way his elegant hands hold a pencil as he draws; how he looks at the clear sky and sees the wind unfurl like tracks on a map; the touch of the very tips of his fingers meeting mine. It's the slightest thread that attaches him to me, nothing more than a hopeful promise, a delicate wish that I'm ready to build an empire of dreams on.

There are no words to my song – none that are recognisable in any language, anyway. At first, it's awkward and halting. Then, very slowly, I forget where I am – I forget my body altogether – and every note that pours out of me is made purely from the contents of my soul. My pitch takes flight, falls and steadies like the flight of an aircraft, and then I find the slipstream, the perfect place to glide.

As I sing, it feels like a thousand, thousand other voices join with mine, echoing and repeating my every note. I'm not sure if it's real or an illusion, but the temple seems to light up, a faint glow coming from within the stones. The oracle chamber awakes, and I think I see the red spirals dance and spin above me, the walls flex and widen like a throat in full voice.

We sing together, all of us, all of me, and the temple teaches me the song of creation: of all time and space. If nothing else, if at any second my song is broken and I remain exactly where I am, then at least I will always have this rarest of experiences, a sense of total unity with everything and everyone that has ever been or ever will be. Whether we know it or not, we each stand shoulder to shoulder, never alone, not in life or death.

Then I see it. At the end of one of the dark tunnels leading off the chamber, a pinprick of light glows, growing larger in rhythmic pulses.

Fear of the unknown takes hold, fear that I won't find what I'm looking for – and fear that I will. Still, there is no other choice.

I don't know where Sal is. I can't see him, and I daren't risk breaking the song to call for him. He will understand,

I'm sure. I hope he understands, and that he has borne witness. I hope he will be able to tell me what happened here one day, not so very far from now when we are safe and at ease.

As I step into the tunnel, my song continues to reverberate throughout the temple, winding its way through and back on itself, like the spirals painted in ochre on the ceilings.

The light grows stronger as the song slowly fades in slight increments, until my song fades away and all I can hear is the sound of my own breathing. The light ahead is now strong enough to slice into the tunnel.

'That's sunlight,' I whisper aloud, stopping short about three metres from the exit. 'Warm sunlight. I came in here after midnight.'

'Yes,' I answer myself, as if there is another version of me standing just out of reach.

'Sunlight, when it must be about one in the morning, and we are far underground.'

'Yes,' I reply. 'When you came in, you travelled through both distance and time – it makes sense.'

'We can only know if we go through,' I say.

'Then we go through – do or die,' I agree.

Someone – I – take my hand, and we walk.

The face of a man I should never have met comes to mind: Danny Beauchamp. Danny was never meant for me, not in this time or the next or in a thousand lifetimes. And yet I know with a greater certainty than I have ever known anything that wherever he is now, he is the guiding light that will bring me home.

Chapter Fifty-Three

Saturday 15th August 1992, 12.32 p.m.

I know exactly where I am.

The Barrakka Gardens, on a bright day of celebration. Joy courses through me. I feel as if several tons of grief and trauma have been floated away out of my body, and I'm light, so light that I could float away into the sky, just like the coloured balloons that sail towards the sun.

Crowds throng around me, humming with chatter and laughter. Children run in and out of adults' legs, some waving British and Maltese flags on sticks. I see the back of heads I think I recognise: a man holding a girl's hand, her dark hair tangled in rat-tails down her back – somehow, I know she hates to have it brushed.

Then I see it, the banner, one of many that have been strung out across the arches that look over the harbour:

1942–1992

I am at the fiftieth anniversary of the end of the siege. Sal was here once – he might still be here. Perhaps I am here to find him.

That's when I see the person I am really here to meet, the soul I've come home to.

Danny is sitting alone on a bench, as if he can't really see all the celebrations going on around him. He's older now, of course, in his seventies. His mop of brown curls has become fine white hair, cut neatly in a military style he never wore as a Spitfire pilot in Malta. He wears a grey suit over a pale-blue shirt that exactly matches the colour of his eyes, finished with an RAF tie. A line of medals is pinned to his lapel. His hands, knotted with age, rest on a walking stick. He is alone, seemingly apart from the crowds, as if he is here for another reason entirely. The sight of him grown old is the most beautiful thing I have ever seen.

My eyes are full of tears as I walk to him. The crowd seems to make a path for me, and I feel as if he and I have moved eons to put aside this moment just for us.

'Flight Lieutenant Daniel Beauchamp,' I say, sitting down next to him and taking his hand.

'Stitches.' Danny turns to look at me, a slow smile spreading over his face. 'I've been waiting for you, Maia. Here you are at last.'

Chapter Fifty-Four

Tuesday 24th June 2025, 12.15 p.m.

'Wake up, Maia . . .' It's Dr Gresch's voice that pierces my dreams. 'Maia?'

Slowly, painstakingly, I climb back into this other body. That's what it feels like – like pushing my way into flesh, dragging myself along every nerve ending and pulsing vein until finally I can open my eyes. The light is bright; the smell is sharp. I feel bereft.

'Hello, there,' she says gently. 'We were a little worried about you – you were hard to rouse.'

'What day . . . what time is it?' I ask, trying to orientate myself. I'm not surprised I was hard to rouse – I didn't really want to come back; I just knew I had to.

Lying back on my clean pillows, I submit meekly as the doctor checks my pulse and points a torch into each eye in turn. She tilts her head when she looks at me, puzzled.

'It's a little after noon. You slept very deeply. Your vitals are all good, but your brain waves were . . . very interesting. How did you sleep?'

She detaches me from a variety of machines, and I rub at the places where the sticky patches have left their residue.

'Terribly,' I say, rubbing the back of my neck. 'I fell in love, met my father as a small child, watched a young woman die, and then came back here to tell my father I'm not staying, so . . . honestly, I could do with a sleep.'

'OK.' She chuckles uneasily. 'That's quite something.'

'It's not a dream or a delusion,' I tell her. 'I have been kind of time-travelling around the universe and . . . well, I prefer it in 1942, so I've come here to sort a few things out before I leave for good.'

There is a long moment in which I am sure Dr Gresch is about to burst into horrified laughter at my crazy talk, and quite a lot of me still wonders if that is what is happening here. The parts of me that matter, though – the parts that aren't tethered to just one reality – don't care.

'I'm not sure I would be willing to admit this to any of my peers,' Dr Gresch says slowly, 'or anyone outside this room, but I think I believe you.'

'You do?' I ask her uncertainly, not totally sure that she isn't just humouring me while she waits for the men in white coats to arrive.

'I don't have any answers for you,' Dr Gresch says. 'This is the first time anyone anywhere has tried to study this theory outside of modelled simulations or on brain organoids.'

'Brain organoids?' I ask.

'Little clusters of brain cells – you kind of put them together and they automatically wire themselves into minibrains.'

I smile. 'Mini-brains? That's mind-blowing.'

'It is,' Dr Gresch says. 'And, please, call me Selena. It makes all of this seem less world-changing somehow if you do.'

'What do you mean?'

'I mean that it's early days and we've only done one session, but . . .' Dr Gresch – Selena – sighs. 'Honestly, I'd rather go back to my friends the organoids than get the results I have with you. But as a scientist, I can't ignore that the brain activity we recorded during sleep wasn't what we'd expect to see when someone is in a dream state. In those circumstances, large parts of the brain shut down – in order to stop you acting out your dreams, essentially. Your thought processes and decision-making take a holiday. But when I watched your scans last night, your brain patterns were those of a waking person – an active, waking person, someone experiencing joy, fear, sadness . . . love. It was . . . as if I was watching you live your life . . . elsewhere.'

'I feel like that, too,' I say. 'I feel like I left a physical place that leaves physical evidence on my body – after all, my hair, my stitches are from 1942.'

'Ah, yes. I'm going to take those mysterious stitches out for you right now,' Selena says, reaching for a pair of narrow scissors. 'I want to get them analysed, see if there's a way to date them. The thing is, Maia, I must be so careful. After all, what are the odds that someone who has these profound, measurable experiences via consciousness might fall into my lap as I am studying that very field? I'm at risk of confirmation bias, trying to find evidence for what I *want* to believe is true. I don't want my enthusiasm to turn my findings into a lie.'

'It's not just me, though,' I tell her. 'I'm not the only person who has vaulted out of one time into another. I've met someone else there in 1942, and he's been there since 1909.'

'Let me guess,' Selena says, picking up a closed paper folder. 'The gentleman you asked me to look for? Professor Salvatore Borg?'

'Yes, yes – did you find him?' I ask her, sitting up. 'What happened to him? Do you know?'

'I found him,' Selena says slowly, holding the folder against her chest. 'I found two of him. Not all that surprising, you may think – there must be many Salvatore Borgs in Malta. If I go outside now and shout that name aloud, there is a good chance that someone will answer. But I think the two men I found might be one person . . .'

'Tell me everything you found out,' I say.

'Tell me what you know first,' Selena says with a smile.

'He was born in 1962,' I say, ticking off all the facts I know about Sal on my fingers as I go. 'He worked and studied in Milan at the university – physics, but at the moment – in 1942, I mean – he teaches English and maths to schoolchildren and squaddies . . .' I pause for a moment to recollect more of what Sal told me. 'He came home to Malta in 1992 with his wife, Elena, who was expecting their first child. He had done something bad in Milan – something he wanted to get away from. They wanted to see his mother and take part in the celebrations commemorating the end of the 1942 siege. It was a big deal, loads of veterans attending – an air show.' A vision of Danny in 1992 floats into my mind, elderly and gallant: a man who has lived a full life, worthy of respect.

'Maia?' Selena prompts me.

'Well, he'd been in a car crash, just like me, and then in Malta, not long after, he went off on a bike ride and got knocked off, knocked out – though he was unhurt. He thought that might be important, Dr Gresch – Selena – that we'd both had accidents in the days prior to . . . Anyway, he passed out in 1992 and woke up in 1909. For a while, as he was – he calls it "settling" – he bounced around time just like I have, trying to leave a trail of breadcrumbs where he could. And then he stayed where he was. He made another life there – he has done for thirty years. He misses his wife and the child he has never known, but he helps a lot of people, teaches the kids and keeps the university going. He volunteers with the servicemen. He is really kind.' I look at her sharply. 'What do *you* know?'

Selena presses her lips into a thin line.

'I found several Salvatore Borgs. I have a list here. But let's just focus on this gentleman for a while. He was born in 1962. In 1992, he was visiting Malta and he was in an accident. He fell into a coma with no clear explanation.'

'Oh!' I cover my mouth, as if hearing bad news of a loved one. Because I *am* hearing bad news of a loved one.

'Sal died?' I ask, faltering, wondering how I am ever going to break the news to him. 'He died here? And there he . . . lives?'

'He didn't die,' Selina tells me. 'He is still alive.'

Chapter Fifty-Five

'He has been cared for in a private facility, which is paid for by his wife and, latterly, his son, for the last thirty-three years,' Selena explains. 'I spoke to his doctor. His health is stable if not good. He still breathes and performs other basic essential-to-life functions without medical intervention, but essentially, he is not there in any meaningful way.'

'Oh, God, his poor wife,' I say. 'Thirty-three years of having and not having him? His poor son. Poor Sal – he'll be devastated. How can I tell him this?'

Climbing out of bed, I start getting dressed in my day clothes, not really clear what I'm doing, where I'm going or what I think I'm going to do. I only know that I need to get out of this room.

'Shall I call Kathryn?' Selena asks, signalling to someone in the room next door. 'I will ask someone to go and call Kathryn.'

'Thirty-three years in a coma?' I ask, ignoring her. 'Is that even possible?'

'It's unusual, to say the least. I can think of only one other patient who has lived in a coma for so long, somebody called Elaine Esposito who was in a coma for thirty-seven years before she died. Mr Borg is very ill, but it's clear that his life is sacred to his family. They are determined to preserve and protect him for as long as he takes breath. They love him deeply. He is still the heart of their family.'

Selena hands me the folder, which I open to find a series of printed-out articles. One, from the *Times of Malta*, shows an image of Sal taken in the last few days before his collapse. I recognise him – albeit a younger, slimmer version of him, with all his hair. He has his hand on his wife's waist. They smile for the camera, their whole lives ahead of them. Then there is a photo of a man propped up on pillows in a bed. The room is clean; there are fresh flowers. He is surrounded by an older woman, whom I recognise as his wife from the first photo, a young man who is the image of him, and a gaggle of children of varying ages: his son and his grandchildren, I presume. All of them are smiling; half a dozen hands rest on him.

Sal, who I know and do not know, lies perfectly still in the middle of all this love, wired up to a monitor with a feeding tube inserted.

'I also found this Salvatore Borg,' Selena says.

This time it's a black-and-white photograph that she shows me. A group of schoolchildren are standing outside a church, all in their Sunday best. I think – yes, I'm right – that is Vittoria, a few years before I knew her, tall and willowy, with eyes full of expectation. And standing with them, his hands crossed in front of him, is Sal, a Sal almost exactly the same as the one I know, and the exact image of the man in the coma.

'That's him,' I say, tears springing into my eyes. 'That's Sal. He lives there, but he's also here. I don't understand how that works.'

'I don't understand how that works either,' Selena says. 'An astrophysicist friend of mine studies the universe, and once, just to pass the time, we compared the structures of the brain to the structures of the known universe and . . . well, they are remarkably similar, so much so that he went away to see if he could show that the universe itself might have consciousness. And if that's the case, then maybe we humans are its creations, made expressly so that it might understand itself – which could mean that how we exist is far more complicated than we are able to fathom.'

'What did your friend find out?' I ask her. 'Is the universe a thinking thing?'

'Well, that was just over a decade ago,' Selena says. 'He's barely started developing a thesis, really. These things take time. But ten years of human time is a blink of the eye in the span of the universe.'

It takes a moment for me to try to line up these big and complicated ideas in my head.

'So, let's say that the universe is just a great big conscious brain,' I ask slowly, 'does that make us figments of its imagination?'

'No, more like manifestations, I think,' Selena says. 'Look, I can't say that I understand what's happening – no one truly understands the nature of our existence, why, where or how we exist. All we can do is to try and try again. In a way, that's what we've been doing since the first human looked up at the night sky. It's always a guess. So, let's theorise, based on the very scant evidence we have, that we exist because the universe wants us to – maybe in more parallel realities than our poor human heads can get around. And if that is so, then having taken that huge, huge, frankly insane leap of reasoning, we could, *perhaps*, extrapolate to a place where the universe organises and reorganises molecules into vessels for our consciousness as often as it wants to. But sometimes, consciousness leaves, and the remnants are left behind. Mostly, this is what we think of as death, but sometimes, basic function remains; a sort of one-in-a-trillion glitch that might lead to a man being in a coma for thirty years and everything that you are experiencing.'

'And what *am* I experiencing?' I ask her.

'Some kind of miracle,' she says.

Chapter Fifty-Six

'It's meant to be closed at the moment,' Kathryn tells us as a security guard lets us into the building that stands above the Ħal Saflieni Hypogeum in Paola. 'They're conducting essential preservation checks, but I managed to get us in for a brief private tour.'

'It feels alive, somehow,' Selena says as Kathryn walks us into a purpose-built room full of incredible artefacts: a skull, an oil lamp, a small statue of a sleeping woman. It's as if it's charged and ready for . . . *something*. 'I'd love to wire the whole place up to understand its electromagnetism and the background sound and radiation levels.'

'I'm almost certain they won't let you do that,' Kathryn tells her. We'd told Kathryn everything we'd discovered on the way here. 'This is a precious place – a world heritage site. It's estimated that about seven thousand individuals were interred here over the period it was in use,' she goes on, in the melodic tone of an expert reciting facts to a bunch of laypeople. Even in the dim museum lighting, I can see her eyes sparkling and the delight in her smile. 'Now, there's a series of metal walkways and steps that we must not deviate from, and please refrain from touching the temple.' She turns to look at me as she says this, knowing that later I will need to understand exactly where to go as quickly as possible if I am to stand a chance of not getting caught. This is a reconnaissance mission.

She leads us through an air-tight door into the upper layer of the temple. It's hard to reconcile what I'm seeing now with the place Sal and I visited in the dead of night. It's been carefully lit and somehow seems tamed by its dedicated protectors into something less feral. Still, I can feel the charge in the air that Selena mentioned, and I hear a faint background hum waiting to rise.

'It's the way it's built that still amazes and confounds archaeologists,' Kathryn says. 'And no, I don't mean we think there's a secret lost civilisation of giants or that aliens did it. I mean that our distant ancestors were incredibly clever, resourceful and remarkable people, able to design shafts and manipulate light from the surface, so that it travelled throughout the complex. We can't know what was in the minds of the builders, but in some cultures, spirals – like the red ones painted on the walls here – are the symbols for eternal consciousness, representing our minds and souls unwinding forever into time and space, even after our physical bodies have turned to dust.'

Selena and I exchange a glance.

'In Christianity, a spiral represents the Holy Trinity,' Kathryn goes on. 'God in all forms, like the spiral of a galaxy or the curve of a shell. It is the form of all creation. The same image is seen time and time again in ancient cultures, across religions, made by peoples who evolved completely separately. But in each instance, it seems to mark the first spark of life, and we can track its path evolving outwards from its conception into infinity.'

'I'm not sure I like the idea of infinity.' I'm whispering for some reason, as if we might be overheard. 'The idea of being lost in nothing forever feels rather frightening.'

'Ah, but there is no nothing,' Selena tells me. 'Even that which seems empty is still full of miracles: gravity, dark matter, the unknowable fabric of our universe – there is no void, only mystery.'

Kathryn bows as she leads us into a long, rectangular chamber. 'But it's here, in the Holy of Holies, as some call this room, or the oracle chamber, that their ingenuity is truly breathtaking.' Her enthusiasm makes me smile, and seeing the temple lit so carefully here gives me an entirely new view of the dark and mysterious place I visited once before.

We step into the largest chamber we have entered so far. There is a rectangle in the centre, surrounded by curved walls forming an elongated oval. Long, beautifully hewn steps lead down to a central floor. The same design is repeated on the ceiling. You could turn the room upside down like an hourglass, and everything would look exactly the same. Even the long tunnels leading off into the dark match one another with fearful symmetry.

'The oracle chamber,' I say, feeling a sense of recognition in the air.

'Yes.' Kathryn nods. 'The room where you say you began your journey back to us from 1942. You sang your way home?'

'Well, it wasn't a direct route,' I tell her. 'It felt like leaving home, if I'm honest.'

'Oh, Maia,' Kathryn says. 'I don't know what's happening, but I do wish more than anything that I could find a way to make you feel that you have a home here.'

'You did,' I reply, taking her hand. 'You gave me an idea of what family could be like. That's why I recognised it when I found it in . . .' I look around. 'Another place. But there are people I have to say goodbye to here, and things I need to say.'

Kathryn nods. 'I thought there might be.'

Just at that moment, a security guard coughs politely in the tunnel outside the chamber.

'Apologies,' Kathryn calls. 'I'll bring them out now.' She turns back to us. 'The moisture in the air, even in your breath – all of it can be damaging to the integrity of the temple. That's why visitors are so strictly limited. We'd better go.'

The last to leave, I take one final look at the chamber before following the others out. There's a whole museum built over the site now, complete with state-of-the-art security. But somehow, with Kathryn's help, I'll need to find a way in here later tonight. This is the only way I can be almost certain of getting back to Stella in time to save her life.

Chapter Fifty-Seven

'Well.' Dr Selena Gresch and I stand in the hospital corridor outside my father's room, before Selena makes her rounds. 'I suppose I ought to wish you good luck, though I do wish you'd hang around and let me study you.'

'I know.' I smile. 'Well, if I'm still here tomorrow, you can, but then again, if I'm still here tomorrow, I doubt there is much worth studying about me.'

'True,' she replies, with a laugh. 'I wish you the best of luck, Maia. Wherever you are tomorrow, just know I will be thinking of and wondering about you for the rest of my life.'

'That you haven't had me locked up in an institution is something I will always be grateful for,' I tell her. 'Thank you for believing me, or at least pretending to.'

'Can we . . . ?'

'Please . . .'

We hug briefly, and Selena shakes my hand.

'Safe journey, Maia Borg.'

★ ★ ★

All my life, I've wanted my dad to greet me as if he loves me. Today, I am trying to find a way to do something I've done in a hundred ways over the years: to say goodbye. And I'm struggling to find the words.

'Vanessa?' I am a little surprised to find my dad's fourth wife sitting next to his bed, packing my father's things into a suitcase, but I'm relieved, too. Ness is a nice woman, kind and generous. She makes the room a kinder place, somehow: a place I can be brave enough to say the difficult things.

'I told her not to come,' Dad grumbles, more to himself than to me. 'I'm perfectly capable of looking after myself – I told her.'

'Hello, Maia.' Vanessa gets up in a cloud of floaty linen and gives me a kiss on each cheek. She smells of roses and lemon. 'I had such high hopes for your trip. I'm so sorry it went wrong.'

'I'm sorry I nearly killed your husband,' I say. 'Do you still get life-insurance payouts at his age?'

Vanessa chuckles and finishes the packing.

'So, you're leaving?' I say, looking at the case. 'They've given you the all-clear?'

'Not the all-clear exactly,' Vanessa says. 'It's more that your father insists on leaving.'

'I'm being discharged into my wife's care. We will fly home tomorrow,' he says.

'I'm going out to find something delicious for my dinner,' Vanessa tells us. 'I'll leave you two to it.'

'Will you bring me back something . . . edible?' Dad calls after her. 'Hospital food.'

'Are you still in pain?' I ask, when Vanessa has left.

'Well, at my age, that's a given,' he replies. 'Reminds you you're still alive.'

I take a deep breath. 'Look, for what it's worth, Dad – that you even suggested this trip, it does mean a lot to me.'

'It was Vanessa's idea,' Dad tells me, fixing me with his hooded eyes.

'I know!' I smile wanly. 'But you went along with it when you didn't have to, and that counts for something. You wanted to try. That means a lot.' I pause for a moment, trying to find exactly the right words for what I want to say. 'I used to think that it was your fault, our terrible relationship,' I tell him. 'And then for a long time, I felt like it had to be my fault, like I wasn't good enough or interesting enough . . .'

'Maia . . .' he begins.

'No, let me finish.' I sit down next to him, taking his hand. 'It's no one's fault. We are both victims of circumstances that were outside our control. We both lost our mums; we have both had to fend for ourselves. It made us into people who found it hard to connect. So, I just wanted to say: I'm sorry about the crash, and I forgive you for not being the ideal dad. I hope you can forgive me.'

'For what?' he asks.

'For anything and everything,' I say. 'And please know that I do love you. As best I can.'

Our eyes meet, and we hold that gaze for a long time, so long that his age melts away from his face and it's David I'm sitting opposite, his small hand that I hold in mine.

'Why do I feel like you're saying goodbye forever?' Dad asks me, puzzled.

'Because I am,' I confess. 'I'm leaving here, Dad, and I'm not planning on coming back. If things go the way I hope, you will probably never hear from me again.' I laugh wryly. 'But I do hope that you will have a life better than you could once have imagined. I really do.'

'Maia.' Dad leans towards me. 'You're not making any sense. You aren't planning to do anything stupid, are you?'

'No.' I shake my head. 'No, I'm just planning to travel, to find myself – you know, the sort of hippy journey of discovery that Mum would have loved to have gone on.'

'I did love your mother, you know, in my own way,' Dad says. 'When she died, I mourned her.'

'I know,' I say.

He doesn't need to say more, I can feel everything in the slight squeeze of his hand and the look in the depths of his starlit eyes.

'Goodbye, my girl,' he says.

'Goodbye, Dad,' I say.

I get up to leave when he catches my hand.

'Wait – I do have something for you,' Dad says.

'A parting gift?' I laugh. What could he give me now when he never remembers my birthday?

'In a way,' he says. 'A memory. It came to me in the night last night, as clear as if it happened just the day before and not eighty-three years ago.'

'What memory?' I ask.

'You wanted to know why I named you Maia,' Dad says. 'Well, last night I remembered. It came back to me in a Technicolor rush, clear as Saturday-morning cinema. I was very small during the war, you see – so vulnerable, afraid most of the time, and often lost. Lost in this huge, grown-up thing that had nothing to do with me but that I couldn't escape from.'

Drawing in a slow breath, I hold it and wait.

'But there was this girl, a woman about your age now. For some reason, this young woman noticed me and singled me out for kindness. She was brave; she was gentle. She was a shelter to that little boy.'

'She sounds pretty neat,' I say, my voice barely more than a whisper.

'Yes,' Dad says. 'Yes, and her name was Maia Borg.'

Chapter Fifty-Eight

'How are you?' Kathryn asks me.

She has brought me out to eat in a little place she knows where the tables are balanced precariously on the steep slopes of a street leading down to the harbour. Fairy lights criss-cross the narrow lane, and the air is full of the smell of good wine and the sound of easy chatter. I'm wearing a lilac tea dress that I hope won't stand out in 1942, and Kathryn has brought a tote bag with her, laden with objects heavy enough to pull the linen straps. But there's an air of tension around her. Something she is carrying lies heavily around her shoulders.

Sitting at this table in the warm evening, in the beautiful rebuilt city of Valletta, with more food than I can possibly eat before me feels like a forbidden luxury, and one I am ready to enjoy tonight. Modern Valletta is a place where I think I could be almost happy. But actual happiness is waiting for me in the rubble this city will rise from – a city I want to help rebuild.

'I don't really know,' I tell her. 'I just know I want to get back to where I need to be, so that I can stop Stella being killed. Imagine if I do, Kathryn – you'll have a grandmother that you grew up with, and Dad . . . Dad might be an altogether different person.'

'And what happens if he stays happily married to his first wife and never meets your mother, and you are never born? What happens to you in the past then?' Kathryn asks.

'It won't matter,' I tell her. 'I won't be in the past – not from my perspective, anyway. I'll be in the now.'

'Then tell me everything, please,' she says as the waiter fills our glasses. 'Tell me all about Danny and how you met him, and . . . just everything. Tell me your story, so that when you're gone, even if I don't remember it, it will still be in my heart.'

'Well,' I say with that particular smile that always accompanies talking about someone you love, 'it did begin with him saving my life . . .'

I'm not sure how much time passes as I tell Kathryn about Danny, Sal, Christina and Warby. When I tell her about Stella and the chubby baby that becomes her mother, she is thrilled. When I talk about Vittoria, her eyes fill with tears.

'You were there,' Kathryn tells me. 'I know you were there. And I hope you will be again, even if it breaks my heart. You deserve to feel at home.'

Kathryn's brow furrows. I can see her trying to find the words to voice her worries. I decide to buy her some time to think with some small talk.

'What's the bag for?'

Her face blanches; it seems like I've accidentally stumbled into big talk.

'What is it, Kathryn?' I ask her. 'What have you found out?' A realisation hits me: I think I understand why she seems so troubled. 'Oh, did you see the line, in a footnote somewhere, where it says someone with my name died on the day before the siege ended?' I'm not sure if it's the wine going to my head or a new kind of optimism that seems ingrained in me, but I feel remarkably blasé about reports of my death. 'Because you don't need to worry about that. I've got it worked out. Like I said, there is no past or future, only a series of nows. So, when I'm back there, nothing is written in stone . . .'

'I didn't read that, actually,' Kathryn says, her dark eyes shining with almost-tears.

Reaching across the table, I take her hands. 'Look, I *know* I can change things – I just know it.' I hear the almost manic tone in my voice, the desperate need to be right. 'It will be fine – I promise you. You have to believe me; it will be better than fine. It will be beautiful, because that's how I'm going to make it.' Of course I am trying to convince myself – I see that now. I have to if I'm going to have a chance of succeeding.

Kathryn nods. 'I believe that you can,' she says. 'I need you to believe that I believe in you. Do you?'

'I do,' I say. 'But tell me why you're so certain now.'

Kathryn reaches into the bag and takes out a small metal model of a Spitfire and a battered teddy bear.

'My mum gave me these,' Kathryn said. 'They were her and your dad's most precious things. She said that David flew that little Spitfire around constantly, pretending to be a pilot. But when he got sent to the UK after Stella was killed, he must have left it behind. And that's Mum's teddy. She has kept that safe for all these years.'

'You believe me because of these toys?' I pick up the Spitfire. Almost all its paint has gone. It's mostly just a dull grey now, but still the shape and spirit of the little aircraft, her sleek lines and inquisitive nose, are unmistakable.

'Yes, for two reasons,' Kathryn tells me.

'Go on?' I lean forwards, holding the aircraft close to my heart.

'That particular brand of toy Spitfire wasn't made until 1968,' Kathryn says. 'I looked it up. And see how that teddy has a label round his neck? Read it.'

I pick up the bear, turning over the dog-eared, parcel label. I have to hold it closer to the tealight that flickers in the centre of the table. The handwriting is faded by age, but I recognise it. It's mine. It reads: *Love from Maia.*

'But . . .' I look up at her. 'When did I get these?'

'I don't know,' Kathryn says, shaking her head. 'Maybe tonight, from me. But I do know that I want my mum and uncle to have these things, these things they loved that were made decades after they were small children.'

'I'll take them to them,' I promise.

Kathryn nods, her expression very grave. 'It must have been hard for your father, just a little boy, sent away from everything he knew to go to school. Even though she was raised by neighbours, at least Mum grew up feeling like she belonged. I'm sure everyone thought that was the best course of action. But I can see why it hurt him so much. Once, he had something; then, he had nothing but himself.'

'Yes.' I nod. 'I really hope I can stop him going through that. The little boy I know is so funny and kind. I want him to survive, too.'

'I know,' Kathryn says. 'And that's why I believe you. And why I know you're going to save our grandmother. But now I realise there's more you need to know.'

'Tell me everything.' I fill my glass with wine and empty it at once. Something tells me I am going to need more than one drink to face what's next.

'Our grandmother was killed on the evening of 14th August 1942, around 8 p.m.,' Kathryn begins, taking great care with the details she knows I want. 'You probably know about Operation Pedestal?'

'I'm afraid not,' I say. 'History was never my strong point.'

'The Allies repeatedly tried to get several convoys of supplies to Malta, from Gibraltar. Food, parts, most crucially fuel, but they were never successful. The ships were sunk or turned back. The Axis always seemed to know they were coming. But when the US entered the war, Churchill saw a chance. Bigger ships, more fire power. One final push to save Malta before she fell to the Nazis: Operation Pedestal. There was a terrible price to pay for those brave souls who were part of the convoy – many lives lost, many ships sunk. But two ships survived, just, limping towards Valletta with hulls full of fuel and food. They finally made it into the harbour on 15th August. It was a turning point in the war for Malta, and it took on even more significance because 15th August is a feast day here: Santa Marija.

'But the night before that, on 14th August, there was a fierce battle in the air. Axis air forces knew that time was running out to break Malta. Many were killed, and Stella was at Luqa, treating the wounded in a field hospital. A pilot was shot down right over the airbase. He crashed badly, his plane in flames, and it seemed like he couldn't get out – he was about to be burnt alive.

'Stella ran straight to him. She got there even before the ground crew could. He was unconscious. She hauled back the hood, dragged him out of the Spitfire with superhuman strength. Some say she knew him, that they were friends. But that's just people talking. Stella was the kind of woman to risk her life for others no matter who they were. That was just who she was – a true hero, you know?

'Anyway, she got him clear of the plane before the flames took hold, but the aircraft that shot him down came round again and mowed them both down with machine-gun fire. They both died. My mum and your father – they were there. Saw it all. Thank God Mum doesn't remember any of it.'

In my core, I know the answer to the question I am going to ask her next, because it answers my own question, too. 'Do you know the name of the pilot?' I ask.

'I do.' Kathryn lowers her eyes, thinking for a long moment before sliding a small, flat, rectangular object out of the bag. 'Quite a few of the pilots that were stationed here during the war kept diaries, and some of them have been published since. Not very widely – local presses mostly. So I thought I'd have a look around some bookshops today, while you were speaking to your father.' She hands me a slim, hardback book, its boards faded with age. 'Open it.'

'I turn to the first page. Under the title *Malta Spitfire* is a photograph of Danny Beauchamp. My Danny Beauchamp, clean and well-groomed, likely taken before he saw any service at all – but there he is, smiling back at me as if he can see me sitting here and he thinks I'm terribly foolish for falling in love with a man who died more than eighty years ago.

'Hello, you,' I say to his photograph, my eyes filling with tears.

When I turn the page, I see a sketch of a girl sitting on a beach, shy and hesitant. A drawing of me.

'It was Danny, my Danny, who Stella was trying to save.'

'Yes.' Kathryn nods. 'The way the history books record it now, they both die. And according to you, there's an account that you die that night, too.'

'That won't happen. I've seen Danny as an old man, so I know there's a version of the future where I succeed. It's not set in stone; there is only now. But I know it's possible. And if it's possible, I have to make it real. I have to go. I have to go *now*.' I stand up. 'There's no time to waste. Can you get me in?'

'I understand the urgency, I do.' Kathryn reaches for my hand, gently tugging it so that I sit down again, drawing concerned glances from our fellow diners as I do. 'But it's too early. I can get you in, but we have to wait for most of the staff to go home before we go back to the temple. At least another hour. And maybe this will be the last hour I will ever spend with my favourite cousin. So, please, let's eat, let's talk.'

Our lives are a series of nows, and it's so rare to know when one now is the very last of its kind. So as the clock ticks on towards midnight, I forget about everything else except Kathryn, my cousin and friend, who believes that anything is possible in Malta.

PART THREE

'I've dreamt in my life dreams that have stayed with me ever after, and changed my ideas: they've gone through and through me, like wine through water, and altered the colour of my mind.'

Wuthering Heights, Emily Brontë

PART THREE

Chapter Fifty-Nine

Getting back into the hypogeum is much easier than it probably should be. Kathryn has all the entry codes and knows the security team like old friends. It's a different shift from earlier, which is probably a good thing. They greet each other in Maltese, but still, I get the exchange of family news and standing jokes. She swiftly introduces me as her English cousin, waving her hand over me as if she is rather hoping they won't notice me at all. In a way, I already feel like I'm not here – that this is just an empty husk standing here, smiling and laughing as she makes jokes and small talk, and that the essential part of me is already far away.

'I'm just picking up some books I need for a lecture tomorrow,' Kathryn tells them with an authoritative air that doesn't invite scrutiny. 'I'll be ten minutes maximum!'

As Kathryn enters the security codes, I take my phone out of the tote bag that she gave me. I wasn't planning on taking luggage, but I hope I can take the toys through. Not my phone, of course – that is staying here. But there is just one last thing I need to look up.

I search for serious road-traffic accidents in Milan in 1992. There's not much – just a line in Italian in an archived newspaper article. Doing my best to commit it to memory, I close the app and turn off my phone, setting it down on the floor.

We are out of the reception building and into the first underground layer of the temple before I really understand what Kathryn is risking for me and my insane notions. If she gets caught smuggling her cousin into Malta's great treasure after hours, then her career could be in ruins. It makes no sense that she is doing this for me, and yet here we are.

'Maia, Maia,' she repeats my name, clicking her fingers until I focus on her face. 'You need to concentrate! It's not every day I break into an ancient monument.'

'Kathryn,' I say, 'we need to go back. This is crazy. I can't let you get into trouble for me.'

'I'm not doing this for you; you are doing it for me.' She smiles, tears shining in her dark eyes. 'I have loved these temples all my life, and I have longed to understand them – not just to make guesses or assumptions but to *know*. Don't you worry about me – I take after our grandmother; I will be fine. All I want you to do is prove me right.'

'I will,' I promise.

'Right, pay attention.' Kathryn is laser-focused. 'I can't go any further with you – you'll have to find your way on your own. I'm going back to the front desk now to tell them you wandered off when I wasn't looking, then we are going to search for you. Either we'll find you in about fifteen minutes or you will have vanished into thin air and we can create an urban myth about you, the woman who vanished into the past.' She grips my hands tightly in hers. 'I will miss you.'

'Kathryn,' I whisper, 'thank you. For everything. You took me to your heart about five seconds after we met. I will never forget that.'

'And you've given me an understanding of these temples and islands that I could have lived a lifetime without having,' Kathryn says. 'And this is going to sound weird, but I hope you make it, Maia. I hope I never see you again.'

We hug, briefly but tightly, and Kathryn hurries back to the front desk.

'Fifteen minutes,' she calls back.

The temple welcomes me into the folds of her belly, and together we begin to sing.

Chapter Sixty

Tuesday 11th August 1942, 6.30 a.m.

It's the golden light of an early dawn. Everything is still. The night sky still lingers over the lilac horizon. A pale moon sinks towards the sea.

The bag Kathryn gave me is still slung over my shoulder, the toys safely inside.

The streets are almost silent. I have stepped out of time into Floriana. I start for the half-house, knowing my way by heart by now, waiting for the city around me to pull itself from fevered sleep and face another day.

Then I see fishermen heading down towards the harbour, caps slouched low on their foreheads, shopkeepers keeping a resolute schedule, sweeping the paths in front of empty stores. I pass a poster for a Victory Kitchen and some women already starting work on cooking that day's communal meal.

I see a boy carrying a sheaf of precious single-sheet copies of the *Times of Malta* under his arm.

'May I look?' I ask him.

He hands me a sheet and waits. I read the date: *11th August*. The day after Sal sent me back. Four days until the siege is broken, one less than that until Danny and Stella are killed.

When I was about eight, Mum used to take me for midnight walks. She'd wake me up and tell me she wanted to show me the moon or the stars – or how the deer seemed to float above the mist on the hillside. It always seemed unfair to her, she'd told me when I was older, that little children never get to see the magic of the night when they are most receptive to its wonders. And it is true that I think I remember watching fairies dance in a woodland clearing. They were probably fireflies, or it was just my imagination, but now it is embedded in my mind as something real that happened: me and Mum leaning against the silvery trees, my hand enclosed in hers, as we watch the magical creatures flit and fly. It doesn't matter to me if it actually happened or not. All that matters is that it feels like it did. And that helped a lot after she died. She showed me all the magic she saw in the world, gave me faith in its power – and that was her greatest gift to me.

'Where are you off to at this hour?' A familiar voice stops me in my tracks.

'Hello, Christina,' I say with delight as I race to her side. 'I've missed you!'

'Darling, I haven't been anywhere.' Christina lights a cigarette, blowing smoke into the air as we begin to walk together towards her lodgings. 'Well, except at work. What a night it was. They are hitting us harder than ever now, don't you think? We're days from running out of food, fuel and ammo. God knows what then.'

'Did we lose many of our boys?' I ask her tentatively.

Christina searches my face for a moment. 'Danny Beauchamp is fine,' she tells me. 'And my Warby came home safe, thank God. But there will be a good few sweethearts waking up from dreams of beaus they don't know they've lost yet. God, I hate this bloody war.' She drops the end of her cigarette and stamps it out vigorously. She turns her face away. Her shoulders tremble.

'Me too,' I tell her, taking her hand and pulling her into a hug. 'It must be unbearable seeing those aircraft vanish from the map, especially when Adrian is in the air.'

'It is, rather.' Christina straightens her shoulders and lifts her chin. 'But it's the least I can bloody do, isn't it?'

'Actually, Christina,' I tell her, 'I think what you do goes above and beyond – you're a hero in this war.'

She smiles at me, tears shining in her eyes. 'Thank you, old girl. But don't be too nice to me. I shan't know myself.' She kisses me on the cheek. 'Now, I want you to do something for me.'

'Anything,' I promise her.

'Tell me to buck up and get on,' she says firmly. 'And come to my party.'

'You're having a party?' I ask.

'Yes, tonight. It's very short notice, I know, and of course it might seem in bad taste, fiddling as Rome burns . . . But Alex and I thought that after the losses we've had in the last few weeks, and poor Vittoria, we all needed a bit of a lift. So the Whizz Bangs are reforming for one night only. We've asked if we can hold a dance at the officers' club tonight, and the powers-that-be have said yes! You and the prof are both invited, of course! You will come, won't you? Danny will be there.'

'Danny and I are just friends, you know,' I lie badly, and she laughs.

'You might think that, but everyone else who has seen the way you look at each other knows better.'

'Well, I have nothing to wear, but I will come.'

'I can see that, darling.' Christina looks me up and down. 'You come to mine, say around 6 p.m., and we'll fix you up *somehow*.'

'All right,' I say, unable to keep back a smile. 'I'll be there.'

'Good,' Christina replies as we arrive at her front door and she heads back into her lodgings. 'It's been ages since we've had a good romance to gossip about round here. We are all living for you and Danny to get on with it.'

Danny.

It seems like years since he and I swam in the warm waters of Mellieħa, although here, it was only yesterday. In those few golden hours, there was more than one moment when it felt like something real and true was drawing us closer together – something so powerful that I would walk across universes to reach him.

Chapter Sixty-One

I am almost back at the half-house when I hear Stella's voice calling urgently from the end of the street. When she sees me, she leaves David standing with the pram and runs towards me.

'Come here – I need you!'

I run to meet her.

'You weren't at home,' she tells me, a little breathless. 'But you are here now – this is good. Come with me, this way. Hurry, hurry.'

Taking the handle of the pram, I trot after her, following her down one street and then another, until we come to a crossroads where dozens of people are gathered. Stella gestures at the remains of a hollowed-out house, damaged far worse than Sal's. Its splintered floorboards jut out into the air like broken bones. A heavy oak bed has paused mid-slide towards a gaping drop onto the rubble below. The house groans and trembles over its wounds.

'Hit in last night's raid,' Stella tells me, breathless. 'The boy and his mother stayed at home; I don't know why. Mother, dead. The boy, trapped. His leg must be amputated now if he is to have any chance to survive. We have to get him out before he is crushed, too.'

'And you need me?' I ask.

'You are calm; you are unafraid. I need you,' Stella tells me. 'You agree?'

I accept the job with a single nod.

The scene is alive with action. Maltese, civilians and soldiers, off-duty airmen, working together to clear as much rubble as they can away from the gutted building: a chain of people moving as one to try to help clear the way to rescue the child. The irony in contrasting this act of community with the meaningless violence that rains down from the sky is sharply painful.

'Stop!' I hear Danny's voice ring out, silencing the intense activity.

He stands on top of a pile of rubble, his cap on the back of his head, hands on his hips. Shorts, unlaced flight boots. His khaki shirtsleeves rolled up to his biceps. His head tilts as he listens intently to the sounds the house is making.

Now, all is quiet, and I can hear the soft sobs of a child. I feel a hand creep into mine and look down to see David at my side, his head leaning into my hip as he looks up at Danny, eyes wide with a kind of worship. Putting my arm around him, I hug him into my waist for a moment, kissing the top of his head.

'We gotta stop moving rubble.' Danny shakes his head. He doesn't have to shout to be heard; his voice rings around what's left of the tall buildings and narrow streets. 'We move anything else and we risk bringing the building down. That beam up there is currently supporting what's left of the roof, and it's only hanging on by a thread.'

There's a communal murmur that runs through the crowd as they look up. Each and every one of them has seen this scenario at least once before. The Maltese build their houses from the same rock the island is made of, and that has saved them from the horror of fire, but the threat of collapse is ever-present.

'Everyone, stay still and quiet.' He scrambles lightly down stones, and strides towards where Stella is waiting.

When he sees me, he pauses, catches his breath. In two steps, he's at my side.

'You're back.' He scoops me into his arms and holds me tight against him as I pull him close to me. Our embrace is only a few seconds long, but it charges me with courage. 'I had the strangest feeling that you'd gone clean off the face of this earth and that I might never see you again. I didn't like the thought of that, Maia.'

'I didn't go anywhere,' I tell him cautiously, but it's almost as if he knows.

'I missed you anyway.' He nods and takes a breath, then focuses in on Stella. 'Doc? What do you need?'

'Is the surgeon coming from Mtarfa?' Stella asks.

'We sent for him, ma'am,' Danny tells her. 'He will come if he can, but likely not in time. A few pilots injured in that last show have his attention right now. The ambulance is here, though.' He nods over to where a battered old van is waiting, filling the whole of the narrow street. 'Got the road cleared of obstructions, so it will be a quick journey out. And I told 'em to park it just out of sight. Didn't want to spook the kid.'

'Thank you, Flight Lieutenant,' Stella says. 'You have been a great help.' She turns her gaze to me. 'Maia, come. David, let go of her hand. You must stay with your sister. Stay back as far as you can – do you understand me?'

'Come with me, David.' It's Sal, pushing his way through the crowd. 'You are home, Maia,' he says quietly just to me when he reaches us. 'We have much to discuss. After.' Sal offers David his hand. 'You and the baby come with me. We can look after each other, no?'

Nodding silently, David goes to Sal, who takes the handle of the unwieldy pram, dragging it backwards, out of the crowds. Stella sends him a silent look of thanks. Now, all she has to think about is the job in hand.

'So,' she tells me and Danny, 'the bottom of his right leg looks as though it is completely crushed. The pressure of the stone is all that is stopping him from bleeding to death.' I glance over at the rubble where a woman crouches next to the boy, talking brightly in Maltese. 'He is in shock and at risk of organ failure, but he is young, and the young have an amazing capacity to recover. So, I must amputate. I am not a surgeon, but I know enough and will not take too long.' Her hands play out the procedure in the air, an unconscious rehearsal. 'The bone is already crushed, you see. I must only cut what muscles and tendons remain. Two or three minutes, I should think. I have a little chloroform, Maia, which you must administer to him. I cannot tell you how much. He is small, so you will give a little, and then more until he sleeps. Too much at once might kill him.'

'Right.' Fear knots in my stomach, but never hesitation. I know that I can do what she needs me to do, even though I don't know why.

'You were good with Vittoria. You calmed her. You have the right temperament for this situation, yes?'

'I can handle it,' I assure her.

She nods in acceptance. 'The boy is ten. His name is Raffa. He doesn't know yet that his mother has been killed, and he must not know until we are sure he will survive. So you will go to him, lie with him. Talk a little, administer the chloroform, small, small, small. And when you are certain he is ready, I will operate. Most important is to remove him from the site and to stop bleeding, so I will use a tourniquet which I hope will stem the bleeding.' She turns to Danny. 'Flight Lieutenant, you must have two strong, nimble men ready with a stretcher to run him over the stones and into the ambulance, waiting for my word.'

'Ma'am,' Danny says, 'there's an awful good chance you, Maia and the kid could all end up under that ton of limestone that's rocking back and forth up there. I don't want Maia to get trapped under that. Now, I ain't no doctor, but I am a big brother – How about I stay with the kid?'

'No.' Stella shakes her head. 'You are needed in the sky, Flight Lieutenant. You are too precious to risk here. You fight to save the many, not the one. Maia is a capable woman.'

'I can do it,' I tell him. 'I'm not afraid.'

'That's what scares me,' he says, his eyes locking with mine. 'Don't die, you hear me?'

'Enough of this talking.' Stella gestures between us, rolling her eyes. She hands me a small brown bottle and a folded muslin cloth. 'Maia, this is all I have. Please don't drop it. Remember . . .'

'I'll be careful,' I assure her. She holds my hands as she passes me the bottle, her eyes searching mine.

'You are a brave woman,' she says. 'I have faith in you.' She turns to Danny. 'Once we begin, all must be done quickly, smoothly. I will travel with you to the hospital, Flight Lieutenant.'

'Yes, ma'am.' Danny nods. 'We will be ready.'

'My tools have been sterilised. I'll fetch them, and then we begin.'

'Right, then.' I head into the ruin. Danny walks beside me.

Every step we take is observed by the pale, worried faces of dozens of people, my father amongst them. Danny's warm arm brushes against mine. My face turns to his. He takes my hand, gently turning me until we face one another.

'Maia, one thing.' Danny dips his forehead to rest against mine. Our eyes meet; there are only the two of us. 'You are gonna knock this out of the park,' he tells me, before letting me go. 'And I'll be waiting for you when you're done.'

Chapter Sixty-Two

Reaching Raffa is hard. I stumble and twist my ankle, banging my elbows on stone but managing to save the small glass bottle. So I crawl, flat on my belly, over the broken stones towards where the woman had stayed with him for as long as she was able.

A faint cry winds into the air, and I see the red of his mouth first. His teeth have been knocked out. One eye is completely closed and swollen. A small, thin hand reaches out towards me, fingers splayed. Something tears; my skin grates and bleeds, but at last I'm able to reach his hand. I hold it as I manoeuvre my body so that I am more or less lying alongside him. Looking up, I see the blue sky through slashes of broken timber that sway and groan under the weight of the slowly shifting stone.

'Hello there,' I say with a smile.

His face is sunken, skin grey. His eyes are wide with fear.

'I'm Maia. I've come to keep you company while they get you out of here.'

'Where's Mummy?' he asks. 'I was asleep. And now . . . what happened? Where is my mother, please, miss?'

'I'm not sure,' I say. 'But don't you worry, because you will be out of there soon and on your way to the hospital in an ambulance.'

'But I want Mummy,' he tells me, his slight voice trembling. 'Where is my mummy?'

Just behind his head, I see a pale, taut hand reaching out of the rubble – a mother reaching for her son.

'I don't know, darling,' I lie. 'When you are at hospital, everything will be sorted out.'

'I'm scared,' he tells me. 'And cold.'

'I know.' Wriggling closer to him, I ease my arm under his neck, holding him in a kind of embrace. I stay with him amongst the rubble, just as one day I will stay with a dying girl whom I cannot save. But perhaps, here and now, I can save this boy.

Raffa doesn't fight, but his whole body trembles.

'Honestly, I'm scared, too,' I tell him. 'But guess what? I was trapped in a collapsed building once, and it all turned out just fine. We are in this together, Raffa. You and me.'

'I wish my mummy was here,' he whispers.

'The doctor gave me this medicine to help you go to sleep and stop you feeling any pain. All you have to do is breathe it in. It will smell a bit funny, but pretty soon you will be asleep, and then they can get you off to the hospital. Is that all right?'

'Will you leave me when I'm asleep?' he asks. 'I don't want to be alone.'

'I won't leave you,' I promise him. 'I will stay with you until I know you are safely in the ambulance.'

'Will Mummy be at the hospital?'

'I don't know, darling. I'm sorry. I can't tell you.' I tell him lies in a calm, soothing voice. 'Now, we need to get you safe. Will you let me put this cloth up to your nose and mouth, and we'll take some deep breaths together?'

'Maia?' I hear Stella's voice from the other side of the rubble. 'Time is pressing.'

With some difficulty, I uncork the bottle one-handed and pour a little onto the pad. I have no idea if it's too much or too little, so I pour a little more.

'Ready to get out of here?' I ask.

He nods, and I hold the cloth in place. His gaze is fixed on mine. I press my lips to his temple.

'I'm right here with you,' I tell him. 'Let's count backwards from ten, nine, eight . . .'

His stiff body flops in my arms.

'Raffa? Raffa?'

He draws a deep breath.

'Now!' I call out to Stella on the other side of the rubble.

I keep my lips against his temple and my arm around him as she works, feeling the slight tugs at his little body. Then his complexion drains to white. I can smell hot blood in the air.

'Stretcher, now!' she shouts.

Then there are men lifting him out of the wreckage. I feel arms half-lift, half-drag me clear, too. I try to run, but somehow my legs won't work. Three men all but throw me onto the road as the roof falls in behind us, dust enveloping everything in a cloud of white. I inhale, lungs full of pulverised stone, looking frantically around for someone I know. A small figure rushes at me, arms flung around my neck: David, with Sal just behind him, pushing the pram.

'He's gone to hospital?' I ask, wiping at my watering eyes.

'Yes, the doctor is with him in the ambulance.' His eyes are bright with tears as he watches me rock David back and forth. 'You did well, Maia – you helped him.'

'I hope he makes it, poor kid,' I say.

'I am glad you are all right, Maia,' Sal says. 'May I embrace you?'

'You may.'

We hug one another tightly, David wriggling his way into the gap between us.

'So, we have much to discuss,' Sal says, in a lower voice. 'What did you learn?'

'A lot,' I tell him. 'But I can't tell you here. I'm just glad I'm home.'

'You said home,' Sal says, kissing me on each of my filthy cheeks.

'I've made a choice, Sal,' I tell him, 'and I think there's a way you can, too.'

Danny appears from nowhere and, taking my face in his hands, kisses me deeply, passionately. The battered, grief-stricken people around us gasp and smile.

'God, you are magnificent,' Danny tells me. 'I gotta go. But I'll see you tonight, won't I? At the party?'

'You'll see me tonight!' I tell him, watching him run to catch up with the truck that's already leaving for the airfield.

Chapter Sixty-Three

David puts his slight hand in mine as we walk back to the half-house; Sal pushes Eugenie in her pram.

Nicco's car is waiting outside. My hesrt sinks as I remember our meeting. Well, he'll just have to wait while we clean up.

I change into the makeshift skirt and shirt that Alex first altered for me and shove my dress into a bucket of water with the children's things. My bag is covered in dust, but still holds the precious cargo.

Sal starts boiling water, filling the tin bath that resides in the living room, since the bathroom upstairs has only two walls and no ceiling at all. For every pan of hot water he pours into it, he adds half a pan of cold. When there is enough, I help David and Eugenie into the bath, one taking either end. Sal washes out the clothes as best he can, silently noting the new dress I came back in with a raise of his eyebrows.

'These things take minutes to dry in this heat,' he tells me as he goes into the courtyard to find a place to lay them out in the sun.

I find an old bone-handled, silver rattle rolling around in the bottom of the pram, and I offer it to Eugenie. Her small hands grab at it eagerly with babbles of delight.

'Mama says it's too precious for her to play with,' David tells me.

'Oh, well, just a moment won't hurt,' I tell him.

Eugenie bows her head with the kind of concentration only an infant can give to an object they find fascinating. She dips it in and out of the water, listening to the clunk of the brass tag on the bottom of the bath, watching the drips as they run off the key and down her arms.

'Are you all right, David?'

The boy, who has been watching his sister with a faint smile, looks at me, puzzled. 'Y . . . yes?' he says, gesturing at himself as if that were evidence enough.

'I mean, how do you feel? On the inside.' I try again. 'Every day, you see a lot of extraordinary things. Some things must make you feel frightened and sad.'

David watches me. The frown set deep between his eyes is one I recognise. I've seen it constantly on my father's face. I see it often on mine.

'We must each do our part,' David tells me emphatically, repeating a phrase he must have heard a thousand times with more gravitas than any five-year-old should ever have to muster. 'Until Malta is free.'

'Yes,' I say. 'And your mummy does more than her fair share, helping whoever needs it. Your mummy is a hero, and so are you and everyone on the island.'

His frown lifts for a moment; his shoulders straighten.

'My mummy is very brave and clever,' David tells me. 'My daddy told us that every day. My daddy died a hero, too. I will see him again in heaven.'

'He did.' I nod. I'm not sure what I want him to say or what I expected when I asked him if he was all right. Perhaps for him to break down in my arms and sob his heart out, so that, somehow, I can heal all the pain inside him before it has a chance to form a scar. That's not what this little child needs, though. Not David, and not his sister. They need what moments of safety and normality the war-torn existence that has dominated their short lives can afford them – spaces to let their natural hope-filled resilience flourish, reassurance that this life they are being subjected to is not the only life there is.

'One day soon,' I tell David, 'all this will be over. There will be no more raids, and all the houses will be rebuilt, and there will be enough food. One day really soon. You just need to hang on a little longer.'

'Yes,' David agrees. 'A little longer. Mummy says one day soon, the ships will come and we will have food and enough planes to scare away the baddies for good.'

'Yes,' I say. 'One day soon.' I hesitate. 'David, can I tell you something? You might not remember it for very long, and you might think it's silly, but can I tell you something that might help you a long time from now when you are a grown-up?'

David nods, resting his chin on the edge of the bath as he listens.

'All the brilliant men and women that ever lived, the very cleverest people that have been, the ones we call geniuses?'

David nods.

'They have always chosen curiosity over destruction. *Always*. These names might not mean anything to you yet, but Da Vinci, Einstein, Caravaggio, Lovelace, Curie, Shakespeare, Brontë, Zammit – these are some of the few people who have lived who have been able to see our lives as humans on this planet existing in a huge and mysterious universe in a way that most of us can't. They understand how precious and rare life is, how spectacular and magical human beings can be. And when it came to it, choosing to build weapons or go to war, they chose art and knowledge instead. Do you understand what I'm saying?'

'Clever people are curious and kind.' David nods. 'Mummy is kind; Daddy was kind. I am kind to Eugenie. Mostly.'

'You are,' I tell him. 'You are clever and so talented. So remember this: no matter what the rest of the world is doing, even when you have no choice but to stand up and fight wars that you didn't start, you never have to let go of the things that make this world beautiful.'

'I can add and spell and read. And draw really well,' David tells me, ticking off his accomplishments finger by finger.

I smile, recognising that flash of my father's self-confidence in him. 'Right, let's get you out of the bath, and I have something to give you.'

'What is it?' he asks. 'Can I eat it?'

I dry David and Eugenie off with thin towels, then dress them in the clothes Sal has left folded on the table.

Reaching into my bag, I bring out the small metal Spitfire and hand it to David.

His eyes grow big and round, his mouth falling open in a large round 'O'. 'I can hold it?' he asks.

'You can keep it,' I tell him. 'It's yours forever now.'

'Maia!' He flings his arms around my neck and kisses me on the cheek. 'But is it stolen? Mummy won't let me have things that are stolen. She says she has to draw the line somewhere.'

'No,' I reassure him. 'Someone gave it to me, and now I'm giving it to you. And this is for your sister.'

Finding the small teddy bear, I hand it to the baby, who immediately stuffs its ears into her mouth. I return her rattle to the pram.

'Can I play outside?' David asks, excited.

'Don't go too far,' I tell him.

'I'll watch them,' Sal says from the doorway. He comes in and picks up Eugenie with a groan. The little girl takes his glasses off at once. 'You'd better clean up before you see the count. There's fresh water on the stove.'

'Thank you, Sal.'

'Maia, what are you doing?' Sal asks me, concerned. 'Are you trying to catch him in a lie or worse?'

'I don't know,' I tell him honestly. 'You know he runs the black market, don't you? And you still accepted his dinner invitation the other night?'

'I do know, and to my shame I chose to look away,' Sal says. 'A lot of very frightening people are afraid of him, Maia. He would be a dangerous man to anger.'

'I know that.' I nod. 'But I don't have a reason to make him angry. Not yet, anyway.'

'Then just take care,' Sal says. 'You have a very particular war to fight. Don't take your eyes off the battle.'

Chapter Sixty-Four

Nicco waits for me on his roof terrace, where he sits at a blue-painted wrought-iron table drinking strong coffee from an espresso cup. He is wearing a pair of round-rimmed dark glasses, and he gazes out across the island like a king surveying his kingdom. Heat hazes the island, making its golden hues shimmer and dance against the bright sky and sparkling sea.

Relaxed, leaning back in his chair, Nicco lights a cigarette with a gold lighter. He inhales deeply and blows smoke into the air. He does not have the air you might expect from a man dealing in national secrets, as I'm fairly sure he's doing, but then I have met people like him before, so immune to human emotion that they are almost another species. So often they are the leaders, the generals and the dictators, the psychopaths who see the rest of us as pieces in their personal game of chess.

'You are late,' he observes mildly, pouring me a cup of coffee.

From the rich, dark scent I imagine it came via the same channels as all of Elias's stock. To drink it feels like a betrayal, but I do – it's exactly what I need after this morning. My nervous system is still humming.

'Sorry I couldn't come early,' I say. 'One of the bombs crushed a house with a child inside. I helped get him out.'

Nicco takes off his shades and our eyes meet. His are dark and empty but intently focused. Any other person might ask about this event, enquire after the child at the very least. Nicco isn't interested in that kind of minutiae, though. It doesn't impact on his big picture.

'The suffering of the Maltese people in this conflict is unbearable to me,' he says. 'But it is necessary.'

'Is it?' I ask, careful not to show the flare of temper that flashes in my chest.

Nicco observes me for a moment longer before leaning forwards in his seat. 'Maia, the time has come for us to reveal ourselves,' he says. 'I'm no fool. The information you passed to me – it was accurate. Not useful, but verifiable. So, I had you investigated by my contacts, and we've been watching you.'

'Naturally,' I say, although the thought had not occurred to me at all.

'You arrive from nowhere; there is no record or trace of you on the island until last week, when you came to Elias for fake papers. There is no trace of you in England either.'

Do his sources really stretch that far, or is he testing me? The best response is none at all.

'Then you give me information that a man of my standing should immediately have you arrested for.'

'But you didn't,' I say, 'which tells me a lot about you.'

'You are fascinating,' he says.

I tilt my cup to him in a toast. 'As are you, Nicco.'

'Then you strike up a very fast romance with an American airman . . .'

'Canadian,' I tell him.

'Quite the day you spent at the beach,' Nicco says, licking his lips. 'My man was rather hot under the collar after witnessing that . . .'

All of my focus is on maintaining a neutral expression, forcing all gut reactions right to the pit of my belly with a fist of self-control. The moment to catch him out is almost here. All I do is listen.

'And then we observe you and the professor going into the old temple at night. Only the professor comes out.'

'So?' I ask.

'So, my men went down there, and there is nothing. No radio set, no secret bunker, not even tunnels that might lead off the island for a covert meeting. My man lost sight of you until this morning. Where did you go?'

Taking a long, slow sip of the delicious coffee, I think fast. 'Your men did not look well enough,' I tell him. 'I didn't leave the island. I could tell you where I went and who I was with, but all you need to know is that I learnt nothing of use.'

'There is only one subject that matters now, to all sides,' Nicco says.

'Yes.' I nod. 'When will the convoy cross Axis waters?'

'Do you know?' he asks. 'Has your pilot let slip any information into your honey trap?'

'I don't, and he has not.' I meet his eye. 'Do you know?'

'I will soon,' Nicco tells me. 'There is to be a party tonight. Your friend the plotter is throwing it. You will attend, I assume?'

I nod. 'I will.'

'A contact of mine will find you, they will greet you with the phrase, where there is life, there is hope. They will pass you the information. You will bring it to me.'

'Why can't your contact just give the information directly to you?'

'It is best for me not to been seen in public places with the person concerned – not in a room full of service personnel who might make unwanted connections. I have already regretfully declined the invitation.'

'And you will send the news to Sicily at once.' I phrase it as a statement rather than a question. I just need to hear him say who he really is with my own ears.

'There are many people in many places searching for this information,' he replies. 'My compatriots may find it faster and more accurately than I can deliver it. But yes, as soon as I have that intelligence, I will pass it to Sicily. The convoy *must* fail. The island must fall. The British must retreat to leave Italy to control the Mediterranean and, with it, entry to North Africa, and the continent beyond. With those positions secured, it's only a matter of time until the war is won and Malta is released from her servitude, back into the arms of her mother country, my beloved Italy.'

There is not one part of him that sees Malta as its own nation, free from any rule but its own.

'I will do my part,' I say, and that's not a lie. I will.

Nicco nods. He trusts me. 'I have one more question for you, Maia.'

'Ask it,' I say.

'Why? Why are you willing to act against your own nation?'

'I'm only half-British,' I tell him. 'But my heart – my heart is all Maltese.'

If he wasn't so blinded by his own ambition, he might understand exactly what that means. Instead, he believes that Malta can never be her own country, entirely independent. Like so many who have come before – the French, the English included – he wants to claim the island for his own nation.

'Oh, I have a favour to ask you,' I say, taking out of my pocket a piece of paper on which I have scribbled the last piece of information I took from the twenty-first century. 'Please could you translate this for me?'

Chapter Sixty-Five

Christina is approaching the half-house from the other direction just as I arrive.

'What luck,' she says, clapping her hands joyfully. 'I was hoping to find you at home. I need your help, dear heart, if you can spare it?'

'Of course I can,' I tell her with a laugh. 'I have some work to do for Miss Strickland that needs doing right away, but after that, count me in. But what do you need me to do – hang bunting or something?'

'Once you're dressed for the party later, meet me at my place. We have to take all manner of props, instruments and costumes to the club, and of course there's no petrol for transport, so I'm putting together a convoy on foot. Even Miss Strickland is pitching in! We need all the help we can get, there's so much still to do, and I'm rather afraid there are also three cases of Greek wine.'

'Why is Greek wine a bad thing?' I ask her.

'Because they were acquired by *somewhat* underhand methods,' Christina tells me, lowering her voice as she leans in closer. 'Not stolen, you understand. No, my Warby, he is ever the eccentric and always on the look-out for an adventure, as if flying reconnaissance in a war isn't exciting enough. He told Command that he had engine trouble and needed to make an emergency landing in Greece. Of course, he had no such thing – he simply wanted an excuse to stock up on wine and a few other delicacies. Honestly, I don't know what I see in him.'

'I think it's his dashing good looks, his incredible courage and his wine,' I chuckle.

'Darling, do not encourage him,' Christina tells me, breaking into an irrepressible smile. 'But I do so love how he can find joy in everything. It keeps one's spirits up so, don't you think?'

'It certainly does,' I say. 'You certainly do, my dear, brilliant Christina.'

'Oh, for God's sake, don't go on so,' Christina chides me. 'Now, the next time I see you, I expect you to look ravishing. Tonight's the night, after all!'

'I don't know what you're talking about,' I call after her. Nevertheless, the butterflies dance in my belly at the thought of seeing Danny again. The thought of finding a way to be alone with him is even more thrilling. That I have found myself in the middle of an exchange of secrets is less so, but I have half a plan forming in my head – one that I think I might just about be able to pull off.

But first, I need to talk to Sal, alone.

* * *

He is sitting on a chair with a series of half-opened books on the table. David and Eugenie are sleeping one each end of the sofa. In his hand, David clutches his Spitfire.

'Maia.' Sal's smile is a little sad.

I sit down at the table. 'We haven't had any time to talk since I got back,' I say, glancing at the children.

'They are exhausted,' he says. 'What happened with the count?'

'I can't tell you,' I say. 'But it will be OK, I promise.'

Sal sighs deeply. 'I worry for you, my dear. So, tell me everything you *can*.'

'Well, it's hard to know where to start,' I say. 'But I think it all ties together. You, me, quantum consciousness and the temples, and, yes, atonement . . .'

★ ★ ★

When I finish talking at last, Sal simply sits opposite me in silence.

'Are you OK?' I ask, tentatively.

'I am,' he says at length. 'You made it. You went through and you went back to exactly where you left . . . All these years I have been here, and I could have . . . sung my way back?' he asks me, aghast.

'Perhaps,' I acknowledge. 'We can never know, Sal. But you said you had been waiting for me. Maybe I had to arrive for this to happen. And it's not too late for you, if you don't want it to be.'

'What do you mean?' Sal asks me.

'Sal, you're still alive in 2025,' I tell him, reaching for his hand. 'You are in a . . . well, in a coma. Your family – your wife and son – take care of you in a private hospital. You have three grandchildren: two boys and a little girl. They visit you every day. They love you very much, Sal.'

Sal's eyes don't leave mine. I watch the expressions on his face cycle through joy, grief and despair.

'So many years,' he says. Taking his spectacles off, he sets them on the table, pinching the bridge of his nose. His eyes squeeze shut. 'So many lost years. My dear Elena, my son. His name?'

'Salvatore, of course,' I tell him. 'One of your grandsons, too.'

'Oh, Maia, Maia.' He drops his head, his shoulders wracked with sobs.

Getting up, I move towards him, putting my arms around him and holding him close as he weeps.

'My son – I have never seen his face,' he whispers. 'My dear wife. All those years she spent without me. I never found my way back to her. I never had a chance to decide. My fate was chosen for me. All those years alone, and she never forsook me. So much lost, Maia. So much lost.'

Minutes pass, the clock in the hallway ticks each second past with a heavy clank. David and Eugenie slumber on, the little girl pressing her teddy tighter to her chest.

'Sal,' I say carefully. 'Listen, I made a choice, and I am here now, in this time, in this universe. I don't think it's too late for you to make the same choice.'

Sal looks up at me, shaking his head. 'What do you mean?'

'I think you could go back to Elena and your family.'

'I can't,' he says. 'I am not worthy of them.'

'Look, you did a stupid, terrible, dangerous thing,' I say. 'But you were lucky, and the actions you took on the night of the crash . . . maybe they weren't honourable, and they were nothing to be proud of. But making that call for help made a difference.'

'How can I ever know that?' Sal asks, his mouth open slightly.

'Because I looked it up,' I tell him. 'It was the last thing I did in my old life.' I show him the piece of paper, and Nicco's translation:

Grazie a una chiamata anonima, i soccorsi sono arrivati rapidamente sulla scena e tutte le vittime si riprenderanno completamente

> *Thanks to an anonymous call, help arrived*
> *quickly on the scene and all victims will*
> *make a full recovery.*

Sal looks up at me. 'They were all right?'

'Yes – the driver and the children,' I say. 'Look, I don't know the man you were then, but I know the man you are now. And I know how much you miss your wife and the life you never had. Sal, you have atoned. You've seen so many through this war. If there is a chance to go back, and you want to take it, then you should.'

'You really think it is possible?'

'I think so, Sal. I think you could go home.'

Chapter Sixty-Six

Later that afternoon, Sal sits at the table while I wash my face and brush my hair, finally I slip into my lilac tea dress, straightening and smoothing it over my head. When I look in the small mirror over the mantel, I see a tanned face framed in brown curls. Not really glamorous, but it's the best I can do with what I've got.

Eugenie woke up a few minutes ago and is sitting on Sal's lap, playing energetically with his glasses. David sleeps on. I wonder where he goes in his dreams.

'Will you come to the dance after Stella fetches the children?' I ask.

'This evening is for the young,' Sal says, smoothing the curls from the baby's face. 'I have a lot to think about. And you – where did you go to this afternoon?'

'To see Miss Stickland about work,' I tell him, waving it away. 'Nothing to worry about. And what about you? Have you had time to decide if you want to try . . . ? You miss them so much, Sal.'

'And yet,' he says, 'so many years have passed. We'd be strangers.'

Sal smiles at me, wan.

'You're sad, Sal – why?' I ask him, taking a seat at the table.

'Time moves on,' he says. 'It is the only certain thing. Where we are in its flow, it will keep running and running until one day we are left behind – too far behind to catch up.'

'Whatever you . . .'

'I have decided,' he nods. 'I will try, I have to. Tomorrow I will try.'

'And I'll come with you as far as I can,' I promise him. The door opens, making us both jump.

'I am so sorry I was so long,' Stella says, interrupting us as she suddenly walks into the room. Taking the third seat at the table, she folds her arms on the surface and lays her cheek on them. Her face is a picture of near-starvation and exhaustion. The dust from the collapsed house still beads her dark hair. Her eyes close, and I think she dreams for a moment, before forcing herself into an upright position and holding her arms out to Eugenie, who clambers into them at once, pressing her cheek hard against her mother's.

'I must get the children home,' she says, collecting herself. 'David, wake up now, my son. Time to go.'

'Perhaps some coffee first?' Sal offers, and she nods gratefully.

'Did Raffa . . . ?' I can't bring myself to form the rest of the question.

'He will survive.' Stella nods. 'He has a hard road ahead, but he will live. I thank you – for helping with the boy and for taking care of my children. I thought you rather pointless when I first met you, but I see now your Maltese half is very present in you. You are strong and brave like . . .'

'You,' I say with a small smile. I can't resist the urge to put my arms around her and hug her shoulders. 'I would like to be just like you, Stella.'

'Well,' she says rather stiffly, as Sal sets a cup of coffee before her, 'I will drink this, then I will get the children home.'

'Stay here tonight,' Sal all but orders her, gesturing at David, who turns his back on us, pulling a cushion over his head. 'That boy is exhausted. We have been careful, and I have enough food to share. Stay, rest, eat – let the children sleep. I have little comfort to offer, but what there is is yours.'

'I couldn't impose . . .' Stella begins.

'You can.' I take her hand. 'You can accept a little help every now and again. It doesn't make you weak.'

Her eyes glaze with the threat of tears. Nodding, she blinks them away. 'Thank you,' she says quietly. 'You look very pretty, Maia. The dress is a little dowdy, but even so, you will dance with Danny tonight. You will kiss him under the stars, I think. Everyone is very excited.'

Even though I know she teasing me, in her own particular way, I am still shocked that even Stella, so focused, so matter-of-fact, has caught wind of what may or may not be happening between me and Danny. 'Everyone seems to know what I will be doing at this dance tonight apart from me!' I protest. 'But I suppose a kiss is not out of the question . . .'

'Pfft.' Stella exchanges a look and a smile with Sal. 'You go and forget about the war for an hour or two. Go and enjoy being in love. There is nowhere more beautiful to lose your heart forever to another than in Valletta.'

I know that already, of course. My heart has been lost to this place and its people from the moment I arrived.

Chapter Sixty-Seven

'Oh no, that won't do at all,' Christina says the moment she sets eyes on me. 'Alex, that won't do at all, will it?'

'No, that will not do,' Alex tells me. 'We are all pinning our hopes on you, Maia. You can't go to the dance looking like a charwoman. We have hopes and dreams and fantasies that we need you to live for us.'

'A charwoman?' I ask as Christina grabs me by the wrist and pulls me inside. 'This dress was hard to come by!'

Christina looks me up and down. 'What are we going to do with her?'

'I thought this was nice,' I say, pressing my hand against the viscose of my tea dress, trying to smooth out the creases.

'It *is* nice – for a funeral or tea at a maiden aunt's,' Christina says, wrinkling her nose. 'But not tonight, darling. Tonight is about glamour and romance. The gentlemen will be wearing dress uniform, and it's our job to scrub up sufficiently well to make them forget about the war for an hour or two. This is what I'm wearing after our show, see?'

She shows me a gown hanging on the back of a door – a sweeping scarlet affair, with a ruffle running bias-cut down the skirt and a corsage of silk flowers on the shoulder.

'Hopelessly out of date, of course,' Christina says, 'I should think it's ten years old at least, but it will do the job, do you see?'

'I do see,' I say, admiring the gown. 'It's absolutely lovely, but *I* don't have any beautiful gowns tucked away in my pocket.'

'And I don't have any that will fit you,' Christina says, woeful. 'This is dreadful. What shall we do, Alex?'

'Call the whole thing off,' Alex says as he presses his shirt. 'I cannot pretend to live in Daniel Beauchamp's arms if it must be done vicariously through a frumpy spinster.'

'Hey.' I clip him lightly round the head. 'I do have feelings, you know?'

'Sorry, darling.' He flashes me a smile, and I forgive him immediately. 'You know, she looks very sweet in that dress, really. Perhaps it will do. She could probably wear sackcloth; he is smitten, after all . . .'

'It will *not* do,' Christina insists. 'Never mind Danny – I have standards. Not to pile on the pressure, but we all need this particular romance to come to . . . er . . . *fruition* tonight, darling. I won't say that morale is resting on it, but . . .'

'A rather sizeable sweepstake is,' Alex tells me. 'I've got you and Danny sneaking off to bed at 10.43 p.m., if you don't mind keeping an eye on the clock.'

'This is awful – I'm not going,' I say. 'I'm not going to have my . . . whatever this is, being turned into a betting book.'

There is another knock at the door.

'I'll show them in on my way out,' I tell them, my cheeks blazing. Of course I have to go to the dance. There is more at stake than what I'm wearing, and if Danny and I die in the next few days . . . but they don't know that.

'Stella!' I blink, opening the door to my grandmother. 'I thought you were staying with Sal?'

'I was – I am – but I had a thought,' Stella says, rather shy. She is carrying a parcel wrapped in brown paper. 'So, I went home to collect this for you. Your dowdy dress simply will not do for your special night with Flight Lieutenant Beauchamp.'

'That's what I said,' Christina says, coming to the door.

My mouth drops open, then I close it again, speechless.

Stella presses the parcel into my arms. 'We have the same sort of figure, or we used to, before I got so thin,' Stella tells me. 'This dress – I wore it on the night that my husband and I became engaged. I have only worn it once, and here.' She hands me a pair of darkest green patent-leather court shoes with a diamanté buckle. 'I have long feet. I think you do, too.'

'Stella, I don't know what to say,' I say, accepting the parcel and shoes.

'You have been a good person to me – a help,' Stella says, 'and I will not be able to pay you with money, so.' She shrugs. 'You will look pretty in it, I think.'

'Well, come in while she tries it on,' Christina says. 'You have to see the product of your generosity. Take a seat here. Have a glass of Greek wine – we will be back in a moment.'

* * *

'Well.' Christina gasps as she unwraps the parcel, revealing a deep-green dress in exactly the same shade as the shoes. It's made from slippery satin, with a deep neckline and a black tulle overskirt. 'It almost looks as if it was made for you. Put it on.'

As it happens, I need a little help from Christina with the hooks and eyes, and then she examines my face, mercilessly plucking any stray brow and lip hairs she finds. She fetches an almost empty palette of eye shadow, with a few corners of powdered pigment remaining, and dabs a little shimmering emerald-green on my lids, before passing me a stub of orange-red lipstick.

'It's all you have,' I say, shaking my head. 'I couldn't possibly.'

'Yes, but it's a special night,' she tells me. 'A girl can't make love to a boy properly without lipstick.'

'Christina.' I turn to her. 'Are you crying?'

'It's just that you look so very lovely,' Christina says, dabbing at her eyes with the corner of a hanky. 'I'm absolutely furious about it.'

'That's not it, and you know it,' I tell her fondly. 'What's really wrong?'

'I just wish it could always be like this,' she says. 'Dances and gowns – and plenty of lipstick. I wish that a girl could happily fall in love and never have to worry about what will happen tomorrow, because there are no wars or dogfights or young men sent off to die every day. I wish you and Danny could have your night tonight and know you had your whole future ahead of you. I wish we all could.'

'Don't cry,' I say, touching my palm to her cheek. 'You'll give yourself a red nose and puffy eyes. Stiff upper lip, remember?'

'Quite right,' she says, straightening her shoulders. 'Though it is hard to bear knowing that I will be only the *second* most beautiful girl at the dance tonight.'

'Now that,' I tell her, 'really is ridiculous. No one can ever outshine you, Miss Ratcliffe. You are a star.'

* * *

I seem to be holding my breath as I head downstairs towards where Stella is waiting. When she looks up at me a slow smile spreads over her face, and I release a long sigh of relief. Stella stands to greet me at the foot of the stairs.

'You look . . .' She falters.

'Yes?'

'You look like me,' she says, with a little laugh of uncharacteristic delight. 'Like I did two children and a thousand years ago. My dear girl, you could be my sister.' She embraces me lightly, kissing me on either cheek. 'This is fitting,' she says approvingly, 'for a dance with the flight lieutenant.'

'It really is,' Christina says, coming down the stairs behind me. 'And now, you look far too pretty to carry anything. I'll just have to get more lads in.'

'I'll do that,' Alex offers. 'And you do look ravishing, Maia. You truly do.'

'Well.' Stella nods. 'I will go back to Sal. He is cooking for us. Have a wonderful evening.' She thinks for a moment. 'But don't drink too much, and don't get pregnant.'

'Copy that,' I say, saluting her as she leaves.

'Well.' Christina puts one arm around me and one around Alex. 'The hour is upon us at last.'

Chapter Sixty-Eight

'Well, now, aren't I the lucky chap, getting to walk in with the two most beautiful women in Malta?' Adrian Warburton, tall, fair and handsome, offers Christina and me an arm each. The rooms at the ERA club are already packed, and the Royal Engineers band is in full swing. The room smells of smoke and perfume, undercut with sweat and something else, perhaps the desire to throw caution to the winds and forget everything.

A cheer goes up at the sight of Christina, who is immediately co-opted by Alex and taken somewhere he refers to as 'backstage'.

'May I get you a glass of something?' Warby offers. 'Not a huge selection, but we do have some rather nice wine and quite a lot of terrible whisky that will put hairs on your chest.'

'I'll take the wine, please,' I say, and he leaves me standing by a pillar as he heads to the bar. Judging by the amount of times he is stopped, clapped on the back and congratulated for his latest act of daring on the way, I am not expecting refreshment any time soon.

Even in Stella's gorgeous gown, I instinctively feel like a wallflower – hardly surprising when I come from a place where couples dance near each other rather than together, and instead of swirling in elegant unison around the dance floor, we mostly just jig about. Leaning against the pillar, rather hoping that I am more or less invisible, I am content to take in the crowded room.

Everyone here has put on a show, as Christina would say. The women have dusted off long-packed-away gowns, painted stocking seams on their legs and found something to rouge their cheeks with. As for the men – oh, the men. Freshly shaved, uniforms pressed, they all look a million dollars. Yes, if you look very closely, you can see the shadows under their eyes, the hollows in their cheeks, the strain on their faces – on everyone's faces. Yet, for a few hours at least, maybe even a whole night, they have put away their cares and worries to dance.

As for myself, I have a secret rendezvous to wait for. I have no idea who will be approaching me, only that when they do, they will whisper one particular phrase, then we are to find a quiet place to talk. That could happen at any moment. I'm not sure what I'm more nervous about – my meeting with a spy or seeing Danny again.

Except that there's no sign of him. No matter how much I look, while trying my hardest not to look, Danny is nowhere to be seen, and all kinds of terrifying thoughts cross my mind. I am about to go and look for him when the Whizz Bangs appear on the makeshift stage and the crowd applauds wildly. Shrill whistles and shouts of delight almost raise the rafters.

'Back to thrill you for one night only,' Christina purrs into the microphone. 'The famous Whizz Bangs are here to whizz your bang and bang your whizz. Take it away, girls!'

Warby arrives at my shoulder and hands me a glass of warm wine. Christina, Alex and the rest of the concert party kick off their set with a spirited rendition of 'Don't Sit Under the Apple Tree'. The partygoers whoop with every twirl and high kick, catcall and howl with laughter at Alex's saucepan-lid bra.

'Lights up a room, doesn't she?' Warby says fondly as he watches Christina ham it up, a lopsided grin on his face. 'Never met a woman like her, never will again. Rather afraid she's got me for good, you know. Hope she won't mind. Mind you, I'll have to track the wife down and divorce her, last I heard she ran off with a Yank.'

'Just don't break Christina's heart,' I tell him. 'She deserves to be happy, and I get the distinct impression she'd be delighted never to see the back of you.'

'Not easy when your heart's set on a pilot,' Warby tells me, with a kind of paternal concern. 'Christina finds it rather trying sometimes.'

'Is that when you are off on secret missions to buy wine?' I smile.

'Ah, yes, well.' He smiles sheepishly. 'How is it that everyone knows about that particular covert operation?' He spots something out of the corner of his eye and digs me in the ribs with his elbow.

'Ouch,' I protest.

'Attention!' Warby tells me, as if he's issuing a command. 'Target acquired at nine o'clock.'

'I beg your pardon?' I ask him, bemused.

'Action approaching at speed.' He nods at the door, where Danny Beauchamp has just arrived, a different cap under his arm and turned out as sharp as a new pin.

I knew I was attracted to scruffy, unshaven, unkempt him, but now the sight of him makes me go a little bit weak at the knees.

'Will you take evasive action or attack?' says Warby.

My first instinct is to wave frantically at Danny, which I then decide is far too presumptuous and uncool, at exactly the moment he spots me in the crowd with my hand at half-mast.

His eyes widen a little, and he smiles, waving at me as if we're kids in a playground.

'He's coming over,' Warby observes. 'Christina has told me to make myself scarce and to give you this.' He presses a key into my hand

'What's it for?' I ask.

'Key to her place. She and I are lodging elsewhere tonight. Just in case you need a bit of privacy, you know.'

'Oh.' I look down at the key in my palm, my cheeks blazing scarlet, just as Danny reaches my side.

'Maia Borg, as I live and breathe,' he says. 'Damn, but you look beautiful.'

'You don't look so bad yourself,' I say, tucking the key inside my bag, not quite able to meet his gaze.

'I missed you,' Danny tells me.

I smile. 'I saw you not long ago.'

'Yes, and I've missed you since.' He lowers his mouth to my ear.

'I'm here,' I say finally, summoning the courage to look at him. 'This is where I am now.' We hold each other's gaze for a moment, and a smile plays on his lips.

'Will you dance with me?' he asks, offering me his hand.

'I really can't dance,' I tell him. 'No one ever taught me how.'

Christina steps into the spotlight and begins to sing solo, something called 'When the Lights Go On Again', full of sentiment and longing. Couples pair off, embracing as they walk onto the floor and dance close together. Heads rest on shoulders; eyes close; fingers link as the whole room seems to move in unison.

'All you have to do is let me hold you in my arms,' Danny says. 'I'll do the rest, I promise.'

'Well, on your toes be it,' I say.

Taking his hand, I let him lead me to the dance floor. I don't think I'm imagining the murmur that runs through the crowd as people spot us hand in hand – or the succession of heads that turn to follow our progress. Whispers are exchanged, alongside a few notes and coins. None of that matters the moment I am in Danny's embrace.

His hand rests on the small of my back; I feel the heat of him radiate through the thin satin. With a small, knotted smile, he takes one of my hands and places it on his shoulder; the other he holds in his, gently bringing my body flush against his. His eyes find mine.

'Trust me,' he murmurs. 'My ma made me take dance lessons after school for a full year.'

We begin to dance, if you can call it that. I guess this is a waltz or something, but whatever it is, it doesn't seem to matter, because it's as if Danny has magically transmitted the steps I need to take directly to my feet. Somehow, everything falls into place as he twirls me around the dance floor, and I wonder if there is another me in another universe lending me her dancing prowess for a minute or two.

Christina's voice soars and dips, each word laden with longing. The band swings the tune with a perfect sense of aching melancholy, and the more I dance, the more my body melds into Danny's. I luxuriate in discovering the lines of his torso and hips, the curve of his thighs, the landscape of his jaw-line. I feel him take in a deep breath and release a long sigh of longing. His lips graze the top of my head, and I allow my cheek to rest on his shoulder, where I can feel the rapid beat of his heart transmitted along his collarbone. He smells of soap and engine oil. His skin is warm and dry. There's a hollow just beneath his ear that I long to kiss.

When the song ends, it is all too soon, especially as the band transitions into something much more upbeat as the Whizz Bangs take their bows. The other dancers erupt into a frenetic whirling, twirling dance all around us.

Danny and I just stand there, perfectly still, not ready for the moment to be over, reluctant to let each other go. Eventually, we pull apart and make our way through the joyful dancers that fill the floor.

'Want some air?' Danny asks me, suddenly very serious and solemn.

'I do,' I say. 'But I can't yet . . .'

'Why?' he asks, puzzled.

'Danny, I need to tell—'

'Champ, old feller.' A pilot claps Danny on the back. 'How's your evening going?'

As Danny turns to him with a mixture of good humour and genuine annoyance, I feel a soft hand on my arm. Looking up, I see a young woman in a pretty gown, her soft blonde hair styled like a movie star. There's something familiar about her, and then I realise where I have seen her before: in the typing pool at HQ.

'Where there is life, there is hope, is there not, Miss Borg?' she asks me pertly with a lift of her chin.

My God, but she is young, her tightly laced nerves evident under her film-star make-up. Do I really want to deliver this child to the military police? The answer is that I don't, but it's too late now. The wheels have been set in motion. This afternoon, I went to see Mabel Strickland with everything I learnt about the count.

She had regarded me from across her desk for a long thoughtful moment. When she picked up the phone, and asked to be put through to HQ, I thought for a moment that it was me that was in trouble. But she spoke to the general and told him everything I had discovered.

'Very well, Maia,' she said, her expression very serious. 'The story is yours to write, after the count has been arrested. Agreed?'

'Agreed,' I nodded.

'And good work,' she said. 'Very good work indeed.'

It hardly felt real until this moment. Now the trap has been set, and this young girl will be the first casualty.

'That's what I always say,' I reply, using the phrase the count gave me. 'Follow me, please.'

'Maia?' Danny calls after me, as we make our way through the densely dancing crowd. I glance back, showing him my five fingers to signal I'll be five minutes, but as he looks round the room, he is noticing what my contact has not: several sets of eyes following our every move. Danny knows something is off, and he's not about to let me go quite so easily.

'Maia.' He catches my wrist, glancing at the girl, who flutters her lashes at him, and smiles sweetly. 'Where you two going?'

'Just to powder our noses,' I say with a fixed smile.

'Do you two know each other?' Danny notices the four or five men who are also leaving the room. 'Maia, what's going on?' he asks, catching my hand.

'Danny!' I laugh. 'Let me go – I'll be back in a minute.'

'Sure, but it's just that—'

Out of options, I grab him by the lapels of his uniform jacket and kiss him hard.

When I pull away, he looks a little stunned, but he doesn't move to stop me when I grab the girl's hand and pull her towards the doors out of the dance hall. Once we're in the hallway, I lead her to the back of the building, where I know there is a small empty kitchen.

Glancing up the stairs as we go, I see pairs of feet waiting in the dark at the top of the stairs. A door to our left is slightly open, and a shadow moves under it. Danny hasn't followed, thank God. I'm starting to wonder if I should have explained all this to him to start with.

Once we are in the kitchen, I pull the door to. 'I didn't expect to see you,' I say, playing for time. 'You work at HQ, don't you?'

'Yes, for now,' she says airily. 'Been an army baby all my life, dragged out here a few years back by my dad, and somehow got stuck here through all of this. I'd rather be anywhere but here. And I'm never going where my dad tells me to ever again. So I'm saving up, going to get myself a nice place when all this is over and stay there for as long as I want with whomever I want.' She crosses her arms like a petulant teenager, and I think she might actually be one.

'Who's your father?' I ask her, my heart sinking. 'Are you sure you want to go through with this?'

'What he doesn't know won't hurt him. Look, can we get this over with? I spent ages getting ready, and I want to dance with my boyfriend.'

She doesn't hear the footsteps on the stairs or the movement in the hallway. She has no idea that in the next few minutes, the future is about to be ripped from under her feet.

'Look, don't tell me anything,' I say. 'You don't have to.'

Her perfect, red-painted mouth falls open. 'I want my money! Anyway, it's not like what I'm going to tell you is going to change anything, not really. I never tell him anything *really* important. All I do is sell a little bit of information here and there, just things I pick up and overhear.

This time, he just wants to know some details about the relief convoy, and I happen to know what he's after – that's all. The Germans and Italians will know within a few hours anyway, so what difference does it make really?'

'Quite a lot, actually.' It's a military police officer who speaks, opening the door. 'I'm afraid you have made a terrible mistake, Miss Grayson, and I am going to have to take you for questioning.'

The small room is suddenly crammed full of military police crowding around the slight, foolish girl.

'What? What's going on?' The girl stares at me with wild eyes, trying to shove past the officers and into the hall. 'No, this is a mistake. I must go back. My Steven is waiting for me – I have to go back. I'll have you know that my father is your superior officer!'

'Not for very long, I shouldn't think,' one of the officers says. 'Thank you, Miss Borg, for alerting us to this situation.'

'This is just a game,' the girl says, catching at my hand. 'It's just a foolish game.'

'Listen to me, tell them everything you know. Everything, all right?' I look at the military police sergeant. 'She's just a child.'

'She's nineteen,' he tells me. 'There are men younger than her flying against the Nazis every day, miss. And if the other side knows exactly when to attack, they'll be fighting for their lives for longer and harder; more people will die. A few hours make a big difference in war. A few hours can be the difference between life and death. We'll need to debrief you, too, Miss Borg. Tomorrow.'

I nod. 'Of course.'

'But I didn't mean anything by it . . .' the girl cries.

Stepping aside, I turn my face away as the police bundle the girl out of the room and towards the back exit.

After a few seconds, Danny is standing next to me. 'What the hell was that?' he asks, and for the first time since we met, I can see only mistrust and uncertainty on his face.

'A long story?' I suggest tentatively. 'Maybe we could . . .'

'You a secret agent or something?' he asks.

I laugh, but when I see the look on his face, I realise that was the wrong call. 'No. I'm a journalist, that's all. I was investigating Count Nicco and . . .'

'Investigating?' He raises his eyes, his tone insinuating.

'Danny . . .' I step away from him.

'Am I an investigation, too? You seeing what secrets I'll spill?'

'What?' I stare at him. 'What's happening here?'

'What's happening is that I've been thinking about seeing you again every second of every day, and you . . . this whole time, you have been planning some kind of undercover operation I knew nothing about. I thought I knew you. I thought we knew each other. I have put all my cards on the table, Maia, but you've been keeping secrets from me. What else are you hiding? How can I trust you?'

There's a beat while I look at him, shaking my head. 'Danny, there are things I need to tell you – big things, actually. But this – this was my work. Because of it, Nicco is being taken into custody right now, and if the Axis find out details of the convoy, it won't be because of him. I stopped him. To protect you, to protect all the people I love, in the best way I know how. This is all because . . .' I stop, unable to articulate what I have to say. 'Because I needed to leave my mark here. Because one day, I will need someone to know that I was here.'

Danny turns away from me for a moment, covering his face with his hands. He takes a deep breath, and I see his shoulders relax.

'Maia,' he says, turning back to me, 'you are clever and brave and brilliant and . . . extremely surprising. And this . . . this came out of the blue, and I guess I thought you would be mooning around over dancing with me, the way I have been about you, and because I underestimated you, and I guess I'm a dumb chump who just wants to kiss you, if you can still stand to be kissed by this idiot.'

'Danny, the only thing you need to know,' I tell him, 'is that I have crossed universes to kiss you. And I always will.'

Chapter Sixty-Nine

'Come with me.' I think he's leading me back to the dance floor, but instead he takes me to the staircase.

'Oh?' I question.

'I'm not . . . I mean to say, I don't expect anything. I just want to be alone with you. Pretty moon tonight, and the stars are out. We can see the star you're named for.'

'Oh, I'm not named after a star after all,' I tell him. 'Turns out I'm named after me.'

'You are a strange one, Maia Borg,' Danny chuckles.

'Not strange, just nervous.'

'Well, that makes two of us.' He glances back at me with a rueful smile.

How can I tell this man something so unbelievable. I have no answer to that; I only know that I have to. I must honour him with the truth.

He leads me up one floor, then another, and finally up a narrow wooden staircase that is more like a ladder than anything. It leads onto the flat roof terrace of the building, which is surrounded by a wide stone wall. When he closes the door to the roof behind him, the muffled sounds of the party cease and are replaced with the hum of insects singing as they always have. There are a few metal chairs scattered across the surface, as if a conversation has been abruptly interrupted.

It's empty of any other revellers looking for a little privacy, and I'm glad. The perfect dark embraces us fondly as we stroll over to the edge of the building and look out over the city. The inky night is painted from a hundred different shades of deep, dark blue, each subtle gradient delineating a city in blackout. I can just about see the dark shapes of what remains of Valletta hiding beneath the starry sky. The water in the harbour cannot help but reflect the moonlight, and all is perfectly still.

Danny takes my hand and pulls me closer to him. We kiss then, long and languorous, easy and peaceful. The material of my gown rubs against the roughness of his uniform, and all I can think is how I want to search beneath his jacket and shirt, to touch and explore every contour and crevice of him, this beautiful creature that I've somehow found. How I want to luxuriate in his body, in his desire and mine, travelling endlessly together just like this.

My hunger for him intensifies, and, pushing onto my toes, I kiss him harder, almost desperate. My arms wind around his neck: his encircle my waist. Our kisses deepen with promises made. Long gorgeous minutes pass as I revel in the feel of his firm, lean body melded to me. I feel the race of his heart matching mine beat for beat and hear the low moan in my own throat.

We part for a moment, eyes dwelling on each other's faces in the dark.

'Maia.' Danny whispers my name, stroking a loose curl back from my forehead. 'Where did you come from, Maia Borg?'

'I fell through time,' I tell him. 'From more than eighty years in the future. One day, I was just suddenly here. And on that day, I met you and you saved my life.'

'You know, if you *are* a secret agent, you could just come up with a better cover.'

'I'm not a secret agent,' I say. 'And of course, that story sounds crazy, but it's true. And I want you to remember it, because one day it might matter that you believe me.'

'What do you mean, Stitches?' Danny has begun to lay light kisses on my neck. It takes effort to stop him and make him look at me.

'If we lose each other,' I tell him, 'if anything happens to part us . . .'

'Nothing will,' he assures me. 'I won't let it.'

'But if it does, I want you to know that it isn't the end of us. No matter what it looks like, no matter what you think. Just remember that I will find you. Wherever, whenever you are, I will find you. Swear to remember that.'

'I swear.' He smiles. 'I don't understand fully what you are talking about, but I don't think I need to either. I know, in the here and now, that I love you and I trust you enough to leave it at that. But I do swear to you that I will do everything in my power to make sure you stay my guiding light. Wherever you shine in that great sky, that's where I'm heading.'

'Then stay alive for me,' I tell him. 'No matter what occurs, stay alive, Danny. Stay alive.'

Our lips meet again, hungry. Our bodies lean into one another. My breasts press hard against his chest; my arms wind tight around his neck. I want him, all of him, in and around me. I want to be lost in his body.

Danny breaks away. Tipping his head back, he takes in a deep breath. He whispers my name, leaning his forehead against mine. 'Kissing you is like flying into fire. I think I might burn up, and I don't really care if I do.'

'Why did you stop? Don't stop,' I whisper.

'Because of where we are heading . . .' he begins.

'Take me there.'

'I want to treat you right,' he says, breathless, as my hand fumbles with the buckle of his belt.

'I want you,' I whisper. 'Now.'

His eyes widen. 'Here?'

'Here.'

He surrenders to me then. Lifting me onto the wall, his hands find their way inside the bodice of my dress, revealing my breasts to his lips. He groans as he buries his face in me; I tangle my fingers through his hair, leaning back into the night without any fear. I know he will never let me go.

Then I feel his palms slide up and under my skirt. Tulle rustles and silk glides up my thighs as I pull urgently at the waist of his trousers. For one moment more, we look at each other, our gazes full of wonder and discovery. This is what it's meant to be like.

Encircling him with my legs, I pull him hard into me, and our eyes meet, wide with delight.

It's fast and hectic. Every touch and kiss is filled with excruciating pleasure that brings swift hits of delight, one after the other. Danny takes hold of the hair at the nape of my neck, kissing me hard as he comes. I feel him shudder against me.

We fold into one another. Holding hard against the next moment, minute and hour, all we ever want is now. His light kisses cover my face, neck and shoulders. My fingers take flight up and down the planes of his back.

Then a thought occurs to me and a giggle bubbles upwards.

'Don't laugh at the man who has just made love to you,' Danny says with a grin. 'Might give him a complex.'

Stepping back, he starts to redress himself, and I pour myself back into the gown I've spilt out of in so many delightful places.

When he's decent, Danny sits next to me, taking my hand.

'What's so funny?' he asks.

'It's just that this is the dress my grandmother got engaged in. I feel very naughty.'

Danny laughs, catching hold of me and kissing me again. He doesn't question where I might have got my grandmother's dress from, although I'm sure he understands it's a long story.

'What would she say if she knew?' he says instead.

'I don't know, honestly,' I tell him. 'I don't think she would mind too much.'

'Maia, I need you to know,' he says, suddenly serious, 'I intend to marry you first chance I get.'

'That would be lovely,' I say, simply. It doesn't feel like I need to say any more – he already knows exactly how I feel.

His words are delivered lightly and full of sweet sincerity. I never want to let him go. Before, in that other world, I never once believed that there was anyone, anywhere meant just for me. But now, I know it's Danny, and to imagine life without him, even for a second, tears me apart.

Because I know that if I don't find a way to prevent it, the love of my life will be taken from me, alongside my grandmother, and so much love will never be given or felt.

Gripped by sudden terror, I fling myself into his arms and burst into uncontrollable tears.

'Hey, now, hey,' Danny says. 'Don't carry on so. What is it? Do you have regrets?'

'No, no, no,' I say, kissing his face in between each word. 'I'm just afraid, Danny.'

'Me too,' he nods. 'Never wanted to live so much as I do now.'

The door to the roof opens and another couple appears in silhouette, accompanied by a burst of applause and cheering as the band strikes up another tune.

'Want to go back and dance some more?' Danny asks, glancing at the other couple living out their own love story in another shadowy corner. 'Forget about all this until dawn?'

'We *could*, or . . . Christina gave me the key to her flat,' I say. 'She said it was ours for tonight if we want it.'

'Oh, we want it,' Danny says. 'We want it more than anything in this world. Let's get outta here.'

Slipping off my shoes, I follow him, and we run as quickly and as quietly as we can. Danny stops me on one side of the entrance to the dance floor, takes a peek inside and then races to the front door, beckoning me after him. We escape onto the silvery streets in a burst of laughter, twirling and tumbling in one another's arms as we revel in our victory.

Then the weight of the hour settles on our shoulders, and we become quiet and serious, feeling the time we have together slip away, no matter how we want it to stand still.

Walking hand in hand, we head to Floriana without speaking another word, not even when we let ourselves into Christina's flat and fall into bed.

No words are needed now. Everything we have to say has already been spoken.

Chapter Seventy

Wednesday 12th August 1942, 10 a.m.

That night and the following morning pass with a surreal air, almost as if I am dreaming.

Colours are heightened, and I feel as if I have lost a layer of myself somewhere, slipped off along with my gown last night, as Danny's hands and mouth soared across the plains and valley of my body, as I felt every touch and emotion with new intensity. Entwining my fingers in his hair and encouraging his kisses to travel further up my thighs, an idea he seemed only too happy to explore.

Parting is almost impossible. Our limbs seem determined to remain entangled, our fingers holding on to one another, forcing us to say goodbye again and again. But Danny can't be late on base, and I have my own meeting to attend. Still, I cannot bear to let him go.

'I won't see you until tomorrow,' I say.

'I've always hated this war,' he replies. 'But never so much as now when it's keeping me from you.'

We kiss again in the street, only stopping when a gaggle of children start to point, giggling and making smooching noises.

At last, we break apart, giving each other one last look, until Danny turns on his heels and jogs off in one direction.

Chasing the delighted children away with a sudden lion's roar, I head in the other.

★ ★ ★

Mabel is waiting for me, sitting primly on one of the chairs outside the general's office.

'I didn't know you were going to be here,' I say.

'I thought you might like a little company,' Mabel tells me, patting the chair beside her. 'Our friend the count is in custody. Things will likely be very serious for him. Of course, they should have taken him in months ago, just for the racketeering, but he was always so careful to stay out of sight. One ring would be broken down, then another would take its place. I can't imagine he learnt anything of earth-shattering importance from Miss Grayson, but it doesn't have to be earth-shattering, does it, for it to be treason?' She sighs. 'It's her I feel sorry for. Silly, foolish, feckless girl.'

'They won't . . .' I can't bring myself to finish the sentence.

'Hang her? No, I shouldn't think so, but she will serve a long time in prison. The best years of her life. It's all rather heartbreaking.'

The general's office door opens. 'Ladies?'

★ ★ ★

After a brief debrief with the general, he seems happy to let me go, and I spend the afternoon at the *Times* office, drafting my article, listening to the radio and waiting for the familiar warning of raids, but none come. The air outside is eerily quiet and still, like the close sultry hours before a storm.

'They're getting ready,' Mabel says as the afternoon draws to a close. 'When it comes, it will be ferocious.'

I file my copy with a feeling that, finally, I am back where I belong.

Stella and the children are still at the half-house when I get back from the *Times* that evening. We all put our rations together and share them in a meal. Sal and Stella want every detail of what happened at the dance. David is delighted when Sal tells him I was a secret agent, and after dinner, he takes some old brown paper and a pencil stub and draws a comic in which I star. Eventually, Stella takes the children home to their beds, and Sal and I get ready to say goodbye.

'If this evening is my last here, then I'm grateful for my years here for all it cost me,' Sal tells me. 'I haven't had my wife or my child with me these last thirty years, but I have had true friends and a family I love.'

★ ★ ★

The night is quiet and dark, the streets empty and silent. We make our way down into the first and oldest level of the temple, just as we did before. This time, I find and light the lamp easily, and we climb down until we reach the oracle chamber. Lifting the lamp, I look up at the red-painted spirals on the stone ceilings and walls, not turning now, but still and serene. The temple is sleeping, dreaming of us.

'I didn't go right back where I was supposed to be,' I tell Sal. 'Be prepared for that. You told me you thought you were here to atone, and maybe you were right. It's been a long time since you travelled, Sal, so be ready. Anything might be waiting for you. You might make more than one stop before you get off where you want to be, and when you do, you need to hold on.'

'I'm not sure this will work,' Sal says. 'I am afraid, Maia – afraid that it won't work, and afraid that it will.'

'This is what you want, isn't it?' I ask him. 'To rejoin Elena and your son?'

'I think it is,' Sal says cautiously, his tone hushed, 'but is it what Elena wants? I can't ask her, can I? What if I'm forcing something on her that she has learnt to live without? More than that – learnt to be happy without.'

'No,' I say. 'It's a risk. It's harder to go forwards than it is to go back.'

'But if there's a chance' – Sal turns into the chamber – 'then it must be taken.'

'You know what to do,' I say. 'I'll wait until you are gone.'

We embrace for a long moment. When he touches his hand to my cheek, he feels my tears.

'I will miss you,' I tell him when I finally let him go. 'You are the closest thing to a father I have ever had.'

'And I will miss you, Maia, my friend and compatriot in the strange lands we have found ourselves in, my daughter of the heart. You showed me the way when I couldn't find it myself.'

And then, because goodbye still doesn't feel like enough, we shake hands, smiling and crying all at once.

Picking up the lantern, I step back to the edge of the chamber and blow it out. The absence of light is immediate and complete, at least until my eyes adjust and I can pick out details in the scant moonlight that filters through from above.

Sal is self-conscious and uncertain at first. His song begins with a hymn, but gradually I hear it peel away from what is familiar and safe and spiral into the sound of his heart and soul. Slowly, the stone under my feet begins to vibrate and seems to glimmer and glow.

The darkness around Sal intensifies as his song does. His voice multiplies a thousand times, echoing and reverberating into a symphony of hope. The sound builds, becoming so loud I can't believe the people in their houses can't hear it or feel the shaking of the ground, and then . . .

He is gone.

The temple is silent and still, and Sal is gone. No sleeping remnant of him lies crumpled on the ground; no trace of him at all. Wherever he has gone, he has gone entirely.

Relighting the lamp, I walk over to where he was. There is no sign of him and no way he could have exited the chamber without me seeing him – at least, no conventional way. It seems foolish that having made this journey myself, I am finding what I just saw – or rather didn't see – hard to believe. In truth, I'd hoped to see an opening portal or moments of time encapsulated like raindrops cascading down.

But all there was was the song and then silence.

Perhaps that's all there ever is.

Chapter Seventy-One

Thursday 13ᵗʰ August 1942, 6 a.m.

The journey back to the half-house without Sal is long and weary. My sore feet guide me to the broken place that has become my home, but it feels like less of one without Sal. I long to lay my head on the sofa, close my eyes and visit oblivion.

I have slept since I returned to 1942, but I haven't dreamt once. I feel as if I never will again – that I used up all my dreams to get here, and now my sleep will be as untroubled and quiet as the light years between stars.

When I reach the house again, it is morning, and Danny is sitting on the doorstep. He looks up when he sees me coming and opens his arms. I run to him and fall into his lap. He pulls me tight against him, burying his face in me.

'What happened?' I ask. When I look at his face, I see grey exhaustion under his tanned skin. 'Come inside.' Getting up, I pull him to his feet. He doesn't speak, just lets me lead him inside, where he collapses onto the sofa.

When he looks up at me, I see so much sorrow in his eyes I can hardly bear it.

'What happened?' I ask him again. 'There were no raids last night.'

'No raids,' he says. 'But the recon boys were up. And they ain't come back.'

'Warby?' I whisper, thinking of Christina.

'Yeah,' he nods, dropping his chin. 'They sent me out to tell Christina, but damned if I know how to.'

'It will be another one of his pranks,' I say. 'He's probably gone to Gibraltar for an adventure. You know how bored he gets.'

'Maybe,' Danny replies, pulling me against him.

'So, what do you think?'

'I think he went dark over Italy, and that's not good,' Danny says. 'I don't want to be right; I never want to be right when it comes to this. But sometimes you can feel it, you know? Like a light has gone out.'

'Oh, God – Christina.' I never thought to look for their names, to see if they made it. If I had, then maybe I could have done something. Could I still? All these millions of lives lost in this war, and I am only trying to save three, including my own. Guilt washes over me, and I turn my face into Danny's neck.

'Save your tears,' Danny tells me gently. 'Christina will need her friends to carry her through.'

'I should have done something,' I mutter half to myself.

'What could you have done?' Danny asks me.

'I don't know,' I say.

'One thing I've learnt is that you can't fight this war planning to save the whole world,' Danny says. 'Not even one corner of it or all your friends and comrades-in-arms. There ain't no one person in the whole world who can do that. You fight for your life and the lives of the people you love, and you fight knowing that you might not make it. You don't have to accept it. You don't have to believe it. But you do have to know it. Adrian Warburton knew it better than most. That man took risks that few would have the courage to. He rolled the dice; he hoped he'd always win. He always knew he might not.'

'So many,' I say. 'So many lives gone, and for what?'

'For the future,' Danny says. 'We gotta believe that tomorrow will be better because of us. Will you come with me to tell her?'

I nod. 'Yes.'

Closing my eyes, I hold him close for a few moments. I know the peace that Danny longs for hardly holds at all, that the world still tears itself apart in the name of causes he can't even imagine yet. But he needs to believe that his friends are dying because future generations are worth the sacrifice. I need to believe that, too, more than anything. I need to believe that we can be good enough for them.

We walk a little apart from each other to Christina's house; we wait at her door while we hear shouting and laughter inside.

Finally, Christina flings open the door, smiling.

The moment she sees our faces, she knows.

Chapter Seventy-Two

Christina insists we go to the medical room after Danny returns to base. She says it would be better to keep to her routine, and today is the day she volunteers. After all, she says, he's only missing. He's been missing before, and he's always turned up. Once we are there, I telephone Mabel, who tells me to stay with her. My article is going to print in today's edition.

Now we sit in the waiting room silently, side by side rolling clean bandages. David is drawing, Eugenie plays with a rattle in her pram.

'I mean, after all, he's only missing,' Christina says again, as if we are mid-conversation. 'He's been missing before and turned up with a story of some ridiculous adventure.' She forces a smile. 'I'm sure he'll be back with some Cuban cigars or treasure from Tutankhamun's tomb. You know what he's like. So I shan't cry or mourn him. Not until they have his body. Of that I am quite determined.'

'What can I do to help?' I ask.

'Oh, you know me, dear,' Christina says, a tremble in her voice. 'I'm a tough old boot. He'll turn up like a bad penny.' She grasps my hand. 'He will, won't he, Maia? Tell me he will.'

'If anyone can, it's Warby,' I tell her.

'I didn't mean to fall in love with him, you know,' Christina says, standing up abruptly. 'Of course, he is terribly handsome, like a Greek god. But so damned annoying.

So very arrogant and foolhardy. And married! Even if she did leave him after a year. Don't fall in love with that one, I told myself. He will drive you to distraction.'

Helplessly, I watch as she paces back and forth, wringing her hands.

'But the trouble is: he makes me laugh so much, Maia. We just get along so terribly well. It was impossible in the end not to lose my heart to him. Oh, I knew we'd never have a conventional life, marriage and children. I didn't expect that our affair would last after the end of the war. But . . . I do love him. I do love him so terribly much. If he doesn't come home, it really will be quite a blow.'

All at once her knees give way, and Christina crumples to the floor. Rushing to her side, I put my arms under hers and, half-lifting her, guide her back to a chair. David looks up from his drawing for a moment before bending his gaze back to the paper. It's a plane crashing into the sea.

'I'm so sorry, Christina,' I say. 'It's unbearable.'

'He's dead, isn't he?' Christina asks, clutching at my forearms. 'Just tell me he's dead, Maia, and then I can start to believe it. It's the hope that will end me.'

'I don't know,' I tell her. 'No one knows. Not yet.'

'He's dead.' Christina nods, pressing her palm to her breast. 'I feel it – I feel it here. Like a connection has been severed. He's lost to me, Maia. He's gone. We've lost him, all of us. Oh, I know only I loved him, but he was so good at what he did, Maia. He was the bravest and the best. And I suppose that's why he's dead, don't you think?'

The consulting-room door opens, and Stella emerges, guiding a limping woman by the arm.

'Wash it in boiled salt-water three times a day,' Stella tells the woman. 'You must keep it clean – it is imperative.'

The woman glances at Christina's tear-stained face, and lowering her eyes, she leaves.

'Christina, you should go home,' Stella tells her kindly.

'If I were home, all I would do is stare at the wall and scream,' Christina says. 'I *must* keep busy. Let me help here today, and then I have a shift at Lascaris tonight. I need to keep busy. It's the only thing keeping me on my feet.'

Stella frowns. Crossing to the door of the medical room, she bolts it shut.

Then she sits on the other side of Christina, reaching for her hand. 'When my husband was killed, I was unprepared,' Stella says. 'We never really thought the war would touch us here or that, if it did, it wouldn't last. When they came to my door and told me he had been killed in one of the first raids, I simply could not believe it.'

David stops drawing. Climbing to his feet, he crosses to his mother, placing his hands on her knees.

Stella smiles at him, cupping his cheek in her palm. 'The best advice I can give you, Christina, is to let yourself grieve. It hurts so very much, but the sooner you start, the sooner you will be able to . . .' Stella pauses. '. . . to remember him without quite so much pain.'

'I miss Daddy, too,' David says. 'I miss playing horses. He would let me ride his neck.'

'He would.' Stella smiles. 'He was very proud of you.'

'That's the thing, isn't it?' Christina says. 'If I were the only woman to lose the man she loves in this war then I could feel sorry for myself, wring my hands and beat my head against the floor. But I am just one – one of millions. What does my heart matter in the midst of all this?'

'It matters,' I tell her. 'Every heart matters. That's the point. If we don't acknowledge that every life, every heart, is just as important as all the others, if we start to see people as numbers too vast to imagine, then we've lost. Every heart matters, Christina. Every loss must be felt.'

'I suppose you are right,' Christina says, burying her face in her hands. 'I just don't know what to do, how to go from one moment to the next.'

'Stay here,' Stella tells her. 'Go and catalogue what supplies we have left. Write an inventory and pack my medical bag. The skies are too quiet – I don't like it.'

'Thank you,' Christina says, flinging her arms around Stella and holding her tight. 'Thank you, Stella. I'll start right away.'

'I can help,' David says. 'I can read.'

'Yes, you come and help me.' Christina offers him her hand. 'And while we work, you can tell me everything you remember about your daddy. How does that sound?'

'OK!' David hops to pick up the model plane from the floor and runs after Christina, who is unlocking the medical room door and heading down the corridor.

'You saw your flight lieutenant?' Stella asks me. Taking my chin between her finger and thumb, she tilts my face left to right. 'You did. I see he didn't shave today.' She smiles. 'You are happy, Maia,' she says then. 'Being in love suits you.'

'It frightens me, too,' I say. 'Like you say, something's coming. Something big. Stella, when it comes, will you do something for me?'

'What can I do for you, Maia?' Stella asks.

'Will you stay safe, with the children? Go to a shelter and stay there. Will you leave this battle to everyone else for once?'

Stella cups my cheeks with her hands and kisses me gently on the forehead. 'Oh, no, Maia. You know I can't do that. I never leave the fate of my country to be decided by others. Our fight is our freedom, Maia. I will never hide from that.'

I knew that was what she was going to say. But I hoped it might be that easy. Now, fear and death seem very close by. Warby's gone, and Christina's heartbroken. Nicco is in jail awaiting trial, and the sky is holding its breath.

It's down to me to try now, and I'm so afraid I'm not brave or strong enough.

The bell on the medical room rings, and my mouth drops open.

It's Sal standing in the doorway.

Chapter Seventy-Three

'Sal, what happened?' I ask as soon as we are alone.

'Let's walk and find a place to talk.' Sal leads us out of Floriana and towards home. The streets seem quieter than usual. People go about their daily lives as always, but they are quieter, as if they sense the storm building out at sea and are waiting for it to break.

Sal comes to a stop just shy of the street where the half-house is. Looking around, he sees an abandoned shop and ushers me in. Its front shutters and door stand open deliberately to reveal that the shelves are empty of anything worth stealing.

Going in first, I step over broken glass and empty wooden crates to find my way to a small back room with a narrow, barred window. Every surface is covered in dust; a broken sink hangs off the wall.

'Tell me.'

Sal sees an old stool in the corner and, drawing it to him, sits on it. He stares into a shaft of steep light that cuts through the gloom to reveal a million particles of dust dancing in the air.

'It didn't work?' I ask.

'It didn't work.' Sal lowers his eyes. 'Not as it should. I should have woken up there. In the bed, just as you have described. But that is not how it was.'

'Then, what happened?'

'I remembered the directions you gave me to the hospital,' Sal says. 'So much has changed. So many more buildings and people and cars – so many cars. Even more than in the nineties. I thought your time wouldn't be so very hard for me to understand, but I suppose I have grown used to a quiet time, at least before the raids started. Everything was so loud.'

'That's not why you came back, though, right?' I ask.

'No.' Sal glances up at me before continuing. 'I went and stood across the road and waited. You said they come every day, and they came a little after 2 p.m.' He smiles faintly, tears standing in his eyes. 'What a gift to see them, Maia. What a treasure to see again all that I thought lost forever. I saw Elena arrive with my son and, I think, his wife – a very attractive young woman, blonde hair. They had three little children with them, running ahead, taking the steps into the hospital two at a time. Such sweet, happy little souls.' Sal draws in a ragged breath. 'Elena looked so beautiful; in my eyes, she had not aged a day. Her grace, her smile was exactly the same. The way she looked at our grandchildren – my heart almost burst from beating so hard. All the years we have been apart, and my love has not cooled one degree. I burn for her, just as I did on the day we met.'

'Oh, Sal,' I say. 'But why did you come back here?'

'It was then that I realised I had waited too long. There is no way back to that life for me now. That other man who lies in bed surrounded by a family he cannot know – he is lost forever. This body – this is who I am meant to be. This time – this is where I belong. And, at last, I know why. I know my purpose.'

'What do you mean?' I press him.

'I had some time, and I saw a kind of junk shop, full of things no one wants anymore: old microwaves, out-of-date mobile telephones, piles of magazines and books. I thought I could pass the time in there. There was so much to look at, familiar and new – to me, at least. It calmed me. And then I found a copy of a book about Malta during the war. I picked it up and flicked through it. I saw your Danny and some other faces I know. Friends – good friends – staring back at me from these pages like ghosts, as though the flesh-and-blood people that I know were never more than half-forgotten memories printed in two dimensions. It is the way, I thought. It is fitting that the names of people, their lives, fade into dust and are let go. That is how life continues. That is how it should be.' His mouth twitches into a smile. 'And then . . . I don't know why, but it was as if I heard a voice – my *own* voice – loud and clear in my ear, telling me to look in the index. At first, I thought it was the young man behind the counter talking to me, but he had these tiny white plugs in his ears – I think he was listening to music through them. So I looked for my own name in the index. And I found it.'

'There are dozens of Salvatore Borgs,' I murmur. I'm starting to see the path this is taking.

'Perhaps, but this Salvatore Borg is me.' Sal lifts his chin. 'There is no doubt.'

'What did the book say about you?' I ask.

'There was a chapter detailing the worst tragedies of the war, and then, at the end, one that was averted. A bomb fell onto a school where the children were sheltering in the cellar. The building collapsed in on itself, filling the cellar with masonry and sucking out the air. The teacher who was with the children was able to find a tiny hole in the rubble, big enough for the half-starved children to escape through. He saved them, all nine of them, though he himself was lost when a second collapse crushed him.

'You save the children,' I whisper.

'I save the children,' he says. 'Of course I do. I know every one of them. I taught most of them to read. I know their hopes and dreams, what they want to do in the world after the war, everything they have to offer their homeland. And there's more.'

'What?' I ask.

'David and Eugenie are amongst the children I save.'

'But . . .' I falter. 'They were at the airfield; they saw Stella die.'

'Not anymore,' Sal says. 'Your friendship with Stella – your influence – must have made her think twice about that at least.'

I think of our conversation earlier today. She will not stay out of the battle, but she will make sure her children are safe.

I pace from one end of the debris-strewn ruin to the other and back again. 'Sal . . . you came back to die.'

'Not to die,' Sal says. 'I don't want to die, Maia. I came to atone. I can't change what happened in Milan or the man I was then, but here is the chance I have been waiting for: a way to make peace with myself and the heavens. It is written. I must do it.'

'You were so close . . .'

'I cannot let those children die so that I can live. I cannot let your father die. That would mean I would never know you. You have always believed that this miracle happened to you for a reason: to save Danny and your grandmother, to change your father's life and yours. I never knew the reasons why I had been taken from life – until today. I didn't come back so that I might die; I came back so that they might live.'

'But, Sal . . . there is no future, remember? Only nows. If we stay in the nows, then maybe . . .'

'You will not try to talk me out of it,' Sal says firmly. 'You will know that just as some fates may be changed, others may remain the same, and I have chosen which.'

'Of course you have,' I say. 'What other choice would you have made?'

'Then let us go home, Maia. Let us live the rest of the hours of this bright day as if they are our best and our last.'

Sal offers me his arm, and I take it.

All too soon night will fall, and what the dawn will bring, none of us knows.

Chapter Seventy-Four

Friday 14th August 1942, 7 a.m.

Danny comes to the house early the next morning.

'Wrangled an hour or two off to see you before the next big show later,' he explains when I let him in.

Sal is sitting in the corner writing down everything he can remember from his visit to 2025 into his notebook. When he sees Danny, he waves a greeting, then gets up and takes himself into the kitchen.

'You must be tired,' I tell him.

'Not yet. Tomorrow, when all this is over and those boats have steamed into harbour, then I'll be tired. One last push, Maia. We get the fuel and the food, and the siege is over. The war might go on, but things will get a hell of a lot better round here.'

'And what are your orders?' I ask him.

'Well, I can't tell you exactly, but you can assume I'll be up there trying to pick off the bombers while the Axis pilots try to pick me off.'

'And if you get hit, you eject, right?' I say.

'Maia,' Danny says. 'Why all the questions now?'

'Humour me?' I ask him. 'It makes me feel better to understand all the steps.'

'If I'm hit, and there's no chance of landing the Spit, then I'll eject. But if I can get her down, I will. Ejecting right into the middle of an air battle and a gunfight ain't always the best idea.'

'So you'd try to land at the airfield?'

'That's the best way, if I can reach it. They got fire crews, ambulances, doctors.'

'And, say you land, but it's like the other day, and you can't open your cockpit, and this time for some reason, you can't kick your way out, what then?'

'The erks will get me out,' Danny says calmly. 'There's an emergency catch right on top of the hood – looks like two screws. You pull it up, and it releases the canopy. Then they'll cut my belts and haul me out. They are pros, these guys, Maia. It's all been thought through, I promise you, right down to the last detail.'

'Right down to the last detail,' I repeat.

'And what about you, when it all kicks off? You'll get to the shelter, right?'

'Yes,' I lie. 'I'll be safe.'

'Good.' He smiles at me. 'I have to go back, Stitches.'

'Already?'

Our arms wind around each other.

'We will see each other again,' Danny promises me. 'I know it. So you believe it, you hear me?'

'I do,' I tell him. 'I do.'

We kiss, and in that kiss, there is a lifetime – decades of the lives we long to live together, bound and sealed with the vows our bodies make.

'Stay alive,' Danny whispers as he lets me go.

'Stay alive,' I tell him.

He smiles, and then he's gone.

★ ★ ★

After Danny leaves – and it takes every fibre of courage I have in my bones to let him go – Sal and I wait, the only two people in the world who know exactly what we are waiting for.

It feels like there should be a lot to say, but we are mostly silent. We sit side by side, my hand in his, waiting for the hour to arrive, the time when we need to leave to meet our fates. Neither of us needs to say that the other has saved them, given them a family when they'd given up hope of one. Neither of us needs to say that we don't want the other to go – that we want each other to change our minds and stay alive. Both of us know we can't do that.

Sal watches the clock standing in the hall, and he must have decided the time is right. He hands me a letter in an envelope.

'This is for you to read tomorrow,' he says firmly. Getting up, he places half a dozen more on the table.

'To my friends. There is one each for Christina and Stella – make sure they get them.' He smiles. 'Don't worry. I haven't mentioned that I know I'm going to die tonight.'

'Sal.' I stand up, rushing to hug him.

'Now,' he says. 'Now, now. We will not make a fuss, Maia. We think we know what will happen tonight, but we have already changed so much, so we will go to our fates as travellers to a new land. And, you know, whatever befalls us, I am certain that we will see each other again in another life at another time. Perhaps we will not know it or even recognise each other, but I do believe that in some part of our minds, we will know we have always been friends. I trust in that above all else. You have given me that faith.'

'You have given it to me, too,' I tell him.

'Then we are ready,' he says. 'No goodbyes.'
'No goodbyes,' I reply.

* * *

We are outside the school, waiting for the children to arrive as the siren sounds, exactly when we knew it would, screaming out into the hot evening, summoning us to shelters and tunnels. All day I have been restless, pacing back and forth, waiting for it all to begin.

We spring up and head for the door together, pausing outside as people hurry around, scuttling as fast as they can to safety.

'See you again,' Sal says, taking my hand.

'You will,' I promise.

'Sal.' Stella is running towards me, pushing the pram with one hand and leading David by the other. 'Take the children, pease? I have to go to Ta' Qali. There was an oil explosion on the field. It was hit by a shell – no one saw it coming. There are some serious burns. I need as much help as I can get. They've sent a jeep.'

'Of course,' Sal says, hugging Stella. 'They will be safe with me.'

We hear the sound of the first wave of bombers droning louder as a jeep screeches to a stop.

'Let me come with you,' I follow Stella to the car.

'No.' She turns to look at me her hand on the vehicle. 'Not today. You must stay safe, Maia. You are my hope.'

'But...'

The jeep screeches away before I can argue.

For one fraction of a second, I am helpless. Then I know what I have to do. I run after Stella, right towards death.

Chapter Seventy-Five

The sky blackens with the swarm of bombers, all focused on the harbour.

Everything is noise; all my five senses are assaulted by it, a cacophony of violence so enormously loud that it makes tears stream down my face as I run. It opens up the ground around me in a series of craters that seem to come from below somehow. It topples buildings into vicious stone splinters and makes every step I take one into the unknown. Still, I press on with only one thought in my mind: I cannot fail.

The closer I get to the airfield, the more intense the bombardment is. The enemy is targeting the planes on the ground as well, doing their best to churn up the landing strip so badly that it makes it impossible for the Spitfires to take off or land.

I am utterly alone out here and still more than twenty minutes away from Luqa, probably thirty. The impossibility of the task I have been so confident of achieving hits me hard. I can't make it on time. I will die here.

That will be the footnote of my life found at the bottom of a page. The world is ripping itself apart around me. Everywhere I look, I see fire; every breath I take is full of burning oil and dense smoke. I'm tired – I'm so tired – and I know I can't make it now.

Except that I must. I don't care what logic and reason might tell me. Logic and reason have no place in my heart in this moment. I will get there in time; I refuse to allow any other outcome.

So, there's no time to stop, no time to take in this vision of hell or the dangers I am clawing my way through. I must keep going.

Then something cuts through the noise, a thin high screech. Even though it's muted by the noise of war, it still raises hairs on my arms. In the next second, I am knocked off my feet by the force of another body. Sprawling onto the sharp rubble, my palms skid through fragmented debris.

Before I can turn to see who has attacked me, a punch detonates in my face. For a second, everything goes black – then reality roars in again, and it's worse than I could ever have feared.

I see Nicco bearing down on me. Blood runs down his face; his eyes are red with fury; his balled fists smash into my ribs, one after another on repeat. I don't know how he got out or why he's here. All I know as I feel my bones crunch and my organs bruise is that he will kill me.

'No!' I shout into his face, feeling the word vibrate in my chest. Frantically, I try to push him off me, scratching at his wrists and face.

Nicco catches both my wrists with one hand, pressing them into the ground. I can feel the fragile bones in my hands bow and splinter.

His mouth contorts with furious, hate-filled words that I can't hear; spittle from his tirade sprays in my face. As I turn away, his hand gropes for something – then he finds it. He picks up a large rock, some piece of masonry that is more than heavy enough to cave my head in.

Anger burns through me in a wild inferno. No! No, I will not die like this. I will make it to the airfield in time.

With all that's left of my strength, I twist and buck, just enough to unbalance him a little. In that one second, I wrench my wrist free and, sitting up, punch my elbows into his throat. It's not enough to really hurt him, but it gives me enough time to crawl from under him and to scramble to my feet.

Then we stand opposite one another, the world burning around us. The sun is blotted out entirely. He stands in the way of where I have to go.

Nicco rushes at me, the rock held high, ready to strike. All I can do is run at him, shoulder first. He is stronger than me, but he is not a tall man, and when we meet, my shoulder hits him dead centre in his chest. He swings the rock at me but misses.

I try to run past him and as I do, he falls. I keep running, hoping to gain some earth. A fighter swoops down, machine gunfire strafes the ground, a thousand tiny explosions surround me. I fall to the ground, hands over my head. The sound of the fighter recedes, and I turn over. Scratches but no injuries. Then I remember, where is Nicco?

When I turn to look, he is lying prone on the ground. Maybe he is dead, maybe unconscious. I don't know. I could go back, but I don't.

This is war.

Chapter Seventy-Six

The bombing has all but stopped by the time I finally hobble onto the airfield, but the Spitfires still wheel above us, fighting to the death.

The first thing I see is that casualties are lined up in makeshift rows on stretchers on the ground. Seeing me holding one damaged arm to my chest with the other, a nurse runs up to me.

'Medic!' she calls, but I shrug her off.

'I'm fine, honestly. Where's Dr Borg? I have to find her – it's important.'

She shrugs, pointing down the field.

Shaking my head, I begin to limp in the direction she was pointing, my view obscured by drifting smoke. The nurse returns to her work.

Then I see the doctor kneeling over a young man on a stretcher, holding his hand.

'Stella,' I rasp and then again louder. 'Stella!'

'Maia, can you find him water?' Stella hears my voice before she realises that I should not be there and looks up at me. 'Don't you worry, Terence,' she tells her patient. 'Water is coming.' She points at a medic. 'Fetch him some water please.'

Getting up, Stella runs over to my side, where I fling my arms around her, despite the pain that every movement shoots through my body.

Four Spitfires head out onto the pitted runway through the smoke of the fire.

'What happened to you?' Stella looks me up and down. 'You need a stretcher, my dear child.'

'What can they do up there when the smoke is so thick?' I ask as the aircraft struggle into the air. 'What can they see?'

'Light's still just about good enough,' Stella says, her hand supporting me under my elbow.

Dimly, I wonder if I am in shock. 'That's good.'

I want to stop and stare at the sky, as if I could somehow make out Danny's aircraft in the purple sunset. Stella lifts a canteen of water to my mouth. The medic must have returned with some for both Terence and me. I take a sip. It's cool and clear.

When it happens, it's almost as if I am one second ahead of time as it unfolds.

I see a Spitfire swoop in low with a Messerschmitt on its tail. It banks high, hotly pursued, heading steeply into the violet sky. The enemy's chase is relentless. There's no other aircraft from either side in view: just the two of them locked in a dogfight.

I know that it's Danny.

'Maia,' Stella says gently. 'Please let me help you.'

Just then, the Spit is hit. Smoke trails from one wing. The other plane loops around and swoops back in. I can't hear the exchange of gunfire, but I do see another plume of smoke, this time from the Spitfire's engine. My heart pumps blood furiously around my body, and reserves of energy I did not think I possessed surge through me.

The time is now.

The Messerschmitt peels away, and the Spit turns, heading for the airfield. Out of options, Danny needs to try to land.

'Ground crews,' the shout goes out over the Tannoy. 'Fire and rescue, get ready.'

'He's going to have to make an emergency landing,' I tell Stella as she comes to my side. 'It's Danny, Stella.'

'You can't know that,' she replies. 'You can't know it's Danny.'

'But I do,' I say.

When I look at her, she sees my expression and knows it, too.

We watch with bated breath as the little plane judders into position to make a landing on the runway. It seems to fall and level, fall and level, almost like a controlled crash.

'Landing gear is fucked!' someone calls. 'Gonna be a belly flop.'

Firefighting trucks head towards where the Spit will land. Stella and I watch transfixed as the aircraft's engines sputter and cut, smoke pouring from her wounds.

At the very last moment, Danny pulls up and the Spit overshoots the end of the runway, almost skimming the tops of the fire trucks as he tries to avoid crashing into the people on the ground. Somehow, he turns the Spitfire hard and she comes down, ploughing into the earth with a horrifying crunch and screech of metal.

The plane slides through the dry earth, far out of reach of the men on standby, ploughing into the deep-red soil at alarming speed, far closer to me and Stella than to the rescue teams.

I'm running towards it before I'm even aware of what I'm doing – Stella, too. Stella's longer legs and months of constant walking power her ahead of me. The Spit crumples into a low wall, and bright flames burst into life at once.

I catch up with Stella.

'He's not trying to get out,' she says as she runs. Far behind us, we can hear the crews heading our way. 'He must be injured or unconscious.' She glances over her shoulder. 'They won't be here in time.'

Adrenalin pumps through me, my legs fly, my lungs open. Power surges through me, and I feel invincible.

'Stand back,' I order Stella as she is just about to get on the wing. 'Let me! I know how to get the canopy open – get ready for him.'

Smoke fills my eyes and my nose, and I leap onto the wing of the aircraft, heat already singeing the hairs on my arms. Danny is slumped inside, his head lolling forwards. I see the button he told me about, the one to trigger the release mechanism that allows the canopy to slide open, positioned underneath the external rear-view mirror. On my first attempt, I can't quite reach it with enough pressure to push. On the second, it burns my palms. Then there's a small explosive noise, hardly more than a soft pop, and suddenly, small flames appear inside the cockpit.

It's now or never. Launching myself at the button, I manage it. The canopy slides open halfway and then sticks – the heat must have warped it. I don't feel the pain anymore as I wrench it open, wide enough to reach in and release Danny's harness. Grabbing at his Mae West life preserver, I try with all my might to drag him from his seat, but I'm not strong enough. The pain shocks him conscious, and he stares at me, disorientated.

'Danny, you need to get out now or you're going to die,' I tell him. 'Make your legs move. Push up, help me get you out. *Now!*'

With a cry of anguish, he surges upwards. Making use of the momentum, I drag him out of the cockpit and onto the wing, just as the rescue team is arriving. There's no choice but to roll him onto the ground. He screams as he lands. At least he's alive. Frantically, Stella and I pull him across the dirt as far away from the plane as we can get him. Dark blood trails behind him.

'Save his life,' I tell Stella, looking up at the sky for any sign of the returning enemy planes. 'You make sure you save his life.'

'I will,' Stella promises.

The Spit catches fire then, and the ground crew tries desperately to put it out with what foam they have left after the oil fire.

'I need my bag,' Stella says as she examines Danny. 'You stay with him. I'll get it.'

'No! He needs you. I'll get it. You save his life.'

As I run towards where Stella left her bag, I can't hear anything approaching from the sky. Fights are continuing up there, but night is falling in earnest now, and soon pilots on both sides will head home. The first convoy of ships will be heading into the harbour, and before long, the island will wake up on the feast day of Santa Marija to the news that the siege is broken – that they have turned the tide against the Nazis, even though they themselves don't know it yet.

All that races through my head as I hurry towards Stella's bag, grabbing it in a single swoop and heading back. Perhaps the last awful attack won't come now. Perhaps I have altered time just enough to stop that pilot turning back and deciding to finish off the job with one more pointlessly malicious attack.

I'm bearing down on them when I hear it.

The sound of the Messerschmitt screaming towards us seems to come out of nowhere, the open fire of its machine guns heading in a direct line to Stella and Danny with deadly accuracy.

I throw the bag at Stella, then fling myself over them. I shield them both with my body.

I don't feel any pain.

Just the curious push and pull of the bullets tearing through me. The sensation of bones shattering, the gush and flow of hot blood.

The sound of the plane's engines grows fainter. Mission complete.

I can't hear what Stella is saying as she gently moves my body off hers. I can only see that her lips are moving. Her expression is stricken as she takes in my damage. I see her mouth my name over and over again; tears track paths through the grime and smoke that silt her face.

'I'm sorry,' I try to tell her. I'm sorry.

My hand reaches for Danny; his face turns to me. I feel the grip of his fingers as if mine hardly belong to me anymore.

'You save him,' I say to Stella. Even though all I can hear is the sound of ringing in my ears. I feel the words move in my mouth. 'You swear you'll save him.'

Stella nods.

'Maia.' When Danny says my name, I hear it in my heart. Our eyes meet. We tell each other a thousand sweet everythings in that one look. 'Hold on. You hold on, you hear me? Don't you die on me, Maia Borg. You promised you wouldn't.'

Tears track down my face. I shake my head.

'I'll see you again one day,' I whisper. 'Just you wait and see.'

The sky overhead turns from velvet blue to dark, dark night. I see the first stars shining, and somehow, I know they are the very first stars that ever set the universe alight.

I'm going home at last.

Epilogue

Saturday 15th August 1992, 12.32 p.m.

I vowed I'd never come back to Malta, and I meant it, too. On that final day when I got posted to England, I was certain I never wanted to see this country ever again. Sure, it gave me a lot: the best friends I ever had, who taught me over and over what sacrifice means. The brightest and most beautiful moments of my life happened here, right under this perfect sky, memories that still shine so clear and in focus, even all these decades later when everything else seems faded and dull.

Malta gave me the love of my life.

But it was here I lost Maia, too. It was not so very far from where I am sitting right now that she died in my arms. God, I wanted to die with her. I begged to – I'm not ashamed to say it. But Stella told me she'd made a promise, and she wouldn't let me. I hated Stella for a while for that. But only for a while.

Years came and went. Wars were won and lost. Eventually, I got too old to fly and went back to my own quiet corner of the world, where the sky's so big you can dream yourself up there.

I tried to forget. There are some things, some faces, though, that will not be forgotten.

Maia Borg, I only knew you for a few days, but I have loved you always. Sometimes, I think I loved you before I was born, and I will continue to long after this old body of mine has turned to dust.

My bones creak, my heart grows ponderous, and my eyes are cloudy and dim. Sometimes words escape me, and this brain of mine is more and more lost in the clouds, in the high blue spaces, each and every day.

When some gal telephoned me and asked if I'd come back to Malta for the fiftieth anniversary, first I said, 'No thank you, ma'am.'

Then they came back to me, so sudden and fresh and full of colour and heartache: the last words you said to me, Maia.

Then I knew. Deep in my heart, I knew that if I was ever going to see you again, it would be on Malta. So I came, fast as these bowed legs could carry me, took out that one drawing I made of you from where I keep it in my wallet, and I've got it right here – hoping, like the foolish, weak-minded old feller I am, that me and this drawing might act like runway lights, bringing you into land, my love. So here I am, sitting on this bench in the middle of all this fuss and nonsense, waiting for you, Stitches.

'Flight Lieutenant Daniel Beauchamp,' you say, sitting down next to me and taking my hand.

God, your touch – your touch I've dreamt of every day.

'Stitches.' It's been such a long time since I've seen your face, I can't help grinning wildly. 'I've been waiting for you, Maia. Here you are at last.'

'Here I am,' you say. 'Shall we go?'

Funny – when I get up, my knees don't creak no more, and I feel just about as strong and whole as I ever have.

Feel like I could take off and fly right up into the cool blue sky, and I wouldn't need no Spitfire to make it.

'Where we going?' I ask you.

'Anywhen you want,' you say. 'We've got a whole universe to choose from.'

I look back just once. I think I know that old feller, sleeping on a bench, scrap of yellowed paper clutched in his bony hand. Yes, I think I know him, but it don't matter much to me.

Not now the wait is over.

Author's Note

This is a work of fiction inspired by real events and some real people, and I created some events and moved some dates around to fit the narrative. If you want to know the facts about Malta in World War II there are many great books: *Fortress Malta: An Island Under Siege 1940-1943* by James Holland, where you can find out more about the extraordinary Adrian Warburton, a true war hero; *Malta Besieged, 1940-1942* by David G. Williamson; and a selection of books by Maltese author Frederick R. Galea, particularly *Carve Malta on my Heart*, where you can read about the real life of remarkable Christina Ratcliffe in her own words. My versions of these two people and Mabel Strickland are completely fictional creations, made with love and respect.

Danny is a fictional character inspired by two pilots that fought in Malta during the siege: the Canadian ace, George Beurling, who was a man of incredible courage and skill, and Denis Barnham, whose artwork still hangs in museums today, and whose diary gives us a real insight into the strain and stresses of being a fighter pilot under such difficult circumstances.

As for the temples and ancient sites of Malta, a story of a group of children going missing *was* reported in *National Geographic* in 1940, but it is widely believed to be an urban legend. (That never stopped a novelist, though!) However, even if time travel isn't on the cards, these enigmatic sites give us a tantalising glimpse into a long-ago culture of wonderful richness and great ingenuity. Heritage Malta do an incredible job of both preserving and continuing to learn from them. I highly recommend visiting!

Rowan Coleman
Scarborough, November 2024

Acknowledgements

Hugest of thanks to my editor Lucy Stewart, her brilliance and skill have been so important to this book. And to my inspirational agent, Hattie Grünewald, whom I'm always so excited to work with. Thank you to all the team at Hodder who work so hard, and to the copyeditor on this book, Katie Lumsden, who was genuinely heroic in her endeavours to sort out a complicated timeline.

Thank you to the island and people of Malta. Because of this book, I visited the island where my grandmother and father were born and lived for the first time. Without fail, everyone I met was so happy to talk to me, to share memories and to tell me what books to read and where to go to find the history I was looking for. Special thanks to Frederick Galea at the National War Museum, who was so kind and informative, and to the lovely lady I met in the St Cataldus Catacombs in Rabat who *insisted* I take home the history book she was reading with me and refused to take no for an answer. I will never forget her! Thank you also to Umberto Ruggiero, the wonderful and incredibly knowledgeable guide at the Malta at War Museum in Birgu, who brought the public air raid shelters to life for me in vivid detail.

Getting to know the place where part of my ancestry is from was really special for me. Special thanks and love to my friend Julie Akhurt, who came with me on my first visit to Malta and helped make it such a magical experience, and to my cousin Kathryn Borg, who let me borrow her name for this book and who showed me the places where my grandmother and Maltese family lived and loved. To be able to stand in the spot where my grandmother got married really felt like I was standing next to her, for a moment or two.

Thank you to my friends who are always there to laugh and cry with, Angela Clarke, Julie Cohen, Kate Harrison, Clare Swatman, and anyone else that I love SO MUCH but have forgotten right in this moment! To my husband Adam, and my wonderful children, thank you for putting up with me, and coming with me on endless tours of historical sites. Finally, thank you to the three best dogs in the world: Blossom, Bluebell and Rufus.